THE Defilers

Deborah Gyapong

CASTLE QUAY BOOKS

The Defilers

Printed in Canada
International Standard Book Number: 1-897186-02-9

Published by:
Castle Quay Books
500 Trillium Drive, Kitchener, Ontario, Canada N2G 4Y4
Tel: (800) 265-6397   Fax: (519) 748-9835
E-mail: info@castlequaybooks.com
www.castlequaybooks.com

Copy editing by Janet Dimond
Cover Design by John Cowie, *eyetoeye design*
Printed at Essence Publishing, Belleville, Ontario, Canada

Library and Archives Canada Cataloguing in Publication
Gyapong, Deborah, 1949-
    The defilers / Deborah Gyapong.
ISBN 1-897186-02-9
    I. Title.
PS8613.Y36D43 2006   C813'.6   C2006-900736-5

CASTLE QUAY BOOKS

Prologue

I used to believe it was easy to tell who was good and who was evil – until the year I turned thirteen. Then someone who was supposed to be good shattered my innocence.

I grew up in Boston's Jamaica Plain district. Brick apartment buildings, ark-like wooden houses, and tall maple trees crowded the streets in my blue-collar neighbourhood. I remember the clatter of the streetcar, the smell of dusty green leaves after a thunderstorm, and the screaming wheels of the Orange Line rattling the elevated tracks that darkened Washington Street.

A low chain-link fence enclosed our tiny front lawn and a little gate opened to the walk leading to our yellow triple-decker – a flat-roofed building with three identical apartments stacked like pancakes. On hot days when the sun scorched the grass the sprinkler would go *tsk tsk tsk* back and forth, wetting Gran's two-foot-high statue of the Blessed Virgin Mary. Our Lady faced a quiet tree-lined street and a root-heaved sidewalk. She stretched her arms over the crabgrass in the one spot where there was no shade.

Gran used to tell me the Blessed Virgin was my mother. For a long time I thought that made me special. I used to brag about it to my cousins until Aunt Gladys spoiled it by telling me Our Lady was the mother of *all* the faithful. I don't remember my real mother, who died of brain cancer when I was three, but Gran said she was up in heaven along with Jesus and the Holy Mother, praying for me.

I never felt like a motherless child. I had Gran and Gramp who lived on the first floor. I had Aunt Gladys and Uncle Fred and my cousins who lived on the third floor. And I had Dad. He and I shared the second floor, though he was hardly ever home. He was a detective with the Boston Police Department, always busy catching the bad guys.

Gran and Aunt Gladys looked after me when I wasn't at school. Between the two of them I always had plenty to eat and, frankly, more attention than I wanted most of the time. They made sure I respected my elders, did my chores, and said my prayers. I tried to be a good girl, but they told me "mischief" was my middle name.

I must have been a handful for Gran, who sewed me dresses and did everything she could to wrestle the tomboy out of me. But I still did cartwheels and hung upside down from the jungle gym. So she finally gave up, except for insisting I wear the dresses to Mass.

Gran often kept an eye on me from a sagging outdoor couch on her front porch. When the weather was warm enough she'd bring her budgies outside. She'd set their white wire cage on a card table nearby and talk baby talk to them. She'd even bring the ironing board outside. That's where she taught me how to iron my Holy Child Parochial School uniform.

Other girls at Holy Child took ballet or Irish dancing, but Dad put me in karate lessons along with my boy cousins. They called me a showoff, but Dad called me his "little ninja girl." Sometimes I tagged along when he and the other detectives taught karate in Roxbury and Mattapan as an outreach to keep kids from joining gangs.

When I was eleven Dad was trying to solve a rash of drive-by shootings in the Grove Hall section on the other side of Franklin Park. We were so proud he was trying to make Boston a safer city. But a year went by and the bodies kept piling up. Kids shooting other kids caused too much stress, so Dad took time off work and made a pilgrimage to Rome – his first vacation without me. On the bus tour he fell in love with a Canadian woman named Veronica.

Shortly after that trip Dad decided to take early retirement. I remember sitting on the edge of a folding metal chair at his retirement party, listening to his friends swap stories about crimes they'd solved and the stupid things criminals did. They treated me like one of their own daughters, but I longed to be one of them. By then my breasts had grown big enough to prompt Gran to buy me a bra. I hunched over to hide the little mounds that pushed out despite my baggy T-shirt, and wished I were flat-chested like a man.

At that age I was taller than most other seventh graders, especially the boys. My honey-coloured hair was fairer than it is now and I had a habit of blowing my bangs out of my light green eyes. Everyone said my eyes came from Gramp. I didn't like the comparison because he wore Coke-bottle glasses that made his eyes look huge. Aunt Gladys said my olive skin and heart-shaped face came from Nana, my Puerto Rican grandmother on my mother's side. I felt Irish, but I didn't look anything like Gran who was short and round. By the time I was in seventh grade people started telling me I was beautiful and to act like a young lady.

Around then I stopped being Dad's special girl. He had his eyes on Veronica. They got married and their wedding felt like my funeral. I might as well have been a ghost because no one noticed how upset I was. It got worse. Rather than persuade my new stepmother to live in Boston, Dad decided to move to Nova Scotia where she owned an art gallery.

Dad and Veronica gave me a choice. I could come with them right away or stay behind with Gran, do eighth grade at Holy Child, then move to Canada the following summer. Deep down I hoped Dad would argue with me and convince me to go with them, even if he had to force me. But he didn't. I hated Veronica for taking him away from me. If he no longer cared about me, I would pretend I didn't care about him either.

Only one person saw through my mask. My priest.

The previous year Father Ron had appeared like a godsend at Church of the Holy Child, a crumbling red brick building occupying a whole block across the street from my school. Ron filled that dark musty space with his presence, radiating something magnetic that the gentle old priests didn't have. He brought change and life – or so it seemed. With his shoulder-length hair and beard he reminded me of the holy card of Jesus with His Sacred Heart showing, except Ron had ice blue eyes and a receding hairline. He even seemed to have a glow around his head, like the halo around Jesus' head in the picture.

We already had folk songs at Mass at Holy Child, but Ron allowed the Moriarty twins to bring in a drum set and an electric bass. Ron himself could do a wicked Jimi Hendrix imitation on his Fender guitar, though he had to explain to us first who Jimi Hendrix was. Aunt Gladys and her charismatic friends loved his special healing sessions. Others loved how inclusive he was. Everyone loved how much he cared about the poor.

When Gran, who still said the rosary in Latin, got upset about Ron not wearing a Roman collar, he started dressing occasionally in a cassock instead of worn Levis and tie-dyed shirts. He'd always wear a black clerical shirt and collar when he brought the Blessed Sacrament to Gramp, who rarely left the living room because of his oxygen tank. After Latin prayers with him and Gran, Ron would head upstairs to tutor me in math.

At first we really did math, but somewhere between solving algebra equations and making graphs Ron zeroed in on the pain and anger I kept hidden. The first time he hugged me I cried in his arms because he seemed to understand how I felt about Dad abandoning me. Hugs and handholding led to cuddling and kisses. Because he was a priest I did what he wanted me to, even though some things shocked and embarrassed me.

Soon we were meeting not only in my second floor bedroom – Gran couldn't easily climb the stairs by then – but also among the cedars at the Arnold Arboretum. When winter came he started driving me to a motel in Quincy.

That was where he raped me.

He made me feel guilty, like I was to blame for his tremendous needs. Even though he hurt me I felt drawn to him, and went back for more. I was like a zombie with no mind of my own. I couldn't break free.

Ron told me I had to keep what we were doing a secret, as secret as the confessional. But the secret came out when I got pregnant. Turns out I wasn't the only one, and some of the other girls were even younger than I was.

Dad forced me to testify against him. At his trial Ron's lawyer tried to blame *me* for what happened. Made me feel like dirt. And while he tore me apart on the witness stand the baby was kicking inside my huge belly.

Dad and Veronica insisted I move to Nova Scotia with them and give my baby girl up for adoption. After that it was as if I took Gran's iron and seared my heart so I would never feel pain like that again. Dad sent me for professional counselling, but that kind of help meant nothing to me. I'd counsel myself. Around that time going to Mass ceased because I no longer believed in Jesus or the Blessed Virgin.

After finishing high school I got a psychology degree from Dalhousie University and became a Canadian citizen. When I was twenty-three I became a member of the Royal Canadian Mounted Police, one of the most prestigious police forces in the world.

When, years later, other victims of abuse by priests started coming forward I didn't see much in common with them. *Why didn't they just move on with their lives like I did?* I could understand filing a lawsuit because I thought the Church should pay. But I didn't understand why people were suing for loss of religious faith as part of their pain and suffering. So you discover the Christian religion is a sham. It's a hard truth, kind of like learning Santa Claus is really Uncle Fred dressed up in a red fat suit and fake beard. Get over it, for crying out loud. I especially had contempt for people who complained of flashbacks – until I started having them.

It's only recently I've been able to examine my past, or anything about Ron, without feeling like I was about to tackle a suicide bomber with his hand on the detonator.

Fifteen years after the abuse, far from Boston and anything reminding me of my past, my careful cloak of sanity began to unravel. I faced an enemy far more evil and dangerous than Father Ron – a supernatural enemy. Nothing in my police training could help me. This evil used people as pawns and destroyed them. When it gained a choke hold on my soul, I had no choice.

I had to cry out to a God I no longer believed in.

consuming Fire

The day my life began to unravel, I was driving my police car through Nova Scotia's first snowstorm of the season with Constable Will Bright directing me from the passenger seat. The call came in as we pulled into the Irving Gas Station parking lot. Someone had firebombed a house while a couple and two children slept inside.

How long had it been since I'd felt that adrenaline rush? It was still intoxicating. I became the old Linda, hyperfocused, intent on rescuing those children and catching the bad guys. *Don't get in the way of my fix.* My foot pressed the gas pedal into the rubber mat and the car skidded onto the highway. The slippery road, fog patches, and big wet flakes drifting onto the windshield demanded concentration. Besides, it was still dark. The sun wasn't even up yet.

Will hung onto the handle over the passenger door. "Watch you don't hydroplane."

Ignoring him, I switched on the flashing lights. "How far is this place?"

"A half hour."

I swore under my breath. At least Dispatch had advised us a couple of volunteer fire departments were on their way.

By the time we fishtailed into the clearing the sun had struggled up behind heavy clouds. Half the house was a roaring inferno and the other billowed black smoke. No one trapped inside could have survived.

Orange flames licked at the grey Nova Scotia sky through the peaked roof and crackled through heat-shattered windows. The blaze cast a lurid glow on the wet snow plastering the surrounding forest. The fire fascinated me, consuming me as if I myself were on fire. Big snowflakes drifted down, creating dots like static on a TV.

I burst out the driver's door and splashed through ankle-deep slush to the trunk. Will plunged around from the passenger side. When I opened the trunk he smacked into me, all two hundred plus pounds of him, and bumped me aside causing me to accidentally bite the inside of my cheek.

"Hey!" I sputtered, tasting the rusty tang of blood.

Will rummaged through the trunk, grabbed a battered video camera, and swung the strap over his shoulder.

Before mouthing off any more I clamped my jaws shut and searched for body bags on the muddy snow. *Be a team player, Linda.* The smoke's acrid haze stank of burning asphalt shingles but, thankfully, not burning human hair or flesh. I brushed my stinging eyes with my forearm.

Will prodded my shoulder. "You've got crowd control."

I spun around.

He tossed me a roll of yellow police tape and then slammed the trunk shut.

We slogged toward the red fire engines parked helter-skelter in the clearing. A dozen firefighters in yellow helmets sprayed streams of water onto the blaze.

Will headed toward the fire chief, a short wiry man standing next to one of the pumper trucks. I decided that Will's "orders" to string tape could wait until after the chief had briefed us both.

"Someone threw a cocktail?" Will shouted over the roar of the diesel engines.

"Yup, that's what the man said." The chief nodded in my direction. We hadn't met, but my navy blue uniform parka and Royal Canadian Mounted Police cap were introduction enough. I wore the yellow roll of police tape like a giant bracelet.

A red-hot beam collapsed throwing a cloud of glowing cinders into the air. The interior shimmered a gaseous yellow, the posts and beams glowing like a red skeleton. A ripple of excited shouts passed through the small group of spectators. Sharing their awe I peered through the smoke, wondering if the perpetrator was admiring his handiwork.

"A couple and their two kids were in there!" the chief shouted. "It could'a been real bad!"

About ten feet away, a man with a faded quilt draped over his shoulders held hands with a small girl who was leaning against his thigh. Next to him a woman rocked a chunky toddler in her arms. The baby stared at me over her shoulder. The cold had turned its round cheeks bright red. When the man laid his arm across the woman's shoulders, she shook it off.

"Is that them?" I gestured with my chin toward the family.

"Yup!" the chief shouted. "The man says someone threw an incendiary device through that window." He pointed toward the inferno. "There are some footprints in the snow. I've tried to keep my men away from them."

Will leaned so close to my ear I could feel the warmth of his breath. I flinched and stepped back, trying to disguise the flinch as a stumble. He raised his lopsided eyebrows. He stepped toward me again and leaned into my ear.

I forced myself to stand still, even though my stomach seized and my heart thumped.

"Can you handle crowd control by yourself?"

"Of course." I squinted. *Does he think I'm a rookie?* He was the same rank – constable – and probably didn't have any more years in than I did, so he had no right to order me around, except for the fact that I was new to the detachment.

Will sloshed backward. "How about stringing that tape before the 'evidence eradication team' tramples any more footprints."

I saluted. "Yes, sir."

Will and I had met for the first time that morning. He struck me as overly conscious of his good looks as well as patronizing. Bitter experience on the job had taught me to be cautious around male RCMP members. Bitter experience back in my native Boston had taught me to distrust men, period.

I strung police tape from tree to tree, creating a barrier between the firefighters and the spectators. Wet sooty snow settled like grey lace on the shoulders and bare heads of the men, women, and children I herded behind the tape. Many wore red or green padded work shirts or stained nylon parkas with their sweatpants or shiny polyester slacks.

A steady trickle of newcomers arrived to gape at the fire. I assumed they came from the nearby settlement of South Dare, an appalling stretch of dilapidated shacks and trailers a hundred yards beyond the edge of the clearing. When, after a long upward climb through rocky brush land and scraggly forest, our police car had hurtled through this hellhole toward the fire, Will must have noticed my astonishment because he said, "Welcome to the Mountain. They didn't tell you about this when you signed up, did they?" South Dare looked like Appalachia or something from the Third World. The settlement both fascinated and repelled me. So did its residents.

A man with the wide-set eyes and flat nose typical of fetal alcohol syndrome ducked under the tape and sauntered toward Will. Following him, I tapped him on the shoulder. "Get behind the line, sir."

The man's brown eyes glistened with resentment. I gestured with my head and prodded him until he shuffled back under the tape. Power and the hint of danger heightened my senses, making me feel alive instead of numb. The inner flames I craved leapt up again. If only I could keep them from burning me out. Keep the flames, but under control like fire in a wood stove.

A van swished into the clearing. Eight or nine women wearing identical green parkas poured out of the vehicle.

"The Ladies' Auxiliary is here," one of the firefighters said. Under his yellow helmet sweat beaded his ruddy face. "Get yourself some coffee, hon."

Hon! I wanted to roll more than my eyes – his head! – but I resisted. "Thanks. Maybe later."

The women placed a big stainless steel coffee urn and plates of sandwiches at the back of the van. The locals tromped over to the food. Despite the snow few children wore hats or mittens, their ears and little hands red with cold. *When had any of them eaten a decent meal?*

I sloshed over to the man draped in the comforter. His untrimmed beard seemed to drag his long face down, and his wiry greying hair bushed out like an Old Testament prophet's. Tall and lean, he stood six inches taller than my five foot eight. Will was searching the bushes between the burning house and the woods. I half expected him to barrel over and shove me aside as soon as he saw me doing an interview.

"This was your house, sir?" I slipped my notebook from the bulletproof vest under my parka. It took the man a moment to tear his eyes away from the fire. I could feel the heat on the side of my face.

"Yes." He turned and his penetrating brown eyes seemed to bore right through me. I averted my eyes as a papery ash settled on my bare hand. When I tried to brush it off it disintegrated into an oily smear.

I searched my pockets for a tissue. "May I get you and your family some sandwiches? Coffee?"

"Someone's bringing us something. Thanks, though."

His deep voice rumbled. He told me their names: David and Anne Jordan.

"I'm Constable Linda Donner from the Sterling RCMP detachment. Are you all okay? Any injuries?"

Anne shook her head and bit her lip, tears clumping her eyelashes together.

I turned to David. "You want to tell me what happened?"

"About 6:30 this morning I heard glass breaking and a man shouting."

"You were both upstairs?"

He shook his head. "No, I was in the kitchen. Anne was."

"Did you recognize the voice? See anyone?"

Anne shook her head. "I was in the back bedroom with the baby." She handed the squirming toddler to David who threw him fireman style over his shoulder.

"Where is or was the kitchen?"

The girl leaning against his leg began to cry and so did the baby. David handed the baby back to Anne, and picked up the girl whose light brown hair clung to her high rounded forehead.

He pointed to the right, near the scorched family car. "In that addition by the laneway."

"The fire started there, on the opposite corner, right?"

"Yeah, in our parlour. I ran in there and found flames shooting up around a wine bottle lying on the rug. I tried to roll up the rug, but the flames were too high. Then the chesterfield burst into flames and so did the curtains."

"Chesterfield?" My eyes darted over to see if Will was watching me. He was filming the crowd.

"The couch."

A wet snowflake landed on my notebook paper, blurring the word "wine."

"Describe the bottle. Was it broken?"

"Not broken. A regular green wine bottle full of kerosene with a rag stuck in the neck. A Molotov cocktail, I guess."

"Kerosene? How did you know?"

"I could smell it. I ran upstairs, grabbed my daughter. Anne took the baby and we climbed out the back window over the wood-shed. Once everyone was safe, I dashed into the kitchen to call the fire department and grab the coats and boots we kept by the side door. That's when I heard gunshots."

I wrote on the damp page. "You see anyone?"

"I was still indoors. My wife saw something."

He flung his free arm over Anne's shoulder.

She jerked away from him. "I heard noises like firecrackers going off and saw a flash of light off in the woods."

David and I locked eyes. He knew his wife's jerking away like that didn't sit well with me. His stare was like an X-ray of thoughts and feelings flitting through my soul that I could barely see myself. He gave me the creeps.

"Who did this to you?"

"I don't know." He finally looked away.

Anne glared at him, trembling, her eyes bloodshot, her brown hair hanging in tangled wet strings. "You know it's one of them. Tell her."

The little girl in David's arms shivered, a tiny furrow in her brow, her lower lip trembling. Her nylon parka was soaked. I had to get the family out of there. A group of men wearing dirty padded shirts and hostile expressions pressed around us.

I shoved past them, shepherding the family toward the police car. The men followed. Their filthy clothes, misshapen bodies, and expressions of hostile defiance matched the sickening squalor of South Dare.

Anne clutched my arm. "They never wanted us to start a church here. They threw rocks at us when we drove through. They came into our house when we weren't home. They made threatening phone calls. They poisoned our dog."

I waved my hand toward the road. "The building on the corner with a fresh coat of paint? That your church?"

"Yes."

"These people want to give South Dare a bad name," interrupted a pot-bellied man in a dirty red work shirt. The deformed fingers of his left hand were fused together like a lobster claw. "You cops only come this way to harass people. The pastor, he set fire to the house hisself." A murky light flickered in his eyes.

Still holding the little girl David stepped toward him. "Gordon, why do you say these things? What have I or my family ever done to you?"

Gordon averted his eyes and stumbled backward.

David's lanky hand grabbed his arm. "We're here because we want to share God's love with you. That's all."

Purple-faced, Gordon shoved David into me. I lost my balance and toppled against one of the men who pressed around us. The men began shoving Anne and David, shouting curses. Focused on protecting the Jordans I planted my feet in the snow, and time slowed down. I whipped out my baton. The men howled in surprise at how effectively I could deal painful blows, even while showing restraint.

"Please leave us alone!" Anne cried. "Haven't you done enough?"

David slung his arm around his wife again. Her shoulders went rigid at his touch. The man in the red work shirt leered at her obvious discomfort, revealing yellowed decaying teeth. I pushed the men aside and prodded the family forward to our police car. We didn't have far to go.

Gordon ground his pot-belly against me and tried to heave me aside.

"I'll have some questions for you in a moment." I gestured with my head for him to leave. His warm sour breath filled my nostrils.

The other men pressed around us. I breathed in slowly and focused.

"Hey, hey!" Will shouted. "Calm down, folks. Come on!" His affable crooked grin beamed at the locals as he waded through the crowd. Maybe he thought his charm disarmed them, but Will stood a head taller than almost everyone except David, and his size probably intimidated them. My legs twitched and the rushing sound in my ears began to fade.

Will laid his huge hand on the little girl's wet head. "We've got to get you out of here."

David nodded, wiping the blood off his mouth. When Will clasped Anne's shoulder she began to sob. He chewed his lip, his hand still resting on her, seeming uncertain what to say. *Are they Will's friends? Why didn't Anne recoil from **his** touch?*

Will and I ushered the Jordan family through the crowd, which had doubled since our arrival. To my relief two more RCMP cars rolled into the clearing.

"Pervert!" someone behind us shouted. A man spat a long string of tobacco juice toward David, splattering the snow with brown splotches.

"Someone slashed our tires." David waved his hand toward an old maroon Chevy with singed paint and flat tires. "Margaret said she'd give us a ride to Cornwallis Cove, so we don't need to go in your car."

Margaret, a dark-haired woman wearing thick glasses, unlocked the doors of a green station wagon and helped the children inside. After David had made arrangements to come to the detachment the next day, Margaret drove away.

Will grabbed my shoulder and leaned into my ear. "I told you to look after crowd control, not start a riot!"

Flabbergasted, I staggered backward.

Will's blue eyes iced me. "Do you want to get us killed?" He wagged his finger at me. "Take your cues from me, understand?"

I brushed his finger out of my face.

He leaned forward, eyebrows raised. "Got it?"

"Yeah, I got it." *Jerk.*

Will put me back on crowd control, though now he had a few more of us to order around.

Gordon slipped under the police tape. He waddled toward Will, who was taping a weathered baseball bat caught in the singed twigs of a bush not far from the house. Others followed him.

I slipped up behind Gordon and grabbed his damp shirt. "You can't stand here."

South Dare men surrounded us, all wearing the same smirk, the same unblinking stare, the same contempt for my uniform and gender. They repulsed me and seemed to sense my reaction. *Be careful. Don't let revulsion colour your judgement.*

"On the other side." I held the tape up high enough for Gordon to duck under, my heart pounding, trying my own version of an affable grin on him. When he wouldn't budge I reached out and dug my fingers into a pressure point between his neck and shoulder. He winced with pain as his knees buckled. *There, that's more like it.*

I smiled, my eyes squinting. "I'm interested in what you said over there." Letting go I ducked under the tape ahead of him. He followed and so did his buddies.

"What's your last name, Gordon?" I wrote his first name in my notebook.

Rubbing his shoulder with his claw-like hand, his eyes glistened with resentment. "Dare. Gordon Dare."

"Who wanted the pastor out badly enough to burn his house down?"

"I told ya. He done it hisself."

"Why do you assume we did it?" interrupted a younger man with brown hair cut short and spiky in the front and dangling to his shoulders in back.

"Just a minute." I sounded defensive. My emotions wouldn't leak out next time.

The younger man shoved his face inches from mine. "You don't care if the pastor's a child molester?" His breath stank of chewing tobacco. The men around him murmured and nodded, reddened faces twisted with hatred.

Turning to the spiky-haired man I flipped a page over in my notebook. "Your name, sir?"

"Lonnie. Lonnie Dare." Tobacco juice dribbled out the side of his mouth.

"What did you say about a child molester?"

"You want us to do your job? Forget it!" Lonnie spat a wad of tobacco into the muddy slush.

I sloshed toward a group of women standing inside the police tape who scattered like a flock of chickens. I approached another group. Some of the teenaged girls had pretty faces, but women only a few years older had bent spines and large coarse-looking hands. A couple of women had dyed their hair platinum blonde, but one was missing chunks of hair from her scalp. No one would talk to me.

My stomach knotted. I'd blown my chance to redeem myself in Will's eyes. Surveying the crowd I plotted my next move.

For every adult there seemed to be four children. A boy, about six or seven, squatted and defecated like a dog next to the police car. Will nearly stumbled over the child pulling up his pants. Ignoring the steaming pile Will tousled the boy's hair. Soon, several of the children were hugging Will's legs, making it difficult for him to move.

I herded the kids away and prodded and pushed them behind the police tape, back to their miserable lives.

A blue Toyota wagon swerved into the clearing. My neighbour and new friend Catherine Ross, editor of the weekly *Sterling Spectator,* jumped out of her car, her designer haircut and stylish leather jacket making her look like a model from a plus-size catalogue.

Snowflakes and ash began to settle on her swept-back curls. "The Jordans okay?"

"Yeah. Someone just drove them to town." I glanced at her vehicle. "You can't park here."

She raised a small digital camera. "Let me take some pictures first, okay?"

I shrugged. Catherine took pictures of the dying flames. A number of beams had collapsed and glowed red hot, while those jutting toward the sky were charred black. The burning house now made me feel desolate and exhausted. I craved another rush of adrenaline.

"This is so weird. I was inside that house yesterday." Catherine aimed her camera at Will. "You're working with Constable Bright, eh? You lucky dawg."

"Why were you here?"

"To talk about David Jordan's new church." Catherine slipped her camera inside her jacket to protect it from the still-falling snow. "I'm not surprised this place burned down. Trouble seems to follow him."

"Seems to me he asks for it," I mumbled and immediately regretted saying it. I wasn't used to having civilian friends. Friends, period.

Catherine dropped her jaw in fake disbelief. "How did you know?"

"Choice of neighbourhood." I widened my eyes and grimaced. "What is South Dare, the set for *Deliverance*?"

Catherine laughed. "I always think of that movie when I come out here. Some of them even look like the banjo player."

"Tell me about it. This is his hometown."

When I reviewed my notes later at the detachment some questions nagged me. Why would a white-collar guy like David Jordan endanger his family by living in South Dare? Why did the locals have such animosity? And what was up between him and his wife? I couldn't rule anything out at this stage. I'd longed for a file like this, but my previous detachment back in British Columbia had been so big, everyone specialized. No matter how hard I tried to get ahead I always got stuck with traffic control, or busting prostitutes and johns, or worse, counselling battered women or rape victims.

The inner flames burst into life.

The firebomber was mine.

the Neighbour

At day's end I stored my pistol in its metal case, stowed it in my locker, then showered and changed into jeans and a sweater. As I drove my red Jeep away from the grey slush and bright lights of Sterling's strip malls I felt drained, like a drunk with a hangover. *Why couldn't I love justice without becoming someone I couldn't control?*

The Jeep tires swished on the wet highway and the full moon gleamed on the snowy fields. Across the water the lights from the village of Cornwallis Cove twinkled. The Annapolis Valley radio station played *My Achy Breaky Heart*. Then a weather report promised more snow and unseasonably cold temperatures for early November.

When I turned onto the road leading up the hill to my farmhouse, the heavy snow weighed the tree boughs down so they arched over the road. Snow coated every twig. The Jeep's headlights illuminated the beauty, reminding me of my childhood and how a snowfall would transform Boston's Franklin Park, covering the cigarette butts, condoms and bottle caps, decorating the leafless maples and oaks, and making even the shabbier areas near my neighbourhood look festive. Driving under the arch I felt like I was passing through a magic gateway, and for a few moments, the hell of South Dare seemed like a bad dream.

At the top of the hill several small farms spread before me. Snow frosted the spruce trees and roofs of the houses. Except for some wet tire tracks even the road ahead was white. A public service announcement about hunter safety blared on the radio. I shut it off. The beauty and wholesomeness of the countryside was as calming as the fire and South Dare had been intoxicating. Even the snow looked different here – fresh and pure instead of cold and dead. Warm yellow light shone from the windows of the farmhouses. TVs flickered in some of the front rooms and woodsmoke curled from the chimneys. This achingly beautiful place was my neighbourhood now. I'd traded a studio apartment in Surrey, British Columbia, for a nineteenth century farmhouse on sixty acres of pasture and woodlot with a small barn I used as a garage.

The sight of my darkened house almost broke the surrounding beauty's magic. Though I loved the old place with its peaked roof and single dormer window over the front door, tonight it seemed empty and cold in the stark moonlight – so unlike the happy-looking homesteads I'd just passed. An icy bough had snapped off the old maple tree and lay across my front lawn. At least I'd left the light on over the back steps.

Sniffing the fragrant woodsmoke in the chilled air I tromped through the wet snow to the back door. I glanced across the white meadow to Catherine's place. Her kitchen windows glowed and her wagon was parked in her laneway. I wondered if she'd already filed her story about the South Dare fire and put her weekly newspaper to bed.

A bare bulb cast a harsh bright light on my damp cold kitchen. Years of footsteps had scuffed a brownish trail on the faded flowered linoleum. A few dingy white cabinets hung over a worn porcelain double sink. The previous owner's aqua and chrome table and chairs still occupied the room's centre.

The kitchen had lots of windows, though I had no blinds for them yet. The oil stove dominated the interior wall. Its weight made the floor sag, tilting the monster so one of its warming oven doors hung open. I cranked up the oil and threw a lighted match into the carburetor. The fuel oil smell and the fan's annoying rattle had taken me a while to get used to. Aside from the stove the other homey touch was the single bed under the back windows.

Many of the older homes in Nova Scotia still had a bed in the kitchen, going back to the days when it was the warmest room in the house. Though I hated the frilly yellow bed covering, matching pillow covers and curtains, my budget and schedule didn't allow me to do everything I wanted to right away.

No, my farmhouse didn't feel like home. It felt like an investment, something I'd scrimped and saved for, and the home I hoped to create was still somewhere in the future. That made me glad Catherine was expecting me for supper. I insisted on throwing in some money toward groceries so as not to be obligated to her. After shovelling my back steps I sprinted across the snowy meadow for supper.

The fire in Catherine's cast iron stove hissed and popped, radiating warmth. The wide pine floorboards, braided rug, and stained glass lamp hanging over the table comforted my senses. I stretched my legs across another chair toward the stove. Catherine grasped the neck of a large screw-top bottle of white wine and plunked it on the table. I poured myself a glass to help get my mind off the firebomber.

Typically I would have done an exhaustive post mortem on the investigation, replaying over and over what had happened at the crime scene. This time I refused to beat myself up for how things had gone. I'd moved back to Nova Scotia to start a new life, and one of my goals was to stop being a workaholic perfectionist. I needed balance, a life outside work. It was okay to enjoy Catherine's friendship. Catherine padded to the table with a couple of placemats and a fistful of tableware.

"Where's Grace?" I hoped it wasn't too late to see Catherine's six-year-old daughter.

"In bed. Her nose was running and she was pretty cranky." Catherine took two earthenware bowls from the cupboard and ambled over to the woodstove.

The news disappointed me. Grace was one of the new joys in my life. In recent years the only children I'd ever seen were victims of porn or abuse, or they were pawns in domestic violence. What a change to be around a happy, innocent little girl who loved teddy bears and horses.

Catherine ladled stew into the bowls. "Edna's stew is fantastic. I've already had some, but I think I'll have a little more." She opened one of the wood stove's warming ovens and removed a pan of fresh rolls. She sat across from me and poured herself more wine in a goblet-sized glass.

"Your housekeeper's a great cook." I unfolded a paper napkin on my lap. "She cost an arm and a leg?"

"Edna costs less than putting Grace in daycare. And she cooks and cleans. It's like having a wife."

I laughed. "I could use a wife too. Someone to iron my shirts…"

Catherine bit into the crusty golden bun and winced with pleasure at the taste. "These rolls are better than sex."

I laughed again and raised a spoonful of stew to my mouth. *When did I start laughing when a conversation made me uncomfortable? I* reminded myself to cut the laugh track. It made me sound nervous.

The beef was moist and tender, but needed salt. As I reached for the shaker I felt Catherine staring at me and looked up at her shining brown eyes. "What?" I grinned.

"Nothing. It's nice to have you here." She smiled, a dimple forming in her left cheek. "Speaking of sex, why don't you bring that gorgeous Will Bright by here some evening?"

I stiffened. "I don't socialize with people from work."

Catherine grinned. "Whoa! Sounds like I hit a sore spot."

Under the table she poked my shin with her slippered toe. "You have a crush on him, don't you?"

"Puhleeze." At least I didn't laugh.

"I bet he flirts with you, doesn't he?" she smirked, poking me again. "Some girls get all the breaks. You are so drop-dead beautiful, Linda."

I hunched over the stew, rolling my eyes. *Beautiful.* My looks made me feel like prey so I deliberately played them down.

"My ex-husband ran off with Will's fiancée. Ever since then he has avoided me. I mean, it's not my fault she dumped him, you know?" She took another sip. "And why his fiancée would prefer Michael to him sure beats me."

I shook more salt over my stew, surprised by this little tidbit of information. Will struck me as someone who broke hearts, not the other way around. This made him seem more human. "Will's personal life doesn't interest me."

"I think it does." She grinned.

"Should I tell him *you're* interested?"

"Tell him he can put his shoes under my bed anytime."

I raised my eyebrows, my palms growing damp. I knew some women liked to discuss their sex lives, but I'd never felt comfortable doing it.

"Just kidding!" Catherine's foot nudged me again. "Actually, I'm dying to talk about the fire."

"What about it?"

"I heard someone threw a Molotov cocktail. And Staff Sergeant Ramsay says you have no suspects."

The wooden chair creaked as my muscles tensed. "It's under investigation. I can't tell you any more than Karen did."

"So there *was* a Molotov cocktail?"

I shrugged.

"Oh, come on! I won't tell anyone where I got my information. You know that."

"Please, I'd rather not talk about work." As much as I enjoyed Catherine there was no way I going to blurt out my need to keep the job from consuming me. Besides, I'd never reveal details of an investigation to a journalist.

A look of irritation crossed her face. "Okay, you can't tell me anything. I understand." Catherine rubbed the lipstick off the rim of her wineglass. "Can I talk to you about it, though? Maybe I can bounce things off you and you can let me know if I'm on the right track. I know some things about David Jordan you might find interesting."

Catherine had hooked me. Maybe she would tell me something that would make up for my lack of success at the fire scene. "Okay." I glanced at my watch, trying to appear blasé. "But nothing that happens between us appears in your paper. Ever."

"Of course!" She pushed a manila file folder toward me. "I did a story on David Jordan when he arrived here a couple of years ago. He's pretty weird."

Inside the file lay a stack of yellowed newspaper stories and pages of notes she must have typed on her laptop.

"About four or five years ago David got fired from a church outside Halifax. From what I could gather he's one of those zealous types with no people skills. His first wife left him at the same time the church let him go. Took the kids."

I rifled through the musty-smelling clippings. "The kids I saw this morning didn't exist four or five years ago?"

"No, this is a new marriage. New kids. His first wife divorces him. The denomination he works for doesn't take kindly to divorce so they kick him out. He's broke, depressed, can't earn a living. Then he's diagnosed with cancer. The doctors tell him it's terminal. He becomes jaundiced, pencil-thin, except for a belly like he's nine months pregnant. There's a picture of him with the article."

"And God intervened," I deadpanned. *How is any of this relevant?*

Catherine chuckled. "Yes. He believes it was a miracle. His doctors called it 'spontaneous remission.'"

"So, he's out to save the world now, is he?" I spooned carrots and potatoes into my mouth.

"Out to save the world. Yeah, right!" Catherine grinned.

For some reason my heart began thudding and my mouth grew dry. My mind drifted. *Save the world.* Ron seemed like a saviour to us at Holy Child. Suddenly, I saw him standing in my bedroom in Jamaica Plain. The memory was so vivid I almost choked. He popped a clerical collar from around his neck, and placed the stiff white band on the dresser next to the gowned replica of the Infant of Prague Gran had given me.

I was perched on my single bed under a poster of Pope John Paul II, wearing my school uniform, my navy blue and green skirt hiked up so the woollen afghan tickled my bare thigh. My heart fluttered with anxiety as I thought about how much I wanted to please him. "Are you scared, sweetheart?" he asked. He sat down next to me, making the bedsprings groan. He gathered me in his arms, stroked my hair, then loosened my blue tie and unbuttoned my white blouse. I heard the scratchy sound of his fingers on the cloth and smelled his oniony breath.

Feeling my stomach curdle I fought to hear what Catherine was saying. *Don't think about Ron. Don't.* I hadn't thought about him in years. *Why now? Is David Jordan another Ron?*

"David Jordan came here as an associate pastor at Cornwallis Cove Baptist. I guess he had to take a junior position to redeem himself. At least they were willing to overlook his divorce."

"So what's up with the church in South Dare?" The flashback had made me so tense.

"He's still at Cornwallis Cove teaching Sunday school. But he started the new church – meets in the afternoon – and moved to South Dare. Maybe he wants to get out from under the authority of the Baptists. Start some kind of cult. I don't know."

Unable to concentrate any longer I feigned a yawn and covered my mouth. My watch read 9:07.

"I can't talk about this now." I spoke more abruptly than intended. "I've got to wind down so I can sleep."

Catherine's plucked eyebrows shot up and her mouth formed a small *o*. "I haven't even told you the juiciest stuff yet!"

I carried my wineglass, bowl, and utensils to the dishwasher, opened the door, and looked for a place to put them. "I have to get up at five. Going for a run tomorrow morning."

Catherine padded behind me. "Did something I said upset you?" Catherine tugged the sleeve of my sweater. "Are you alright?"

"I'm fine. If you tell me more, I'll be up all night thinking about it."

I couldn't look at her. Ron's face flashed through my mind again. "Let's go in the other bedroom, sweetheart. That bed is bigger." I felt the goosebumps on my knees. I was thirteen again. I couldn't go into Dad's bedroom, even if he *had* moved out to live with his new wife. Even if he'd never know. I placed my spoon in the caddy and my bowl on the top rack.

Catherine slid my dirty wineglass toward the sink. "Well, okay. But you might want to hear this. David was active in the anti-abortion movement. He was charged with – "

"Not now, Catherine." As I interrupted her, my cheeks flushed and my heart pounded. "I need to sleep. If I'm not alert and rested tomorrow, someone could get hurt." I slid my arms into the sleeves of my parka.

"I'm sorry. I didn't mean to upset you." Catherine's voice shook a little. She padded back to the kitchen table and fumbled with the file.

"I'm not upset. Tired, that's all."

Catherine searched my face. It astonished me how much she seemed to care, how much she seemed to fear damaging our new friendship. The sudden affection I felt for her hurt like a numb arm when the blood starts circulating again. The mask I'd spent years moulding slipped for a second.

"You could read this tomorrow." She offered the file to me like an olive branch. "Please forgive my pushiness, but there's stuff you need to know about David. Make sure you look at the affidavit from his ex-wife."

the **Preacher**

With the file clamped under my arm I stumbled across the snow-covered grass clumps back to my house. Thin clouds raced beneath the full moon. Tears stung my eyes but the wind dried them up. Feeling sorry for myself was out of the question. I couldn't even remember the last time I'd cried.

I tossed Catherine's file onto the kitchen table and headed straight upstairs to run a bath. Into the churning tap water I threw a handful of Epsom salts and sprinkled several drops of lavender essential oil. I avoided my reflection in the mirror.

In my bedroom I stripped off my clothes. Every item had a place and every action was part of a sensible routine that kept me sane and my house tidy, no matter what stress work threw at me. Catherine had convinced me candles, hot baths, and essential oils relieved stress, so it was off to the bathroom with the box of wooden matches.

The vanilla-scented candles Catherine had given me flickered on the bathtub's edge as a cool draft blew the flames sideways. Fragrant steam wafted up from the full tub. My house was chilly and my skin prickled with goosebumps as I slid into the water.

I leaned against the back of the tub, feeling the water seep into the hair pinned up at the back of my neck. Despite my efforts to relax, David Jordan dominated my thoughts. *Why did he trigger such a vivid memory of Ron?* Ron seldom crossed my mind anymore, and when he did I usually felt nothing. My mind replayed the way David's wife had either flinched or shaken his hand off every time he touched her. The men from South Dare called him a pervert, a child molester. Said he set his own house on fire. Yet how credible were those swamp dwellers? I surged out of the water.

Five minutes later I was downstairs at the kitchen table reading Catherine's file, shivering in a white terry cloth robe. I cranked up the heat and filled the ceramic kettle with water. The oil stove fan rattled. The headline of the first yellowed article read: Pastor claims miracle cured his cancer.

The picture of David Jordan sick, emaciated and bald shocked me. His basset hound eyes, even in the old newspaper photo, had a compelling stare. Another picture showed a smiling Jordan, his hair growing back, no beard, and his smiling new wife Anne. Happier days. What a change from the radiant young woman in the picture to the angry woman I'd met at the fire.

Thumbing through more of the articles I came across a copy of an affidavit signed by a woman named Barbara Jordan. As I skimmed the pages it dawned on me that Barbara Jordan was David's first wife. I clamped my fist against my mouth. In her sworn testimony taken during their divorce proceedings she accused David of sexually abusing their seven-year-old daughter. I thought of Catherine's sweet little daughter Grace sleeping innocently in her upstairs bedroom. My knuckles pressed against my teeth. I tried to slow my breathing.

There he was again. Ron. Memories of how he discarded me like a used condom after he raped me, and moved onto his next victim. It was like stitches in a deep wound had torn open and pain gushed out like hot blood. The water boiled in the ceramic kettle. I had overfilled it, and droplets bubbled out of the spout and sizzled and bounced on the stove's smooth hot surface. I jumped up, bumping my knee against the chrome table leg. With shaking hands I poured water into a mug over a peppermint tea bag.

Scraping the chair across the linoleum I sat down again and flipped through the remaining articles, looking for information about any criminal charges against David. I pulled out an article from *The Halifax Daily News*.

Police charge anti-abortion pastor with fire-bombing abortion clinic. I peered at the picture accompanying the yellowed article. It showed David Jordan chained to the stair railing under the abortion clinic's sign.

Jordan pleads not guilty in clinic firebombing, read another headline. The article showed a picture of David walking away from the Halifax law courts accompanied by a priest and a female lawyer wearing a black legal gown.

Then I read: Police drop charges against anti-abortion pastor; Abortion clinic firebombing remains unsolved.

Under the articles were copies of handwritten notes from an interview between Catherine and a Halifax police detective.

"Jordan's a fanatic," I read. "He believes doctors are murdering babies when they do abortions. People like him see bombing an abortion clinic on par with blowing up railroad tracks to a Nazi concentration camp, though he denies the comparison."

"The Crown couldn't pin anything on him," the note continued. "He had an alibi, but he could have been part of a conspiracy. Other anti-abortion types accounted for his whereabouts. These groups are tight-knit, so it's hard to infiltrate them."

David Jordan came across like a fascist vigilante. I clutched my stomach, willing my body to stop trembling.

My instincts told me he was the firebomber, but I needed to calm down, develop a strategy, and prove a case against him. I grabbed a notebook and wrote down the detective's name. When I noticed some transcripts of TV news reports by a journalist named Heather Franklin I made a note to contact her as well.

That night my thoughts raced like a revving engine. Over and over I rehearsed my questions for the appointment Will and I had with David Jordan in the morning. Whenever my mind slowed down it filled up with memories of Ron's muscular body pinning me to my creaking bed, his mouth crushing mine. I could feel his teeth clacking against mine and his probing tongue making me gag. I choked for air. I shifted my thoughts to the fire, to David Jordan, to anything but Ron.

Early the next morning thin shapeless clouds raced across the dark sky as streaks of white and pink light glowed in the east. A warm damp wind blew in from the south, carrying the smell of woodsmoke and wet leaves. I hadn't eaten breakfast or made my lunch the way I always did before leaving. Nor had I gone for my usual morning run. I tried to blank my mind by focusing on my senses, centring myself in the present as best I could.

At the detachment I changed into my uniform, donned my Sam Browne belt, and stuck my pistol in the holster. I flicked on the fluorescent lights in the office area and logged onto one of the three computers we shared. The keyboard felt tacky. Grimy fingerprints surrounded the on/off button. I downloaded information on David Jordan and then printed it out. There wasn't much. Nothing about sexual abuse allegations.

Catherine's file would have to be returned so I made copies. As I leafed through the first stack of copied pages, still warm from the copier, I saw a woman's magnified eyes behind thick glasses staring at me from a newspaper photograph. It was the same woman who had driven the Jordans away from the fire in her station wagon.

`Social worker fired for whipping up devil hysteria.`

The article quoted David Jordan as saying, "Margaret Roach had the courage to call our attention to abuse that has been going on for years in South Dare. In my opinion, the hysteria comes from her accusers. They're lying. A lot of people around here are in deep denial."

The copier whirred. As I copied further sections of the file I tried to read some of the articles I hadn't looked at the night before.

`Judge throws satanic ritual abuse case out of court.`

Satanic ritual abuse! *Come on!* Making a face I slapped the article onto the glass, closed the cover, and pressed print.

That wasn't the only article about satanic ritual abuse, or SRA as I'd seen it referred to somewhere. I copied them all and then leaned against the copier to read them. The accused man, Reginald "Rex" Dare, was from South Dare. Yellowed newspaper pictures showed him having a thick moustache and slicked-back hair. I didn't recognize his face or name from the fire at David

Jordan's. And Constable Will Bright was mentioned as one of the investigating officers. That explained his connection to David Jordan and the social worker. My already low estimation of Will plummeted even further. *How could he believe this satanic ritual abuse garbage?*

I darted into the conference room that doubled as the staff lounge and plugged in the electric kettle. While the water came to a boil, I paced. Once I'd made myself tea I tried to read the Halifax daily paper. The print swam in front of my eyes.

At 8:15 Will came in with a fried egg sandwich and a large Tim Horton's coffee. He eased into a chair across from me, his big teeth bared in a wide-mouthed grin as he unwrapped his breakfast. His copper-coloured hair was damp and he smoothed it, probably trying to get rid of the imprint from his hatband.

We exchanged greetings, but I looked away so as not to encourage him. When he'd first seen me the day before he'd done an involuntary double take and then stammered, "I, I didn't expect you to be so, so stunning."

No matter what I did to downplay my looks guys like Will never took me seriously. Some female Mounties were happy in what I called the "pink ghetto," assigned to counselling battered wives and sexual assault victims. Not me. Socially my looks weren't such a great advantage either. I became the object of gossip and sexual innuendos. I didn't want the problems I'd had in British Columbia to start all over again. My mind drifted back to the satanic ritual abuse case and our upcoming interview with David Jordan. Will's voice jarred me back to the present.

"I hear you bought the Harrison place in Cornwallis Cove." His deep blue eyes crinkled around the edges.

"That's right." I glanced at my watch.

"Beautiful spot." His voice had a Nova Scotian twang. "That house must be 150 years old. Have you done a lot of work?"

"Some." My shoulders stiffened.

"Now that the leaves are gone I bet you can see the water from some of your windows." He sipped his coffee. "I've got a place out in Cornwallis Cove too, but on the other side of the village. Sterling County's God's country, isn't it?"

"Yes, it is beautiful." I still avoided looking at him.

He studied my face, which made me self-conscious. "You were out in Surrey, right?"

My heart sank. *Had he already been checking up on me with members in British Columbia?*

"I hear the cost of living out on the West Coast is something terrible," he continued. "How did you ever save up enough money for a down payment with the rent they charge out there?"

"I won the lottery," I quipped, then plunked my notebook on the table. "I have some questions."

"Shoot." A tiny piece of Kleenex clung to a little dot of blood on his neck. He must have cut himself shaving.

"Why would a firebomber fill a cocktail with kerosene?"

"To keep from getting injured. Gasoline fumes can explode prematurely." He wiped some egg yolk off his chin with the back of his hand.

"Exactly. You know Jordan was charged with firebombing an abortion clinic?"

"So?"

"Maybe he did his own place too." *Could Will see how my temples throbbed?*

"That case in Halifax was a joke! Everyone in the pro-life movement was a suspect. Little old ladies with blue hair were suspects. The media propelled that bandwagon." He gulped his coffee, then took another bite of his sandwich. "David didn't firebomb the clinic. Or his house, if that's what you're getting at."

"We shouldn't rule him out."

Will stifled a burp. "I wouldn't put too much weight on anything the people from South Dare told you yesterday." He stood. "One of them did it." He glanced at his watch. "We're not raising the abortion clinic angle."

He crumpled the trash from his breakfast and tossed it at the wastebasket. He missed, but had already swaggered out the door. Mimicking his last words I scooped up his trash and hurled it into the wastebasket.

David Jordan arrived at 9:06 a.m., a little later than expected. A smarmy air of serenity and charm replaced the sad, stunned manner he'd shown at the fire. He was too calm, too cheerful. His emotional state under the circumstances seemed weird to me, like a sociopath's. David's heavy-lidded eyes moved from Will's face to mine, then rested there.

"Why didn't you notify us when you moved to South Dare?" Will asked.

"Notify you?" David grinned. "Why would I do that?"

"Didn't it occur to you that Rex would be out to get you?"

David shrugged, his attention still focused on me. "I wasn't worried about Rex."

Will shook his head.

David's stare made me self-conscious. "Why did you move out there?" I asked.

"We wanted to develop trust because we saw the need for a church there."

Need for you to rip them off? I felt my face grow hot. "Your wife said your place got vandalized?" I tried to keep anger from leaking into my voice.

"Someone broke the windows in our woodshed. We had our tires slashed. Sometimes people threw rocks at our car. I think someone poisoned our dog."

Will leaned on his elbows. "You should have reported this."

"What for? I expected resistance. We decided to trust God for protection."

I snorted. "Obviously God wasn't protecting you when your house burned down."

An uncomfortable silence settled over the room. David looked down at his long narrow hands and made a steeple with his tapered fingers.

"You seem awfully calm for someone whose wife and kids nearly died in a fire." We locked eyes.

"I thank God for getting us out of there safely." David emphasized every word like a hypnotist.

"You put your family at risk by living out there." My voice rose. "Your house burns down and you barely get out with your lives and you're…"

David's eyes bored into me.

I steeled myself and stared back until he looked down.

"God led us to South Dare. Placed a burden on our hearts. I thought we'd be safe." He spoke softly, gazing again at his steepled hands. He was good! He had the hypnotic showman shtick down pat.

A derisive smile crept across my face. "God told you to go?"

"I'm happy to answer your questions. But I didn't come here to have my beliefs ridiculed or things I say twisted."

Will shook his head. He slouched in his seat as much as his muscular body would permit. "No one's trying to ridicule your religious beliefs." He shot me a warning glance.

I concentrated on my pen scratching words on the page, feeling oddly anxious and disoriented. Ron flashed through my mind again. I saw him take off his black clerical shirt and hang it on the doorknob. Goosebumps covered my knees. I hugged them to my chin, feeling the tightness of my bra and white cotton panties.

I remembered the rumble of his voice. "You are so beautiful. Remember, you are the Bride of Christ. And I am the Bridegroom. There is nothing wrong with what we are doing, but we have to keep it a secret because this is like the confessional, right sweetheart?" I remembered being spellbound, knowing something was terribly wrong, but worshipping him and assuming if he thought it was okay, it must be. He unbuttoned the fly of his faded Levis, stripped to his jockey shorts. The bed springs jangled. The vividness of the memory nauseated me. I shook it off. I glanced at David, terrified he'd been reading my mind. But he and Will were deep in conversation. *How long had I zoned out?* I glanced at my notebook and saw I'd been recording their conversation, even while lost in the awful flashback.

"The satanic ritual abuse is still going on," David said. His eyes kept coming back to me, like searchlights.

"You know we've investigated the rumours," Will said. "We've never been able to find any proof of a cult. Sexual abuse, yes. But no cult."

"Most cases of SRA have been proven to be bunk," I said.

David leaned toward Will. "Look, I share your reservations. I know these things can be blown way out of proportion. But something unspeakably evil is still going on out there." David's eyes were on me again.

The hairs on the back of my neck lifted. *You! You're the evil.*

The room seemed to lose oxygen. The green walls started closing in. I felt an almost overwhelming urge to run out of the room.

My heart was firing like a machine gun. *This is crazy. Get a hold of yourself.* I looked down at my ballpoint pen and noticed the ink was almost gone. To drive off my panic I concentrated on it. Told myself my blood sugar must be low because I'd skipped breakfast. Flipping a page I peered at the questions I'd prepared, focusing on them. I forced myself to breathe slowly so I wouldn't gulp air.

I squared my shoulders. "People in the community think you set your house on fire."

"I heard that." David continued to study me.

What is his problem? He was making me angry now. "This isn't the first time you've been suspected of firebombing a building, is it Mr. Jordan?" My voice was steady now, even hard.

He looked hurt. "Are you considering me a suspect?" he asked Will.

Will glared at me. "No, we're not."

After David left I offered to bring the car around. I needed a few minutes alone to collect myself. When I'd calmed down I drove to the front door and waited for Will. Our next stop was an appointment with David Jordan's wife who was staying with the children at the Baptist parsonage in Cornwallis Cove.

I checked my watch again. *What's keeping him?* A few moments later Will burst through the front door, barrelled down the short flight of stone steps, and heaved his large body into the passenger seat.

He twisted his torso to face me, baring his teeth in a wide crooked smile that didn't match the cold look in his eyes. "I thought we agreed the abortion clinic bombing was irrelevant." He pulled the door shut.

I shrugged and flicked on the turn signal. "I don't recall agreeing." Looking straight ahead I inhaled slowly, and released my jaw when I realized I was clenching my teeth.

Will was still facing me. "Don't you think you were a little hostile back there?"

"Hostile?" I adjusted the rear-view mirror. "Maybe I was compensating for how nice you were. He a friend of yours?"

"David Jordan did not firebomb his own house." His knees

scraped the dashboard, even though he'd pushed the seat back. He sprawled, his shoulders almost touching mine.

I kept my mouth shut. No point arguing.

Cornwallis Cove Baptist Church was built into a steep hill that fell to a narrow tidal inlet. The parsonage, a huge three-storey red house, loomed over the sidewalk just up the hill from the church. The parsonage's small laneway, just big enough for two cars side by side, was empty so I parked there. We climbed out. Without saying anything to me Will bounded up a steep flight of wooden stairs to a door on the second level.

My muscles were tense, so I stretched my arms over my head and brought them slowly to my sides. The snow melted into a rushing, rattling torrent along the gutter and gurgled into a big storm drain. I tried to imagine my anxiety going down with the water, being carried out to sea with the tide. The village below was laid out like a scene from an old-fashioned Christmas card.

Wooden houses clustered on the hillsides. Main Street cut sharply down the hill, crossed a causeway and a narrow bridge over a creek that emptied into the cove, then climbed the steep hill on the other side. Old wooden buildings perched on pilings lined the causeway, housing the Cove pharmacy, the Co-op that sold groceries and hardware, the Cornwallis Craft Association gift store, the Royal Bank, and the Crow's Nest bookstore. Since it was now high tide blue-grey water almost licked the bottoms of the buildings.

When a matronly white-haired woman answered Will's knock I sprinted up the wooden stairs to meet Ruth Harwood, wife of the senior pastor at Cornwallis Cove Baptist.

We stepped onto a plastic boot tray inside the orderly kitchen. Years of scrubbing had faded the green and white counters. A portable dishwasher hooked up to the sink whirred and hummed, sending the abrasive odour of detergent through its vent. The smell competed with the scent of cinnamon and fresh bread baking. Will surprised me by unlacing his boots, stepping onto the kitchen floor in sock feet, and heading for the living room. *Why hadn't he asked for Anne to come to us in the kitchen? What if there was an emergency call and we had to make a quick exit?* But I was the newbie here, so I reluctantly stepped out of my boots too and followed Ruth and Will into the living room, where Anne sat in a green upholstered rocker.

Her narrow face was blotchy, her eyes red from crying. She wore a black turtleneck under a long brown corduroy jumper. Will asked her many of the same questions I'd already gone over with her the previous day.

"You've been through a rough time." I sat across from her on a wooden chair.

Her trembling hand reached for a tissue. She blew her nose. "We really believed God called us there." She sounded like her husband's parrot. "Then something like this happens."

Will shifted in his seat on the couch. He flung his arm across the back.

Anne sniffled. "Before this happened I thought I was afraid because my faith wasn't strong like David's."

"Maybe your fears were trying to tell you something." I tried to sound kind.

Anne burst into tears. "I'm sorry. I really can't help you. I don't know who started the fire. My husband might know."

"Why is that?" I asked.

Anne reached for another tissue and wiped her nose and eyes. "People confide in him. But he won't tell me or anyone else what they say. I don't know anything."

"Could your husband have set the fire himself, Mrs. Jordan?"

Will groaned and shook his head.

Anne set her shoulders. "Absolutely not!"

Ruth stood in the doorway, twisting her hands in her apron. "You couldn't possibly think that David..."

"These are just routine questions, ma'am." I turned back to Anne. "Do you have insurance?" I felt sorry for her, so I made my tone as gentle as I could.

I had to ask. Maybe he had a policy she didn't know about.

"No, we don't. We lost everything." She sounded defensive.

Will cleared his throat. "David says you'll be moving temporarily into the church in South Dare." His voice sounded syrupy with concern. "Is that where we can contact you?" He stood to indicate the interview was over.

Anne shook her head. "David is. The children and I will be staying here until we find an apartment in Sterling." The little girl with the high round forehead peeked around the door. Ruth shooed her upstairs. So, I was right. There was big trouble between Anne and David. Will was eyeing me, so I slipped my notebook into my pocket and stood up.

Ruth brushed past us and wrapped her arms around Anne who had started sobbing.

"We'll show ourselves out," Will said.

He clomped out the back door and down the outside stairs, making the old wooden building vibrate. Still inside, I laced my boots, collecting my thoughts. I could hear Ruth trying to soothe Anne.

"Where is God right now?" Anne sobbed. "Why didn't God protect us? What are we going to do?"

Ruth murmured something.

"I have no home for my children. We have no money, unless I can get more work at the hospital. *I've* been providing. Not God. *I'm* the one carrying all the weight of this family, while David tries to save the world. I'm sick to death of it."

As I closed the back door behind me with a gentle click I remembered the Infant of Prague replica in my childhood bedroom. The doll-like figure had a crown and royal robes, with his little hand raised in blessing. It was supposed to represent the Baby Jesus. The Holy Child. The Infant of Prague sure didn't protect me when Ron pinned me to the motel bed and tore my panties. Neither did the Virgin Mary.

And God didn't protect me from getting pregnant either.

the Molester

On the way to South Dare Will gave me the silent treatment, speaking to me only when giving me directions. I wasn't sure which I preferred because he had been way too chirpy and talkative earlier that morning. He had me on a seesaw – overly friendly one minute, cold and distant the next. A control thing. I wasn't going to fall for it.

We took the back road from Cornwallis Cove instead of the highway. The sun had melted most of the snow into big puddles, which shimmered in the light. Outside the village we passed several houses with long rows of small cages in front. A peaked shingled roof covered each line of cages, protecting some kind of animal from the weather.

"What's in those cages?" I asked.

"Mink or silver fox. Mostly mink around here. Some people from South Dare muck out the cages for a living."

The tires swished through a deep puddle, spraying muddy water on either side. Then the pavement ended and the gravel road's potholes rocked the car. Bare maple saplings and scrubby brush hugged the road until we passed a swamp where rotted trees poked up through the rippling water.

We turned right onto a dirt track full of boulders and water-filled ruts. Gravel popped under the tires. Weedy-looking trees and brush closed in around us until we reached a clearing where an ugly two-storey house with a crooked picture window loomed over three shacks and a trailer. A massive rusting satellite dish stood next to the house.

"What's going on?" I braked to a stop. "I thought we were supposed to meet the IDENT guy, what's his name."

"First, we're going to see the unofficial mayor of South Dare."

A couple of snarling dogs greeted us until a man with a bushy lion's mane of shoulder-length hair called them inside.

Will opened the door without knocking, and the first thing that hit me was the humid smell of beer, stale sweat and dog feces. The picture window had black curtains blocking most of the light, so it took my eyes a few moments to adjust. It looked like a makeshift tavern instead of a living room. The room had about six white plastic tables and at least twenty chairs. Bluish light flickered from a big-screen TV.

At one table sat Gordon Dare and another man whom Will introduced as Rex Dare, Gordon's younger brother. He wore a nylon mesh sleeveless undershirt, his hairy chest and arms sporting green tattoos of dragons, skulls and naked women.

Was this Reginald "Rex" Dare, the man I'd read about this morning who had been charged with satanic ritual abuse three years earlier? Catherine had said that incest ran rampant in these poverty-stricken isolated communities. Was this the man who'd orchestrated the abuse of his own children? I tried to keep my face from showing my disgust.

Rex bared big yellow teeth in a smile. "So, this is the new constable. Welcome to South Dare." His left eye focused on me while his right eye wandered. He had a few days' worth of stubble on his chin.

Will strode around the room. "Didn't see you at the fire, Rex. You never showed up to admire your big blaze."

"You have a warrant?" Rex's good eye glinted. When he sipped his beer his bushy moustache brushed the foam. Gordon leered at me.

"Don't need a warrant to ask questions." Will opened the curtain hanging in the doorway to the adjoining room. Beyond I could see a storeroom containing stacks of cardboard boxes full of beer, packages of chips and cigarette cartons. I didn't need a degree in rocket science to figure Rex was a bootlegger.

Will peered into the storeroom. "Why are you trying to burn the pastor out?"

"Sit down. Relax." Rex kicked a chair toward him. Will came around and stood next to me. Rex gestured with his thumb and Gordon fetched two beers from an old fridge in the corner, clutching them with his deformed fingers. He twisted off their caps and pushed them toward us. The blue light of the TV flickered and out of the corner of my eye I saw the white curvaceous forms of two naked women writhing together.

"Turn that off," Will ordered, "or I'll arrest you for pirating that signal."

Rex clicked the remote to a shopping network, then sipped his beer and wiped his moustache with the back of his hand. "What I hear, the man set his own house on fire."

"You gotta do better than that," Will said. "I could have a warrant in no time and be all over you like a bad smell."

"Hey, I'm being for real here. My nephew Alan was out checking his rabbit snares yesterday morning and he seen the pastor in his front yard with a baseball bat. He seen him break his living room window and throw in a cocktail."

Will grimaced. "Aggie's son? Come on."

Rex turned to me. "You're way too beautiful to be a cop. You must have all them other Mounties in a frenzy."

Gordon flicked his pink tongue at me.

"Stop it, Gordon!" Rex shifted toward me in the white plastic chair. "She's a lady." He puffed out his chest like a peacock fanning his tail. "You married?"

I narrowed my eyes. "We'll get a statement from your nephew."

"Do I stand a chance with you, gorgeous?" Rex grinned.

He radiated sexual magnetism that made my blood fizz like acid.

Will caught my eye and made a subtle gesture toward the door with his head. It bugged me that he was calling all the shots, but I wasn't going to complain about it in front of Rex and Gordon. In unison, Will and I strode to the door. When Will pulled it open, sunlight flooded the room.

Holding the door open for me Will twisted to face Rex. "We'll be seeing you. And I'll have a warrant."

"You come anytime, sweetheart," Rex grinned. "I'm happy to answer the lovely young lady's questions."

I hesitated in the doorway, but Will prodded me outside. The noonday sun was blinding.

"That pastor, he's got a thing for kids!" Rex shouted after me. "He's a child molester. Some of the women want to make complaints." Will positioned his large form in the door frame, his thick hand clutching the grimy woodwork.

I poked my head back into the room. "Which women?" I asked.

Will did not lower his arm. *How dare he use his physical size to try to keep me from doing my job.* I saw a vision of myself breaking his arm with a karate chop.

"Trudy Cranwell, for one." Rex tipped his beer bottle up to drain the last sip, watching us with his good eye.

Will grabbed my elbow and nudged me away from the door with his hip.

"Trudy? You're not fooling anyone." Will let the door close.

Hey, I want to ask more questions! I brushed by him and reached for the doorknob, but he grabbed my elbow again.

I jerked it out of his grasp. "I'm going back in!"

"If you want to stay out here alone, be my guest." He spun and lumbered down the rocky path to the car.

I glared at him as he circled it, checking the tires probably to see if one of the locals had slashed them. *I've got the keys, buster!* When I'd calmed myself down enough to no longer see myself drop-kicking him to the dirt, I marched down the path and confronted him over the roof of the car. "Who is Trudy Cranwell?"

"Don't go there," Will growled. "Rex is trying to confuse you."

"I'm not the one who's confused."

The pupils in Will's eyes shrank to pinpricks. "Rex Dare is dog dung. He molests his own children." The muscles in his jaw flexed.

"What's up with grabbing my elbow back there?"

"Give me the keys, or open the door!" Teeth clenched, he looked away, took his hat off, and ran his fingers through his hair. Anger mottled his cheeks with red. He checked his watch. In a more conciliatory tone he said, "Charlie from IDENT is waiting."

Silently counting to ten, I fumbled with the key and unlocked the doors.

While driving slowly around the potholes and boulders in the Dare's rutted laneway I observed Will out of the corner of my eye. He looked straight ahead, his face still red, his mouth pursed.

"Don't ever grab me like that again," I said when I'd calmed down enough so that my voice would sound normal.

He shrugged. "Did I grab you? Sorry. Didn't mean to." He glanced at me, apologetically.

I weighed my response. His apology seemed genuine enough. He was doing his seesaw routine again. Remembering my silent pledge to be a team player I decided to accept it. "Do it again, and I will bust your lip."

He laughed. I hated the strange relief I felt that he got my joke. Yet maybe I didn't want him to take it that way. I really could bust his lip. He had no right to bar my way like that.

"Why are you so sure Rex firebombed the Jordan place?"

"If he didn't do it himself, he got somebody else to do it." Will stretched one of his legs as best he could in the confined space.

"Maybe David did it knowing Rex would get the blame."

Will laughed. "That is nuts." He glanced at me. "You're joking, right?"

"It's so funny I forgot to laugh."

"People are beginning to trust David and confide in him. Rex has an illegal empire to protect. He's got to drive David out."

The sun shone directly overhead as we pulled into the Jordans' former laneway. The auxiliaries who'd guarded the scene all night waved to us as they drove away. Inside the blackened shell charred beams lay at crazy angles. I scanned the area, wondering where this nephew of Rex's might have laid rabbit snares. The scrubby woods were thick with underbrush. Maybe Rex was telling the truth about an eyewitness.

Will opened the trunk and took out the case containing the forensic gear. As we began to put on protective oilskins and rubber boots the IDENT arson specialist Charlie Delaney arrived in an unmarked police car. A thin hollow-cheeked man in his early fifties, Charlie's thick white hair had a yellowish tint.

Will passed me a handful of plastic bags. "Linda, you catalogue what we find."

I rolled my eyes. *Team player, remember? Team player.*

Some of the beams were still hot. No wonder we had to wait twenty-four hours before doing this part of the investigation. We slogged through about three inches of sooty water. Charlie recorded his observations on a tiny voice recorder he kept in his breast pocket. We found some green melted glass that could have belonged to the kerosene-filled wine bottle. The heat had exploded all the living room windows outward from the heat, except one, broken from the outside.

Mid-afternoon we called it quits. On the way back to Sterling Will and I observed a couple of vehicles parked outside David Jordan's church, so I turned into the small unpaved parking lot.

Inside, light glowed around bare bulbs suspended from the open rafters. Worn maroon linoleum covered the floor. David Jordan sat on a chair, reading from a picture book to seven children sitting at his feet. They ranged in age from about five to ten. My stomach curdled. Me. Sitting on a plywood chair, gazing at Ron playing his guitar. I dug my fingernails into my palms to block the memory. David nodded toward us and then continued reading. A wooden door at the side of the room opened slightly, then closed. *Who's in there?*

A little blonde girl wearing pink sweats stood apart from the group, leaning against a post. The simpering seductive look on her face jarred me. *Is she another one of David's victims?* I clamped my jaws together and took a deep breath through my nose, afraid my rage was obvious. *The poor little kid.*

Will grabbed a plastic chair from the stack while I lifted up a rubber boot by the door and checked the sole pattern. These boots could have made the footprints Will found at the fire. My eyes were drawn to David's socked feet as one of the little boys climbed into his lap. I was clenching my teeth so hard I could have cracked one of my molars.

Margaret Roach entered through the side door carrying a pitcher and some paper cups. Someone quickly closed the door behind her. *Was someone hiding back there?* Margaret gave me a thin-lipped smile, though her magnified eyes were wary. She set the pitcher down on a corner table next to a box of soda crackers and a jar of cheese spread. At least Margaret provided some supervision for this monster. Or was she an accomplice?

A few times I caught David inspecting me. *What is he staring at?* He radiated charm. The kids seemed to adore him, though that didn't help them behave any better. Will plunked onto one of the plastic chairs and stretched his legs out.

The little girl in the pink sweats sidled up to Will, climbed on his lap, and flung her arms around his neck, her amber eyes gleaming like a cat's. Will gently tried to peel her off. She clung to him, giving him a seductive stare through half-closed eyes. She sure fit the profile of a sexual abuse victim with her inappropriate friendliness, sexual precociousness, and lack of boundaries. Seeing Will's discomfort I lifted her away from him. She kicked and spat at me. When I put her down she scampered right back to Will who stood to keep her off his lap.

David closed the picture book. "Okay, kids. Time for your snack."

The children rushed over as if they hadn't eaten all day. David ambled up beside the girl in the pink sweats. He squatted so he was at eye level with her. "Becky." He placed his hand on her shoulder.

Becky recoiled from his hand as if it were a red-hot iron. She hissed and growled like an animal. The hair rose on the back of my neck. Suddenly, the little girl before us looked more like an evil gnome.

David appeared completely unfazed. The loving expression on his face made his ex-wife's testimony blink in my brain like a flashing light – this man had abused his own daughter. "Don't be frightened, Becky," he said.

Becky whirled around and ran toward the other children. She snatched a paper cup from the table and gulped down the juice. Then she grabbed a handful of crackers and ran off to a dark corner. *That girl belongs in a mental hospital.*

David rose slowly, as if he had trouble unwinding from his squat. He and Will chit-chatted about the investigation. Satisfied Will wasn't going to be giving away any evidence, I left to take a look around the building.

I wove through the gang of children who were jumping, hollering, and racing around playing tag. I opened the side door and entered a shed-roofed kitchen to find an old fridge, stove and a laundry-style sink. A black rotary-dial phone hung on the wall.

The back door was slightly ajar. Opening it I stuck my head out and saw a wooden outhouse at the edge of the clearing.

I froze. A woman leaned against the back of the church only four feet away from me. She jumped. Her deep-set eyes locked on mine, full of fear and anguish. The cold had turned her pale skin a mottled red and white. Her shoulder-length wiry brown hair was full of split ends. Flinging a cigarette onto a patch of snow she bolted toward the woods.

"Wait! Come back!" I shouted. "I want to ask you a couple of questions." I debated whether to chase her, but she was already out of sight.

Inside the church David told me the woman was Cindy Dare, Becky's mother. He said she probably ran away because she was extremely shy. He started summoning the children to join him in a circle, so I left.

Outside, Will slouched against the police car, smoking. The corners of his mouth tipped downwards, his reddish eyebrows almost meeting. He threw his cigarette down and ground it into the squishy clay.

I told him about Cindy running away.

"Cindy is Rex's second wife. The little girl in pink? Their kid." His husky voice shook a little. He searched my eyes for a split second, then glanced away. "Becky's the way she is because of what Rex did to her. He sexually abused several children in South Dare, not only his own. We finally got it to trial and Cindy was one of our key witnesses. She choked on the stand big time. No one believed her." I thought his eyes welled up a little, but I wasn't sure.

So Rex *was* the subject of the witch hunt the judge had thrown out of court. Will had it in for Rex. Maybe that's why he had a blind spot where David was concerned. I unlocked the car door and slipped into the driver's seat. Will heaved himself in next to me.

"I wouldn't be surprised if David Jordan is a pedophile." I braced myself for Will's reaction.

"You don't quit, do you?" Will shook his head. "Don't get sucked into Rex Dare's lies. He lies even when it's to his advantage to tell the truth."

"Look at David's charm. Look at his interest in those kids. Doesn't it seem a little overboard to you? You know the profile. He's reading them stories and serving snacks to gain access." I twisted the key in the ignition, the car fired up, and we pulled away. "Soon he'll be plying them with communion wine."

"Baptists use grape juice." Will tapped my shoulder. "Not everyone who likes kids has ulterior motives. I used to coach Little League – that make me a pedophile?"

"I worked on child pornography stings. I know something about these creeps." My voice moved up half an octave.

"As if I don't!" He gazed out the window.

"What about the boots?"

"So, they match. They match the boots of every farmer in Sterling County."

"I think we should interview the nephew, the one who said he saw Jordan set the fire."

"Give me a break. At 6:30 a.m. it was pitch black. Alan couldn't have seen anything." Will shifted in his seat and clutched the strap as I swerved into the passing lane.

"Alan could have seen him through the window and watched him come outside. The moon was almost full the night of the fire."

"Alan Dare comes from the shallow end of the family gene pool. He'll say whatever Rex wants him to say. Rex's brother Gordon saw me pick up the baseball bat at the fire scene. He put two and two together."

"Well, Jordan's ex-wife accused him of sexually abusing his own daughter."

"Yeah, right!" It took a moment for what I said to register. We exchanged glances. His eyes were full of questions.

Ha, he didn't know this already. "She did. I saw a copy of her affidavit."

"Where did you get that?"

"Catherine Ross. She keeps a file on Jordan."

"People say crazy things during divorces. I wouldn't stake too much on it. It was during a custody battle, I bet."

"You can't automatically assume Rex Dare is lying just because he comes from swampsville."

"Look, I know Rex Dare. I know this community. You don't. These aren't nice people. Whether David was sexually abusing his daughter is irrelevant. Rex Dare or someone he sent firebombed the

Jordans' house. Whether or not we can prove it is another story."

Driving in silence, I made up my mind to interview Rex's nephew Alan and find out one way or the other if David Jordan was a pedophile.

the Child

That evening Catherine's daughter Grace sat at their pine kitchen table in red-footed pyjamas. Her face shone with love for me. "Hi, Auntie Linda." Her little hands were spread over a stack of picture books.

"Hi, pumpkin. What you got there?" I sat across from her and examined the cover of *Green Eggs and Ham* by Dr. Seuss.

"I can read this." Grace opened up the book. "I do not like green eggs and ham. I do not like them, Sam-I-am," she recited.

I glanced at the page. "That's good, Grace."

Catherine, who was wearing a burgundy dressing gown, patted her daughter's head. "Time for bed, sweetheart."

"I want Auntie Linda to read me a story." Grace beamed at me, her legs swinging under the table. "Please?"

Catherine popped some fried chicken into the toaster oven. "This'll take a few minutes to warm up. If you want to, Linda, go ahead."

Upstairs, Grace hopped into bed and arranged herself under her covers. She patted the edge so I would sit next to her. I leaned against the wall and stretched my legs over her patchwork quilt.

Grace cuddled against me, nudging me until I put my arm around her. Grace and I had become buddies when I took some

vacation time in early October to renovate my house before starting work with the Sterling detachment. I had been stacking some
scrap wood in the yard and saw her prancing around in the
meadow. I figured she was pretending to ride a horse. She didn't
see me and pranced onto my laneway and up to my small barn.
Then she pretended to dismount and tie the horse up. She jiggled
the latch on the door and then peeked through the cracks between
the weathered boards. I snuck up behind her. She was so intent on
getting a glimpse inside that she didn't hear me.

"That's a nice horse you have there."

Grace jumped, and then her little body froze with embarrassment.

"I'm Linda, your new neighbour."

She glanced at me with luminous blue eyes, then looked away,
blushing. I regretted startling her.

"Are you a Mountie?"

"That's right."

"Do you have a horse?"

"No, I drive a police car with a flashing light on top."

"Oh." She sounded disappointed. She tucked her hands into the
pockets of her blue denim jacket. The sun brought out the high-
lights in her long reddish-brown hair braided down her back.

I squatted so I was at eye level. "If I had a horse, I'd let you
ride it."

Grace smiled shyly, her trusting, shining eyes melting my
insides.

She asked if I had a red coat, so I brought out my scrapbook
and we sat under the trees while I showed her pictures of me in my
Mountie dress uniform – red serge tunic, Stetson, Sam Browne,
breeches and riding boots. Over the next few weeks she followed
me around while I stripped linoleum and sanded floors in every
room except the kitchen.

Grace was one of the most beautiful children I'd ever seen,
mostly because of her innocence. She was like a little angel. She
reminded me of the baby girl I'd given up for adoption. Maybe
that's why my feelings for her were so strong.

Catherine's warmth and generosity sealed the bond. In no time
I was Auntie Linda and a frequent supper guest. I hadn't allowed

myself to really love since Ron's betrayal. Their friendship had changed all that.

The little bedside lamp created a golden bubble with Grace and me inside. I could feel my heart thawing, and it hurt. But I felt more alive than I had for well over half my life.

"I want to show you something," Grace said, bringing my attention back to the present. She kicked off the covers and freed herself from my arm. Her little feet dug into my thighs as she climbed over me, reached under her bed, and emerged with a hat and child's Western holster with a silver cap gun in it. She buckled on the holster, her brows knit and her naturally pink lips pursed.

"Don't tell Mom," she whispered. "She doesn't approve of guns. I cut the other holster off so it would be more like yours."

Grace beamed. When Catherine called me for dinner a moment later Grace tore off the holster and hat, slid them under the bed, then scrambled over me and under the covers. Catherine trudged up the stairs and into her daughter's bedroom.

After kisses goodnight, Catherine and I returned to the kitchen and wolfed down the most decadent crispy fried chicken I'd ever eaten. Catherine was good for me, teaching me how to enjoy life.

She handed me the latest edition of *The Sterling Spectator*. In her account of the fire she'd written that the Jordans had lost everything since they had no insurance. She even mentioned the rumours circulating that the pastor had set his own house on fire. She countered those rumours with quotes from within the Christian community that Pastor Jordan was the next best thing to the Second Coming. All in all, I thought she was fair. Nothing about Rex Dare's nephew Alan. I had a chance to get to him first.

As I sipped tea, propping my feet up on a chair near the wood stove, I mentally reviewed my plan to go to David Jordan's burned-out house early the next morning. I had to see if there was any way Alan could have seen David set his own house on fire.

Then I'd go see Alan.

the Body

At 4:17 a.m. I was delighted to discover a light snow falling. That meant weather conditions were similar to those the morning of the fire. I decided to put on my whole uniform – gun, bulletproof vest and all – so I wouldn't violate Canada's strict anti-gun laws. I would call it voluntary overtime since I was supposed to be off duty.

Big flakes drifted slowly down, swirling in the glow of my headlights as I pulled into the clearing where David Jordan's house had once been. I drove behind the charred rubble to hide the Jeep from the road.

Tramping through the wet snow I made my way toward the wooded path from South Dare. The moonlight behind the clouds was bright enough for me to navigate without a flashlight. At the edge of the woods I stopped to survey what was left of the Jordans' former home. *If Alan Dare had been out inspecting his snares before dawn, could he have recognized David Jordan, or anyone else?*

The burned shell of the house stood out like a dinosaur's ribcage against the snow. I could make out the silhouette of a fir tree in the small meadow beside the former house, and could see the outline of the bushes where Will had found the baseball bat the previous day. A shadow flitted in the corner of my eye. I whirled around, feeling goosebumps creep up my sides, to see a fir branch waving in the wind. I turned back to the blackened ruins. I might have been able to make out the silhouette of a person in these conditions. *Might.* Maybe Will was right and Rex had cooked up the story about his eyewitness nephew. Besides, it would have been weird for Alan Dare to check his snares this early in the morning.

Heading back toward the house I played my flashlight on the fresh snow, searching for rabbit tracks and snares. Finally, I noticed some fresh rabbit tracks near the fir tree in the meadow and followed them to the edge of the clearing. The underbrush was thick. *Would someone set snares in a tangle like that?*

Suddenly, a roaring grinding noise came from the direction of the road. Heart hammering, I shut off the flashlight and rolled under a fir tree's snowy boughs. The noise grew louder and bright lights lit up the sky on the other side of the house. *What is that?* When a huge eighteen-wheeler whizzed past, I felt silly. *What did I expect, a spaceship?* I shook off a sense of foreboding. When I could no longer hear the truck engine I emerged from under the trees, dusted the snow off my parka and hat, and turned on my flashlight.

With tense muscles and a jittery feeling, I continued searching, playing a beam of light into the brush, looking for signs of rabbit snares. Then I heard what sounded like the engine of a pickup truck, and a snapping rumbling sound as it bumped through the woods in the direction of South Dare. Shutting off my flashlight again I ducked behind a birch tree.

The truck's headlights and a row of lights on top of the cab illuminated the woods separating the house and the settlement. The lights stayed on after the pickup stopped. Several minutes later the sharp crack of gunfire made me dive to the ground, my heart beating so fast and hard I could feel it pulsing in my head. After a terrorizing few seconds I realized the person or people in the truck probably weren't aiming at me, but likely using the bright lights to stun deer. Will had told me deerjacking was a big problem when hunting season opened. A few more loud cracks broke the eerie stillness. The truck lights went off a few moments later.

I wanted to get closer to the deerjackers – if that's what they were – without them seeing me. If I could make an arrest without endangering myself, fine. If not, I could at least try to identify them. Several paths led through the woods to South Dare. The truck headlights, now off, could easily illuminate the paths nearest the house, so I couldn't risk taking one of them. Then I remembered David's church and the path Cindy Dare had taken when she ran away from me. That path might allow me to circle around behind the illegal hunters. I wished I'd broken my pledge to never own a cellphone. Then I remembered Will saying they didn't always work out here anyway.

The church occupied the corner where the road weaving up the mountain ran through the ramshackle settlement and met the back road from Cornwallis Cove. David's house on the back road was separated from the church by a swampy patch of alders, now bare of leaves.

Staying under cover I ran to the road and used the eighteen-wheeler's tracks to guide me to the church. Behind it I sprinted across the meadow to the path I'd seen Cindy take the previous day. I could see the deerjackers' flashlights bobbing through the trees.

In the dim moonlight I stumbled along the wooded path. When I came within fifty yards and could hear the low rumble of their voices, I drew my gun. I assumed they were disembowelling the deer they'd just shot. My ears rang from adrenaline. A snow-covered fir bough brushed my face, nearly taking off my hat. *I should call for backup. Or get out of here.*

The truck's lights came on again. They lit the scrubby woodlot in harsh white light making the stunted trees cast jagged shadows. I ducked, momentarily dazzled. I was right. The men dragged a deer carcass to the truck. The doors slammed. The headlights disappeared as the truck drove off. Then silence.

I snuck forward again, feeling my way in fits and starts, temporarily blinded by the light. *They're gone. Why not go back home now?* Then my boot hit what felt like a tree root, only it had more give. I lurched forward, sprawling into the wet snow, hitting something that felt like a sandbag. I rolled slightly, and the smell hit me – the thick odour of blood and a sweet smell like rotten milk. I scrambled to my feet in revulsion, brushing myself off, a cold sweat trickling between my shoulder blades. *It's an abandoned deer carcass. Get a grip.* I willed myself to calm down by focusing on my breathing, relaxing my shoulders, and emptying my mind of thoughts. Except for a slight rustle in the trees I heard nothing, so I turned on my flashlight.

The light revealed a carcass alright, but no deer. It was Rex Dare. He lay crumpled on his back, his body dusted with snow, his mouth gaping in an *o* of surprise, and his eyes half open.

Resisting the desire to bolt I doused the light. I listened for any signs Rex's murderer was hiding nearby. The darkness grew eerie. Branches creaked in the wind. After a few minutes I squatted and turned the flashlight on to make a quick examination. My fall had knocked some of the snow off Rex's body. Congealed blood covered his shirt and solidified into a frozen liver-like pile beside his ribcage. The odour made me retch. I steadied myself by putting my hand on the snowy ground.

Standing up, I backed away from the body, careful not to disturb more of the scene than I already had. My knees trembled, making me wobble as I tried to fit my feet back into my own footprints.

Keeping my flashlight low I raced through the woods to the church, aware I was making myself a moving target in a place where the residents hated strangers. I banged on the church's back door, then kicked it open.

After I flicked on the lights my eyes took a moment to adjust. The chairs were neatly stacked against the side wall. In the kitchen I used the phone to call the detachment, but hung up when I realized no one would be there and my call would patch through to Yarmouth dispatch. Shaking, I hung up. I leaned against the wall to collect my thoughts. Will would be appalled I was in South Dare.

Fumbling with the phone book hanging underneath the phone I looked up Will's name and dialled his number. A sleepy-sounding woman answered.

"Is Constable Bright there, please?" I tried to steady my voice.

"I think so. Hold on a minute." Bed springs groaned and the woman yelled, "Will! Phone!"

His hoarse voice came on the line. I identified myself.

"Hey, what's up?" The concern in his voice almost made me cry.

I swallowed, refusing to let him hear how vulnerable I felt. "Someone shot Rex Dare. I just found his body." I made my voice flat, almost mechanical.

"No way! Where?"

"Behind the church in South Dare."

"What are you doing out *there*?"

"Voluntary overtime," I quipped. Then mustering a more businesslike tone I asked him to call the detachment's NCO IC – noncommissioned officer in charge – so I could go back and secure the crime scene.

After securing the broken church door as well as I could I raced back to Rex's body. The woods were silent so I holstered my gun and examined the corpse again, sheltering the flashlight beam with shaking hands. I had to turn off the light. I'd seen dozens of dead bodies before, so I had no idea why this one bothered me so much. I looked up at the dark grey sky. Snowflakes melted on my face and one landed on my eyelashes. A feeling of overwhelming loneliness swept over me.

I turned the flashlight on again. Frozen congealed blood covered Rex's blue and green quilted work shirt. The fact he wore no coat and the extent of the body's stiffness indicated he had probably been shot sometime the previous day, which had been much warmer. I expected we'd find footprints frozen in the mud under the snow. My hands and feet ached from the cold. *What's taking them so long?*

Finally, lights from three police cars appeared through the trees near the church. I waved my flashlight so Will could find me. Two lights moved through the brush toward me.

"Over here!" I shouted.

"We see you!" a male voice rang out.

I shone the beam on the body as two officers trudged toward me. I knew from their voices Will wasn't one of them.

"What're you doing here, Donner?" A tall Mountie lifted his flashlight to make a light over our heads. Constable Bob Morin. With him was Constable Eddie Johnson.

I blinked in the light. "Securing the crime scene."

Eddie squatted next to Rex's body. "That's not what he meant. You spend all your nights off roaming around in the woods?"

"South Dare's a happening place. Sure I'd find you out here too."

Will emerged from the dark carrying a video camera and a briefcase of forensic gear.

I played my flashlight on the corpse. "He's pretty stiff. Been dead since yesterday."

Not looking at me, Will set the briefcase off to the side. I cringed as his flashlight explored the outline my body had made in the snow when I'd fallen next to Rex.

Eddie guffawed. "Looks like Donner's been getting cozy with the corpse."

Will squatted next to the body. "IDENT will be kicking butt for all these footprints."

He got up and fiddled with the video camera. "Bob, put up the tape. Eddie, get the debrief."

Eddie nudged my arm with his elbow, his pen poised over his notebook. "You want to tell me what happened?"

"This is my file. I found the body." I wrapped my arms around myself for warmth and stamped my feet.

"This is my file," he mimicked in falsetto.

"You always act like a jerk?"

The sky was brightening and I could just make out the line of Eddie's double chin as I told him what I'd seen.

He seemed especially interested in the deerjackers.

"These people accidentally kill several of their own every hunting season."

"This was no hunting accident."

Eddie nodded his egg-shaped head. "Look at what he was wearing. He should have been wearing hunter orange. He was a fool to go walking in the woods in clothes like that. Whoever shot him probably thinks they got the bear."

I rolled my eyes. "Bear?"

Bob was stringing yellow tape across the path behind us. "A renegade black bear out here mauled a kid last summer."

Eddie chuckled.

"What's so funny?" I clasped my gloved hands tight to keep from backhanding him.

"Some people out here thought Rex could change into a bear," Eddie said. "Maybe they shot the bear and it changed back into Rex!"

I glared at him. "You have a lot of contempt for the people out here, don't you?"

"You will too when you've worked in Sterling County long enough. Listen, honey, just FYI, the staff sergeant isn't too happy you're out here. Karen wants you to report as soon as you've debriefed us. Why *were* you out here anyway?"

Eddie's smirk made me livid. I paused several seconds until I could speak in a professional tone. Then I told him about Alan Dare and his rabbit snares.

"Just like Alice in Wonderland, following a rabbit." Eddie scribbled in his notebook. He grinned, exposing lots of gum and a row of tiny teeth.

Will trudged toward us. "You notice anything? Footprints?"

"Nothing," I said.

"Karen is expecting you." Will still wouldn't look me in the eye. He pursed his wide mouth into a straight line.

"I heard."

Will laid his hand on Eddie's shoulder. "You get your debrief?" When Eddie nodded Will finally glanced at me. "You better go now."

Shaking from anger and the cold, I drove out toward the highway. The snow made the shacks and trailers of South Dare seem even more hopeless. A bare bulb shone through the frost-streaked window of a tarpaper shack. Smoke wafted from a stovepipe stuck through the shed roof. *How fast would news travel that Rex was dead?*

At the detachment I found Staff Sergeant Karen Ramsay standing by her gurgling coffee machine, holding a mug in her hands. She sized me up, then motioned for me to sit down. I shook the snowflakes off my cap. She offered coffee, but I said no. Then she stepped behind her desk and sat down, her uniform perfectly pressed, her frizzy curls escaping the combs she used to pin up her hair. I told her about Rex Dare's apparent murder. She told me she might call on the General Investigation Section, or GIS, from Halifax.

My heart sank at the thought. GIS could end up taking control of the investigation, denying me the career opportunity I had always dreamed of.

"You're not getting paid for this morning." Karen continued to pore over the papers on her desk.

"That's fine. Didn't expect to be. But I'd like this to be my file." I sat on the edge of the seat, my parka across my lap. My boots left little pools of melted snow on the tile floor.

"If GIS comes in, they'll take the file." Karen peered at me. "Otherwise I'll give it to Will. He's got more forensics and he's familiar with South Dare. Right now I'd like you to go home and take your scheduled days off."

"I'm being taken off this file?" *I shouldn't be disciplined for this!* Karen was worse than any male staff sergeant I'd ever worked under. I'd applied to Sterling because I thought a female one would give me a fairer shake.

"Don't be ridiculous. This detachment is too small for anyone to own a file." She wagged her finger at me. "And another thing. You can't go off half-cocked into dangerous areas without backup. If you'd been injured or killed, you might not have been discovered for days."

"I understand. May I go back to South Dare today on my own time?"

"No." Karen's cell rang. She opened it and put it to her ear.

"Yes? Okay. Only a couple of members are here. One's patrolling the town."

She stood up and turned away with a sigh. "Okay, I'll send them now." She edged around her desk and closed her phone. "They need help with crowd control. You're back on duty. But you're off tomorrow and Sunday." She had a warning look in her eyes that made me realize pushing back might land me in deeper trouble.

I rode back to South Dare with the constable who'd been patrolling the town of Sterling. When we arrived a sizeable crowd had gathered in the church parking lot. A dark van had pulled up to take the corpse to the morgue. Anxious relatives, some angry, others hysterical, tried to press through the police tape. The other constable and I had to shove people back behind the tape.

At about noon Corporal Randy Cohen from Halifax IDENT arrived. Sterling Corporal François Jacques, the NCO IC, introduced us. "Linda, can you take Randy to the scene?" François squeezed my arm in a friendly gesture. "Then I'd like you to accompany the body to the morgue in Sterling. The coroner says we need an autopsy. Plan on taking the body down to Halifax on Monday."

"Thanks." I was relieved to be back in the game. So far, in my two weeks on the job, François was the only male at the detachment who was friendly without sexual overtones. Maybe he was more sensitive to the discrimination I faced because his family originally came from Haiti. He was the only "visible minority" in the detachment and Karen and I were the only women, except for two civilians.

I guided Randy through the woods to Rex's corpse. Randy set down his suitcase and shook Will's hand. They obviously knew each other. When they made no effort to include me in the conversation I debated whether to barge in.

Finally, Randy turned to me. "We'll need about an hour. Then have the body removal people come in."

Randy took a little voice recorder out of his vest. He recorded his observations about the stiffness of the body, the wound, and the state of the congealed blood. He put on protective gloves and nudged the body in several places. Then he brushed some of the snow aside to examine the blood splatter patterns. Will took photographs. The two men worked closely, almost wordlessly. With a pair of tweezers Randy picked up a cigarette butt, slipped it into a plastic envelope, and handed it to Will.

After a few more minutes Randy stood up and pointed through a grove of alders.

"I'd say the shot came from that direction. Came in at this angle, from fairly close range." Using his own body as an example he gestured to where the slug had hit Rex's torso.

"Not a hunting accident," I said.

"No. Whoever shot him had a pretty clear line of sight from over there." Randy pointed in the direction he thought the bullet had come from, took a roll of yellow tape out of his briefcase, and asked me to tape off the area where the shooter had supposedly aimed at Rex.

I cut through the brush and found a parallel path less than twenty feet away. I taped off the area, being careful to stay off the path in case there were footprints or other evidence under the snow. After a few minutes of tough slogging through the bush I came to a clearing where Bob was keeping a dozen or so people from tromping on either path.

Behind police tape stood a shack the size of a garden shed, its door gaping open. I poked my head inside and saw a rusted wood stove, a mattress covered with dingy sheets and ratty-looking blankets, stacks of clothes and a metal pail. Clothes hung from several spikes jutting from the wall. Some of the clothes would fit a girl about six or seven.

I glanced at Bob who was unwrapping a peppermint LifeSaver. "Who lives here?" I asked.

"Cindy Dare. Don't touch anything."

I squirmed through the brush back to Will and Randy who told me to tell the body removal people to come in. I jogged to the church where I met two attendants from a local funeral home. They followed me to the crime scene with a stretcher. As Randy zipped Rex's corpse into a body bag I wrote my observations in my notebook.

The crowd at the church became increasingly agitated as the blue body bag strapped to the stretcher came into view. Using my shoulders and my baton to keep people away I made room for the attendants to load Rex's corpse into the van. Inside, one of the attendants unzipped the bag. In my notebook I recorded the date, time, my name, and that the body was indeed Reginald "Rex" Dare. His gaping mouth, bloodstained yellow teeth, and dull half-closed eyes left a mental image long after the zipper closed over his face. I rode with the body to the morgue in the basement of Sterling Hospital.

Under the dim fluorescent lights of the small refrigerated room the attendants slid Rex's body bag into one of the few metal drawers along the inside wall, locked him in, and gave me the only key. The room seemed to get darker. I shook off a sense of dread.

After leaving the hospital I stopped by the detachment, showered and changed, then filled out the paperwork. At the copier I made extra copies of my notebook pages and left them on Will's desk for the Rex Dare file.

My trip to Halifax with the body would also include several interviews with people who could tell me more about David Jordan. I made several long distance calls to line things up.

Then I asked Debbie and Maureen, the civilians who handled the clerical work, to give me the number for Rex Dare's sex abuse file. I found a box of files in the file room and signed it out for the weekend.

With the box on the front seat I drove down the hill toward Sterling's waterfront commercial area and headed for the Crown prosecutor's office. I left the blight of the strip malls surrounding the detachment for the white, yellow, and grey clapboard houses studding the hillside overlooking the harbour.

Old wooden buildings with grey weathered shingles lined the downtown business district along the waterfront. On the harbour side they sat on pilings over the water. Though some owners had renovated with vinyl siding or fake bricks, most of the street retained its historic charm. Bright green, red, and blue fishing boats bobbed along the public wharf, riding the high tide.

I parked in front of an office on the harbour side, walked in, and asked a chubby girl in her early twenties, who appeared to be the receptionist, for the Crown prosecutor, Michael Ross. A handsome large-headed man about my height came out to meet me. *So this is Catherine's ex-husband and Grace's dad.* I could see where Grace got her periwinkle blue eyes. I extended my hand and introduced myself.

He clasped my hand with both of his. "My daughter is quite smitten with you. The Mountie next door."

I withdrew my hand. "I need to borrow the transcripts and files from the Rex Dare case."

"You're not trying to resurrect that mess, are you?"

"No. The mess is past resurrecting. Rex is dead."

"I heard." Michael shook his big head in mock seriousness. "The king is dead," he smirked as if enjoying some secret irony. "Murder?"

"Looks like it. Someone shot him."

"And I'll no doubt have to prosecute the hero who did us the grand deed." He smiled again, his blue eyes crinkling. "Just kidding. You didn't hear me say that."

While the receptionist gathered two generous cardboard boxes full of papers and a few videos I used her phone to call David Jordan. No answer at the church, so I tried Anne at the Cornwallis Cove parsonage. She told me David had left the previous afternoon to visit his children at his ex-wife's. She gave me Barbara Jordan's number in Halifax, and I asked her to have David call me at the detachment.

Arriving at my farmhouse with the boxes of evidence I retrieved the mail from the mailbox at the end of the laneway.

When I got out of my Jeep by the back door the wind felt mild and damp and smelled of rotting leaves. Water dripped from the eave-stroughs and the moon shone between patches of cloud. I glanced next door, but the lights were off at Catherine's house.

Once inside my kitchen I leafed through the mail. Flyers. A few bills. A coral-coloured envelope addressed in familiar artsy hand-writing. *Veronica.* The sight of my stepmother's letter annoyed me. *What could she possibly want now?* I threw the mail unopened on the kitchen table. Dad had died a year ago. I no longer had to pre-tend to like her.

Because I'd missed my morning routine again, I changed into sweats and headed for the living room where the freshly sanded floors made an ideal workout surface. The room still had no furni-ture except for a reclining chair, a TV, and a set of free weights. I turned on the TV and began to stretch. My father had had a simi-lar ritual. He used to work out early in the morning or before sup-per in our spare bedroom back in Boston.

Afterward I took a hot shower. Thanks to the new pump I'd installed the water beat against my skin so hard it stung. I let it massage my sore muscles. When I came downstairs in a clean pair of sweats the lights were still off at Catherine's, so I fixed myself a ham and cheese on whole wheat. I fell asleep reading transcripts of Rex Dare's trial.

the Blame

When I awoke the next morning the clock radio read 5:55 a.m. I fumbled with the dial to find the local news. While I listened to a female announcer give a brief report about Rex's murder investigation my body lay rigid. I unclenched my fists.

"The RCMP are tight-lipped today about whether a man found shot dead in the woods near South Dare is Sterling County's first murder victim of the year. Reginald 'Rex' Dare was found early yesterday morning about a kilometre from his home. Police refuse to say whether Dare was murdered or died as a result of a hunting accident. Three years ago Reginald Dare faced trial on charges related to satanic ritual abuse. A judge threw the case out of court before a jury could render a verdict."

I kicked off the covers and put on some black spandex shorts, a black sports bra, and a bright green T-shirt. Downstairs I eyed the files sitting on the daybed while I poured myself a glass of water and downed a fistful of vitamins. I gulped one glass down and refilled it, then went into the living room to stretch and do my exercise routine. Today was to be spent with Catherine and Grace. I was off work and would set it aside.

Back in British Columbia police work consumed me and I had no time for a personal life. That led to trouble sleeping, nervous stomach cramps, and other signs of burnout. And now, despite all my resolutions to maintain balance, similar signs of strain were back. But the stress in Surrey had been much worse, especially after one of my male colleagues started circulating a picture of me taken while working undercover as a prostitute. The snickers and jokes turned out to be nothing compared to the cold hostility and lack of co-operation when I told the jerk I wouldn't tolerate his behaviour. Maybe he feared a harassment complaint from me, but I didn't need a human rights tribunal to fight my battles.

Shortly after that the staff sergeant hauled me into his office for a performance review, saying I wasn't a team player. A coincidence? Maybe, but doubtful. I kept my mouth shut and soon asked for the posting to Nova Scotia, hoping to leave my stalled career, sleepless nights, and rotten attitudes of my colleagues behind me.

While doing lunges I mentally rehearsed the day I would spend with Catherine and Grace. I visualized our time together, hoping positive thinking could allay the gnawing feeling in my gut about work, and the way my thoughts drifted to the crime scene and Rex's frozen corpse. I yearned to be with the team investigating today, but I was ordered to take the day off. I *would* take it off and enjoy myself.

After stretching and some rope skipping I showered and dressed in jeans and an aqua sweatshirt. I blow-dried my hair and twisted it into a single braid. I needed a trim. Veronica was always nagging me to get my hair cut and highlighted. Her letter, still unopened, sat on the kitchen table. Just before leaving for Catherine's I ripped it open.

Dear Linda,

Welcome back to Nova Scotia. I hope you're settled in by now. I'm so glad you're close by and I'd love to have you come and visit. You're welcome anytime. What are your plans for Christmas? Please come and celebrate with me. I think your father would have liked it if we could be together.

Love, Veronica.

I tore up the letter, threw it into the plastic wastebasket under the sink, and slammed the cabinet door. How dare she write about Dad to me! Saddened by the memories I grabbed a paper towel and wiped my eyes. *For crying out loud, Linda! Stop that!* I glanced at the Rex Dare files sitting in the kitchen, and the image of his corpse competed with a memory of Dad packing the Buick for his move to Nova Scotia with Veronica.

I forced myself to focus on my present surroundings. In the mud room I laced up my boots, then felt along the upper shelf for some gloves. My fingers touched a stack of framed photos I intended to hang. I took the top one down.

There we were – Dad, Veronica, and me at my graduation from the RCMP Academy, Depot Division, in Regina, Saskatchewan. I wore my red tunic and my hair pinned up under my Stetson. Dad, his hair trimmed close like a Marine, wore a beige raw silk sports jacket that looked great on him, but I didn't like because Veronica had chosen it. I stood in the middle, towering eight inches over her, but only an inch shorter than Dad's five foot nine.

His square face beamed in the photo. He seemed proud of me that day, but I didn't feel much of anything. After Depot I took a posting with the gigantic Surrey detachment in the urban sprawl between Vancouver and Seattle, putting a continent between me and my memories. I hadn't seen much of Dad and Veronica over the next ten years. If I hadn't seen much of Dad while he was alive, there was no reason to start seeing Veronica now.

Outside, the brisk wind made it feel cold, even though the sun was melting the snow, leaving bare patches of brownish-yellow grass. I sprinted across the semi-frozen meadow to Catherine's and slipped into the toasty warmth of her kitchen. The smell of brewed coffee and fresh baking filled the air. Grace, dressed in bibbed ski pants, sat at the table nibbling on a muffin. Her face lit up when she saw me.

"Where's your mom?"

"Upstairs. She said help yourself."

I poured myself a mug of coffee and took a muffin from the tin on the edge of the wood stove. Then I tried to concentrate on the little girl at the table with me, the aroma of the coffee, the texture of the cranberry and walnut muffin, resisting thoughts of work or Veronica.

Catherine came down wearing bright orangey-red lipstick and smudged dark-green eyeliner around her eyes. She wore a dressy

camel-coloured parka with a fur-trimmed hood. She looked especially pretty, her naturally wavy hair in a chin-length bob swept
back from her oval face. She had a long neck and delicate features,
but she thought she was plump and hated her figure. I imagined
men found her voluptuous. She wore a long black skirt and reddish-brown leather boots.

Catherine's blue Toyota station wagon was nearly out of gas, so
we piled into my Jeep and headed for the craft fair in the next
county, the last outdoor fair of the season. Catherine and Grace
kept up a steady conversation during the half-hour drive, helping
me stay focused. We drove into Annapolis Royal, a tourist destina-
tion boasting an old fort, museum, and streets lined with histori-
cal buildings, many brightly painted in pastel shades of blue, yellow and beige.

The craft market occupied a square across the street from a
gravel beach where a green and white scallop dragger rested on a
wooden haul-up. The sun shone through a thin layer of high white
cloud. Wind whipped the grey water of the bay into whitecaps and
buffeted the outdoor tables. Some men unloaded baled Christmas
trees from a truck.

Not many craftspeople were braving the winds and cold temperatures. A man stood next to stacks of kindling and firewood in
stove lengths. A woman in a big padded coat displayed winter
squash partially wrapped in newspaper for insulation. A man next
to her sold wooden bird feeders and bags of seed. Catherine
seemed to know almost everyone and she flitted from conversation
to conversation.

Grace held my hand as we walked among the tables. "See the
squash, Auntie Linda? I don't like squash that much." She wore
a woollen hat with her parka hood over it. The wind had turned
her cheeks bright pink and brought tears to her eyes. She wiped
her nose with the tissue I gave her. She leaned over to smell a
balsam fir.

"Smells like Christmas." Grace beamed up at me. "You know,
Santa Claus isn't real but some little kids think he is."

I leaned over and inhaled the wonderful scent.

"I want a Britney Spears doll for Christmas but Mommy does-
n't like them," Grace said.

While Grace prattled on I enjoyed experiencing life through her senses, seeing everything as fresh and new. Someone had set up a small petting zoo and offered pony rides. She rode around the little circle on the pony, looking so solemn and proud of herself while Catherine took photos. Time slipped away. Soon it was almost noon.

A man in a red woollen work shirt ladled steaming cider into paper cups. Grace and I each took a sample. As I blew on the cider to cool it Catherine gestured to me, indicating the restaurant across the street. Then she crossed over and disappeared inside. As soon as we finished our cider Grace and I followed.

Bells jingled as I pushed open the door. The sound of trumpets playing *Hark the Herald Angels Sing* competed with the din of conversation and clattering dishware in the darkened room. People who had been outside checking out the wares had ducked inside to escape the wind. A bright orange fire crackled in a huge stone fireplace along the far wall, scenting the air with woodsmoke.

Catherine waved at us from a table by the fireplace where she sat with two men. I didn't want to sit with other people. I gestured toward an empty table, but Catherine smiled and beckoned me over. The burly bald man with her wore a charcoal business suit and sported a well-trimmed grey beard. The smaller man was about twenty years younger. Darkly tanned, he had a soft sensual mouth, shining dark eyes, and a perfectly chiselled bone structure. Catherine and the older man leaned their heads close together as they talked, while the younger man watched Grace and me walk over. *Catherine wants us to eat with these guys? This isn't what we planned.* I tried to hide my dismay.

I helped Grace remove her parka and hung it over her chair. As I lifted off her hat static made some stray hairs rise. She extended her hands toward the fire's warmth and grinned at me. "Auntie Linda, do you like the fire?"

Nodding, I patted her shoulder and then pulled her chair out for her. This was a great table near the fire, so how could I insist on that empty table by the door?

"Linda, this is my good friend George Hall," Catherine said.

Both men leapt to their feet.

"And this is Rafe. I'm sorry, I don't remember your last name."

"Lupien." He extended his tanned hand. His smile, shining eyes, and the charge of energy from his warm handshake nearly bowled me over.

Catherine introduced me as her next-door neighbour.

"*Constable* Linda Donner," said George Hall as he held my chair for me to sit down.

"That's right."

We all sat and George handed me a menu.

Rafe offered his hand across the table to Grace who hesitated before taking it. He started going over the menu with her. She kept looking to me for cues. Catherine, though, was quite pleased Rafe was showering attention on her daughter. She wanted to switch chairs so she could share her lunch with Grace. I ended up sitting across from George who watched me with merriment dancing in his grey eyes. In his dressy suit he looked out of place in rural Nova Scotia.

"So, you're the latest addition to the Sterling detachment." His teeth appeared to be expensively veneered. They glistened almost blue-white when he smiled.

"That's right."

"Among my civic duties I chair the Police Services Committee for Sterling County."

"So, you're my boss' boss." I glanced at him and smiled. That wasn't technically true, but I knew Karen was doing her best to keep a cordial relationship with county and town officials. Cutbacks in Ottawa forced the RCMP to rely on contract policing in places like Sterling to compensate for shortfalls in federal funding.

George laughed and raised his water glass to me in a mock toast. Then to Catherine he said, "To community policing and Staff Sergeant Karen Ramsay!"

"George has been one of my most valuable contacts," Catherine gushed, clasping my forearm.

George eyed me. "You're the one who found Rex Dare's body yesterday."

I pretended to pore over the menu. "Sorry, can't talk about that." It creeped me out that he seemed to know so much about me. Catherine and I had talked about Rex's death briefly that morning.

I was so wound up I couldn't remember if I had told her I'd found his body. That wasn't like me.

To change the subject I turned to Rafe. "You're obviously not from here."

"No, Florida. I'm talking with George about a job."

"What job?" Catherine asked.

"Rafe produces videos and does Web design," George said. "He's even won awards for some of his travel documentaries. I need some promotional stuff done for some of my businesses here in Nova Scotia and New Brunswick."

"Florida's pretty far away," I said.

"Not with the Internet," George said.

"Is that how you found out about each other?" Catherine asked.

George laughed. "No. We're old friends. We met ten years ago in Thailand. He and I share an interest in exotic travel."

"Thailand?" *Do they smuggle drugs?* I handed the menu to the waiter who stood by the table, ready to take our order.

"It's a beautiful country," George said. "You go away from the big cities and Thai society is pretty much like it's been for centuries. None of the decay you find in places like Bangkok. Lovely people. Fascinating culture."

"I love Thai food," Catherine said. "George is a great cook. Thai, Italian, Indian, you name it."

We ordered lunch. Catherine buttered a piece of warm bread for Grace who cradled her chin in her hands and looked as glum as I felt.

"George said you won an award?" Catherine said to Rafe. He smiled at her and pushed a large brown envelope toward her.

"I won an award for a documentary on the Aztecs in Mexico. There are some clippings if you want to take a look."

Catherine slid a copy of a magazine article out of the envelope and scanned it. "Wow, I'm impressed."

"I have done travel documentaries for some of the cable shows down in the States, but this was for PBS. I specialize in religious monuments off the beaten track. It's a hobby of mine."

"Oh, you're interested in spiritual things? Like Stonehenge?"

"That's right." Rafe smiled. "I did a piece there too."

"I'm interested in spirituality," Catherine said. "At university we studied the parallel themes in mythology. I visited the Mayan ruins near Cancún last winter. I could feel the spiritual energy. It was awesome."

Rafe had shifted his interest from Grace to Catherine. He focused on her, his dark eyes sparkling, white teeth gleaming. Her face flushed – she smiled back at him. Catherine sounded like a flake when she talked about spiritual things, and her response to Rafe's magnetism embarrassed me. Her cheeks were growing rosier by the minute. By the time the waitress brought our food my appetite was gone. This was not the day I had mentally rehearsed. I couldn't care less about spiritual things, so that left me listening to George who droned on and on about Sterling County politics.

"Every year we have to fight to keep the contract with the RCMP," George said.

I picked at a salad of baby greens. "Is that right?" The sound system was playing *Carol of the Bells.*

"We have some dinosaurs on the town and county councils who want to set up a regional police force. They think it'll be cheaper and they'll get better police coverage."

"Hmm." I forced some linguini and scallops into my mouth. I should have stayed home and finished reading the Rex Dare files.

"Either you keep the costs of the RCMP contracts down or municipal police forces start looking really attractive, but I think the RCMP are more professional and worth any extra cost," George continued.

I nodded politely. Catherine and Rafe were engaged in a conversation so intense George, Grace, and I might as well have not been at the table. That made me bristle with annoyance. The lunch hour crowd thinned out leaving the restaurant almost empty.

"I want to go home!" Grace rested her chin on her hands, then pushed away her half-eaten ravioli, nearly toppling her glass of water. She swung her legs back and forth under the chair.

"Don't whine, honey." Catherine smiled apologetically at Rafe and George.

I offered to take Grace with me to the bathroom. I felt sorry for both of us. When we returned to the table I mentioned to

Catherine I had to get back home. While I helped Grace get her coat on, Catherine said goodbye to her friends – reluctantly.

As soon as we were on the road back to Cornwallis Cove, I asked Catherine if she'd told George about my finding Rex's body. My cranky tone probably gave away my suspicions that she had betrayed my confidence.

"It's not exactly a trade secret," Catherine huffed. "I have sources in the detachment other than you, you know. You're my friend, not a source, okay?"

The sun, though low in the sky, sent shafts of golden light through the trees along the highway. I glanced in my rear-view mirror at Grace. She had fallen asleep using my parka as a pillow.

"Isn't Rafe gorgeous?" Catherine mused.

"A little short for my taste." *Is this woman man crazy? First it was Will she was raving about. Now she's gaga over this guy after one meeting. Give me a break.*

"We have so much in common. And he was so sweet to Grace. Oh, Linda, that smile. I could have slid under the table every time he flashed those beautiful teeth at me."

Doesn't she know they're probably caps?

Catherine invited me for supper and a movie later. I declined. Day off or not, the Rex Dare files were waiting for me.

When I pulled into Catherine's laneway Grace was still asleep, so I offered to carry her inside. The wind had died down and a huge red sun hovered above the horizon. Our houses were among six old farms built on narrow strips of cultivated land on the hillsides over Cornwallis Cove. Below the road the tree-covered hill fell steeply to the water. I paused to take in the beauty of my neighbourhood. *Am I trying to punish Catherine by refusing to eat with her?* I pushed the thought aside.

Through the bare maple trees the cove was in shadow, its water dark but sparkling with reflected light. The tide was high. At low tide the wide expanse of water would turn into vast tracts of mudflats. The big bare maples along the road cast their shadows on the muted pastel colours of the homes and the brown fields dotted with patches of wet snow. The reflected sun glared in the second-storey window of the house just beyond Catherine's. I squinted in the blazing light.

As soon as I scooped up Grace from the back seat she woke up and flung her arms around my neck. Her cheek felt warm against my chin.

Inside Catherine's chilly kitchen I set Grace on her feet so we could remove our boots. Catherine moved to the stove and sighed as she poked the cold ashes. She began crumpling newspaper into balls and stuffing them into the firebox. I saw she had no kindling and her woodbox was empty, so I hauled my boots back on and brought an armload of wood in. I made a second trip and found some pieces of bark and smaller dry pieces of wood that would help get the fire going. I lay the kindling on top of Catherine's crumpled newspapers and watched as she lit the papers and the flames licked them. A papery ash floated up. Catherine seemed so disorganized and unable to take care of herself.

But was she?

the Molested

Back at my place I slid the kettle on the hot part of the stove and arranged the Rex Dare files on the kitchen table. First, I read the lawyers' summations at the end of the trial transcript.

According to Crown Prosecutor Michael Ross Rex Dare had orchestrated the ritual sexual abuse of a group of five children. One of them was his daughter Becky. Though Rex hadn't actually taken part in the sexual acts himself, he had procured the children for other adults. All of the children were violated, some of them repeatedly. What I read revolted me. But I had to admit the prosecution didn't have much of a case. The children's testimony was contradictory and the adults' was bizarre and unbelievable. The chief witness was Rex's ex-wife Cindy.

Rex had a first-class lawyer from Halifax. He tore the children's testimony to shreds because the Crown had no corroborating evidence. Through expert witnesses he showed how the evidence resembled the lies and accusations in the daycare trials of the 1980s when satanic ritual abuse, or SRA, was the fad and many innocent people went to jail. He brought forward evidence from the '90s when these cases were discredited. Rex's lawyer tore apart the social worker Margaret Roach. An expert from the United States said Roach's leading questions planted suggestions in the witnesses' minds. Another expert described how rumours of satanic ritual abuse are a form of hysteria overwhelming a community experiencing other stresses, such as high unemployment. Well, Sterling County had its share of economic problems. *Where had Rex found the money to mount a defence like this?*

I opened a cardboard file from the detachment evidence room. Among the file folders were several videos labelled with the names of the five violated children. I popped Becky Dare's tape into the VCR.

A blonde five-year-old girl came on the screen. She resembled Becky, the little girl I'd seen that day at the church, but much younger. Instead of that simpering, sexually precocious child the video showed a frightened, vulnerable, deeply traumatized little girl. I leaned forward, resting my elbows on my knees. *These are the tapes of Margaret Roach's interviews the judge had ruled inadmissible.*

"Did your daddy touch you on your private parts?" Margaret asked off-camera.

"No." Becky squirmed. She seemed uncomfortable. Scared.

"Did your daddy tell other men to touch you on your private parts?"

"My daddy was the devil." Her remarks were odd, as if she were describing what he wore for Halloween. Her eyes had glassed over.

"Did your daddy kill a baby?"

"The baby was on fire. I have to go potty." She was acting coy and squirming.

There was a moment of static, then Becky was back on-camera five minutes later according to the time code.

"What happened when your daddy killed the baby?"

"He was the devil. He danced around a fire. He tied me up."

"What happened when he tied you up?"

"A man with a donkey head hurt me."

"How did he hurt you, Becky? Can you show me with these dolls?"

It took several minutes as Margaret coached Becky using anatomically correct dolls to piece together what sounded like an orgy involving men wearing animal masks, dancing around a fire, and sexually abusing Becky and the other children. Yes, the social worker was asking leading questions, but Becky's testimony deeply disturbed me.

Toward the end of the interview something happened to Becky that gave me chills. The shy little girl transformed into a brazen foul-mouthed gnome. An Academy Award-winning actor could not have done a better job. Suddenly, she was talking about sexual acts most adults have never heard of in the most eerie, repulsive way imaginable. *Was this multiple personality disorder?* I had read about it, but had never seen anything like this. I clutched the recliner's leather arms, my palms clammy. No wonder ignorant, superstitious people confused mental illness with demonic possession.

The tape creeped me out so much I checked the locks on the doors and turned on every light downstairs. Then I listened to the other children's interviews. One described Rex as a priest with a long black robe. They all mentioned a baby, but one said it was thrown into the fire, another said its head was cut off. Still another said it was stabbed. It sounded to me like these kids had watched too many heavy metal videos or cheap horror movies.

Margaret Roach praised the children every time they made a lurid accusation. She did seem to be rewarding them for giving the answers she wanted.

There were three consistent elements in the children's testimonies. Rex Dare played some role, though what he was described as doing varied wildly. Each of the children did show physical evidence of repeated sexual abuse.

The abuse involving Rex allegedly took place in the "Pizza House." *Where was that?* I thumbed through the more than three hundred pages of transcripts. I searched the evidence envelopes and found some photographs of a corrugated metal Quonset hut that had previously housed a pizza franchise. The sign was partially missing, but I could see the word "pizza."

Photos showed the building was gutted to the bare metal inside. The fixtures, wallboards, and wiring had all been removed. I recalled passing this building, which was on a back road to Sterling. Its big plate glass windows were now boarded up. The defence summary said the police had found no evidence to link the children to this Pizza House. Not a fibre, not a hair, not a drop of blood.

The prosecutor declared Becky's mom Cindy, a former prostitute and alcoholic, a hostile witness. The children's statements to police differed wildly from their video interviews. The judge had no choice but to throw the case out of court.

I noted the names of the officers. Of course Will Bright was one of them. The other officer was Corporal Earl Broadfoot who was no longer at the detachment.

The phone rang. Catherine. She pleaded with me to come over to stay with Grace so she could go to dinner at George Hall's. I knew she wanted to see Rafe, and that made me annoyed and uncomfortable. On the other hand I was ready for something to eat, and Catherine's fridge would be full of goodies. And any time with Grace was precious to me. So, I set my uneasiness aside, rounded up some files to read after Grace fell asleep, and headed next door.

Grace and I played checkers and watched "The Simpsons." I helped myself to leftovers in the fridge and later made microwave popcorn. We curled up on the den couch together under an afghan made of brightly coloured squares. When she fell asleep I carried her to bed.

I read more trial transcripts from an unwieldy stack of copies until I dozed off. When I awoke at 2:03 a.m. Catherine still wasn't home. Uncertain whether to be worried or angry, I picked up the phone on the end table to make sure an extension hadn't been left off the hook by accident. Dial tone. I threw some more wood into the stove in the kitchen, banked the stove in the den, and closed down the dampers. Then headlights swept the front hall and car tires crunched the gravel in the laneway. I walked over to the window and saw Catherine's Toyota wagon roll to a stop by the back door.

I folded the afghan on the couch, gathered up my files, and reached the kitchen just as Catherine stepped through the back door carrying her boots and grinning.

I didn't grin back. "It's two o'clock in the morning. I was worried about you."

"Sorry to be so late, but, oh, Linda, I had such a good time. Please don't be mad!"

"Why didn't you call?" I opened the door to the mud room and took my jacket off the hook.

"I tried to call – I meant to call you when I left George's. I ended up going for a drive with Rafe. Then we stopped and talked. I didn't realize how late it was."

Catherine laughed. She smelled of wine and cigarettes. "Come on, let's have a nightcap. I want to tell you what happened."

"Tell me tomorrow." My coat on, I scooped up the files and headed home.

"I really am sorry," she called after me, sounding like she really meant it. But I didn't have the stomach for hearing her swoon over Rafe.

When I unlocked my back door the phone was ringing. I hung up my jacket and took off my boots, in no hurry to answer in case it was Catherine. *Let her stew.* It continued to ring. I padded into the kitchen on sock feet, flicked on the ceiling light, and picked up the receiver. "Hello."

"Hello, Constable Donner?" asked a resonant male voice on a line full of static.

"Who is this?" I glanced at my watch. Two-seventeen a.m.

"David Jordan. Sorry to call so late, but I've been trying to reach you all evening. I want to report someone missing."

"Why are you calling me?"

"Remember the woman you saw running into the woods the other day? Becky's mom? She never came back that afternoon to pick up her daughter. She's gone missing."

"Not much I can do right now. You can go in tomorrow and file a missing person report." My colleagues would already be looking for Cindy since her cabin had been roped off. *What was David up to in calling me? How did he get my unlisted number?*

"Can you meet me tomorrow?"

"What for?"

"I can't talk about it over the phone."

I considered for a moment whether it was wise given Karen's explicit orders to take days off. But no one besides me considered David a suspect, so I arranged to meet him at Cornwallis Cove Baptist Church in the morning when the service ended.

I had to get to the bottom of this.

the Conflict

Later that night I awakened in a strangely paralyzed state. When I tried to move, my body lay motionless. I tried to cry out, but no sound came out of my mouth. My heart pounded like a jackhammer, but I still couldn't move. I sensed the same hideous shadows that had terrified me in the woods when I found Rex's corpse. Finally, a little croak came out of my throat. I sat up, sweating, and turned on the light on the night table. My light blue duvet, the spare lines of the natural birch chest of drawers, and the newly sanded floors assured me I was home, and safe.

The clock showed 6:04 a.m. Though still my day off, routine prompted me to get out of bed even if the sun wasn't up. I opened the window and shivered in a gust of cold air. A rooster crowed. The fresh air smelled faintly of creosote and spruce.

Wearing a pair of snow joggers, my blue nylon shell and splash pants, I headed outside. The streetlights were about a hundred yards apart, but when my eyes adjusted I found I could just make out the shoulder of the road.

All Catherine's inside lights were off except the fluorescent light over the kitchen sink. Her outside light was off too leaving her station wagon in shadows in front of the small barn. The smell of fresh manure wafted toward me from the farm on the other side of Catherine's. I could just make out the outlines of several Hereford steers in a pen near the barn.

As I ran I was aware of the pounding of my feet and the rustle of the wind in the dry maples. Soon I was in the village of Cornwallis Cove where the houses were perched close together on the hillside. As I began my descent the sky was lightening in the east. I stepped onto the one-lane bridge running over the creek and leaned over the rusty railing. The tide was out, and below the bridge a narrow swath of dark fast-moving water cut a groove in the silt.

A car whizzed past, rattling the bridge. It wove up the hill in the direction I had just come. Because it was speeding I made a mental note of the license number. I jogged in place. The long uphill climb toward home lay ahead of me.

When I passed by Catherine's I saw a strange car in her laneway – the same car that sped by me on the bridge. Light glowed from her kitchen window. My feet broke a puddle's thin ice as I walked toward her back door. Looking inside her window I was shocked to see Rafe and Catherine kissing, his hands moving up and down her back, rubbing her white flannel nightgown. My stomach churning, I ran home and bolted upstairs to the bathroom.

I felt strung out for the next couple of hours. I paced from my kitchen to my living room and back again. *Why am I in such turmoil?* My thoughts jumped from Catherine to David Jordan. I dreaded meeting him now. I stretched in the living room and used every relaxation technique I knew to calm down, but found myself compulsively looking out my window to see if Rafe was still next door. What about Grace? *Does Catherine always get so quickly involved with a new boyfriend?*

I decided to go and get dressed for church to stop thinking about Catherine's lousy mothering skills. The new paint made my closet door stick. I yanked on the doorknob to view my limited civilian wardrobe. I found a dress Veronica had bought me when I graduated from Depot. It was something she'd wear – a soft, flowing, feminine dress with bold crimson flowers on a black background.

I tore open a new package of pantyhose, something I seldom wore, then dug a half-slip from the back of my drawer. I slipped on a pair of low black pumps. I studied my face in the mirror. My eyes were a little puffy from lack of sleep, though the run had heightened my colour. My honey-blonde hair still had sun-bleached streaks and my bangs had grown long enough to tuck behind my ears. I combed my hair and decided to pull it all back and pin it up. I glanced out the window next door one more time before I dusted off my black purse, and put my wallet, keys, and a notebook inside. I caught a glimpse of my reflection in the full-length mirror in the hall and was surprised by my feminine curves. The dress accentuated my small waist and its mid-calf skirt showed off my ankles. A bulletproof vest, utility belt, and straight-cut slacks tended to square off any figure. I pulled my magenta and turquoise ski jacket on over my dress.

As I opened the door I saw a tall woman with a frizzy perm get out of a pickup truck next door. Then I remembered Catherine telling me her housekeeper Edna came on Sundays to take Grace to church. She wore her usual navy polyester slacks over her narrow hips and a light blue parka around her stout upper body. I waited until I saw Grace, dressed in a green wool coat and matching hat, step out the back door. The affection I felt for her made my heart ache. Rafe's car was still parked in the laneway.

Inside, the church smelled of lemon furniture polish, wool coats and cologne. Grace slid into a pew halfway up on the right-hand side. She gestured for me to join her. Edna had paused to chat with some friends. When she started looking for Grace I stood and waved.

Cornwallis Cove Baptist seemed austere with its frosted windows, wooden pulpit, and table with some flowers I supposed was the altar. Fatigue washed over me. At least this church didn't have statues, stained glass, and flickering red and blue votives. Catholic churches repulsed me because of Ron. In this bare place I felt only mild contempt.

Ruth Harwood, the senior pastor's wife, sat at an electric organ readying some music. Then she started playing. The congregation sang the words to the songs via an overhead projector. Pastor Don Harwood, a thickset man with a big double chin and glasses, led the singing with his booming voice. When the music stopped he asked David Jordan to lead in prayer.

David stalked over to the podium and set his Bible on it. As he adjusted the mike, the room fell silent.

He cleared his throat. "Let us pray." Then he stood for what seemed an eternity, saying nothing. Even the children were still. The anxiety plaguing me earlier returned full force. My senses heightened, making me aware of feet shuffling, the man behind me blowing his nose, a baby fussing. Out of the corner of my eye I saw a young woman rise carrying an infant.

David scrunched his eyes shut and made a fist out of the hand that rested on the podium. "Lord, we come before you broken and humble. We lay our needs before you. We thank you that you hear our inward cries, that you are a God who answers prayer, who delivers us, who heals us. We praise you, Lord."

As he droned on, my anxiety grew. As I sat there feeling more and more anxious I realized part of me was serenely observing my anxious self. *Am I dissociating?* David had a beautiful, soothing voice. A hypnotic voice.

"Father, this has been a difficult week for me and my family. I thank you so much that you protected us from injury in the fire. I thank you for the love and generosity so many people have shown us. Amen."

I remembered how Ron's deep, soothing voice had thrilled our youth group, how all the kids, even the boys, seemed to have crushes on him. I ground my teeth. My nose began to run as tears stung my eyes.

Edna passed me a tissue. Embarrassed, I took it without looking at her.

David announced it was time for the children to come forward. Grace stood up and brushed in front of me toward the aisle. Other children also moved up front. They sat on the floor around David who now straddled a chair backward. As he told them a story about Jonah in the belly of the whale the children were spellbound. When he finished he led them like the Pied Piper to a stairway down to the basement. My eyes followed Grace as she skipped by in her black tights, green jumper and white blouse. My throat constricted. I could feel Ron's mouth over mine, and I couldn't breathe. I clutched the back of the pew in front, ready to spring up after her, but then saw Anne and Ruth follow him. David was supervised.

After the seemingly endless service I noticed other children came upstairs, but no Grace. When Anne and the other ladies appeared sweat trickled between my shoulder blades and my chest felt tight. *Grace can't be alone with that monster for one second.* I jumped up, walked to the door, and swung it open. There, at the top of the stairs, stood Grace holding hands with David. She looked up at him with that same open innocent affection she gave me. Her neck looked so delicate, scarcely strong enough to support her head.

"This is Auntie Linda. She's a Mountie."

"I know," he said.

"She's my friend." Grace beamed up at me. She handed me a drawing on blue construction paper. She'd glued cotton balls to it and pointed to them. "Those are clouds. Do you like it?"

"Yes. Who's that?" I pointed to the three stick figures holding hands.

"One big one is you. The other big one is Mommy." Grace rose on her tiptoes. "The little one is me. You can have it, but I have to show Mommy first."

Finally, Grace was out of David's clutches. While Edna was helping Grace on with her coat I made a mental note to tell Catherine, among other things, not to send Grace to this church.

"Mom wants you to come for dinner today," Grace told me. "See you later!"

After she skipped off with Edna David led me downstairs by some Sunday school classrooms to a small cubbyhole jammed with stacks of construction paper, glue and felt-tipped markers. He motioned me toward a wooden chair and scraped another across the cement floor so he could sit near me.

It unnerved me to have him sit so close. I took my notebook out of my ski jacket and made a blue squiggle with the pen to test the ink. I wondered if my pounding heart was visible through my dress.

David's eyes pleaded with me. "You are the last person who saw Cindy before she disappeared. Did she say anything to you? What direction did she go in? We need to find her."

I shrugged. "She disappeared into the woods. That's all I know."

"Becky's with the Roaches, but I don't know how long Margaret will be able to handle her." David picked a piece of pink construction paper off the floor, then stood. "Cindy hasn't contacted me or anyone else about her little girl. I'm afraid something bad's happened to her. Otherwise she would have called."

"After we saw you last Thursday at the church, how long did you stay there?"

"I left for Halifax right after you and Will drove off."

I wished I knew the exact time of Rex's death. Randy had made a rough estimate at the crime scene based on the extent of rigor mortis, but it was a range including Thursday afternoon through early evening. I doodled with my pen so my hand wouldn't shake. David could have done it after Will and I had left the church. Before his trip to Halifax.

David stared at me. "I'm afraid Rex has done something to Cindy. She was about to come forward with more information about the ritual abuse."

"You must be glad he's dead."

"Rex is dead?"

He seemed so genuinely surprised I was taken aback. If he was acting, it was pretty convincing. I watched him through narrowed eyes. *Didn't he ever listen to the radio? Didn't someone tell him?*

"What happened?"

"He's dead. That's all I can tell you."

He sat there looking at his hands. Then he wrung them and looked off to the side, deep in thought, his brown eyes heavy with sadness. "How did he die? Was he shot?"

"I'm not supposed to say."

"Was there any sign of a struggle at Cindy's?"

I shrugged. *How clever. He was trying to implicate Cindy. That's why he wanted to talk to me.* "If I knew, I couldn't say."

"She wasn't the best housekeeper." A half smile flickered on his lips.

I smiled back at him. "You think Cindy might have done it?" I saw through his game.

He shook his head, his eyes damp. "Cindy couldn't shoot Rex. She's a timid soul. Even in self-defence, I doubt it."

He used the word "shoot." I'd never said anything about the cause of Rex's death. He was implicating himself. *How can I get him to incriminate himself even further?* I asked a throwaway question to plot my next move. He thought he was so smart. "Does she have any friends or relatives?"

"Margaret has contacted them. She said no one's heard anything."

"Did you kill Rex?" *Real subtle. What did I say that for?*

A look of dismay crossed his face. It suddenly dawned on him I suspected him all along.

My throat constricted and my pulse throbbed in the back of my skull. "You had reason to. You think he burned your house down. You think he masterminded the ritual abuse of children. You were out to get him."

"I wanted to bring him to justice, Linda. Using the proper authorities. I do not believe the end justifies the means."

He bowed his head and steepled his hands. *Is he praying?* His false piety offended me. Then he stared at me for a few seconds. The anxiety and sense of panic I'd felt during our first interview at the detachment returned full force. I saw an image of myself running out of the room, screaming. I began to silently gulp air. I gazed at my white-knuckled hand clutching the pen. I thought about his ex-wife's affidavit swearing he abused their children.

"Constable Donner, I'm not your enemy. We're on the same side."

I jumped away from him, wobbling on my heels, making the chair skid across the floor. "Same side? How dare you patronize me!" I shouted. "You fake! You child molester!" I let out a string of obscenities.

Suddenly, the fear, the desire to flee, switched to rage. I fought back. My mouth started moving, but I had no idea what I was going to say next. My fists jabbed the air. Suddenly, I understood what criminals meant when they confessed to some violent act by saying *I felt like I was watching a movie.* There I was, screaming at the man.

He reached out and touched my arm. His fingers sent a charge of energy through me. I shuddered and recoiled. *What is he doing to me to make me feel this way?* Terror seized me and it must have shown in my eyes.

"It's okay. Don't be frightened." He faked a concerned expression.

Had he put suggestions in my mind? Was he causing me to have these irrational feelings? The rage came back and I shouted at him some more.

"In the Name of Jesus Christ I command the spirit of rage to loosen its hold on Linda Donner right now!" The authority in his voice shocked me like a slap.

The anger vanished. All that was left were feelings of deep shame. I couldn't look him in the eye. My chest started heaving.

"It's okay. Let it go," he said softly.

Sobs wracked my body. I gulped air.

"Look at me." He touched me again. This time I did not recoil, but still could not look at him. Twisting from his grip I edged toward the door. I stifled the sobs.

"May I pray for you?"

"No! Thank you." My voice shook. "I shouldn't have blown my stack like that. That was unprofessional. I apologize."

When reaching for my purse and ski jacket I glanced at him. His stare felt like an assault, as if he'd reached into my soul and dragged up every secret, every hate, every betrayal, every time I had deadened myself to block the pain. I couldn't bear the look of phony compassion on his face – it made me feel humiliated and unworthy. I bent over to get my notebook, which had dropped to the floor. He picked up my pen and handed it to me.

"Everything's going to be alright." He tried to lock eyes with me.

I moved the wooden chair out of my way. "Why don't you go to the detachment tomorrow and see Constable Bright." My legs wobbled as I staggered out of the room. *Damn heels.*

I drove home in tears. I had laundry to do, and not being one to let feelings of any kind interfere with my routine, I sobbed as I carried the laundry basket down to the washer in the basement. While the washing machine was running I lay in my bed in a fetal position, drenching tissue after tissue. When lying down didn't help I paced a little circuit from my kitchen to my living room, still crying. I scoured my sink and scrubbed my cupboards and counters, bawling most of the time. I hadn't cried like this for as long as I could remember. *Why? Why am I so upset?* Thoughts tumbled in my mind like clothes in the dryer. *Ron. Catherine. Veronica. Will. My job. Nothing is working out. Loneliness.*

Catherine called three times, but I didn't pick up the phone. She left messages on my answering machine, apologizing for being late the night before, begging me to come over for dinner. I was in no condition to face anyone.

Confusion and anxiety crushed my chest. I ached for the connection I used to feel with Dad before Ron spoiled everything.

Then something broke, like a dike holding back an ocean. I wept because Dad was dead. All the hurt, longing, regret, and sorrow I never allowed myself to feel overwhelmed me. I'd never see Dad's chipped-tooth smile again. I'd never be able to tell him I forgave him. His square face kept flashing in front of me, his Boston accent, his thick fingers, the white grizzle on his chin when he'd stop shaving for a few days. I recalled how awkward he seemed when he tried to get me to talk to him about my work, and how coolly distant I was. I'd been so cruel. *I'm so, so sorry.* I recalled his puzzled look of concern, the sadness in his eyes. The feelings were almost too much to bear. I felt wicked, unclean. *What had he done to me, really, except fall in love and find happiness? Am I so self-centred, so selfish, that I begrudged him that?*

The self-condemnation was unbearable, so while I paced I found myself compulsively looking for ways to blame David Jordan for making me feel so terrible. But my efforts couldn't block the grief for Dad. The last time I'd been convulsed with emotion like this was when I discovered I was pregnant and "Father" Ron accused me of sleeping around. That was fifteen years ago. I contemplated seeing a doctor to get some medication.

I slowly and gradually regrouped by concentrating on work. Rex's autopsy was the next morning in Halifax and I still had a box of files to read. I called the detachment and found out Karen had asked GIS to take over the Rex Dare file. GIS members along with Will and other Sterling County Mounties were already scouring South Dare for evidence. Though I hated not being with them, I looked forward to going to Halifax to do some extracurricular sleuthing. Focusing on my theories steeled my nerves as I methodically pressed my regulation slacks, ironed my shirts, and hung them one by one in my closet.

I would nail the firebomber. His name was David Jordan.

I only had to prove it.

the Investigation

My clock radio glowed a red 5:04 a.m. Feeling haunted I stumbled to the window and stared out into the darkness. Rafe's car was no longer parked next door. At least Catherine had *some* sense and didn't let him stay the night. I decided to write his license number down in my notebook since I'd memorized it when he'd sped past me on the bridge. Then after a run, showering, and putting on my uniform, I ate a muffin and cheese, fixed a thermos of hot tea, and took off in my Jeep for the morgue in Sterling.

The man from the body removal service met me in the lobby of the hospital. He was young, in his early twenties, dark-haired, earnest, wearing a cheap black suit and red and gold striped tie. He introduced himself as Kyle Murphy, an employee at Calhoun's Funeral Home. We went downstairs to the morgue. I unlocked the body, examined it again, and logged everything in my notebook. The morgue attendant helped Kyle get the body onto a gurney and into the van.

The van barrelled down the dry salt-stained highway bordered by dirty snowdrifts toward Halifax. The asphalt cut through a brown and white landscape of rolling hills, farmers' fields covered with scattered patches of snow, and woodlots of balsam fir, spruce and leafless maples. Every now and then I saw a farmhouse trimmed in Christmas lights off in the distance. Kyle, who seemed nervous and eager to please, made several attempts to start a conversation. I just didn't feel like talking.

We made good time until we got caught in early rush hour traffic outside the city. Eventually we pulled into the parking lot for the hospital, a huge brick complex in the city's fashionable south end. Kyle drove up to an annex containing the pathology lab and the morgue. Inside, Dr. Walter Munson, the forensic pathologist, emerged from behind his desk to greet me. A grey-haired man with black-rimmed glasses, he had an odd smile on his face as if death were somehow humorous to him.

Soon Rex's corpse lay face up on a stainless steel table in the autopsy room, clothed in the bloodstained blue and green shirt. A microphone attached to a recorder hung over the table. Randy Cohen from IDENT arrived carrying a clipboard and a legal-sized file folder. Wearing a uniform, minus his cap, he stood five foot nine with a receding hairline and a moustache. He readied a camera with a powerful flash. He recognized me from the crime scene. We exchanged greetings, then I asked him to bring me up to date on the investigation.

"We found a few shells. No useful fingerprints, though."

"What kind?"

"Twelve-gauge shotgun. Remington 870. No sign of the gun. I understand it's a common firearm out in South Dare."

"Are you folks ready?" Dr. Munson asked. He'd donned a white apron and pulled on some opaque rubber gloves.

First, he started the recorder, said the date and time, and named himself, Randy, and me as present. Then, while Randy snapped photos the pathologist examined Rex's clothed body, commenting on the bloodstains and looking for any evidence. He noted a burn mark on Rex's quilted work shirt and noted that it may have been made by a burning cigarette butt. He turned the body over. Then he carefully cut away Rex's clothing. Randy filmed the procedure.

Soon Rex's body lay naked on the stainless steel table looking waxy and unreal. Congealed blood smeared his torso. His green tattoos stood out against his grey skin. Dr. Munson described where the shotgun slug had entered and the condition of the wounds. Then he began to slice around Rex's face. After some deft cuts he peeled Rex's face off his skull. Then he sawed a hole in the top of his head, lifted his brain out and weighed it. He worked systematically, examining organs that appeared to have nothing to do with the shooting. He extracted a misshapen metal slug from Rex's spine. Randy leaned against the wall making calculations based on the slug's trajectory and velocity. I found the procedure fascinating. I had always prided myself on my objectivity and ability to control my emotions in the past, so it felt good to be hitting my usual stride again.

The whole process took most of the morning. Randy and Dr. Munson offered to have typed copies of their notes ready for me to take back to Sterling later that afternoon. Randy offered to buy me lunch in the hospital cafeteria, but I told him I had plans. I arranged to meet Kyle later that afternoon at Dr. Munson's office before returning to Sterling.

I used the pathologist's phone to call Heather Franklin. She agreed to meet me.

I took a cab over to the TV studios, arriving at 12:31 p.m. A thin woman wearing a short navy skirt and matching tailored jacket came down the stairs to meet me a few moments later. She was tiny, four foot eleven maybe, and radiated energy and will. I introduced myself.

Heather's handshake felt powerful for a child-sized hand. "I'd love to tell you about that slimeball, but I have to go out on a shoot. Is the clinic firebombing case opening up again?"

"I don't know. I'm investigating another firebombing."

Heather eyed me. "His house, right? Ha! That's poetic justice for you."

"You're certain he did the clinic?"

"Oh, he did it alright." She glanced at her watch. "I could put you in a screening room with some of my items. You can take a look at my files too."

She nodded to the security guard, and I followed her through the glass doors to the stairway and up to the production area on the second floor.

"I hope David Jordan gets nailed. He is bad news." Her heels clicked on the tile floor.

She had me wait in a tiny screening room with a video machine and a TV. In a few minutes she returned with a cardboard box of videos and file folders. After demonstrating how to work the video machine she showed me how she'd labelled the tapes so I could easily find what interested me.

After she left I put the first tape in the machine. It looked like tape right out of the camera. First, it showed a wide shot of a building I assumed to be the abortion clinic due to the placard-waving crowd in front. The camera suddenly zoomed in and focused to show David Jordan chained to the wrought iron railing along with two other men. He looked harsher, younger, his colour more sallow. *Was he already sick with cancer by then?*

The tape showed Halifax police officers forcing their way through the crowd. They cut David's chains and carried him away. A group of pro-choice demonstrators screamed and cheered. One of the women spat in his face. I saw his cheek twitch. I paused the tape.

The door opened behind me. Heather squeezed into the room and stood next to me. "I don't have to leave after all. They just killed my story." She pressed play. The screen showed a close-up of David Jordan's face as the police carried him through the crowd.

"That pig!" Heather muttered. "That self-righteous fascist pig! Look at him!"

David had turned toward the woman who'd spat at him. His lips moved, but the noise of the crowd drowned out what he said.

"The women at the clinic always said he was the worst one," Heather snorted in disgust. "He had this stare. This judgemental stare that made vulnerable women feel tormented. I can't tell you how much he offended people."

I knew all about that stare.

Heather showed me her stories about the firebombing and let me skim over her files of newspaper clippings. The clinic showed hardly any damage, just some smoke around the door.

"You don't believe his alibi?"

"David was the ringleader of the movement. When he said jump they asked how high."

"Yeah, but none of what you've shown me is proof he did it."

"I talked to a disaffected member of his group three years ago, and she all but accused him of the firebombing. She wouldn't go public, though. And she wouldn't co-operate with the police either. She was scared of him."

"Where is she now?"

"I'm not sure. She's from the Sterling area, though. Maybe you'll find her up there."

Heather wrote a name down in her spiral notebook. She tore out the sheet and gave it to me.

"Her name's Cindy Dare, but she doesn't have a phone."

Cindy Dare! Heather picked up the box, examined the label on the back, and put it down. Picked up another, then another, until she flipped a tape out of the box, put it in the machine, and hit fast-forward. The numbers scrolled on the counter.

Then she hit play.

"There's Cindy."

On the screen a woman stood on the sidewalk near David Jordan, clutching a pro-life sign. She held it against her body like a shield. Her hair, bleached platinum blonde, was shoulder length but uneven in thickness as if she had some bald spots she was trying to cover over with the remaining hair. Because of the hair colour I couldn't be sure if the woman on the video was the same woman I'd seen behind the church.

"Did you tape your interview with Cindy?"

"Oh, no. She was literally quaking with fear. But I took notes."

"Where are those notes now?"

She hesitated a moment. "I shouldn't be letting you see any of this stuff without a subpoena." She reached for a folder on the floor, withdrew some typewritten notes, and leafed through them. "Take them. Don't say you got them from me."

I folded the notes and put them into my jacket pocket. Heather gave me David Jordan's ex-wife's phone number at work, warning me that Barbara Jordan was mentally unbalanced. When I reached Barbara she agreed to meet me for a late lunch.

It took me about five minutes by cab to get across town to Barbara's office. Nova Scotians for Life occupied a two-storey wooden building on a street of old row houses. I pushed open the red-painted wooden door into the hallway where a staircase went up to the second floor. The front room on the first floor had been converted into an office. Barbara wore her red hair chin length in a blunt cut. I hadn't expected her to be so serene. I had imagined her bedraggled and forlorn like Anne.

Barbara and I strolled along the sloped sidewalk to a Chinese restaurant on Gottingen Street. Inside, a young woman brought us a white teapot. As Barbara poured the tea the scent of jasmine wafted from the steaming cups.

"What can I do for you?" Barbara smiled faintly.

"I understand David Jordan was investigated for firebombing the abo_ion clinic. Can you give me any information about that?"

Barbara exploded. "That was a crock! The media were out to get him. Nobody asked about who benefited from that bombing. Certainly not us. Radical pro-abortionists benefited because of the propaganda value. Which they still exploit to smear us."

Barbara paused her ranting for a moment. She no longer seemed warm and friendly. I could see what Heather meant about her being unbalanced.

"Why would you ask about that? What does that have to do with David's house getting firebombed?"

"Probably nothing. But I have to cover all the bases."

"He loves his kids. He loves Anne. He would never, ever risk hurting them. I can assure you of that." She watched my reaction, then looked at her menu.

I nodded, making my face seem sympathetic. "You seem to think pretty highly of him." *How could she if he abused their children?*

"The idea that he would do anything violent. I mean, this is a pro-life movement. Pro-life! We don't approve of bombing abortion clinics or shooting abortion doctors." *Born again Barbie! A pro-life fanatic.*

She must have seen my eyes glaze over because she stopped. The waitress took our order.

"Are you a Christian?" she asked.

I grinned. "I was brought up Catholic. Does that qualify?"

"Of course. David has special gifts. Do you know about spiritual gifts, Constable Donner?"

I racked my brain to think of something fast. The story of his miraculous healing popped into my mind. "Gifts like healing?" *Let her assume I'm on the same page.*

Barbara smiled. "That's right. Gifts of healing, discerning spirits, words of knowledge."

"I know he was healed himself. Can he heal the sick?"

"Well, not everybody gets healed. But I've seen him pray for people and some do get better. And sometimes he knows things about people's lives that only God could reveal to him."

"He's clairvoyant?" My stomach tightened. *Could he really see through me?*

"No, not clairvoyance. That's occult. Christians call it 'words of knowledge from the Holy Spirit.'"

"May I ask, Mrs. Jordan, why you aren't still married to him?"

"It's a long story."

"I've got time." *How can I get her to open up to me?* "Did he leave you for the woman he's with now?"

"Oh, no." Barbara shook her red hair. "I left him. David would never have married again except he thought he was dying and his nurse – that's how he met Anne – wanted to take him home to die at her place. He didn't think that was proper, so he married her. Then he got better. God does have a sense of humour."

The waitress placed some spring rolls in front of us. I popped one onto my plate and spread some plum sauce on it.

"You left him because...?"

"I didn't bear up well under the pressures of being a pastor's wife. I couldn't say no to people. And he just wasn't there for me. He had his causes." She smiled to herself as she sliced her spring roll. "He's grown a great deal since our divorce. We've made our peace with each other. Why is this important to the firebombing?"

"You don't mind him spending time with your children?"

Barbara stiffened. "Why should I? He's an excellent father."

"Didn't you accuse David of sexually abusing your daughter?"

Her cheeks reddened. "Hold on! I withdrew those accusations. They aren't supposed to be on record anywhere. How did you know I made them?"

"They were false?"

Barbara gripped the tabletop. "Yes, they were false. He was trying to get custody of the children. I was desperate. It's the worst thing I've ever done. I want any record of those false accusations removed!" She shoved her untouched spring roll away.

"Where were you Thursday evening?"

"Why do you want to know? I don't understand where any of this is leading. You think I firebombed David's home?" Barbara signalled to the waitress. "I am not going to have lunch after all. Can you bring me my bill please?"

"If you want to help David, the best thing you can do is be honest. Where were you Thursday afternoon and evening and what were you doing?"

Barbara glared at me. "I was at my office in the afternoon. Then I was upstairs in my apartment straightening up and preparing supper. David arrived just before we were going to sit down to eat."

"You have an exact time?"

"No, but we usually eat around six and I didn't serve supper any later than usual, so I'd say he got there at about quarter to. He ate with me and our two children and later he crashed on the futon downstairs in the office. He spent Friday working with me until the children finished school, then drove them to my parents' cottage in Hubbards."

"You know Cindy Dare? She's gone missing."

"I hate to sound uncharitable, but I don't care. No more questions. I think you've taken enough advantage of me." Barbara removed a ten dollar bill from her wallet, shoved it under her plate, and left.

Barbara's testimony was favourable to her ex-husband, but her rote fundamentalist rants on the abortion issue and her ex-husband's alleged supernatural powers convinced me I was on the right track. If David arrived at her place around suppertime, that gave him a small window of opportunity to shoot Rex after Will and I had left his church that afternoon. Then he could have hopped in the car and sped down the highway to visit Barbara, who would probably lie for him and say he arrived earlier than he really did. I glanced at my watch. I had to drop by the pathology lab to pick up the Rex Dare file and meet Kyle for the ride back to Sterling.

I took a cab to the morgue and picked up the manila envelope containing the autopsy report. Scanning it quickly in Dr. Munson's office I saw that it jibed with what I had witnessed in the morning. The time of death could have been anywhere from 3 p.m. to 7 p.m.

the day before I found the body. Randy included his calculations and diagrams. Will would find these pieces of the puzzle meaningful. Kyle arrived with the van.

Before leaving Halifax Kyle drove me to the Halifax Police Department for a last appointment with Detective Patrick Ryan who had investigated the clinic firebombing. He told me nothing I didn't already know. I feared my search was going nowhere until he pulled his notes from the firebombing file.

His black eyebrows twitched like caterpillars as he read.

"Someone broke the window first and threw a bottle with kerosene into the room. The bottle hit a wall, but didn't break. The kerosene caught fire from the burning wick. But it didn't spread so it burned like a smoking lantern without a chimney. There was a man from a cleaning service in the building at the time who reported the fire. Then he turned a fire extinguisher on it and put it out before the firefighters got there. Not much damage. Nobody was hurt."

"Sounds like a pretty amateurish job to me." I could scarcely contain my elation at the similar modus operandi between the clinic firebombing and that of David Jordan's home.

He shrugged and the eyebrows jumped up. "It was more of a political statement, or a warning. Whoever did it wanted to make sure the fire wouldn't get out of control. It shut down the clinic for a while and created a political firestorm. David Jordan had a good alibi, fortunately for him. When you have a priest and a nun ready to swear on a Bible that you were with them it looks pretty good to a jury. I thought maybe he could have done it. But with Jordan's military training he could have made a much more lethal bomb if he'd set his mind to it. So, when he came up with the alibi, I was like, okay. But one of my partners was convinced there was a conspiracy and these people cooked up a story to cover Jordan. I believed that at first. Now I'm not so sure. It's been a long time."

On the return trip to Sterling with Kyle my mind drifted over the interviews of the day. Barbara Jordan and her pro-life rant reminded me how desperately I wanted to abort Ron's child, but Dad and Veronica had stopped me. So I went through with the pregnancy because I had to. The nurses sedated me during labour, and I planned never to see the baby because I had already agreed to give her up for adoption. But the night she was born curiosity got the best of me, and I asked the nurse to bring her to me. As I slid aside the white flannel receiving blanket I saw a perfect, tiny hand. I touched it. The skin was so soft. Then she gripped my finger. This was *my daughter*. She was real. Alive. Trembling, I lifted the blanket corner hiding her little face. There she was, this red-faced wrinkled little being. A love like nothing I'd ever experienced, even for Dad, settled over me. I would have died for her if I'd had to. I burst into tears. I felt so guilty for hating her because she was Ron's child. The nurse, seeing how upset I was, swept my baby daughter out of my arms.

I looked out at the dark landscape, aching for my lost child and my dad whom I would never see again. I wiped tears from my eyes, hoping Kyle didn't notice. I wanted her to know, wherever she was, that I loved her more than I thought it possible to love anyone. I tried to push the image of her tiny red face out of my mind.

the Suspects

At 8:32 p.m. Kyle dropped me off at the detachment. Will sat in the conference room that doubled as the staff lounge. He slouched in one of the chairs, his feet up on another, saying nothing to greet me when I handed him the findings. His eyes were bloodshot with fatigue and the corners of his mouth sagged. I left him reading while I did my continuation report.

About fifteen minutes later Will brought me up to date on the investigation. He told me no one in South Dare was talking, and how a thorough search of Cindy's cabin and Rex's big house had turned up nothing. GIS considered Cindy a suspect, but he doubted she'd be capable of killing Rex.

We were both hungry so he drove me downtown to a coffee shop on the waterfront. Fog rolled in off the harbour, creating a grey mist that obscured the twinkling lights of buoys on the dark water, and the outlines of fishing boats banging against the pilings at the public wharf. The tide was out and the mudflats smelled of seaweed. A drunk sat in the doorway of the lawyer's office next to the coffee shop.

He scrambled to his feet and clutched Will's sleeve, asking for some cash.

"Not for booze, Stan."

Stan was weeping. His breath reeked of the sweet smell of Lysol. He lurched toward me, forcing me to step back.

To my surprise, Will put his hands on Stan's shoulders and pushed him into the coffee shop ahead of us. The owner came to the door, distressed.

"Get Stan the special. I'll pick up the tab," Will said.

The owner glanced at his other customers, his lips pursed, then nodded. He told Stan to sit down in the booth close to the door. Will and I sat down a few booths away. A waitress came over and I ordered the special myself – liver, bacon, onions with mashed potatoes. Will reminded the waitress to give him Stan's bill.

"Why did you do that? Buy his dinner?"

Will looked away, then ran his hands through his hair as if wondering whether to tell me.

"My father was an alcoholic."

"Oh."

"Is that all you want to know?"

I averted my eyes. "Yeah. Sorry."

Our orders came and we ate in silence for several minutes as I wondered how to discuss what I'd learned that day.

"Heard you saw David Jordan on Sunday." Will seemed to be studying my response.

Did David Jordan mention my meltdown? I blushed. "Yeah. He was a big help." I changed the subject. "Did you know that kerosene filled the bottle used to firebomb the abortion clinic?"

"So?" A cynical smile curled Will's lip up on one side of his mouth. "Still trying to catch the firebomber, eh? You think David Jordan killed Rex too?" His fork dug into the cherry pie, then he shovelled it in.

I felt my cheeks flush with anger. "He's got a motive."

"Well, hey, I've got the same motive. Rex Dare was probably the most evil person I've ever met. Maybe you should consider me a suspect."

"Where were you on Thursday afternoon?"

He knit his brows as if trying hard to remember. Then, looking down, he smiled to himself.

"If I recall, ma'am, I was with you." He smiled. "You're okay, Linda. You've got a sense of humour."

I drove home through a fog so thick the usual landmarks were missing. The windshield wipers scraped a fine drizzle off the windshield. I leaned forward, peering into the heavy white mist, navigating by following the road's yellow centre line. Once in my laneway I could barely make out the outline of Catherine's station wagon. The light from her kitchen window brightened the chilly fog. I set my jaw and headed into my cold dark kitchen.

The phone rang. I ignored it as I unlaced my boots, hung up my coat and hat, and did my usual routine with my uniform and gear. Once upstairs in my bedroom the red message light flashed on my answering machine. I hit play.

Catherine's voice came on. "Linda. I know it's late, but can we talk? Please pick up the phone."

I was no longer angry with her, but feared her intuitiveness and questions. Dressed in sweats I watched the late news in the living room. Someone banged on my back door and persisted until I opened it. Catherine stood under my porch light, her eyes blotchy from crying.

"Are you going to throw away our friendship because I made one mistake?"

"It's not that. Not that at all."

"What is it then?"

"I don't..." I paused, struggling to keep my feelings from welling up. "I don't want to talk about it. I'm sorry. It has nothing to do with you."

Catherine grabbed my arm. "Linda, what's wrong?"

"I can't." I shook my head and averted my face. Her warmth and concern for me made me clench my jaw to keep my eyes from filling with tears. I stepped aside so Catherine could come into the mud room and I could shut the door to keep the cold outside.

"Well, that's okay. You don't have to talk about it. But please don't stay away. Grace kept asking for you yesterday when you didn't come over for dinner."

"You already had company. Now that you have Rafe for a friend, you don't need me." I surprised myself at the bitterness in my tone. *What am I saying?*

An odd look passed over Catherine's face. "Linda, your friendship is important to me. But you don't have the right to make me choose. I'm happy for the first time in six years. Please don't begrudge me that."

"You've known this guy for less than three days and he's making you happy? You don't even know if Rafe Lupien is his real name!"

"I don't want to argue. My relationship with Rafe is my business. But it means a lot to me that you and I stay friends."

"Maybe I'm being your friend by telling you to watch out for this guy. It's not a good idea to trust people so quickly."

"Okay. Thank you. Warning noted. Are you going to boycott me until I see things your way, or are you going to come over and eat some supper?"

"I've already eaten. It's late."

"Come over for dessert then. Some tea? Please?"

I stuffed my feet into my rubber boots, grabbed my parka, and followed her outside. She put her arm around my back and hugged me to her for a moment. The clumps of dead grass were mushy and wet as we sprinted through the fog and drizzle.

The next morning at the detachment someone had commandeered my desk and covered it with files. A few unfamiliar members sat at the other desks. I assumed they were from the Halifax GIS. As soon as I wrapped up some initial paperwork all the members working on the Rex Dare murder investigation convened in the conference room.

Will sat sideways at the table, facing an equally large man who had short dark hair and a permanent five o'clock shadow. Will introduced me to Sergeant Pete Surette from Halifax. He rose partway to shake my hand, chewing gum and apparently sizing me up.

The other two GIS members came in with Staff Sergeant Ramsay and Corporal Jacques.

Sergeant Surette brought us up to date on the state of the investigation. He drew a diagram on the flip chart showing Cindy Dare's shack, the path and location where Rex's body was found, and the parallel path where the shotgun shells were found. He flipped the page over and began to write the names of people the GIS team and Sterling members had already interviewed.

"We have a warrant out for Cindy Dare's arrest. She's our chief suspect. We haven't ruled out a family dispute. Rex's oldest sons by his first wife Ma Lorraine have been vying for control of the bootlegging and drug smuggling business out there. The older son Lance already has a power base in the community with his bingo hall. The younger son Lonnie hates Lance. He's jealous of Lance's competence. Lonnie's close to Rex's older brother Gordon, and Gordon and Lonnie were running Rex's bootlegging operation. Lance could have done his father in to increase his own empire. Or maybe Lonnie and Gordon got tired of the control Rex had over them."

I raised my hand. "You should include the pastor of the church, David Jordan, as a suspect."

Pete glanced at Will, then nodded and wrote David Jordan's name on the flip chart.

"Linda, you can debrief us in a moment."

Pete pointed the felt-tipped marker at the names. "Basically, it could be anyone out there. I want you to lean on these people. Get search warrants for minor violations. Seize any improperly stored shotguns and send them for ballistics tests. We've already seized five. We didn't get much from our interviews so far. Will and Linda, I want you to spend a lot of time in South Dare. Cultivate contacts, keep your ears to the ground. Linda, you see what you can learn from the women out there."

"If you need a warrant, Robert or Maurice will handle it. Get them for anything – bootlegging, stealing juice from the power grid, selling smuggled cigarettes, growing weed. Karen says no one works alone out there, especially now. Understood?" He glanced at me.

Pete had me go next. First, I debriefed them on the autopsy, though Will had already given each of them a copy of the report. Then I laid out my case against David Jordan, building fact upon fact. Will hunched in his seat, elbows on the table, chin in his hands, tensely coiled like an angry snake.

"David Jordan is a fundamentalist who believes a satanic cult is operating in South Dare," I said. "I think we can make a case that he killed Rex Dare to destroy the cult. A TV reporter from Halifax says Cindy Dare told her she saw David Jordan firebomb the Halifax abortion clinic three years ago. Someone threw the same kind of kerosene-filled cocktail into Jordan's house in South

Dare. Maybe he wants to make sure he looks like a victim to hide his tracks. If he thinks he's serving God by bombing an abortion clinic, it's not that big a stretch to murder a man he sees as the servant of Satan. I haven't been able to follow up on this, but Rex Dare told Constable Bright and me that some women were coming forward to complain Jordan sexually abused their children. His ex-wife filed an affidavit that he abused their daughter."

Will traded glances with Pete. Will shook his head so slightly it was almost imperceptible. I wanted to kick him. The rest of the members looked at me, faces blank. Then the others each got up and shared the results of their investigations.

When the meeting was over, Will bought a Sprite from the pop machine and left the conference room. Now I was the one holding my head in my hands, hunched over the table, ready to explode with frustration. Seconds later he poked his head in to say we were going to South Dare.

I twisted to face him. "Thanks for heading me off at the pass. You made sure no one would take my ideas seriously."

"That's not true."

"Whatever." I turned my back to him. I sensed him standing there for several seconds.

He exhaled in frustration. "We're leaving in half an hour." Then he lumbered away.

To take my mind off *my* frustration with *him* I decided to run a check on Rafe. Then I heard Debbie paging me. I stuck my head out so she could see me from the glassed-in area where civilian members worked. I told her to send the phone call to me in the conference room.

Who would be asking for me by name at the detachment? Hardly anyone knew me in Sterling County.

the Photo

I picked up the warbling phone to find Veronica on the line, her voice sounding faint and tremulous.

"Is this a bad time?" Veronica didn't sound at all like the crisp controlling woman I remembered.

I rolled my eyes. "I've got a moment. Shoot."

"Have you given any thought to the holidays?"

I stared at the fake wood grain of the dark brown conference table. "I'm the new kid on the block, so I'll probably be on duty."

"I'd love to see you." Her voice trembled.

"Okay. I'll see what I can do." I had no intention of seeing her, but I didn't want to be rude.

"There's something I need to tell you."

"Shoot." I felt my chest tighten and my shoulders tense.

"I'd rather tell you in person."

I was shaking when I hung up. I looked down at my spiral notebook and forced myself to concentrate on Rafe's license plate number. Stuffing my notebook in my vest pocket I repeated it like a mantra to block my feelings. I walked over to a computer and logged on. The phone at my elbow rang, and as I reached to answer it I hit a half-empty can of Sprite. It spilled across the desk and onto my slacks. Furious, I jumped up, receiver to my ear with one hand, keyboard in the other to get it out of the way of the spreading liquid.

A familiar deep melodious voice asked for Staff Sergeant Ramsay. I transferred the call to Karen, hung up, and sopped up the mess with paper towels from the bathroom. Will was always leaving his half-empty coffee cups and pop cans around. *He* should have been cleaning up his mess. I then returned to the bathroom to get the pop off my slacks.

In the mirror my light green eyes were wide and wild looking, my lips pursed, my jaws tight. My hair was up, but several strands had escaped and fell in loose waves to my shoulders. I looked like Medusa. I pinned the strands back and splashed cold water on my face.

I strode down the shiny waxed hallway toward the room containing the universal gym and free weights. I overheard Eddie Johnson say, "Hey, Incest Kid, take a look at this."

"Don't call me that!" Will said.

"Some photo, eh?" Eddie said.

"That's Linda?" Will said. "You've got to be kidding. Hubba, hubba!"

When he and Eddie laughed I felt sick in the pit of my stomach. Their banter brought back the horror of my time in Surrey.

"Where'd you get this?" Will asked.

"Someone from my troop at Depot is a constable out in Surrey. He took this off the video someone shot while she was undercover busting johns. Quite the butt on her, eh?"

I leaned against the hallway wall, feeling the cool of the green-painted cinder blocks. The photo had followed me to Sterling. In it I wore fishnet stockings, platform shoes and a micro-miniskirt, and I leaned on the door of a black Ford Bronco, but had turned my head to give the finger to someone. I wore a black wig and my face was plastered with garish makeup.

"My buddy says the members in Surrey used to joke that Donner looked more like a transvestite than a chick. You know how mannish she is."

"Ouch!" Will said.

Now I understood why Eddie had such a negative attitude toward me. He'd checked me out with his buddy before I even came to Sterling.

I heard some mumbling I couldn't understand, then another voice laughing. It sounded to me like Bob Morin. I started to walk away.

"Linda's going to South Dare with me to get the women to open up," Will said. He and the others laughed.

"Yeah, yeah, the Ice Amazon's really going to provide the sensitive warm environment, right?" Eddie said.

"Tell me about it," Will said. "You guys don't have to work with her."

"You think Karen's got the hots for her?" Eddie asked.

"Come on, Eddie," Will said.

I'd heard enough. I strode into the exercise room.

They froze. Will tried to hide the photo behind his back. He and Bob couldn't look at me, though a sneer curled up Eddie's lip.

I planted myself in front of Will. "If I don't like how you're doing your job, you're going to hear it from me. I won't go behind your back. I expect the same of you."

Will blushed. I grabbed the photograph. Sure enough, there was my butt sticking up in the air in that short miniskirt. I folded it and stuck it in my pocket.

"What jerks!" I turned and strode back toward the office.

Will followed.

"Linda, hold on."

"What?" I stopped, but kept my back turned.

He touched my elbow. I shook off his hand and turned around. His freckled face seemed earnest and contrite. "I apologize. That won't happen again."

I shrugged. "Yeah, sure." I raised my chin to look in his eyes, which looked surprisingly kind. "You got a bone to pick with me about something?"

"Well, okay. I do have a problem." He sounded a little nervous, as if confrontation made him uncomfortable.

"I've got problems with you too, Bright. You want to go first?" I realized I'd put my hands on my hips, and let them drop to my sides.

"Okay. Look, I don't want to be unkind, but..."

"Just say it! I'm not going to break."

"We are a tight-knit group and we want to make you part of the team. But you hold yourself apart. You disregard everyone else's feelings and only talk when you're irritated about something or want to have your own way."

Have my own way? Look who's talking! "You make me feel so welcome," I smirked.

Will glanced at the weight room door. "Don't judge the whole detachment because of that. I'll make sure nothing like it happens again."

I gave him a cool stare, but his eyes stayed kind. It would have been easier to hate him if he glared back.

"I'm not saying this to offend you, Linda, but I have wondered if you hate us because we're men." He crossed his arms.

I groaned and rolled my eyes. "That's ridiculous. All I want is to be treated like a member, period, not like a female member."

"Can we start over?" He offered me his hand to shake. I reluctantly took it.

"Okay." I felt oddly touched and could feel the expression on my face softening.

"We can start over on one condition. You don't leave your half-empty pop cans around. And clean your trash out of the car at the end of the day."

That behind me I headed to the parking lot to leave for South Dare, wondering what Veronica could possibly have to tell me that she couldn't say over the phone. *Maybe it was about my daughter.* I clutched my stomach. A wave of grief surged through me. *Get a grip, Linda.*

Instead of insisting on driving I brushed past Will and got into the passenger side, nauseated by the turmoil Veronica's phone call and the photo had triggered. Will paused for a moment, trying to catch my eye, then got into the driver's seat. He started the car and glanced at me again. I leaned forward, still clutching my stomach, reached for my seat belt, and pulled it across.

"You okay? Did I come down on you too hard?"

"No. Not at all."

I glanced at him and felt my mask slip away for a second. To my extreme embarrassment my eyes watered and my face puckered. *Damn!*

"Hey, she's human," he said, gently. He reached into the footwell where he had crushed innumerable coffee cups and came up with some clean paper napkins. "My trash comes in handy for something." He passed me the napkins.

I laughed and blew my nose.

In South Dare we hiked through the scrub, alders, and poplars to the place where I'd found Rex Dare's body. The police tape was in tatters. Will surveyed the scene. "What are they gonna use the tape for, souvenirs?"

"Nah. Repairs."

Will laughed.

The branches were covered in a thin coat of melting ice. The temperature was rising so the path was muddy. The nearby woods were silent, except for the sound of constant dripping.

"This is where you found Rex." Will took out copies of Randy Cohen's diagrams. He beckoned to me. "You stand here, okay?"

"Do I have a choice?" Branches cracked as I stepped toward him.

"Hey, the old Linda's back!"

"Look, about what happened in the car. I wasn't upset about our conversation in the hall. I don't want you to think I crumple with a little criticism."

"Were you upset about the photo?"

"You've got to be kidding. I've got a thicker skin than that."

"Well, it would have bothered me." Will pushed through the brush.

"I'm used to it. I just thought maybe you guys would have a little more originality."

"I wouldn't let a thick skin become a wall. Stay there please, okay?"

Will continued to plough through the brush like a mini-bulldozer, holding his copies at shoulder height. I hated it when he patronized me and ordered me around. He stopped and examined the papers, then tossed me the measuring tape and asked me to extend the tape to him. He grabbed the flopping end of the tape, then pressed backward several feet through the brush.

"Hold it right by the tree. Tight."

"Yes, sir!" I clicked my heels together and saluted.

"This is where whoever shot Rex was probably standing. We found the shells over here."

The line of sight was clear to the other path. Though the woods were fairly thick with young trees, the area Will had ploughed through was mostly bush no more than four feet high and, with most of the leaves fallen off, not that thick. Will beckoned me with his head and I cut through the bush to join him.

He stared across to the other path where I'd found Rex's body. "Nice place for an ambush." He kept zipping the end of the measuring tape in and out.

Standing next to him I followed his line of sight and remembered how Rex's crumpled corpse had fallen. I remembered the cigarette butt Will had found near the body and the burn mark on the dead man's shirt. "So, Rex was smoking a cigarette when he turned to face the shooter."

"Yeah, that's right. We found some frozen footprints. They indicated Rex had been walking toward the church. Then he stopped and turned in this direction. Whoever shot him probably called his name or made a sound. I suspect it was someone Rex knew. Someone who wanted Rex to know who was going to kill him."

"Like the pastor?"

Will groaned. "Give it up. And Cindy couldn't have shot Rex like that. He'd have been able to talk her into putting the gun down."

"You make Rex sound like a magician."

"He knew how to manipulate people and make them dependent on him. If kindness didn't work, threats and cruelty did."

"I think you're giving this guy more credit that he deserves. Rex may have been a sociopath, but he was no genius."

"He didn't need to be a genius around here. He persuaded people he had supernatural powers and claimed he could turn into a bear and harm them. They believed him."

We trudged back toward the church, surrounded by the sound of dripping water and the sucking of our boots in the mud.

"You think you or I could have heard the shot from inside the church?" Will eyed David Jordan's sagging white building, now called South Dare Community Church according to the sign out front. It had a square vent on top like on the roof of a barn, resembling a stunted steeple on the pitched roof. Fir boughs banked the outside of the building to insulate against the cold weather. The building sported a fresh coat of paint.

"I don't know. It was pretty noisy in there with those kids running around." I shuddered as I recalled how Becky Dare had hissed and growled like an animal after David had touched her.

Will shrugged. "Rex probably got shot right after we left and Cindy saw it happen. We found some prints that might be hers. Duck boot prints."

"But there were lots of other footprints, right? David Jordan could have come up this path looking for Cindy after she ran away. And he could have shot Rex just before he took off for Halifax."

He grinned and shook his head. "You are like a dog with a bone. But you're right, there were lots of footprints. We have to find Cindy. Then we'll be able to put a lot of this together."

As we tromped back to the police car Will noticed several rabbit snares.

"Looks like Rex's nephew Alan *has* been out here." Will pointed to some wire loops in the brush. "See the snares?"

Since Will and I were getting along I decided not to press my theory just yet.

Next stop was Rex Dare's place. The door of the main house hung open. Smoke curled from one of the surrounding shack's stovepipe. The other shacks clustered around the big house showed no signs of life. Someone moved inside the heated shack's dirty window.

"Company!" Will said as we climbed out of the police car. We strode up to the open door of the big house and knocked. No sign of the dogs. Inside the room I flicked on my flashlight. The place had been looted. All the neatly stacked cases of pop and groceries were gone. The tables were broken, upended or pushed aside. The big-screen TV was gone. The room smelled dank. Old newspapers, empty beer bottles, and broken cardboard cartons covered the floor.

"GIS responsible for this?" I said.

Will laughed. Members working in the boonies like Sterling County had a love/hate relationship with GIS. They came in, took over our desks, used up the overtime budget, and got all the glory when, most of the time, the local members ended up solving the case on their own.

Will picked up a crowbar lying on the floor, examined it, and put it down. "Rex's body isn't even in the ground and the power struggle has already started."

"That bad, huh?"

"Oh, yeah. Rex kept a lid on things. He was the unofficial mayor, banker, landlord and warlord. It's going to get violent because even though they're inbred as hell, they all hate each other. But, they hate outsiders even more."

Will kicked a cardboard box out of his way. "You should have seen this place Saturday. Most of them were here. The whole crazy family. Everyone except Rex's oldest son Lance. Lance and his brother Lonnie can't stand each other. Their mother, Rex's first wife Ma, was here. She's a piece of work. And Rex's present girlfriend Dodie and her little girl. And Gordon, Rex's older brother, and Gordon's wife and kids. Oh yeah, Rex's sister Aggie was there and her son Alan, the one you're so eager to meet."

"You ask Alan about what he saw the night of the fire? Did he see Jordan firebomb his place?"

"I told you, Alan isn't all there most of the time."

Will must not have asked him, or he'd discounted anything Alan said. *I should have been there.*

As we examined the other rooms in the house we discovered most of the furniture was gone, and what remained had been trashed. There were dirty clothes and papers lying on the floors, and the upstairs stank of dog feces, which dotted the newspapers lying in the upstairs hall. *How could these people have lived with the stench?*

Once outside we made our way to the one shack where I'd seen someone moving inside. A woman with thin platinum hair opened the door to reveal neatly arranged stacks of clothing, a box of Tide, packages of Kraft Dinner, and other supplies cluttering her tiny living space. A gigantic pot of water boiled violently on top of a rusted barrel serving as a wood stove. A child wrapped in a tattered pink towel eyed us with wary curiosity. The little girl's hair was wet with glistening hair dye that filled the air with the acrid stench of ammonia. The woman's arms shook and she was unable to look us in the eye. Will introduced me to Dodie LeBlanc, one of Rex's girlfriends. The little girl was Rex's daughter Melodie.

"Lance cut off the electricity," Dodie said. "He and Ma even took the generator. He took all the food from the big house. Lonnie's gone. I can't live here by myself."

"Ma'am, we could put you in touch with a social worker in Sterling," I said, trying to be as soothing as possible. The woman began to wail and moan. The child shrank away from us and began to cry.

the **Family**

Dodie sat in the back of our police car with little Melodie whose wet hair was now bleached the same platinum blonde as her mother's. While Will drove through South Dare I sat in the front seat trying not to let my jaw drop too far at the squalor around me. *How could such Third World poverty exist in Canada?*

We passed through what looked like an old cottage development on a small lake with water so dark it was almost black. Big boulders and dead tree trunks rose from its murky depths. Shacks clad in fake brick siding encircled the eroded beach, their sills sagging on concrete blocks.

We passed through an area of alders and frozen cattails and came upon the "new" part of South Dare – a row of about twenty bungalows built maybe twenty-five years earlier. Each occupied about a quarter of an acre and was perched high on concrete foundations. The bungalows sported stained and warped vinyl siding and aluminium storm windows with torn screens. Cardboard replaced broken glass panes.

Will parked in front of Lance's place, the only house looking like it had had any maintenance in twenty years. A shiny grey Ford pickup truck sat in the steep laneway.

Dodie and I walked up to the side door. A weary-looking young woman answered. Next to her was the boy I'd seen defecating outdoors at the fire. The woman's otherwise pretty face was flushed, her thick brown hair dull and her lips cracked. She said her name was Marie Dare.

Dodie elbowed me and forced her way to the step next to me. "Where's Lance?"

"At the hall." Marie wouldn't look either of us in the eye.

"He had no right to take those things," Dodie said. "Rex would have wanted me to have them."

"Lance is gonna look after you, Dodie." Marie looked at the floor. "You'll get your fair share."

Dodie spun around and thumped back down the badly constructed wooden steps.

When we had both climbed inside the police car Dodie slumped down next to her daughter, who sucked her thumb and twisted her hair. Dodie slapped Melodie's hand away from her mouth. That made Will and me twist around in our seats and order her not to hit her daughter.

Dodie asked us to take her to Lance's bingo hall at the lodge by the lake, so we backtracked.

Will wove the car among the lake shacks through a tag-playing group of children. They ran behind the car, banging the trunk with their fists. A rock dinged the passenger door. We passed through a muddy rut-filled area serving as a parking lot to the lodge, which was a long one-storey building with warped plywood siding painted the colour of dried blood.

Dodie stomped in first, clutching her daughter's hand. She trembled, but our presence seemed to increase her courage. Will and I followed.

Inside, Lance Dare – a younger, handsomer version of his father, though without Rex's moustache and bad eye – mopped the floor. He had the same mane of dark shoulder-length hair and his eyes glowed with resentment. He wore faded black jeans and a grey sleeveless undershirt that displayed the tattoos on his well-developed arms.

"What do *you* want?" Lance glanced at Dodie and nodded at Will, but kept mopping.

Dodie surveyed the room with its dozen or so long tables and stacks of chairs along the walls. Chest heaving, she pointed to several rows of boxes containing bags of chips, chocolate bars, pop, and several thousand dollars' worth of cigarettes. Next to these an old generator sat on cinder blocks with newspaper underneath.

Dodie planted herself in front of the goods. "There! See? Lance stole this. He has no right to it."

"Get off my property." Lance wrung out the mop in a chrome bucket. Judging by the wet sheen, he'd already cleaned most of the yellowed linoleum tile. "I brung it here to keep it from getting stolen. I'll make sure everyone gets their fair share."

"Yeah, right. Lonnie isn't going to – " Dodie said.

"Lonnie can't do nothing about it," Lance interrupted. "Ma!" he shouted.

Lance's pudgy mother emerged from the hall's small kitchen. She had pulled her thin hair into a greasy grey ponytail and her dark malevolent eyes glittered over round chipmunk cheeks. She sucked her stained dentures off and on revealing bare upper gums. So, this was Rex's first wife Ma Lorraine. Lance and Lonnie's mother.

"I told Lance to bring the stuff here," Ma said.

"You don't care that I'm freezing out there and I got no food?" Dodie said. "Aren't you going to arrest them?" Dodie asked Will. "Lonnie says they had no right to steal – "

"Lonnie's a fool," Lance said. "And you're a fool to hitch yourself to him." He spat into the bucket. His mother's sides shook as she laughed and cackled. Lance grinned at her. He had the same big teeth as his father, except his weren't yellowed...yet.

"Let's go," I said to Dodie. "We'll take you to town."

"I gotta use the bathroom," Dodie said. She staggered over to the women's bathroom, which was located along the back wall next to the kitchen.

A burning cigarette dangling from her lip, Ma Lorraine grinned at Melodie and broke open a box of Oh Henry! bars. She gave her one, then wandered back to the kitchen. Soon I heard the crackle of fat frying. Melodie sucked on her huge chocolate bar and, with her free hand, spun the seats that ran along the snack counter. The whirling seats made a grinding noise that was getting on my nerves. I stepped closer to listen to Will and Lance's conversation.

"I'm trying to run a legit business here," Lance said. "I ain't gonna live off welfare like Lonnie and them."

After Will introduced us Lance explained he had a charitable license to run the bingo hall.

"Stop that! Stop spinning them chairs!" he shouted at Melodie.

Melodie stopped, but as soon as Lance resumed talking she started again. Will asked him who he thought killed his father.

Lance shrugged and swished the mop in the bucket of dirty water. Melodie had two chairs spinning.

"Well, it wasn't Cindy." Lance cracked a contemptuous smile. "She's a bowl of jelly. She couldn't have shot Rex. Except maybe in the back."

"Did you shoot Rex?" Will asked.

I saw Lance's jaw clench. He whirled and shouted at Melodie. "Stop that, you little..." He pushed her flat on her bottom. She shrieked.

I rushed toward the child and helped her up. "Listen, buster!" I pointed my finger at Lance. "We could charge you for that."

Melodie pummelled me with her free hand and then scurried over to the bathroom, sobbing. She rattled the doorknob, waving the chocolate bar in her left hand.

"I didn't have no time for Rex," Lance said. "I hated his guts. But I didn't kill him. If you wanna know who killed him, ask Lonnie." He glanced at the bathroom door. "What's that witch doing in my bathroom?"

He stomped over and beat on the door. Melodie howled. Will bumped him aside and pounded on the door. "Dodie, open up!" Will ordered. Melodie sucked on the chocolate, her body occasionally shaken by a sob.

Lance grabbed a key off a nail on the wall by the cash register, and passed it to Will who unlocked the door. When the door swung open, I gasped. Dodie had cut her hand and smeared blood on the walls. She'd drawn a pentagram in blood on the mirror and some other symbols like ram's horns and upside-down crosses.

Lance grabbed Dodie and yanked her out. Will broke Lance's hold and I grasped her wrists. Her blood trickled over my hand. *What if she has HIV?*

"You stupid witch!" Lance shouted in her face. "You think that stuff scares me, huh?"

"I curse you, Lance Dare," Dodie hissed. "I curse you and hope you die."

"Shut up! Shut your trap! I can call the devil right back on you."

I led Dodie around to the sink behind the counter and ran water over her cut. Then I yanked some paper towels out of a dispenser and pressed them into her palm. While I rinsed my own hands Ma Lorraine leered at us as if enjoying the tension.

Just as Will and I were preparing to leave with Dodie and her daughter I noticed through the window two trucks pull into the yard. Lance's wife Marie got out of the new grey truck with her son Cody. Lonnie and his Uncle Gordon got out of a rusted brown pickup. When the two men came inside the hall Lonnie smiled obediently at Will and me. I recalled meeting Lonnie at the fire. The spitter. He resembled his brother Lance, except he wore his hair short and spiky in the front with wavy dark curls falling to his shoulders in the back.

"Hello, officers. I hear you been looking for me." Lonnie hooked his thumbs inside the waistband of his shiny blue and grey track pants. His big thick-soled running shoes gleamed white. Lonnie ignored Lance.

Dodie darted toward Lonnie and wrapped her arms around him. He tried to disentangle himself. *Was Rex hardly cold in the morgue and his girlfriend was already taking up with his son?*

"I told you the stuff was here. There's the generator," she said.

Lonnie pushed Dodie away. "It's okay. I told Lance he could take it."

A puzzled expression slipped across Lance's face. That told me Lonnie was lying. Probably for our benefit. As much as they hated each other, they hated us more.

Ma Lorraine waddled in from the kitchen area carrying a plate of fries and a red plastic ketchup container. She set them down on a table and beckoned to Melodie.

"Hey, Lonnie." Ma grinned at him, her eyes glittering. "Lance says you're a fool."

Lonnie's smile froze. "Is that right, Ma?"

Lance's hair fell forward as he wrung the water out of his mop. He began mopping behind the counter.

"That's right, Lonnie. Lance called you a fool." Ma began to cackle with laughter.

Lance straightened and shook his hair back. His jaw muscles were working. "Shut up, Ma."

"He also said you know who killed Pa." She continued cackling.

"That's right, Ma. I do know who killed Pa," Lonnie said in a singsong voice. "Lance killed Pa. Your favourite boy killed Pa." Red faced, Lonnie glared at Lance. "You called me a fool?"

"You *are* a fool. Look at you!" Lance said in disgust.

Lonnie dove across the counter and grabbed Lance's throat. The cords on Lonnie's neck bulged. Ma giggled and cackled. Dodie whimpered. Gordon backed toward the door, a hint of a smile flickering on his face.

Will scrambled over the counter and pulled Lonnie away from Lance who was grinning contemptuously at his younger brother. Then Will frogmarched Lonnie outside. Gordon, Dodie and Melodie followed.

"What did you do that for?" I asked Ma Lorraine. Then I noticed Marie and Cody standing near the bathroom with Lance. Marie looked pale and Cody was crying. As I walked over to them I smelled feces.

"Did you mess your pants again?" Lance hollered at his son.

"Lance, please," Marie said.

"Shut up!" he snapped.

"You shut up!" I stepped between him and his wife. "Mrs. Dare, if he so much as lifts a finger to touch you or this boy you call me, and I'll make it my personal project to put him behind bars."

But when I offered it to her, she wouldn't take my card.

When Will came back inside I debated whether to join his conversation with Ma. With my back to Lance and Marie I overheard Lance apologize to his son. That made him seem a cut above his relatives.

Then we heard the crash of breaking glass. We rushed to the windows and saw Lonnie throw a crowbar into the back of his pickup. He drove off with Gordon, Dodie and Melodie, leaving Lance's new truck minus a windshield.

Marie slipped her hand into Lance's. Ma Lorraine sat at the table eating another batch of fries, erupting every few seconds into hyena-like laughter. She made me shudder. Lance refused to file a complaint against Lonnie. Why he showed him any loyalty was beyond me.

Marie and Cody followed Will and me outside to survey the damage.

"Lance ain't like them," she said. "But sometimes his hate for Rex makes him act like him. He don't want to be that way."

Marie then gave Lance an alibi. She told us he was in Halifax buying a new bingo machine the day Rex was shot, and she had a receipt to prove it. Will couldn't shake her story. When he asked about Cindy she discounted the rumours. She mentioned others were saying David Jordan killed Rex, but she didn't believe that either.

"What about Lonnie? He kill Rex?" Will asked.

"He's too weak. Gordon too. They couldn't a done it. They always done what Rex told them, their whole life. Now they don't know what to do with theirselves."

Marie glanced furtively over her shoulder and saw Lance watching us from the window. "I gotta go." She grabbed Cody's hand and scurried back inside the lodge.

"Rex sexually abused Lance," Will said as he drove out of South Dare. "Lance said Rex abused all his kids. People would come from Sterling on drunken tears and Rex would offer them his children."

"Lance ever testify?"

"No. He hates outsiders seeing South Dare as a hotbed of incest and inbreeding. He told me he'd deny everything."

"That's why this place never gets cleaned up. Who from Sterling?"

"Never said. Twenty years ago a Sterling doctor used to go slumming out there, but he committed suicide long before I got posted here. There are lots of wild rumours swirling around this place about prominent Sterling people."

Why any prominent person would venture out here was beyond me. We passed a cinderblock foundation covered with corrugated metal. A smoking stovepipe poked through the rusted steel into the air. A dozen rusted cars and trucks were strewn in the surrounding bush.

Will continued in his chatty mode. "One of them probably killed Rex or had him killed. Lance was a bit outside his father's sphere of influence. Had his own sphere with the bingo hall. Now he's made off with the loot from Rex's place. Did he kill Rex for it? Doubt it. Must drive Lonnie crazy that he has it. It'll be interesting to see what happens. Gordon and Lonnie owed everything to Rex. That kind of dependency can breed hatred."

On Wednesday Will and I visited Margaret Roach at her farm on the back road connecting Cornwallis Cove to South Dare. The sun shone brightly in a blue, nearly cloudless sky. The air was cold enough to fog our breath and freeze the reddish-brown mud. As Will turned into Margaret's laneway a man I assumed to be her husband was tending several long rows of mink cages in front of the house. He waved and then joined us in the yard. Will introduced him as Wallace Roach.

Wallace's jovial-looking blue eyes twinkled behind his glasses as he led us to a weathered barn behind his bungalow. About ten head of beef cattle milled around the barnyard. Steam rose from the fresh manure. He led us around to the chicken coop where Margaret and Becky Dare gathered eggs in the dim light. As we entered, Becky pushed a hen off its nest who then clucked and flapped her wings. Then Becky grabbed the egg and slammed it against the wall. The gooey contents dribbled down the barnboard carrying with it bits of brown shell.

"Becky, you reach under the hen gently to take the egg. You don't have to be mean to the chickens," Margaret said.

Becky's face and hands were covered with bruises and cuts as if she'd been beaten. As we asked a few questions Becky flailed her arms at Margaret. The blows must have been painful, but Margaret's severe expression never changed. Then Becky threw herself against the barn wall and banged her head against the boards. *Were the Roaches responsible for the recent wounds?* Margaret said something sharp and authoritative to Becky that I couldn't hear over the squawking chickens. Becky stopped hurling herself, though it was like something was still lurching around inside her body as she wobbled and tried to see us out of the corner of her eye. Maybe she was making a huge effort to resist her involuntary tics. Wallace led the child outside.

Margaret's magnified eyes had the David Jordan stare.

"How did Becky get all those cuts?" I asked.

"She throws fits. The demons in her do that."

Demons. Indeed! "Becky should be in an institution, under medication." I disliked this woman intensely. She gave me the creeps.

Margaret eyed me through those Coke-bottle glasses. "Medication wouldn't help. Put her in a stupor, that's all. We're the best chance this little girl has."

"Still no word from Cindy?" Will asked.

Margaret shook her head. "She's disappeared before, and sometimes it's taken her months to remember who she is. She goes into fugue states and another personality takes over. Worst case of multiple personality disorder I've seen."

Oh come on! Multiple personality disorder is another discredited theory, along with satanic ritual abuse. What a backwater this place is.

Margaret droned on. "One time Cindy ended up selling her body on the streets of Halifax. That's when Pastor David met her. When she came to herself she had no idea she'd been prostituting herself like that."

"She worked with him in the pro-life movement, didn't she?" My interest was picking up.

"David had her come along with him so he could keep an eye on her. She'd left Rex, but Rex wouldn't let her take the child with her. Becky was two, maybe three. That's right. She's left Becky before. Then Children's Aid took Becky from Rex and turned her over to us. We were Becky's foster parents for several months when Cindy disappeared that time."

"You think she's gone back to Halifax?" I asked.

"Maybe. David's cast out demons from her before, but Cindy won't put into practice what she knows from the Word, and soon she's in bondage again. I think Cindy likes the attention, myself. She used to go from pastor to pastor for deliverance. Maybe she likes creating a spectacle and shocking people. Since Pastor David's been counselling her she's a lot more integrated, but one of her other personalities is treacherous like the people she comes from."

"You still believe there's a satanic cult?" I asked, trying to disguise my contempt.

"I don't know what's out there, but I know it's evil. I know Rex dabbled in the occult. People were scared silly of him because he said he could lay curses on them. He said he was a warlock and could turn into a bear." Margaret shrugged her thin shoulders.

"You know a wildlife officer shot the bear," Will said to Margaret.

"I heard. Isn't it interesting they only got the bear after Rex died."

These gullible people made me want to shake my head in disbelief.

Will took out his pen and notebook and drew some of the symbols Dodie had drawn in the bingo hall bathroom. Then he pushed the notebook in front of Margaret and asked if they were familiar.

"Those are all demonic symbols. The pentagram, that invokes the devil. Those are upside-down crosses." Margaret nodded. "Yup. That's a goat's head. Now, whether people saw these in a rock video or a horror movie, I don't know. But I tell you, there really is a devil, and you call his name long enough, even in jest, he's gonna show up and put you in bondage. So these people might not think they're serious about worshipping the devil at all. Just putting on a show. But they're still serving him. Look at the evil fruit. Look at the destroyed lives."

To keep myself from screaming at her for her ridiculous comments I yawned and stretched, then examined my nails. They needed trimming.

Our next stop was Gordon's place. Rex's brother lived a few doors down from Lance in the newer section of South Dare. Lonnie's brown truck was outside. The yard was full of old appliances – a few stoves, a couple of fridges, a dishwasher with its door swung open, a rusted wringer washer. A vinyl shower curtain dotted by puddles of dirty water partially covered the stoves.

Inside, Lonnie leaned against the counter, his dark eyebrows pulled together into an angry furrow. Gordon sat legs splayed apart at a chrome kitchen table piled with dirty dishes and papers. The floor was covered with several inches worth of newspaper covered in cat feces. The stench gagged me.

A fat sloppy-looking woman stood by the cluttered counter, stuffing fresh meat into freezer bags from a brown cardboard box on the floor. Her hands and lower arms were bloodied. Every now and then she kicked cats away from the box. She had chipmunk cheeks like Ma Lorraine's and her lower jaw jutted forward.

"Moe, make these officers some tea," Gordon ordered. Moe walked by the counter and, with her bloody hands, filled a chipped kettle with water and set it on the stove.

"No, thanks. We just had coffee," Will lied.

The upholstery on the seat of the chrome chair was torn and laced with cat hair and sticky food residue. Moe continued her bloody work, ignoring us. Gordon was enjoying my apparent discomfort. Will and I remained standing while we asked him questions.

Gordon lit a cigarette and took a drag to make sure the tobacco had caught fire. "I seen the pastor out there in that cabin with Cindy. I looked into the window and they was goin' at it like a couple of dogs."

"When was that?" I asked.

"Last Thursday. The day he shot Rex."

Will shook his head. "Last time you said he was a child molester. Now he's having an affair with an adult. You expect us to buy this?"

"Go ask Trudy Cranwell. She says he abused her children. I seen him abusing Becky while Cindy watched. Then the two of them was doin' it."

This didn't sound so preposterous to me because David had been out at Cindy's the morning of Rex's murder.

Will called Gordon a liar.

"I know what I seen. You Sterling and Cornwallis Cove people think you're so much better than us. But you come here after dark and use our women." A look of hatred replaced Gordon's leer.

Outside I took several deep breaths of fresh cold air to remove the stench from my nostrils. Once inside the car Will glowered at me from the driver's seat.

I crossed my arms. "I think we should go see this Trudy Cranwell. And Alan." A bossy tone crept into my voice.

"Trudy's probably got an IQ of about sixty. And Alan's got fetal alcohol syndrome. Even if they had something to say nothing would hold up in court. Both of them can be easily manipulated."

He twisted the key in the ignition. "You'll see."

the Witnesses

Will parked in front of Trudy Cranwell's hovel, a tall narrow flat-roofed building clad only in tarpaper. None of its crooked windows matched and someone had stuffed pink insulation around their frames. If despair had an address, this was it.

The shack door opened revealing a thin woman with an extremely overshot lower jaw, a rounded back and long arms. She had dull brown hair and shiny brown eyes.

I greeted her, but Trudy didn't answer. Instead she left the door open for me and shuffled back inside. The car door slammed, so I waited until Will joined me at her door before following her inside.

A fire roared in a black metal barrel hooked up to a stovepipe, creating oppressive heat. The counter surfaces and tabletop were clean but streaked with residue from an abrasive cleanser that made the room smell like bleach. It was like Trudy had been trying to wash away a bloody tragedy. She sat listlessly at the table near the sink wearing a sleeveless green dress. A boy about nine or ten lay on a cot by one of the windows. His naked torso and arms were covered with raised scar tissue.

Will walked over to the boy and shook his hand. "Hi, Darrell, how're you doing?"

"Fine." Darrell's voice was higher and more childlike than I expected.

Will shot me a glance. "Darrell got mauled by the bear I told you about."

Trudy made an agitated sound from her throat, stood up, and pushed away her chair. She started to pace in front of the stove, back and forth, while Will examined Darrell's scars and asked him if the wounds still hurt.

Dark-eyed like his mother, the boy shook his head, then focused on a black and white TV flickering in the corner. Holes in the stovepipe the size of quarters drew my attention. Through the holes I saw flames shooting up the flue. *Fire hazard.* Will sat down at the table and asked Trudy to sit down. She edged toward a chair and plopped down across from him. I decided to pull up a chair beside him.

"Do you know Pastor David Jordan?"

"Yesh." She swung one leg back and forth under her chair and the table, vibrating her whole body.

"Do you have a complaint you want to make about him?" Will repeated.

Trudy's brow furrowed, her eyes flitting from side to side.

"Did he do anything to hurt you or your family?" I asked, figuring she didn't know what "complaint" meant.

"He seshly 'bused my kids," Trudy said in a monotone voice, disconnected from her agitation.

"Darrell?" Will asked.

"Tanya and Sharah." Trudy stared at a ladder going to a square hole cut in the ceiling.

She screamed her daughters' names, her yells almost splitting my eardrums. Two girls about five and six climbed down the ladder. They were plain-looking with dark hair like their mother's. The younger one was slightly cross-eyed. The older one was overweight, round like a beach ball. We tried to question them, but they were either too shy or too slow to answer.

"Rex told you to say that, didn't he?" Will said to Trudy.

"Rex never told me nothing." Trudy's voice had grown shrill.

Will leaned toward her. "He did. He told you to say that Pastor David sexually abused your kids."

I tugged Will's sleeve. "What are you doing?"

Will glared at Trudy. "Rex told you he'd send the bear to hurt your girls if you didn't."

Trudy began to quake. She hugged the girls to her, eyes glistening with tears. "The pashtor abushed my kidsh," she said in her flat voice.

"Rex told you to say that."

Through his thick jacket I pinched Will's arm to make him stop badgering her. But he kept on. "What did the pastor do to your kids?"

"He abused them," she repeated, unable to look us in the eye. The girls started to cry.

"You're lying, Trudy," Will said. "Your parents taught you not to lie."

She shook her head from side, her sad-looking little girls like baby chicks under her outstretched arms.

"The bear is dead, Trudy," Will said.

"Rex said the bear can come anytime," Darrell piped from the daybed.

"Rex is dead, Trudy. He can't hurt you." Will's voice became soft.

I kicked Will's boot under the table, and asked if Trudy would be willing to come into Sterling to file a complaint and bring her daughters to be interviewed by a social worker. She didn't have a clue what I was talking about.

Will eyed Trudy. "The pastor didn't abuse your kids, did he? Say he didn't."

"He didn't," she said.

I'd seen enough. I jumped out of my chair. "Thank you, Trudy." I smiled my squinty-eyed professional grin, then without waiting for Will, marched outside.

As soon as he got into the car I shouted at him, "What did you do that for?"

"To show you how easily she can be told what to do."

"Bug off! You had no right to do that! You probably ruined her as a witness!"

"You just saw what a defence lawyer could do to Trudy on the witness stand. You want to go and see Alan Dare now?"

"Don't you pull a stunt like that again." My hand shook as I buckled my seat belt.

"You sound like a schoolmarm." He glanced at me as he backed up the car, and laughed. *How dare he manipulate a potential witness like that! And where does he get off treating me like I'm some kind of joke?*

Will drove past the church and the charred remains of David Jordan's house, then another kilometre or so to another tiny shack in a clearing. Around the shack someone had strung several clotheslines and pinned up rabbit carcasses in various states of decay. I covered my nose with my arm. *"I'm* doing the interview," I said. "You keep your mouth shut."

Will ducked under a clothesline and grimaced. "Don't know why Alan snares these. He never eats them or does anything with the hides."

We traipsed across a muddy strip of dead weeds and knocked on the shack's door. A white-haired woman with red-rimmed eyes answered. Will introduced Aggie, Rex's older sister. A cigarette dangled from her lip. She left an odour of gin as she wobbled on thin legs toward an upholstered chair almost blocking the door to an adjacent room.

"What Alan done now?" she asked in a gravelly voice as she sank into the chair. Will and I squeezed into the room. Some dented white metal cabinets hung on the wall on either side of a small sink under a grimy window. On the narrow counter sat a filthy two-burner electric hot plate, piles of clothing, boxes of corn flakes and macaroni, magazines, a laundry basket, and a big open box of No-Name detergent. A single bulb and a bug-covered strip of fly paper dangled from the ceiling.

In the next room I discovered a young man sitting in a ratty armchair watching TV, flicking the remote control through such an array of stations I figured they must have satellite. Sitting with his mouth open he had the wide-set eyes and flat nose characteristic of someone with fetal alcohol syndrome. Cigarette smoke curled from a butt left in a brass ashtray on a stand. He ignored me, but reached for another smoke from the front pocket of his red plaid work shirt.

A double bed filled the room. Stacks of clothing and girlie magazines lined the walls around the bed. *Where did Alan sleep? Did Alan and his mother share this bed?* I glanced back into the kitchen at Aggie whose goat-like eyes seemed to be reading my thoughts and mocking my revulsion. The house stank of human waste. Edging closer to see the other side of the bed I noticed a commode chair whose contents explained the smell. I couldn't wait to get out. Then I saw the Remington 870 twelve-gauge shotgun propped against the outside wall.

"Whose gun is that?" I asked. I heard the floor creak as Will made his way through the cramped kitchen to the door frame.

Alan sat in a daze, eyes on the TV, exhaling smoke through his slack mouth. "What?"

"It's illegal to store a shotgun like that," I said.

Alan remained passive, vacant. *Is he stoned?* I had no sense he was violent, but had seen people like him go from passive to extremely violent in a matter of seconds. Will was now between Alan and me, so I pulled on some gloves, picked up the shotgun, and smelled it. "It's been fired recently." I cracked it open. "It's loaded."

"Stand up, Alan," Will said.

"You're in my way," Alan whined, trying to see the TV.

Was this the murder weapon? I carefully made my way past the commode chair, quelling the urge to retch. I had to squeeze by Will who had pulled Alan to his feet and was patting him down.

"Where you taking my gun?" Alan asked.

"To Sterling." I brushed past Aggie's bony knees and took the gun outside. *Have we found our murderer? Are we in danger here?* My instincts, usually trustworthy, told me no.

After bagging and labelling the shotgun and locking it in the trunk of the car I took an arrest form out of my briefcase and brought it inside. I cleared some space on the table to lay my new file folder. Will prodded Alan through the crowded kitchen and squeezed him into a kitchen chair.

"Arrest him," Will said. "But we don't need to take him in. Just tell him his court date. I'm going out for a smoke."

"Wait a second."

Will beckoned me to follow him outside. I climbed onto the frozen mud and waved my hand in front of my nose, grimacing. I asked Will why we weren't taking Alan in.

Will shook his head. "He won't run. He's too stupid to go far even if he did." He opened the police car door, fumbled in the glove box, and drew out a cigar wrapped in Cellophane. He unwrapped it and lit it. He puffed on it a bit and blew smoke through his nose. He passed it to me. "Clear your nostrils of the stench."

I shook my head. "What if that shotgun's the murder weapon?"

"We've found at least four like it out here. All recently fired. Don't worry. Alan's not an escape risk even if he did off Rex. Just fill out the paperwork and tell him to appear in court. You know the appearance days?"

I nodded. "You owe me, pal." I headed back into the stench.

I read Alan the standard police warning telling him he had a right to call a lawyer, and that he had nothing to fear or gain from talking to me, but that anything he said could be used against him in court. Aggie answered most of the questions. Alan seemed to zone out behind glazed eyes. He seemed every now and then to strain to hear the TV.

"Alan, the day of the fire at Pastor David Jordan's, did you see anything?" I asked.

He mumbled something I couldn't understand. Alan's eyes had a strange gleam and he jiggled his knees and drummed his feet on the floor. Aggie hawked and spit into the sink.

The door creaked open and Will came back inside, chomping on the cigar. He asked Aggie if she minded if he smoked. She shrugged.

I tried again. "Alan, where were you the day of the fire at David Jordan's place?"

"Huh?" Alan fiddled with a cigarette rolling machine buried among the junk on the table.

Will passed Alan a cigarette from a stack of new ones. "Were you out at your rabbit snares the day of the fire?" he asked.

Alan stared at us for several seconds with his mouth open, eyes glazed. "I checked them that morning, early. I seen you out there the next day."

"Did you have this gun with you that day?" Will asked.

"I don't shoot rabbits with a shotgun," he said with disgust.

"Do you know who killed Rex?" Will asked.

There was another long open-mouthed pause. Alan was miles away, lost in thought. "No," Alan said finally, still eyeing the TV. "I seen you all, though."

But he couldn't answer when. I asked him about the fire. After a frustrating pulling-teeth exercise of one-word answers he appeared to be saying he did see David Jordan set his own house on fire.

"Tell me what you saw," I said, hoping for a better version.

Alan became agitated. "I don't know."

"When did you fire your shotgun?" Will asked.

"I didn't."

Will leaned over him. "If *you* didn't, who did?"

Alan began to cry, sobbing like a little kid. "I don't know. Leave me alone," he whimpered. He seemed to have the mental age of an eight year old. Soon it was clear we could get no more information out of Alan or Aggie, so Will and I returned to Sterling.

Back at the detachment, I took the shotgun to one of the GIS members who placed it in one of the holding cells he'd converted into an evidence room. Inside I saw five similar shotguns, all tagged the same as this one.

In the office area Pete Surette asked Will and me to go to Rex's visitation at the funeral home that evening. Will said it was a better idea to send someone they didn't know.

"No, you two go," Pete said. "In civilian clothes. Continue leaning on those buggers. We need to create pressure and uncertainty so the killer will slip up. You can log the overtime."

By the time I drove home the sun had already set. Anger at Will nearly made me a road rage hazard. I deliberately had to loosen my grip on the steering wheel and lighten my foot on the gas. *What happened to balance in my life? And to my friendship with Catherine?* She never called anymore because Rafe was always there. So much for our suppers together. As I jumped out of my Jeep I glanced over next door at the glow of her kitchen lights. Rafe's rental car was parked in her laneway. I stomped inside my mud room telling myself I couldn't care less.

For our upcoming funeral home surveillance I changed into the flowered dress, then ate some ham and cheese on whole wheat while I read the latest edition of *The Sterling Spectator*, forcing myself to concentrate.

Church faces protests over Dare funeral, read the front-page headline. Rex's funeral was going to be in Sterling's biggest church – St. Thomas' Anglican – tomorrow. Many of the upper-class Sterling parishioners were incensed at the prospect, but Rex was on the church rolls so they couldn't refuse to bury him. Just as I wiped my mouth on a napkin I heard Will's truck crunching the gravel in my laneway.

To make space for me in the cab Will stuffed some papers and a pair of gloves behind the seat. He smiled at me and told me I looked nice. I ignored him. He wore a sports jacket and tie. It felt weird, like we were on a date.

We rode in silence to Sterling. Because the moon was waning, the trees along the side of the road looked especially black, and the golden lights from the houses especially warm. As we turned off the highway onto the main road into town the lights from the fast food stands and gas stations turned the streetscape a garish orange. A woman with a young child picked her way along the roadside. Will pulled over, engaged the two in conversation for a few minutes, then brought them to the truck. It was Marie and Cody.

I slid over to the middle of the seat and Marie climbed in with her son. He climbed up on her lap. He stank as if he'd soiled himself. Marie hugged him close. Then Will climbed in, and I was jammed between his wide shoulders and thigh and Marie's sharp elbow and bony shoulder.

I wondered if he had another cigar in his glove box to get rid of this stink.

the Funeral

Marie told us Lance was drunk and on the warpath, so she had left. We dropped them off at the women's shelter in Sterling, then drove to Calhoun's Funeral Parlour, a newer building covered with brick halfway up and white vinyl siding on top. About a dozen men and women milled about outside, smoking and drinking from paper bags. Children played on the steps and among the shrubs, which were covered with burlap to protect them from the cold. The little girls wore party dresses and the little boys wore suits under their dirty torn parkas.

Lance leaned against a white stretch limo. His hate-filled eyes shone with an unearthly light as if the booze had given him a personality transplant. Lonnie climbed out of a black limo and Lance staggered into an embrace.

Gordon sucked on a cigarette. He spat on the ground when he saw me and told Will and me we were not welcome.

"Don't you have any respect?" Lonnie lurched toward Will, but Lance grabbed him and held him back.

The click of high heels hitting the pavement made me turn to see a heavy-set platinum-blonde woman strutting toward us. She wore a shiny black plastic raincoat with dirty white stitching along the cuffs and collar. The coat opened revealing a low-cut black dress displaying melon-sized breasts.

"Get outta here, Dawn!" Lance said.

"I gotta right to be here," she said in a husky voice. She took out a cigarette, then glanced over at Will. She had painted her tough square face with bright red lipstick, purple eye shadow and pancake makeup, which looked pasty under the yellow outdoor lights. Her platinum-blonde hair was cut mid-cheek in a plain straight bob with heavy bangs across her low forehead. A cartoon dominatrix.

"Rex's other girlfriend," Will whispered as he took my elbow and guided me toward the stairs. I shook his hand off and followed him up. From the landing I turned to see Lance push Dawn onto her behind. As she fumbled to get up her pantyhose split into huge holes around her knees. She cursed Lance with a stream of obscenities. The Dare men laughed. Dawn kicked Lance in the shin. He howled in pain while Dawn, despite her stilettos and hefty build, sprinted up the stairs past us into the funeral home.

Dawn radiated an excessive sexuality that matched her overpowering musky perfume. She told Will she was staying with her brothers on Cape Sterling.

She looked him up and down hungrily, licked her finger, then ran it along her cleavage. Will looked away. She acted like she knew him intimately, but maybe she was doing that for my benefit. *My benefit? Why would I give a hoot about what Will does in his private life?*

Will introduced us, then wandered away to check inside. I asked Dawn for her address on the cape. "*He* knows," she purred suggestively, eyeing Will's back.

I resented the way she inferred we were in some stupid whores' fight over Will. "Do you want me to take you to the detachment?"

"Go to hell." Dawn shoved me aside and lit a cigarette.

I counted to ten to make sure my response was appropriate.

"I'm sorry, ma'am, you can't smoke in here." Kyle Murphy wore a black suit for his job ushering visitors down the hall.

Dawn ignored him. I slammed her against the beige vinyl wallpaper, knocking the cigarette from her mouth. She wheezed as she tried to suck air into her lungs. Kyle jumped to retrieve the burning cigarette butt from the red carpet.

"Answer me or I'll book you for assaulting a police officer." I felt Will's warm breath over my neck and his hand on my arm. Her eyes danced with contempt. But strong as she was she realized she was no match for me.

Seething with resentment she told us where her brothers lived. She also said she had not been in South Dare for a few weeks. When the brief interview was over, Will and I followed her into the funeral home's viewing room.

Rex's body, dressed in a tuxedo, lay in a silver matte coffin at the back of a large well-lit room. A serene expression, helped by thick makeup similar to the junk on Dawn's face, replaced the open-mouthed shock of his death mask. How they got his mouth shut was an industry secret. Ma Lorraine sat near the coffin in a grey dress, sucking her dentures in and out.

A steady stream of people from the mountain greeted Ma, then shuffled past Rex's corpse. Dodie and Melodie sat in the middle of a row of chairs on the opposite side of the viewing chapel. Dodie wept inconsolably, while little Melodie, her platinum hair set in big curls, played with a dirty plastic figure of Pocahontas.

Dawn eyed me malevolently as I sat down. She stood near the door arching her back and rocking back and forth on her lethal-looking heels. Dodie kneeled by the coffin. I wondered how Ma, Rex's first wife, and his two girlfriends past and present, Dodie and Dawn, felt about all being together in the same room.

What are Will and I doing here, acting like voyeurs on the Dare suffering? Yeah, maybe the murderer was here, but among these sociopaths I doubted he'd give himself away with a tearful confession over the coffin. Besides, in my mind I knew who the murderer was – David Jordan. We were wasting our time. And it annoyed me that we had no focus, no game plan, no sense of organization to make this overtime stint worthwhile. I liked to plan an investigation. Develop a strategy. When Will sat down next to me I asked him what we were supposed to be looking for.

He gazed straight ahead. "I want you to see that any one of them could have killed Rex."

I gave him a disgusted look and he grinned at me. Now I was sure he enjoyed annoying me. After he left the room I tried to engage visitors and family members in conversation, but those I spoke to ignored me or moved away.

Suddenly, the room was abuzz with indignation and everyone's eyes turned toward Rex's body. Dodie had climbed into the coffin and was lying on top of the corpse, wailing hysterically. Dawn rushed through the crowd, grabbed Dodie by her hair, and tried to lift her out. A clump of hair came out in her hand. *Is that where Dodie's bald patches come from?* Dodie screamed. Dawn grabbed her hair again. I shot over and so did Kyle who now had beads of sweat on his forehead. I pinched the pressure points on Dawn's shoulder until she winced and bellowed.

A bald man who was apparently the owner of the funeral home scurried into the room. "Please, ladies and gentlemen, show respect to the grieving family! Oh, my goodness."

I pushed Dawn aside and seized Dodie around her ribs. Dodie flailed her arms and legs as I heaved her out of the coffin. She struggled to get back in, screaming the whole time. Little Melodie, lost in her daydream world, stood next to us stroking the long hair of the plastic Pocahontas. The bald man ushered Dodie into the lounge. I followed.

The lounge was full of smoke despite the No Smoking sign. Gordon, Lance, and Lonnie sat in a corner drinking, all holding lit cigarettes. Alan stood by the coffee maker drinking vodka out of a pint bottle. Someone had crushed a cigarette butt against an Oreo cookie on the cookie platter.

"I hope you charged a premium for the funeral," I whispered to Kyle. He rolled his eyes.

Will appeared in the doorway and gestured with his head for me to come out to the hall. Glad to leave the smoky room I walked over to him. "Had enough?" I almost had to shout over the growing din. Will loosened his tie. "Yeah, let's go."

As Will drove us back to Cornwallis Cove I watched the dark scenery pass. Lights from a buoy flickered on the water of the bay.

"It's like that every weekend in South Dare. Every weekend, every holiday, every government cheque day," he said. "They fight and break stuff over each other's heads."

"So what? Rex wasn't killed in a drunken brawl."

"Drunken brawls create hard feelings."

We drove in silence until both our beepers went off. I used Will's cell to call Dispatch only to find out the Dares and Cranwells were trashing the funeral home.

Back we went. The parking lot was nearly empty except for a police car, a few vehicles belonging to employees, and a couple of hearses. Empty beer bottles, paper bags, and fast-food containers littered the pavement. Inside we found Kyle with a swollen split lip and a bruised eye, holding an ice pack to his injuries. Bob Morin had his notebook out. He told us he had everything under control and to go home, but we looked around anyway.

The viewing room was empty. Some of the chairs had been knocked over and the floral arrangements were strewn across the carpet, though Rex's body lay undisturbed. The lounge was another story. Someone's body had left an imprint in the drywall. Blood and coffee splattered the carpeting, the chairs were overturned, and the window was broken.

I wondered if we would be blamed for failing to prevent the trashing. I mean, we saw it coming. But we'd been sent to ferret out the murderer, not act as security guards.

The next morning I awoke to the sound of rain pounding on my roof. I threw the window open, peered through the fog, and inhaled the muggy air. The warmer wind carried a pulp mill's rotten egg smell.

Rafe's car was still in Catherine's laneway. So, he was staying the night now, after they'd known each other only a week. Disgusting. My chest felt hollow and my ribcage ached as if the emptiness inside would make it collapse.

At the detachment later that morning Pete swaggered into the office and loomed over me, waiting for me to vacate my desk. Water dripped off his jacket.

"Don't worry, sweetheart," Pete said. "We'll be gone soon, and you'll have your desk back. There's not much more we can do from here."

He gave me a flirtatious little grin and stood just a little too close as I gathered up my stuff and edged out of his way. I avoided Will until we left for Rex's funeral.

St. Thomas' Anglican Church loomed over a Sterling neighbourhood of big Victorian houses, towering trees, and soggy brown lawns. Bells pealed from the tower of its high squared-off steeple. The hearse, its headlights shining through the rain, led a procession of black limousines and dilapidated pickups and cars. The trees in the churchyard dripped rain, their thick grey trunks soaked almost black. The wind blew the rain in sheets.

As I ducked into the church's foyer, folding my umbrella, I saw Catherine taking pictures of the pallbearers bearing the coffin up the church steps. Kyle Murphy and Ray Calhoun held black umbrellas over them. The Dare men, looking pale and hungover, wore the same black suits from the previous evening, only now their trousers bagged at the knees and their shoulders were spattered with rain.

Catherine and I slipped into a pew near the back. Cheeks flushed, eyes dancing, she looked radiant and at least ten pounds slimmer.

"Sorry for not being in touch," Catherine whispered. "I've been so busy with work and keeping up with Rafe."

"No problem."

"Linda, I'm so happy. I think he's the one."

Her words made my stomach roil. The organ began to play and Catherine craned her neck to scan the room. Then she leaned toward my ear again. "We have to get together soon for one of our chats."

"Yeah, sure." About two hundred people packed the wooden pews, mostly folks from South Dare. Their children roamed the aisles and scampered in the balcony upstairs. The ushers tried to keep them from knocking over the floral displays or throwing brochures from the table at the back.

I spotted Will sitting a few rows ahead near the aisle. A blonde man wearing a priestly robe read some passage from the Bible about corruption and incorruption.

During the prayers I heard male voices arguing. People stared as Lonnie stood at the front of the church and then bellowed, "Murderer!"

In unison, we turned to see that David Jordan had entered the church with Marie and Cody Dare. Lonnie, Gordon, and Lance burst from the front pew and strode down the aisle, their fists clenched, faces red. I slid out of my seat and so did Catherine. We headed for the foyer. When I got there Lonnie was shaking his fist in David's face and screaming, "You and Cindy murdered my father!" Spittle sprayed from his mouth.

Lance grabbed Marie and marched her into a corner. Cody cowered by her side. David brushed past Lonnie and tapped Lance on the shoulder. Lance whirled around and landed a wild punch that glanced off David's cheek and knocked him back a few steps. Marie began to cry. She fell to her knees and wrapped her arms around poor little Cody.

"Ladies and gentlemen, please. Return to your seats," the priest pleaded over the microphone. The ushers joined us in the foyer. Catherine's camera shutter clicked repeatedly and her flash went on and off like a strobe light.

Will and I placed ourselves between David and the Dares. Lance resumed screaming in Marie's face. "You think you can take Cody away from me?"

"You want to lay charges?" I asked David, glaring at him to let him know I was onto him. He shook his head.

Will and the others returned inside the main part of the church leaving me with Lance and his family. David said something in a soothing voice to Lance. Lance turned to face him, his face contorted, his rib cage pumping like a bellows. Then he dissolved into sobs. David's power over people terrified me. He embraced Lance who cried like a baby.

"This is not like you. You were doing so well," David said.

Rattled, I returned to my seat, swallowing my frustration. Why wouldn't anyone in Sterling County press charges or even report criminal activity? No wonder the bad guys got away with murder. David Jordan certainly was, and no one saw him for what he was, except me. There he was, playing the "turn the other cheek" Christian for show.

I was going to bring him to justice. I didn't care how good his act was.

the **Boyfriend**

Shortly after Rex's funeral the GIS team returned to Halifax, giving me a chance to investigate the murder and the fire-bombing myself. Or so I hoped. I got assigned to patrol the town of Sterling. If it wasn't a break and enter, it was public drunkenness or fender benders. My files started filling up with family violence, drug dealing, and other run-of-the-mill crimes. I complained to Karen that we were dropping the ball on the Dare case and she snapped, "I can't afford to tie up two members to go out there all the time." She pointed at me. "No one is to drive out there alone. That means you, Linda."

The murder investigation stalled. There was little community pressure to solve it, and even when we were able to double up and venture into South Dare to ask questions, none of us found anything helpful. We had all those shotguns to test to see if the slugs pumped into Rex matched, but the ballistics were delayed because some key individual in Halifax was on vacation.

My personal life reflected the same holding pattern. I still saw Catherine occasionally, but only when Rafe wasn't there. The woman couldn't seem to bear being alone, so she'd call me on the odd days his car didn't show up in her laneway. I felt used. On the days when I came in handy to keep her company she told me Rafe was hunting with George Hall, who had a fancy hunting lodge out in the bush.

Catherine had lost at least fifteen pounds since meeting Rafe. The few times I did stop in and have a meal with her the former food junkie served herself tiny portions. She seemed lost in her romantic daydreams and easily distracted. I could tell little Grace felt neglected. Catherine talked about Rafe constantly. Making coffee instead of her usual tea she would say, "Rafe brought me some fresh roasted beans from Montréal." Playing a CD of Latin American music instead of her usual Dido or Cranberries she would say, "Rafe loves this kind of music." It was alarming to see how she was taking on his identity.

One evening he happened to drop by while I was there. He was charming and friendly toward me, but I remained aloof. He laid a big plastic bag of extremely red meat on the counter and told her he and George Hall had shot a deer.

"Thank you, honey." Catherine embraced him. He nibbled her ear and patted her shrinking behind. "We're going to have venison, Grace!"

"I don't like venison." Grace sat at the table, her chin in her hands, frowning. Her legs swung under the table.

"You don't? How 'bout I take you to McDonald's then, sweetheart?" Rafe said.

"Edna will make me eat it," Grace frowned.

"Stop whining," Catherine said.

"I'm not whining. I don't like venison." Grace clutched her head.

"Go to your room if you're going to keep that up," Catherine snapped. Rafe's arms were still wrapped around her and their hips pressed together.

I offered to read Grace a story. Catherine was gazing at Rafe, transfixed by his shining eyes, and didn't answer, so I took Grace's hand and led her upstairs. When I lay on her bed and draped my arm around her, her little round face was solemn. She sifted through the pile of picture books on her lap. It took several minutes for her to warm to me and lean against me the way she used to. Then she asked me to read story after story. I must have stayed for a half an hour, maybe more, treasuring my time with her.

Then Rafe stomped upstairs and burst into the room. "What's going on here?"

"What do you mean?" I said.

"You've been up here too long." He leaned in the doorway and made a jerking gesture with his thumb for me to leave.

Ignoring him I got up and tucked Grace in. It had taken me so long to coax a smile out of her and now her lower lip was trembling. I pushed some wisps of hair off her forehead. Rafe whistled behind me like I was a dog he was calling off.

"Hey, little one," I said.

Grace flung her arms around my neck. I wanted to push the jerk down the stairs. I gently disentangled myself.

When Catherine came to the door I brushed past her and Rafe and waited for them in the kitchen. "What was that all about?" I asked when they came downstairs.

"You were up there too long, sister," Rafe said. He slung his arm over Catherine's shoulders. "Tell her."

"We, uh, I have some concerns that maybe your attachment to Grace isn't healthy." Catherine's voice shook.

"You have concerns? You're neglecting the poor child. You've known this guy for less than a month and you're totally obsessed with him."

"Get out!" Rafe ordered. He pointed to the door.

"No, Rafe. This is my house." Catherine's knees were trembling.

Rafe grabbed his leather jacket off the wall hook. "Catherine, one of these days you're going to realize I'm right." Then he stormed outside, slamming the door behind him.

"Rafe, please!" Catherine stuffed her feet into rubber boots and followed him outside without her coat. Through the window I saw them hugging and kissing, then he drove off. She came back in looking relieved.

"What's his problem?" I asked.

"He thinks you're too possessive of Grace. And of me. He thinks you're jealous of him." Catherine gazed at the floor.

I placed my hands on my hips. "Is that what *you* think?"

This time she riveted me with her eyes. "Well, you have been acting kind of weird. I can't understand why you aren't happy for me. Maybe you *are* jealous."

"You're acting like an addict, Catherine. This guy is bad news. He's probably up here smuggling drugs."

She frowned and shook her head. "He produces videos. I've seen his work."

"Good cover."

Her mouth formed a thin line. "Maybe we need a rest from each other." Catherine studied the floor again. "Our friendship doesn't seem to be working right now. I'm sorry."

"Fine." I strode to the mud room and pulled on my boots and parka.

She followed me. "You have to accept that Rafe is part of my life now and that he's going to be for a long time."

"*You* have to accept that Grace is more important than your boyfriend." I slammed the back door behind me.

That night, to work off my anger, I spent a couple of hours kicking a heavy bag suspended from the beams in my basement. I was still upset when I awoke the next morning. At the detachment I found the notebook where I'd written the license plate number of Rafe's rented car and asked Debbie to do a search. It was registered to an agency in Halifax. I phoned, identified myself as a member of the RCMP, and left the license plate number with the sales agent.

Eventually, he phoned me back with a Florida driver's license number in the name of Raphael Lupien. He also faxed me a copy of the rental application with his signature on it.

One of the women who'd been in my troop at Depot was assigned to the force's drug section in Yarmouth. I wondered if she had some good contacts in the US Drug Enforcement Agency, so I looked her up.

Dorothy McQuaid wasn't exactly a close friend, but we had weathered the intensive basic training at the Regina training depot together.

Dorothy seemed delighted to hear from me. We engaged in small talk for a while, bringing each other up to date on the details of where we'd been posted over the years. She knew Sterling County well since there had been some major drug busts in recent years on the cape.

"There's someone up here who's dating a friend and I have a bad feeling about him," I told her. "He's got a Florida driver's license. You got any contacts in the States with the DEA who might run some checks on him?"

"Sure. We have DEA contacts. We can start a 'check mate' service."

I e-mailed Dot Rafe's info, then faxed the rental application. The detachment office had been nearly empty, but soon François and Karen were huddled outside Karen's office door. Something was up from the buzz of activity and the serious expressions on everyone's faces. As François donned his parka he told me a cleaning woman working at a Sterling motel had found a teenaged girl dead of a drug overdose. Lying near the body were crack pipes and hypodermic needles. An IDENT team was on its way from Halifax and other members were already at the scene. They'd identified the girl as the daughter of a prominent Sterling physician.

I wasn't needed to help out, so I slipped away to Cape Sterling for a third time to try and find Dawn Cranwell, to question her about Rex's murder.

The cape's picturesque patchwork of fields, woodlots, and fishing villages hid the fact that some of its residents were as lawless as those in South Dare. We seldom got complaints from the cape because law-abiding folks feared retribution, and the detachment was too far away for us to answer calls quickly. Poaching was a way of life among the low-lifes, who often smuggled drugs using small fishing boats to off-load shipments of marijuana and harder drugs from mother ships coming from places like Colombia.

I drove an unmarked car and kept my police cap off, hoping the informal phone relay of watchful neighbours wouldn't alert Dawn that I was on my way. This time I was lucky. When I arrived at the rectangular bungalow on the highway between the villages of Brier Cove and Little Harbour, music boomed from the house.

Like most of the bungalows along the main road its picture window faced the highway instead of the bay, which was grey and white-capped beyond the frozen brown fields. Clear plastic covered the windows to hold in the heat. The smell of dead fish wafted from a stack of lobster traps next to the laneway. Thick curtains prevented me from seeing inside. I banged on the door several times until a heavy-set man in his early thirties opened it. His pupils were dilated – he seemed stoned on something.

Inside the darkened living room two other muscular men wearing T-shirts and faded jeans sat listening to pounding heavy metal music. They told me they were Dawn's brothers. The scent of incense and hashish filled the room, but any other evidence of their activities had been cleared out of sight. When I asked for Dawn the brother who'd answered the door picked up a remote and flicked off the sound system. My ears rang in the silence.

"She's in the bathroom," said the brother whose head was completely shaved.

They must have been smoking something really mellow because they had silly grins on their faces. Since I was alone they probably knew I had no plans to arrest them on drug charges. I sniffed the air. "Mind if I go talk to her?"

The brother shrugged. I heard a metal cigarette lighter clang shut. One of them burst out laughing. Then they were all laughing. Soon, the music was pulsing again.

Dawn emerged from the bathroom. She staggered by me toward the living room. I figured I had probable cause, so I proceeded into the filthy bathroom. Muddy footprints covered the warped linoleum and mildew blackened the tiles above the bathtub. She must have just flushed the toilet because water rushed into the tank. I lifted the cover and saw the black ball bobbing on the rising water, but no drugs or alcohol hidden inside. Nothing except the usual inside the medicine cabinet. I rifled through a pile of dirty laundry in the corner, wishing I had my rubber gloves with me instead of outside in the car. I washed my hands under the tap.

Back in the living room I asked Dawn to accompany me outside.

"I'm not goin' anywhere with you." She sat next to her brothers on the couch under a painting on black velvet of a stag with massive antlers. They all had square faces, broad muscular bodies, and stupid but dangerous grins.

I told her to meet me at 9 a.m. the next morning at the detachment with her lawyer.

She never made it.

the Overdose

When I arrived at the detachment the next morning François told me Dawn Cranwell was dead.

I gaped at him in disbelief.

"Drug overdose." He handed me a report from Eddie Johnson who had worked the night shift. "Read this, and see how you can help."

Shocked, I started reading the file on the way to my desk. Eddie's notes said that the bartender of the Legion Hall in Brier Cove had called with a complaint that Dawn Cranwell was "going mental" in his bar. By the time Eddie got there Dawn was having convulsions. An ambulance took her to hospital in Sterling.

According to eyewitnesses Dawn had entered the bar alone. She started screaming at people and got into a shoving match with a woman. The bartender called the police when Dawn became hysterical and started hallucinating. Eddie's report described her as running around the bar, tearing at her clothes, screaming that bugs were crawling all over her.

Dawn was dead on arrival at Sterling General. The doctor on call suspected a drug overdose. Turns out she'd swallowed cocaine inside a condom, which had leaked into her intestine. *Was that what she'd been doing in the bathroom yesterday?*

That evening Will and I took his truck to Lance's bingo hall to see if reaction to Dawn's death would point us to anything new in the Rex Dare case. We went on our own this time because Karen claimed there was nothing left in her budget for overtime. A bare yellow bulb over the hall entrance was the only outside light.

Inside, Dodie sold bingo cards. A few hundred people packed the tables, each playing several cards at once. Burning cigarettes smouldered in metal ashtrays. Smoke curled around the suspended light bulbs like a soupy yellow fog. At the far end of the room Lance pulled balls from the shiny new bingo machine, his voice booming the numbers over a scratchy PA system.

Will lumbered over to Ma Lorraine who leaned over the counter at the canteen serving cans of pop, packs of cigarettes, chocolate bars, and cardboard plates of fries that littered the long tables along with the many bingo cards. *Where did the people get the money to play?* I heard most of them showed up every night of the week.

I found an extra chair and pulled up next to Dodie who ignored me. *Why is she working for Lance? Are he and Lonnie friends now?* I asked her if she'd heard about Dawn's death. Finally, a response.

"Good riddance," Dodie snorted.

"Dawn have a drug problem?"

"Don't know what her problem was." Dodie lit a cigarette.

"You didn't like her much, eh?"

"Hated her guts. The feeling was mutual."

"Did you hate Rex too?"

Dodie slapped her stack of bingo cards down. "How could you say that?" Her face scrunched and her eyes watered. "I loved Rex."

"I heard he preferred Dawn."

Dodie jumped up. She bent from the waist and hissed. "Rex loved me. But he changed when Dawn was around. She liked hurting people."

"I heard Rex hurt you too."

"Rex got mad sometimes, but Dawn, she was evil." Dodie grabbed the bingo cards and flitted toward Lance.

I followed her as far as the canteen counter to listen to Will's conversation with Ma Lorraine. She told him, "Dawn, she was alright. She didn't get in my way – I didn't get in hers."

The smoke bothered me, so I went outside for some fresh air.

"Cody! Cody!" A woman shouted from the parking lot. It was Marie, her eyes darting left and right, shoulders hunched. She asked if I'd seen her son.

I told her I thought I'd seen him inside. Then I asked her what kind of relationship Dawn had had with Rex.

Marie looked frantically around the parking lot. "I've got to find Cody."

"Did she have something on Rex? Did she control him?"

Marie hugged herself as if she were cold. "Where'd you hear that?"

"Something Dodie said."

"Dodie was real jealous of Dawn."

"Dawn used to beat her up?"

"Dawn used to beat everybody up, except for Ma."

"Rex couldn't stop it?"

"You kidding? Rex got off on it. He was a monster and Dawn was his sidekick. She's the only one Rex treated like an equal. The other women were like sex slaves. Except Ma."

"So, what was his relationship with Ma?"

"Like she was his mother, not his wife. Ma and he was alike. They loved it when everyone was fighting. Like it gave them energy or something."

A group of children came into view from among the cars in the dark lot. Cody ran to his mother. Then the bingo hall door swung open. Will stood in the doorway talking with Lance. Marie and Cody vanished into the shadows.

On the way back Will and I traded information. Ma Lorraine hadn't revealed any more than I had heard, except to repeat the rumours about David Jordan's affair with Cindy Dare, which of course Will still dismissed as ludicrous.

Several days after Dawn's death Karen asked Will and me to join her at a special meeting of the Sterling Municipal Council. The weather was foul, with high winds and sleet that pricked our skin and coated the ground with greasy slush. Will drove the three of us down the street to the modern yellow brick building housing the council chamber. About a hundred people stood on the wide steps leading to the glass front doors, some of them holding placards that twisted in the howling wind.

The hand-lettered signs read: Stop the Drugs! and Kerry Browning didn't have to die! We pushed through the crowd to find more people packing the foyer and the hallway. Inside the chamber the councillors sat at individual desks of blonde wood arranged in a semi-circle. The warden sat at the centre desk and the clerk and staff secretary sat at a table nearby. George Hall sat at one of the councillors' desks. He nodded hello to us.

"Ladies and gentlemen, we'd like to call this special meeting to order," the warden said, but the crowd drowned him out. He looked around the room, licking his lips and wringing his hands. Angry people filled all the available seats and stood in several rows behind them.

"No justice, no peace! No justice, no peace!" a man shouted. The crowd picked up the chant and waved their placards. Some showed pictures of a pretty teenaged girl. "Kerry didn't have to die! Kerry didn't have to die!" came another chant.

The warden cleared his throat into the microphone when the chants died down. "First, we'll hear from Dr. Philip Browning. Then the staff sergeant of the RCMP will give her report. I would appreciate it if the audience would hold the questions until both the doctor and the staff sergeant have finished their reports."

"We want our own police force! The Mounties don't care about Sterling!" a woman shouted, waving a copy of the latest *Sterling Spectator*. That started another wave of chanting.

I looked at the newspaper sitting on a man's lap near me. Two dead of drug overdoses: Is there a crack epidemic in Sterling? screamed the headlines with pictures of Kerry Browning and Dawn Cranwell.

A slight middle-aged man with a large moustache and tiny black-rimmed glasses moved to the podium to address the chamber. When a camera flashed I twisted to see Catherine taking pictures.

"Mr. Warden, councillors, ladies and gentlemen," he began. "I'm Doctor Browning and I want to thank all of you for coming today to show your support for our family. We've suffered a great loss. Kerry was a beautiful girl, a figure skater, a good student, a dearly beloved daughter. There is no reason why she had to die alone in a motel room with drug paraphernalia around her. We opened our medical practice here because we thought Sterling would be a good place to raise our children." Tears wet the faces of many in the crowd.

Dr. Browning's voice choked and he gripped the edges of the podium. "And now we find out another young woman has died of a drug overdose. Where are the drugs coming from? This is Sterling, not Halifax or Montréal." He waved a sheaf of papers. "Here's a petition signed by over a thousand residents of this county. We want the flow of drugs stopped. We want the RCMP to make this a priority."

Karen was next. She wore her formal uniform – scarlet tunic, riding boots and all, minus the Stetson. The crowd chanted some more before allowing her to speak. She pleaded for members of the public to report anything suspicious, reminding them that Sterling County's long coastline was like a sieve for drug smuggling.

I could see the political pressure building on our detachment as Karen promised to pour all possible resources into stopping the drug trade. Our detachment had too few resources as it was for the huge area we had to cover. This promised shift in focus would mean little opportunity to work on the Rex Dare file or the fire-bombing of David Jordan's house. *Doesn't anyone care about solving these cases but me?* A rich girl dies and everyone cares about that, but not about a South Dare victim.

I left Will and Karen behind talking to Catherine, who I ignored, and ran back through the sleet to the detachment, my feet splattering slush onto my slacks.

Back at my computer, Dot's reply was in my inbox.

Hey Linda,

Your boy Raphael is known to my DEA contacts, but he's kept his nose clean or at least he's never been caught. He runs with the shady crowd, the money launderers, the drug dealers, that kind of thing. He's got a computer business with his brother and he owns an interest in his sister-in-law's travel agency. He shoots travel videos, but the DEA guys think that's a cover. One of the guys had heard Rafie-baby was charged a long time ago with living off the avails of prostitution, but never convicted. You could check with local authorities in Miami about that. All in all, girlfriend,

I wouldn't want a friend of mine dating this guy. I've attached the picture on his Florida driver's license. Let me know what happens. It was great to talk with you the other day. Yours, Dot.

As time went on Catherine and I were still not speaking, so I didn't share the information with her right away. By mid-December, though, I realized I hadn't seen Rafe's car in her laneway for a couple of weeks. Maybe she had sobered up on her own. I hoped so. But I never phoned her. And she never phoned me.

One evening I drove home from work through a gentle snowfall that covered Sterling County in white. Multicoloured Christmas lights decorated shrubs and trees and houses. Instead of soothing me the beauty struck me as fake, as if I were trapped inside a little snow globe from a tacky souvenir shop. I could feel myself growing emotionally numb again, doing it deliberately. I disciplined myself not to stare at Catherine's glowing lights, or even check her laneway for Rafe's car. When I pulled into my own laneway that evening I discovered a strange car had been parked there long enough to be covered with snow. I dusted off the license plate and saw the dealer's logo – Lunenburg Lexus-Toyota.

Veronica.

the Stepmother

I scraped off enough snow to make sure she hadn't fallen asleep inside, but it was empty. When I retrieved my mail I found a sheet of paper on top of the envelopes. Under the streetlight I could just make out what it said.

Hi, Linda. Veronica's here. She's waiting for you at my place. Come on over for supper. Catherine.

I dropped my jaw and gazed at Catherine's brightly lit windows. She had no right to interfere in my life. I could just imagine the information she was prying out of Veronica about me. I marched to my back door, unlocked it, then paused among the shoes and jackets hanging in my mud room. Turning around I stomped outside, slammed the door, and marched through the snow over to Catherine's, still wearing my uniform, gun and all.

Grace opened her back door to my pounding, jumped up into my arms, and tried to hug me around the bulk of my Kevlar vest and parka. In the soft light Veronica sat at my usual place at the pine table across from Catherine. They were leaning their heads toward each other, but looked up as I came in.

I squatted and tried to pry Grace gently away from me.

"I missed you so much!" Grace seemed overexcited, as if she'd eaten a whole box of chocolates.

"I missed you too, little one." I stroked her hair, which was coming out of its long braid. I exchanged hellos with Veronica.

"Please come in," Catherine said, her now gaunt face smiling. *Is she on crack?* What a dramatic weight loss.

"I'm not staying." I got up with Grace still clinging to me and stepped onto the braided rug inside the kitchen door. She buried her head against my shoulder and wound her arms tightly around my neck. Catherine and Veronica both had big grins on their faces as if they were plotting something and felt silly about it. Veronica had aged a great deal since my father's funeral. She had always been thin, but now she seemed unhealthy.

Catherine helped Veronica with her coat as they mumbled small talk. Grace took off my hat and put it on her head. It fell over her eyes and she giggled.

"Gotta go, pumpkin." I lifted my hat off her head.

Outside, Veronica moved unsteadily so I offered her my arm. "Would you like me to bring the car around?"

"No, I can walk." She slipped her arm through mine. "Isn't it beautiful out?"

Snowflakes drifted down and formed a fluffy light blanket. We took the long way, down Catherine's laneway to the road, then up mine to my back door because the clumps of meadow grass could be hard for Veronica to cross. She barely came up to my shoulder, and through her coat her bones were light and birdlike.

I led her into my kitchen, turned on the heat full blast, and suggested she leave her coat on until the house warmed up. Firing up the oil stove I put the kettle on. We said nothing until I sat down across from her. The overhead light was harsh and stark, accentuating the hollows under her eyes. Her short hair as usual was perfectly coiffed.

I steeled myself and asked the question terrifying me ever since I'd received her call. "Is this about my daughter?"

"No. It's about me." She paused. "Linda, I have cancer. I don't know how long I have to live."

"Cancer?" I was stunned.

"I had a breast removed last summer, and I recently finished a bout of chemotherapy. I won't know for a while if the chemo has been successful."

"Oh," was all I managed to say. I looked at my white-knuckled fingers digging into the aqua tabletop, overwhelmed by conflicting emotions. When I looked at her again I realized she was wearing a wig.

Veronica placed a veined bony hand on mine. "I'm here to make amends. I want to tell you how deeply sorry I am."

"For what?"

"I was so selfish when I married your father. I didn't want you with us. It's my fault you remained behind in Boston, and I blame myself for everything that happened after that." Her voice quavered. "He so much wanted you to come with us. I persuaded him that you'd rather stay with your friends in Boston."

"I don't know what to say."

"I got between you and your father."

"Well, I guess he let you." My own words shocked me. Suddenly, I realized how much rage I felt toward Dad. She'd been a foil, a target for rage that I couldn't bear to feel toward him because I loved him so much.

My knees began to knock. Then I leaned over the table and clutched my head, unable to hear what Veronica was saying. I took a long jagged breath. Then I could hear her again. Just barely.

"Men don't see these things," Veronica said. "You never let him know you were upset. He didn't want to push you to come to Nova Scotia against your will. I knew he should have worked harder to persuade you to come. I sensed how much it hurt you, but the last thing I wanted was a surly teenager to ruin our romance. I am so, so sorry."

"I don't think I can handle talking about this right now. It's been a long day."

"Carl made a mistake. We both did. He paid for it for the rest of his life. He always loved you. But you know how hard it was for him to put his feelings into words. He didn't know how to reach out to you, to connect with you the way he wanted to. Even after you came to live with us he knew you were shutting him out. He blamed himself, thought he failed you as a father. I want to make amends for both of us."

My shoulders stiffened in an attempt to block my feelings. Pain formed a crushing band around my chest. My heart beat madly, and I tried to slow my rapid breathing.

"Can you forgive me?"

"This is pretty overwhelming, Veronica. It's going to take me some time to process it all."

Veronica asked to lie down, so I dashed upstairs to change the sheets on my bed, grateful for a few minutes alone to try to compose myself. That night Veronica slid under my down comforter, still wearing her raspberry-coloured sweats. She seemed so weak and small. Then she mustered her strength. "That's not all I'm sorry for."

"Let's talk about it tomorrow." I edged toward the bedroom door, my face averted. "Save your energy."

That night as I lay in a sleeping bag on an air mattress in the living room I remembered my father's hurt and astonishment when Veronica told him I was pregnant. I rolled into a fetal position, sobbing at the memory of the disappointment in his eyes.

Dad and Veronica had returned from Nova Scotia for a visit. Back in our large second floor apartment in Jamaica Plain, the place Dad had abandoned me, the scene of much of the crime with Ron, Veronica convened a "family conference" at the kitchen table. She told Dad she had found a pregnancy test in the trash.

"Pregnancy test?" My father looked at me, his square face pale. "Are you pregnant?"

Veronica butted in. "The test strips indicate she is."

"Linda, you want to tell us who the father is?" His voice quaked. Veronica covered his hand with hers. Her nail polish was coral coloured.

"Why don't you ask Veronica?" I sneered. "She seems to know everything."

My dad's eyes widened and his mouth turned down. He grabbed my wrist across the table. "Who is the father?" His eyes filled with tears, but I felt the anger in his touch.

I jerked my wrist out of his fist. "It doesn't matter." I blew my bangs out of my eyes and then glared at Veronica. "What right do you have to go through my trash?" I had stuffed the stupid test strips inside a green garbage bag with the rest of the household trash and she *still* found them.

Veronica ignored me. Instead, she concentrated on my father. "Honey, I overheard Linda on the phone trying to book an appointment for an abortion."

I jumped up. "You listen in on my phone calls too?"

"Linda, sit down," Dad ordered.

I slouched into the chair.

Dad's face crumpled and his voice choked up. "Did this happen, sweetheart, because we left you here alone?" I had never seen my father cry. At least not that I remembered.

"I told you I wanted to stay here," I said hotly. I clenched my teeth so I wouldn't burst into tears.

"Who is the father? Please tell us how this happened," Dad pleaded.

"How do you think it happened?" I wrestled with anger and shame that made my face hot. I hated Ron for making me believe in him. I had recently seen him with one of the other girls in my youth group, kissing behind a hedge at the Arnold Arboretum where he used to take me. I hated Veronica for getting in the way of my plan to end the pregnancy and put this behind me.

"Who's the father?" Dad roared. He'd never yelled at me before.

Setting my jaw, I stood and stomped away from the table. Dad bolted out of the chair and grabbed my shoulder, spinning me around.

"Tell me." Dad's eyes had a wild look, though his voice was measured.

I stared back for a few seconds, then spat out the words: "Father Ron."

"Father Ron? The new priest? I don't understand. We should ask Father Ron?"

Out of the corner of my eye I saw Veronica's coral-coloured lips form an *o*.

I lifted my chin and bit my lip to keep it from quivering, furious that he didn't believe me. Dad's grey eyes searched mine.

"Father Ron. The priest. He's the father of your baby?" he asked softly.

My eyes must have been blazing. I felt my chin thrust forward and my mouth purse.

Bam! Dad punched the avocado green refrigerator. His fist thudded with such an impact it shook the contents inside, rattled the motor, and left a dent in the door. I jumped. Veronica gasped.

"Are you telling the truth?" he shouted. He cradled his injured fist. His knuckles were bleeding.

"You calling me a liar? You think it's my fault?" I shouted. "I'm not the only one! I saw him with Tammy Moriarty at the Arboretum!"

He stormed down the stairs. My devout Catholic father stormed over to the Moriarity's house and confronted Tammy. That hurt. And it made me furious because it seemed he didn't believe me until after he spoke with her.

That night Dad begged my forgiveness for leaving me alone in the apartment after he married Veronica, for not protecting me. He made sure charges were laid against Ron, and then he and Veronica forced me to move to Nova Scotia and start high school there. We returned to Boston when Ron went to trial. I waddled into the courtroom, almost due to give birth. I could feel the baby kicking as I testified. I numbed myself to survive.

That evening, as I sweated in the sleeping bag in my dark living room, I realized that my anguished feelings had always been there, no matter how much I tried to deny them or push them aside.

Sleep didn't come that night. My memories were vivid and dreamlike. I cried until my diaphragm hurt from sobbing. I got up just after sunrise. By the time I returned from my run the sun shone in a cloudless blue sky. Icicles along the eaves glinted in the sun as drops of water formed at their tips and fell to wet holes in the snow. I felt drained.

I phoned Karen and told her I needed some time off. She didn't pry. She told me to stay off until next Tuesday if I wanted.

I tiptoed into my bedroom for a change of clothes and then took a shower. I glanced at the stepmother I'd hated for so long. The frail woman sleeping in my bed was not the monster I had imagined. She'd asked my forgiveness. Maybe I could try to give it. I wished I had forgiven Dad while he was alive. The thought choked me up.

Downstairs I checked the fridge to see if I could offer anything for breakfast. I fired up the oil stove, put the kettle on, and removed a carton of eggs and a loaf of whole wheat bread from the fridge. I dreaded having Veronica see how the onslaught of memories had devastated me.

A faint rapping sound came from the mud room. Someone was knocking on the back door. I opened it to find Grace bundled up in her parka, cheeks rosy and a big smile on her sweet face. She carried a basket covered with a napkin. It was as if joy itself had come to visit. She told me her mom had made the muffins for me and Veronica.

Grace stepped in. I took the muffins and saw a note stuck in among them. Grace took off her boots and handed me her coat and hat. I hung them next to my parka and police jacket.

"I made a snowman and used Craisins for his mouth." Grace sat near the stove, prattling on about this and that. Veronica came down and we ate blueberry bran muffins and chatted. Grace's presence was a relief because it prevented Veronica from starting any heavy conversations.

I stuck the note from Catherine into my jeans pocket, unread. Catherine's sending Grace over was a sign she wanted to be friends again, but I needed time to sort out my feelings. Then I heard the crunch of snow and whine of a motor as a car pulled into my laneway. I stepped to the window to see Will climbing out of a police car carrying something in a paper bag. I opened the back door before he reached the bottom step.

"I heard you were in bad shape, so I brought you my sure-fire cure." Will handed me the paper bag. Inside was something in a round Styrofoam container.

I lifted the cover to see soup full of egg noodles. It had cooled considerably on the ride and grease pooled in little circles on top, but the savoury smell of chicken, celery, and onions pricked my appetite.

Uninvited, Will removed his boots and tromped into the kitchen. I introduced everyone. He helped himself to a saucepan from the dish drainer, poured the soup into it, and moved it to the warm part of the stove.

"Mrs. Donner, I want you to make sure she eats this chicken soup," he said to Veronica.

Grace giggled. "Soup for breakfast?"

After a few more minutes of small talk, I followed Will out to the mud room and closed the door to the kitchen to give us some privacy. I asked if there was anything new on either Rex or the drug trade. There wasn't.

I punched Will's shoulder. "Hey, thanks."

"For what?" He bent over to lace his boots.

"The soup. Thanks for thinking of me."

He rose to his full height, smiled at me, and punched my arm back. "You're welcome."

I could smell cinnamon and a hint of tobacco on his breath. I glanced up at his face and suddenly I was afraid he might try to kiss me. I froze.

"I just wanted to make sure you're okay." He squeezed my shoulder, put on his hat, and left.

That day, much to my relief, Veronica and I didn't get into any more heavy conversations about Dad. Instead we discussed her cancer treatment, my home renovations, the weather. After Grace scampered home we analyzed Catherine's relationship with Rafe. Finally, I read the note Catherine had sent with the muffins.

Dear Linda,

I'm so sorry about what's happened between us. I hope I can repair the damage I've done. It's really humiliating to admit this, but maybe you were right about Rafe. He's dropped out of sight, with no explanation, no phone calls. I have a real problem when it comes to choosing men. Obviously.

Please forgive me.

Love,

Catherine.

At Catherine's that evening for dinner I didn't ask about Rafe, and Catherine didn't volunteer any information. She was her usual animated self. Every now and then when the conversation hit a lull her face fell and the corners of her mouth turned down. I could see the hurt in her eyes and I hated Rafe for putting it there.

Grace spent a good part of the evening sitting on my lap. For the first time in weeks I felt happy and relaxed. Catherine and Veronica hit it off well and somehow I got roped into plans for all of us to celebrate Christmas together. Slowly, I let down my guard and decided to like Veronica.

Maybe I could forgive the person she was now.

the Prayer Meeting

On returning to work the next Tuesday I felt much better. My recent meltdown had merely been a delayed reaction to my father's death and had now worked through my system. I updated myself on various files and found out the Children's Aid Society had sent a social worker to Margaret and Wallace Roach's farm to remove Becky Dare. The couple had refused to surrender her. Then François handed me the legal papers and asked Will and me to take the child.

Five inches of fresh snow capped the wooden roofs over the rows of mink cages. Our tires rolled over the ploughed laneway. Wallace, pulling a beige jacket around his heavy-set frame, came outside to meet us. His eyes were serious behind his steel-rimmed glasses. The wind whipped his thinning grey hair.

Will removed the legal document from a pocket in his parka. "We have instructions to apprehend Becky Dare for Children's Aid."

Wallace's eyes grew hard. "Becky's not here. She left with Margaret about an hour ago. Don't expect them back until tonight."

Wallace explained he needed to feed the chickens and limped on bow legs toward the barn.

"I bet he'll call ahead to warn her we're looking for Becky," Will said as he backed the car out of the Roaches' laneway.

"Probably. I bet they know where Cindy is too. She could be in Sterling County, right under our noses."

We drove to Sterling to the red brick three-storey apartment building where the Jordans were now staying. My palms grew damp as we got closer. I hadn't seen him since Rex's funeral. I felt my chest tighten as we made our way down the long dark hall toward #302. Will knocked on the door. Anne answered and told us David was out.

She looked wary and tense. "I don't know where he is now. But tonight he's going to be at the church in South Dare." Her little girl joined her at the door, leaning against her leg, a pink barrette holding back wispy brown hair.

"What's going on at the church?" Will asked.

"I can't say."

"You don't know?" I asked. "Or you won't tell us."

She shrugged and repeated, "I can't say. Sorry. Please excuse me. I hear my son crying." She closed the door in our faces.

Will and I checked back at the detachment, but nothing was going on that needed our attention, except the ever-expanding sea of paperwork. We decided to sign out a police car to go out to the church together that evening. All afternoon my anxiety grew so that I could barely concentrate. I could feel my muscles stiffening. I braced myself to resist David's strange power to throw me into a panic attack. My rage toward him began to make me feel alive in that toxic way I both loved and hated.

By mid-afternoon I suggested to Will that we head out before sundown to George Hall's spread near South Dare. I told him my suspicions about Rafe and what Dot's DEA contacts had said about him. We picked up some subs to go before we left Sterling.

When we drove past the charred remnants of David's house my back stiffened. I needed to focus so I could be alert for nosing around George Hall's place. "I saw a tractor-trailer heading out here the night I found Rex's body," I said.

"So?" Will checked the rear-view mirror.

"Well, what's a tractor-trailer doing out here? Picking up bales of marijuana? Cocaine dropped into the airfield and stuffed into fish carcasses?"

He grinned at me. "You've got a vivid imagination."

"So, you like this George Hall?" I shifted in my seat to face him.

"I don't feel one way or the other about him. He's been helpful to us. He seems to have come by his money honestly."

"Birds of a feather. Why is he friends with Rafe?"

"You know, nothing surprises me anymore." Will flicked on the signal and steered the car onto the access road to George's hunting retreat. Someone had recently ploughed the snow into fresh white drifts on either side of the laneway. The lodge looked like a Swiss chalet that had spread to many different levels, all with similar peaked roofs and balconies.

I thought the lodge, its three outbuildings, the parking area, and the small artificial lake were the extent of the developed property. But Will told me that beyond the trees George had a grass airstrip, a hangar, and beyond that hundreds of acres of private game preserve, which backed onto several thousand acres of crown land.

Will followed the road cleared by the snowplough through a gap in the trees to the snow-covered airstrip. The sun, now a huge red disc, seemed to sit on the tips of the silhouetted spruce that formed a jagged black line on the horizon.

A massive tractor-trailer with Hall Seafood stencilled on the side was parked by the corrugated metal hangar. Our boots sank into the fresh snow. I tried the door and it was locked. I tried to shine my light inside, but the window glass was tinted black.

Will examined a small plane hidden under a tarp. Cables tied the plane to ground stakes to keep the wind from toppling it.

"Why is this plane outside?" I asked.

"Yeah. That's what I was thinking. What's in the hangar? None of this makes sense. It's not like he's running a seafood restaurant out here and needs raw fish."

We turned at the sound of an engine and tires scrunching on the packed snow.

A black Mercedes SUV bounced up the road toward us. George Hall got out, his ample frame enclosed in a grey cashmere coat and a Russian-style fur hat covering his bald head.

Smiling, he waddled up to us and shook our hands as if we were old friends. "Is something wrong?"

"No, sir." Will grinned. "We were on patrol, checking for vandalism or break-ins."

"Well, it's nice to see my tax dollars going for something." Still smiling, George took a set of keys from his coat pocket.

"We're doing some work inside." He unlocked the double doors and let them swing open. He switched on fluorescent fixtures that cast a dim flickering light over an interior large enough to hold at least a few small planes and other equipment. The room was bare except for some unassembled metal grids and coils of electrical cable. The polished cement floor shone with a dull shine and was as smooth as a baby's behind. The hangar smelled of new wood two-by-fours and industrial plastic.

"We just laid and polished the floor. We're rewiring the place too. I want better lighting so I can work on my planes all year 'round," he said as we stepped inside. "That little plane out there? I built her. It's what I do to unwind. And of course flying them is one of the dividends."

He was so charming, so relaxed, I doubted my earlier suspicions. Maybe he had used the tractor-trailer to haul supplies for the renovation. George checked his watch. "I've got to get back to town. Thanks very much for including this place in your rounds. I come out here regularly myself and post guards here at night."

I traced my foot along the smooth floor of the hangar. George opened the door to the outside and flicked off the lights. As we tromped through the snow to our vehicles we discussed the Rex Dare murder.

"I've heard preposterous rumours from some of my South Dare employees," he said. "I'm sure you heard that Rex's ex-wife Cindy was having an affair with a married man of the cloth who was also abusing children out there. They say this pastor killed Rex because he threatened to expose them."

"We heard similar rumours," Will said. "In fact, Rex spread some of those stories himself before someone knocked him off."

George brushed snow off the top of his SUV's side mirror. "I agree, the stories are preposterous. I never believed the allegations against Rex either, frankly. I think all this satanic abuse stuff is way overblown."

The sun had dipped behind the trees, leaving streaks of pink and orange on the horizon. In our car Will and I followed George's SUV out of his compound. He turned toward the highway, while

Will and I headed into South Dare by the "new" section where Gordon and Lance lived, and then by the bingo hall. Except for the beams of our headlights the night had turned inky black. Even the pale yellow lights inside the shacks and trailers barely lit the interiors. I realized it was so dark because South Dare had no working streetlights. The few they had didn't work because someone had shot the bulbs out.

We headed back through South Dare toward George Hall's property again. I rummaged around the footwell for the bags containing the subs we'd picked up in Sterling. Will backed the car onto a logging road. I set a flashlight between the seats. It gave us enough light to see our food.

"Well, so much for my theories about George Hall," I said as I peeled back the wrapper on my sub. My stomach was in knots, but I didn't want to risk low blood sugar and dizziness.

"I disagree. I think you're right to be suspicious."

"Yeah?"

"The overly friendly treatment he gave us? He's hiding something."

"What. That's the question." I took a big bite. "What's his relationship with Karen?"

"Karen? You noticed that, eh?"

Noticed what? "The other day I transferred a call to her at the detachment, and I'm sure now it was George."

"He calls her all the time. They've got some kind of thing going. You see them together at some of the big town functions. I think she's sweet on him."

"I heard she's a lesbian." I regretted the words as soon as they left my mouth. I felt I was betraying her.

"Oh, Eddie thinks that. He thinks George is gay and he and Karen use each other as a front. But Eddie's a jerk. Bob and I don't pay attention to him."

We ate in silence for a minute or so.

"Can I ask you something?" Will asked.

"Yeah, go ahead." I braced myself. *Is he going to ask me if **I'm** a lesbian?*

"Have you given up trying to nail David Jordan?"

I sighed with relief. "I haven't changed my mind."

We sat in silence for a few more minutes until a car whizzed by toward the turnoff to George's lodge. I shut off the flashlight. Then a truck raced by. Then another. We counted seven vehicles. Most were pickup trucks or SUVs. Some of them sounded as if they desperately needed new mufflers.

"Should we go back to the lodge?" I asked.

"Nah. They could just be using the back way to Lance's bingo hall."

As Will drove the car toward the church another vehicle nearly side-swiped us as it sped past. Will ignored it and kept on driving.

When we arrived we saw the church was brightly lit from inside. Three cars, Margaret's station wagon, and a pickup truck were parked outside. A single bulb under the eaves of the church cast a yellow light over the freshly shovelled steps. A slight wind felt cold against my cheeks, and Will's breath made a cloud in the winter air. The snow squeaked under our boots.

Then the screaming started.

It began as a horrific guttural wail that rose to a high-pitched screeching, then trailed off into animal-like growls. It had an eerie supernatural quality that froze my heart. Will grabbed my arm. Then we both drew our guns. The uncanny howls continued. When Will banged on the door the horrific noise stopped.

"Open up! Police!" Will shouted, standing clear of the door.

We heard footsteps, and the door opened a crack. An athletic-looking man at least six foot five slipped outside. He closed the door softly behind him. When Will said his name – Earl – I realized it was Earl Broadfoot, the retired Mountie.

The screaming started again. I reached for the door, but Earl barred my way. "I can't let you in there."

Will stepped closer. "It sounds like you're torturing someone."

I pushed against Earl with my hip and lunged for the door. It was locked.

"Open it!" I ordered, waving my pistol. I noticed Will had put his back in its holster.

"A group of people are praying for Becky Dare. We're praying for deliverance. That's one of the demons you hear. You must not come in now." The overhead light shone on Earl's thick slicked-back grey hair. "It could be spiritually dangerous for you to come in right now."

"You're doing an exorcism?" Will asked without any of the usual humour in his voice. The screams were too harrowing for any joking.

"They could be killing that child!" I shouted. "I heard of a little girl dying from a botched exorcism!"

"Earl, we have to go in," Will said. "You can let us in, or we'll do it ourselves."

Earl grimaced. "We'll have to go around back. I don't have a key."

I holstered my gun and beamed my flashlight on the path as Earl and Will went on ahead.

"Please wait until it's over. I beg you," Earl pleaded.

My knees knocked from the adrenaline.

We have to rescue that poor child from these fanatics!

the **Deliverance**

New screams and growls, more intense than before, greeted us as Earl pried open the back door. We followed him through the dimly lit kitchen into the main part of the church, where all the lights blazed and candles burned on a table serving as an altar. Nine adults sat in chairs in a circle around Becky who wore a blanket around her tiny shoulders. I froze, riveted by the expression on her face.

The child was staring right at me with a hatred and malevolence that shocked me to the core. In a split second a dark ghostly shadow seemed to invade my being just below my ribcage. I gasped for air, staggered, and wove to keep from falling.

Then I blacked out.

When I came to I found myself sitting on a white plastic chair with my head down between my knees. Will squatted next to me, his hand on my back and an anxious look on his face. Earl threw a flannel blanket over my shoulders, then handed me a glass of water. Becky was quiet, and the adults around her prayed softly. I felt dazed and strangely paralyzed, as if watching everything in slow motion. Becky screamed and howled. Dread froze me to the chair.

Will pulled up a chair next to mine, as did Earl who spread a big Bible on his lap. "Heavenly Father," Earl prayed, "please protect Will and Linda so that no demonic forces can harm them. I plead the precious blood of Jesus over them."

The words nauseated me. With horrified fascination I gaped at Becky whose face contorted as if made of plastic. Her eyes bulged. Her tongue lolled obscenely. At one point she broke out in huge dark red welts all over her face. She retched convulsively, then threw up. One of the women caught her vomit in a stainless steel bowl.

David Jordan and the others prayed as if nothing unusual or frightening was going on. *How could they not find Becky's transformation terrifying?* Though they occasionally touched her, they weren't holding her down or doing anything that could harm her physically. *Was that just because Will and I were there? Would they have beaten her or tried to force water down her throat if we weren't?*

Pastor Harwood and his wife Ruth from Cornwallis Cove Baptist, Margaret Roach and her husband Wallace, and the young Anglican priest from Sterling were among the adults praying. I didn't recognize the other three men in the prayer circle or the other woman. Deep shame spread like acid inside my chest at having passed out, at having shown any fear or weakness around Will or these religious fanatics.

David, holding an open Bible in his hand, stood over the writhing child. "Spirit of lust, in the Name of Jesus Christ I command you to leave Becky. Now!" His voice rang with authority. I hated the way my trembling knees and shivering body betrayed me.

A booming male voice throbbing with hatred rang out. "You have no power over me. Becky is mine." To my horror I realized that Becky's lips were moving and her face had twisted into a horrible leer. *How could a little girl have a voice like that?* It was physically impossible. The child's neck cords bulged. "She's mine!" the voice boomed.

David leaned toward Becky's twisted face. "In the Name of Jesus, I command you to be silent."

Suddenly, Becky's body flew out of the chair onto the floor as if a supernatural force had flung her like a rag doll. I lurched back in my seat. Becky writhed and convulsed for several moments, undulating sometimes, jerking at others, while her face took on a hooded cobra-like look.

"Becky, you don't have to do that," David said. "Don't believe what the demons are telling you. Becky, I know you love Jesus. I know you asked Jesus to come and live in your heart, and I know He's living in you right now. These demons have no right to bother you, honey. Jesus is stronger than they are. Tell these demons to let go of you in Jesus' Name. Say it, honey. Just say, 'In the Name of Jesus, get lost!' You have the authority as a child of God."

I could hear Becky trying to speak, but her words were choked. David helped her sit on the chair again.

The lights dimmed and the candles flickered. Terror seized me again. Becky went limp. She slid toward the floor, but David caught her. Silence. The church lights seemed to grow even brighter. The circle around Becky was bathed in light. My teeth chattered and my knees jumped so that the water in the glass sloshed into my lap.

"You tell them to leave, Becky. God has given you the authority as His child. Say, 'I am a child of God. I belong to Jesus. In Jesus' Name, I command you to leave my presence right now. You have no hold over me,'" David said. "I want you to see that you can do this yourself in case the demons try to come back again."

"I belong to Jesus," Becky whispered.

Something in me shrank in terror at the word "Jesus." Hatred toward Jesus bubbled up, hatred that contradicted the respect I'd always felt for Christ as a great moral teacher. I felt split in two because while I hated Jesus, at the same time another part of me was rooting for Becky to be free. *Am I going crazy? Is this David's doing?*

"Say, 'In the Name of Jesus, I command every evil spirit to leave me right now,'" David said.

"In the Name of Jesus, I command every evil spirit to leave me right now." Becky's little girl voice trembled.

I felt an awful swirling of vile energy around me, but Becky seemed to be growing stronger, more childlike and innocent.

"Anytime they try to bother you again remember that Jesus is living in you and He is stronger than they are," David said. "Order them in Jesus' Name to get lost."

The child sniffled and sobbed, "I want my mommy."

"I know you do, honey. We'll find your mom. First, let's make sure we close any opportunities for those demons to come and bother you again, okay?"

Becky nodded. Margaret had thrown a skinny arm over the girl's shoulders and wiped her upturned nose with a tissue.

"Becky, let the demons know you've forgiven your dad and all the other men who hurt you," David said. "Say it out loud so the enemy knows it."

Her forehead shone with sweat. She paused for a long time. Her little shoulders heaved up and down as she suppressed some terrible inner battle. After a few minutes she looked straight at David and whispered, "I forgive them."

Outrage flamed in my gut. *How could he insist she forgive men who abused her? Wasn't she the victim?* I hated David for what he was doing to her.

Earl continued praying softly. I closed my eyes. I felt a black abyss inside me. I had stopped believing in God after Ron's seduction and betrayal, but now that unbelief was mixed with hatred of Christ. I struggled against the feeling, it seemed so toxic. Then a deep sense of unworthiness, of being vile, washed over me. I clutched my head and rocked until I realized that Will and the others might be watching me. When I dared to look at Becky again the praying had changed to praise and thanksgiving. Becky rested in David Jordan's arms, sobbing, while he caressed her hair.

I glanced at Will to see if he was watching my meltdown, but he was caught up in what was going on in the prayer circle. He was leaning forward, elbows on his knees, hands cradling his chin. Light glistened on what must have been a tear on his cheek. David strolled toward us, still carrying Becky. Ashamed of my ugly thoughts and hatred I dreaded his approach. I'd just seen something that shattered my entire world view – or had I? *Could David be tricking all of us?*

David, still holding Becky in his arms, sat in a chair opposite Will and me. The child glanced at me, but there was no sign of that evil presence. Her amber eyes were clear and she seemed an ordinary little girl again, sweet and innocent like Grace. She buried her face in David's neck. His face shone. He looked holy. My eyes and ears were telling me I'd witnessed something beautiful, but my feelings responded as if I'd just witnessed something revolting. I averted my eyes and hunched over.

David tapped my shoulder. "May we pray for you?"

Something deep inside me shrank in terror. Though I recoiled from his touch, I managed to make my voice sound somewhat normal. "No, thanks."

Just then a loud *bang!* startled me. We heard male voices shouting outside. Then the lights went out. The only remaining light came from flickering candles on the front table. Two more loud crashes shook the building. Will drew his gun and loped to the front door. Earl followed. Somehow, I staggered there too.

In the parking lot a ball of flames consumed our police car. In its orange glow I counted six bandana-wearing men running for trucks and SUVs parked in the shadows.

"Get back!" Will shouted. He pulled the door shut and ordered everyone out of the church. What must have been a gas tank exploding shattered the church window just as the last of us slipped into the kitchen. I heard a smaller crash as if a glass bottle had struck the church's wooden door. Smoke poured in from underneath. When we were all safe outside Will used his cell to call the detachment – miraculously he got a signal. Then he started giving orders, his voice hoarse, words clipped. This time I didn't mind him taking charge. We heard a couple of other loud explosions.

Guns drawn, Will, Earl, and I ran to the front of the church, but all the men in the bandanas had fled. The police car was ablaze, and so was a Ford pickup and the Chevy Capri next to it. Someone had also set the church entrance on fire. Flames blistered the new white paint.

"Linda, see if David has a hose or a bucket!" Will barked.

I raced through the shadows and discovered David kneeling by an outside tap. "No electricity, so the pump won't work."

"You have buckets? Bowls?" I said, thinking of the standing water in the ditches and the nearby swamp.

In seconds we created a small bucket brigade to the nearby ditch using an old watering can, a cleaning bucket, and plastic salad bowls to try to douse the flames licking the church entrance. After several minutes our efforts brought the fire under control. A broken wine bottle, the remains of a Molotov cocktail, lay on the concrete landing in front of the door.

A crowd soon gathered, filtering in from the nearby settlement. I was sure the perpetrators, minus their bandanas, were among them. I spotted Gordon and Moe, Lonnie, Alan, even Aggie. I was so grateful for the external excitement to distract me from my inner turmoil.

Fear and awe mixed with the hatred I'd previously felt for David. I doubted everything now, even my previous assurance he was Rex Dare's murderer. My mind was a whirlpool of thoughts, all arguing vehemently with each other. If he were evil, he couldn't have helped Becky. If demons were real, maybe that meant God was real too. No, it was fake. The "exorcism" wouldn't last. Becky would revert in no time because the child was mentally ill. The ritual was a travesty. Something alien got inside me and made me pass out. I could feel it. *Stop it.* I was just overly stressed and had gone into shock. I hated David. I loved David. I hated Jesus. I loved the idea of a Jesus who could set people free. Mostly, though, I felt condemned.

Will tapped my shoulder. "You okay?"

"Yeah, sure." I couldn't look at him so I stared straight ahead.

"That stuff with Becky was something else. I don't think I've ever literally shaken in my boots before." Will stood so close his arm touched mine. For a moment I wanted to lean against him.

"You think this crowd is dangerous?" I said, changing the subject, surprised at how normal I sounded.

"Not now. They're cowards, basically. Hit and run."

The flames, the stench of burning plastic, the smoke and shadowy figures moving around with flashlight beams resembled a scene from hell. But I didn't believe in hell. *Or did I?* A fire engine arrived along with volunteer firefighters in their pickup trucks.

Margaret Roach led Becky Dare in sight of the milling crowd of firefighters and spectators. Even in the flickering light the change in the child was so obvious I could see astonishment ripple through the crowd. Marie Dare burst into tears, and David flung his arm across her shoulders and placed his hand on her son Cody's head. I could hear him praying for her and Cody. Others from the prayer circle gathered around. I hated the power he had over these people.

The fire had blackened the door frame of the church and the surrounding clapboards, but the damage was more cosmetic than structural. However, the vehicles in the parking lot were a total loss. Bob and Eddie arrived in separate police cars.

When Will and I were sure everyone had transportation out of South Dare we returned to the detachment with Bob. We filled out our paperwork and then I excused myself to take a shower. I gazed at myself in the mirror, wondering if I looked as undone as I felt. My skin had lost the summer tan and looked almost greenish under the overhead lights. While shampooing the stench of burning rubber and plastic from my hair I kept seeing Becky while the demon possessed her. I couldn't get the hate-filled uncanny look of recognition the demon gave me out of my mind. I leaned a hand on the blue shower tiles to steady myself.

I felt as if I were at the bottom of a mineshaft, condemned, hopeless and alone. I took my time drying my hair, hoping Will would leave before I had to face him again. When I returned to the office wearing a fresh uniform Will sent many worried glances my way, but I avoided his eyes. He asked if I wanted a lift home.

I shrugged. "What for? I have my Jeep. See you tomorrow."

the Oppression

That night, for the first time in my life, I inspected my medicine cabinet to see if I could find something to help me sleep. I found a bottle of cough syrup and an old prescription of painkillers with codeine. Suddenly, an awful compulsion to take all the medicine at once came over me. *Drink it! Swallow them. End your misery.* My thoughts were like voices, screaming. An image of me dead on the floor, empty bottles beside me, flashed through my mind. Clutching my head I stumbled out of the bathroom, but as I turned I caught sight of my razor on the rack across my big bathtub. *Kill yourself. It's hopeless. The razor will be painless.* I had a ghastly image of myself lying in the bathtub in water red with my own blood. Leaving the lights on I climbed into bed and huddled all curled up under the covers. *Take your gun out of the cabinet. Pull the trigger. It'll be fast. You'll have peace.* I could see my brains splattered on the headboard and my waxy-looking body beside the smoking gun. I couldn't bear to be alive, and I was scared to death of dying. I was afraid to call an ambulance because the attendants would think I was going insane.

For what seemed like hours I quaked with fear. The images continued to haunt me. Eventually I must have fallen asleep because early in the morning the phone jarred me awake. Too terrified to answer I cowered under my covers as Karen left a message ordering me to report for duty immediately.

Ten minutes later the phone rang again. Will's voice came on the answering machine. "Linda, are you okay? Please pick up the phone. Come on. I've got to talk to you."

About a half an hour later he tried again and left another message. I got up and staggered to the bathroom, then dove back into bed. Utterly exhausted, I could not muster the energy to go into work or even phone in sick. And I didn't care about the consequences.

The sun shone through the opaque window blind. I heard a car turning into my laneway, then loud raps on my back door. My heart pounded with anxiety and I gulped air. Then I heard heavy thuds as someone kicked my back door in. I hid under my covers.

"Linda? Linda, are you here?" Will shouted from the kitchen. The house rattled as he thumped around the first floor, then bounded up the stairs. He knocked on the bedroom door, then turned the doorknob slowly.

"Linda?" His voice shook. He peeled back the covers.

"Gosh, woman, you nearly gave me a heart attack!"

"Get off my bed." I pulled the covers over my head.

He remained seated, his parka and boots still on. I felt a mixture of relief that he was there and embarrassment at how crazy I was acting.

"Come on downstairs and I'll make you some breakfast. Get up." He tore back the covers, gripped my arm, and hauled me to a sitting position. He slid my slippers under my feet.

"Get up," he insisted.

I glanced at him. His face was stricken with concern.

"I'm sorry. I feel really weird." My voice quavered. I stared at the weave in my grey knit sweatpants, afraid Will might hug me. Instead he did something even more intimate. He touched my cheek with his knuckles and gently pushed my matted hair back. I stiffened and averted my eyes.

I heard the sound of heels thumping downstairs. "Linda? Linda!" Catherine's voice rang out. "Is everything alright?" Her steps echoed in the stairwell.

She entered the bedroom. "Linda, what's wrong?"

I looked away and shook my head.

Will stood. "I'm going to go down and light the stove and make her something to eat."

He left me alone with Catherine who took me in her arms and rocked me. "What's wrong? Talk to me."

"I think I'm having a nervous breakdown," I quipped. I tried to laugh.

"I know what that's like. Do you want me to call Veronica?"

"No. She's got enough on her plate."

"She'll want to be here for you." Catherine reached for the phone on my night table. "She's in Lunenburg, right?" She picked up the extension. Then she put it down.

"Will's using the phone. Sounds like he's talking to David Jordan. Do you want me to call your doctor when the phone is free? Maybe you should see her."

Catherine made me get up and wash my face and brush my teeth. She chattered about work, about the fire last night, about Grace. It kept me from thinking. I combed my hair and examined the dark circles under my eyes. I looked gaunt and haunted. Catherine persuaded me to take a bath. She stayed with me and kept talking. She seemed attuned to exactly what I needed. She brought me a towel, then went to my bureau and pulled out a clean pair of sweats, some underwear and socks.

When we went downstairs Will had made coffee and scrambled eggs with ham. He popped some bread into the toaster as we came into the kitchen. He set a glass of orange juice in front of me and insisted I drink it. He served me breakfast and made sure I ate a few mouthfuls of everything. Then a car pulled into the laneway.

I clutched the edge of the table.

"It's okay. I'll go see who it is," Will said.

He came back inside with David. I slumped over the kitchen table, my chin resting in my hands. I watched the dust float in the beams of sunlight coming through the window. Will had left eggshells on the counter, the bread bag still open, and the milk carton out of the fridge. I didn't care. My mind churned and so did my stomach. The men joined Catherine and me at the table.

"Whose car burned last night?" Catherine asked.

Another wave of nausea passed over me.

"Get the details from Staff Sergeant Ramsay," Will said.

Catherine searched her purse and drew out a notebook. "Oh, come on." She scribbled with her pen to get the ink flowing and glanced at David. "What were you doing at the church last night? I heard it was an exorcism."

"I'm sorry, I..." David fingered the blue satin ribbon bookmark in the leather Bible he'd brought.

"Look, I'm hearing all kinds of rumours," Catherine said. "Can't you at least tell me something off the record?"

Will shook his head. "We can't help you. And right now we need to discuss some confidential matters with Linda."

Catherine peered at him. "It was your car last night! You were at the church." She turned to me. "You were there too."

I couldn't focus. I hardly recognized Catherine as the person I'd become friends with. *Who is she really?* In the last six weeks she had lost at least twenty pounds making her cheekbones stand out and totally altering her formerly round face. She looked glamorous, unreal, like a movie star. *Why is she wearing makeup at this time of day?* Her face flushed with anger. I reminded myself she was my friend.

"I'm not going to take anything confidential and put it in the newspaper," Catherine said. "But I do have a responsibility to this community, and rumours are out there that a group of people performed an exorcism on Becky Dare last night. And I hear that two Mounties have been suspended for making an unauthorized trip in a police car while off-duty. I hear people in South Dare set their police car on fire."

Will shrugged. "Maybe your source isn't telling you the truth."

"Constable Donner, may I talk with you a moment? Alone?" David said.

I couldn't look at him. "If you've got something to say, say it. I want Catherine to stay."

David's eyes settled on me. "You put yourself in grave danger last night. Unseen forces may be trying to destroy you."

Catherine stood up. "What kind of garbage is this?"

"Are you suicidal?" David asked me.

"No," I lied.

Catherine leaned toward David. "Stop this. This is spiritual terrorism." Fear made her voice tremble.

"Catherine, please," David said. "This is a matter of life and death."

"Maybe she's just depressed. She hasn't been eating right or getting enough sleep. She's been under a lot of stress lately. You're adding to her depression by talking like this." Cathering grasped my shoulder and squeezed it. "Linda should see her doctor."

She was vocalizing all the rational arguments I'd given myself to explain what happened last night. But David's words chilled me to the core.

"May I pray for you?" David said.

"This is ridiculous," Catherine said. "Linda, don't let them pressure you."

Out of the corner of my eye I saw her grab her coat and hat. I couldn't look at any of them. I couldn't speak.

"I'll be next door, Linda. I'll take you to your doctor this afternoon, if you want." Catherine wobbled on shaking legs to the mud room and fumbled with the back door. As soon as she was outside she slammed it.

"Whoa! What's eating her?" Will said.

"That's okay, Will," David said. "Most people find these matters unsettling."

"No kidding!" Will scraped a chair toward him and sat down. "I never used to believe you when you talked about demons. After last night I sure believe in them now."

"I hope you believe in the far greater power of God in Jesus Christ."

My fingers dug into the wooden seat of the chair as that unfamiliar hatred rose like an evil stench.

"I don't want to talk about this." My stomach churned. "I need to be alone." I jumped up, stomped into the living room, and threw myself into my recliner. I covered my ears to block out the conversation in the kitchen.

Confusion and inner chatter filled my head so completely it took several minutes before I realized I was rocking my body back and forth. Because I heard nothing from the next room I wondered if David and Will had left. I tiptoed in, glanced at David's face, and winced. He shone with an inner light that hurt me to look at. But the light was beautiful. I was both drawn to it and repelled at the same time. *What is wrong with me?* But I remembered how Ron seemed to have a light about him too.

"Linda, please join us," David said.

I shuffled to the chair and perched on the edge, tense and ready to bolt.

David turned to Will. "You believe Jesus is the Son of God. You believe He died for your sins. What's stopping you from turning your life over to Him?"

Inwardly, I recoiled.

"I don't know," Will answered. "We've talked about this before. I can't commit to being good all the time. I can't follow all the rules."

"It's not about rules. It's about a relationship." David's eyes shone. "Give yourself to Jesus, ask Him to come into your heart, and He'll change you. It's about believing the truth, not obeying the rules. Believe in Jesus and soon you'll want to obey Him."

The corners of Will's mouth turned down. "Don't push me, okay?" He ran his fingers through his hair, then picked up the salt shaker and twisted the cap on and off. David leaned back and observed him.

Will raised his head. "It makes me uncomfortable when you stare at me like that."

David looked down. "I'm sorry. I don't mean to. I'm at a loss right now of what to say. How people come to faith in Christ baffles me. Only God knows. Everyone is different."

I jumped up again from the table and strode to the living room.

More silence. I returned to the doorway, thinking David would be fixing his laser glare on Will, but he wasn't. He just sat there and stared out the window. Will was hunched over the table, his hands covering his eyes. I turned on my heel and perched on the edge of my recliner, my knees shaking. David began to pray.

"Jesus said that if any two or three are gathered in His Name, there He is in the midst. Thank you, Lord, for being here. Thank you for ministering to Will through the Holy Spirit," David prayed.

"Father, please give me the words. Draw Will and Linda to your Son. I ask this in Jesus' Name, by the power of the Holy Spirit."

There were several more moments of agonizing silence. *Maybe God* **is** *real. He's not real. This is ludicrous. Please be real. Help me, God. No! It's hopeless.*

"Do you feel like you don't deserve God's love?" David asked.

I couldn't hear whether Will answered.

"None of us deserves it," David said. "Will, can you ask Jesus to come into your heart and turn your life over to Him?"

I bolted from the chair to the doorway. *Stop pressuring him!* Will still hid his eyes behind his fists.

"Yes," Will said.

I stomped away from the doorway, enraged. Confusion clouded my brain as inner voices clamoured for attention. I paced through the living room, flung open my front door, slammed it, and then stomped back into the kitchen. David glanced up at me, his face shining with what looked like love. But I had been seduced and deceived by that look before.

I hated him.

"Will, how about praying this prayer with me?" David asked.

I upended the kitchen table and dishes and mugs crashed to the floor. "You won't say that prayer in my house," I hissed. "I've heard enough of that garbage. Get out of here, both of you. Now!"

Will stood so fast his chair fell backward. At first he averted his face and righted the chair. Then he looked at me, his face a picture of contrition and sorrow. My composure shattered. I hadn't intended to knock over the table and clearly I wasn't in control of my body. Rage turned to terror, then shame. I began to sob.

"Linda, evil spirits are trying to gain control of your mind," David said. "I believe something might have invaded you last night. Let me pray for you, please."

I felt so desperate I allowed him to lay hands on me and pray for me. As he stood next to me, praying, the bleakness and oppression lifted. A warmth passed through my body, and I felt a calm I hadn't felt since I first received Holy Communion as a child. The rage subsided, the voices died down. David seemed to know exactly what was going on in my mind. He prayed against suicide and anointed me with oil, etching the shape of the cross on my forehead. Though embarrassing, the prayers relieved me. I wept in sweet relief. I felt peace that reminded me of my early childhood when I went to church hand in hand with Dad. When I opened my eyes Will's eyes were full of concern.

"Linda, you're back." He squeezed my hand.

I quickly withdrew mine and wiped my face. What an idiot I was to be crying like that in front of Will. But I felt so much better.

Then David took Will's big hands while Will repeated a prayer to accept Jesus into his life. Then both men stood and embraced. A big bear hug. I felt like an outsider when I saw the mutual love on their faces. Confused, I didn't know what to believe.

the Turmoil

After David left, I felt so much better I donned my uniform and let Will drive me to the detachment to face the staff sergeant's wrath over the destroyed police car.

"Haven't you lived here long enough to know that being out in South Dare at night is a provocation?" Karen shouted. "These cars are not for your personal use!"

She said she had launched a disciplinary review and told me she would dock my pay for missing work that morning, even though Will told her I was ill.

The peace I'd felt after the prayers was wearing off. I began to wonder why she cared more about her precious police cars than us. She should be happy we weren't in the car when it exploded!

Karen asked Will to leave her office. I sat there fingering the badge on my hat as a bizarre fantasy played in my mind. I unholstered my pistol, aimed at Karen's head, and blew her brains out against the green-painted cinder blocks. I shook my head to stop the gory images. Karen closed the door behind Will and sat in the chair he had just vacated. She watched me until I looked up. Now I knew David's prayers were a bunch of hocus pocus because their effect had already worn off. Dread gripped my stomach.

"I think I need to go on stress leave," I stammered.

"Maybe you're too involved in this case. It wouldn't be the first time someone's gotten in over their head. Look, when children are involved it's hard to keep the boundaries between us and the awful things involved in the job. But you must keep those boundaries, Linda. You must."

She told me to get a doctor's letter and she'd give me stress leave if I needed it.

After Will and I spent the rest of the afternoon briefing Bob and Eddie about the arson attacks the previous night, Will drove me home in his truck. Sitting in the passenger seat I realized I could grab the steering wheel and force us off the road into the water. I saw myself yanking the wheel and had to twist away so I could resist the compulsion to actually do it. A vision of the truck sinking into the green water and Will and I fighting to get out sickened me. I fought against the image of the truck's headlights piercing the murky water of the cove.

When we came to a stop in my laneway Will turned his large body toward me, one arm resting on the steering wheel, the other across the back of the seat. There was something about the way he looked at me that bothered me. Though I was scared to be alone, I sensed a yearning in him and I couldn't handle any feelings on his part that might have sexual overtones.

"You're making me uncomfortable. I feel like you want to be more than friends."

He smiled his crooked smile. "I thought I hid my feelings better than that."

"I don't feel the same way. You make me uptight." I squirmed on the seat and faced straight ahead.

"I know. I'm sorry."

I glanced at him. "So, what are you going to do? Persist? Crowd me?"

He laughed. Sighing, I opened the truck door.

"Linda, wait a minute. Please. I can't help the way I feel." The back door light sparkled in his eyes.

I thought Will already had a girlfriend. A female voice had answered the phone the day I'd found Rex's body. Maybe they'd broken up. *If not, why was he sniffing around me?*

"I want to be your friend." He made the word "friend" sound like it meant something dear.

"So, what about those other feelings?" I kept the door open to make my getaway.

"I don't have to act on them. I'll try not to crowd you."

"It still feels like you have ulterior motives." I folded my arms across my chest.

"I don't know, Linda. Maybe I got hopes. That's different from motives."

"Forget your hopes. Not interested."

He was smiling again when I glanced at him.

"What's so funny?" I asked.

"You're behaving like your old self. I'm relieved."

I climbed out of his truck and slammed the door. He followed me to my back door, though he kept a respectable distance as I stuck my key in the lock.

Inside I hung up my coat and hat, then switched on the light in the kitchen. It was still a wreck from the brunch Will had prepared.

"What a mess." My voice sounded tight and anxious.

Will offered to help. He lit the oil stove while I ran water in the sink for the dishes. He had already swept up the broken dishes from my embarrassing explosion earlier in the day. The fact he'd seen me in bed terrified that morning, exploding in rage at him and David, sobbing like a little kid, then getting prayed for was unbearably intimate. I hated him seeing sides of me that surprised even me. That made me feel irritated and jumpy.

The phone rang. Will handed me the receiver, which I tucked between my ear and shoulder as I continued washing dishes. Catherine was on the line telling me she'd saved some food for me. I told her I'd be right over, so grateful to get away from Will. I told him about Catherine's invitation.

"That's fine." Will leaned against the counter watching me as I dried my hands on a dishtowel. I quelled the urge to snap the towel in his face to make him stop. The more irritated I got, the more he tried to draw close to me. I sensed his disappointment and it made me want to scream.

"There's nothing here to eat."

"We could order pizza. But go ahead next door if you want. I just didn't want you to be alone."

"I like being alone."

Will took out his notebook and wrote a couple of phone numbers down. "Call me at home or on my cell if you need me. Even if it's three o'clock in the morning."

"You sure your girlfriend won't mind?" The lame remark made me want to kick myself. I really didn't care if he had a girlfriend. *Go home to her! You are driving me crazy!*

"Girlfriend? No one will mind." He looked perplexed for a moment. Maybe it dawned on him that his girlfriend *would* mind.

At Catherine's I discovered Grace was away visiting with her dad. As we ate Edna's meatloaf and mashed potatoes Catherine described a volatile municipal council meeting she'd attended earlier that day. Council discussed the burned police car and Catherine said George Hall had defended Will and me. I didn't care.

Then she told me some Mounties and social workers had successfully removed Becky Dare from the Roach home. That news totally killed my appetite. "What's going to happen to her?"

"They'll put her in a foster home. You know the Roaches wouldn't send her to school."

"I don't think Becky could have coped with school." Becky had probably reverted to her wild state and involuntary tics.

"She *was* the one at the church last night, wasn't she? At the exorcism. *You* were there!"

"Can't talk about it." I stared at my plate feeling nauseous.

"People are saying she was set free, that Pastor Jordan got the 'demons' out of her." Catherine wiggled her fingers when she said "demons" like the word was a joke.

I shrugged, though my heart banged in my ribcage. "Did you see Becky today? How was she?"

"No, I never saw her. By the way, I thought that David was completely out of line with you this morning. Sometimes I think he's a nutbar. He had no right to talk to you like that."

I nodded noncommittally and drank some tea. I had withdrawn into my shell. Edna's meatloaf and mashed potatoes were getting cold and the gravy was congealing. I could barely force down some green beans. I felt like claws were on my shoulders and someone's steel-toed boot was crushing my diaphragm. I couldn't wait to go home, but I couldn't bear to face my dark house alone. Suddenly, the phone rang. I jumped. Catherine padded to the phone and lifted the receiver.

"Hello?" Catherine's voice was tired and heavy. "Rafe!" Her tone brightened, her posture straightened, and colour rushed to her cheeks.

I groaned inwardly. Just when I'd hoped Rafe was gone for good he popped up again.

Catherine's side of what was obviously an intimate conversation embarrassed me. She placed her elbows on the counter. I gathered he was calling from Thailand. I tried not to listen to her love talk.

After telling him she loved him and hanging up she sat across from me like a junkie who had just mainlined the best heroin in the world. She adored this jerk. I looked for a way to break it to her about his drug connections.

"He wants me to come to Florida. Says he'll pay my way. Grace's too. I don't know."

"Doesn't Grace have school?"

"Yeah. But she's way ahead in math and she already reads. What could she miss in first grade?"

"What's he doing in Thailand?"

"I told you. He's got a travel business. And he shoots promotional videos."

"Maybe he travels to smuggle drugs," I suggested, thinking perhaps I'd found the right opportunity.

"Rafe doesn't use drugs. Let's not talk about it anymore."

That night as I jogged across the frozen ground to my place I saw in my mind's eye a gunman wearing a black balaclava. He was hiding in the woods, aiming an AK-47 at me. I ran toward my house. As I unlocked the door I imagined a wild-eyed maniac with a blood-smeared face hiding in one of my closets, ready to jump me and slice me up with a switchblade. Heart racing, I switched on all my lights and systematically searched every room, every closet. The pictures in my imagination were so vivid my palms were sweating and my ears rang.

I saved the basement for last. A dank smell of heating oil and damp earth greeted me when I opened the door off the kitchen.

The rough wooden stairs groaned as I descended, playing the beam of the flashlight on the rough stone foundation. My hand brushed cobwebs as I pulled the string to turn on the single bulb hanging from a wire. Clammy with sweat I probed the dark corners with the flashlight.

The new oil furnace hid behind an old cast iron wood one. Its twelve-inch diameter ductwork looked like the tentacles of a monster, the chrome grate over the fire box like a hellish open mouth. I backed up and banged my head against one of the ducts and the hollow *bang!* echoed throughout the house above. Something darted in the shadows. I whirled with the flashlight and saw nothing. My skin felt like something was crawling on my cheek, down my back. *Someone's down here!*

Stop this, Linda. You're imagining things.

the Hit and Run

The next day my doctor confirmed what my rational mind had been trying to tell me: I displayed symptoms of a nervous breakdown and clinical depression. She advised me to take stress leave for the rest of December, and wrote me out a prescription for a medication she said might take as long as six weeks to kick in. I never filled it.

Instead I stayed busy, pumping natural endorphins into my system through intense physical workouts. I jumped rope, lifted weights, practised my martial arts forms, and ran almost every day, even if the weather was bad. I continued the renovations on my house and filled cracks in the plaster, painted the living room and two upstairs bedrooms. I shovelled snow and cross-country skied. Too busy to think during the day I fell into bed, dog-tired. The bouts of terror and suicidal flashes, however, continued. They would come in the middle of the night. I'd wake up, terrified, hearing rapping noises or creaks coming from the stairs. My fear-filled closet-by-closet searches and tours of the basement became a ritual. I knew it was crazy, but my anxiety would build if I didn't calm it by checking the whole house, sometimes three times or more.

One morning I awoke before dawn shouting because I felt someone lift the edge of my duvet and sit on the bed. In my rush to turn on the light I knocked over the bedside lamp and it smashed to the floor. Then the furnace ductwork contracted several times with loud bangs. Trembling, I pulled the drawer out of the bedside table so fast it came loose and the flashlight thudded to the floor along with the pens, notebook, and AA batteries I kept in there. I bolted across the floor in bare feet to the light switch by the door. Nothing. *Linda, there's nothing here. You're going crazy.* I shook glass from the broken lamp out of my slippers, squinting in the bright overhead light.

Someone's downstairs. Flashlight in hand, flicking lights on, I crept down the creaking stairs to the kitchen. The room was cold and clammy despite the rumbling of the oil furnace. I jiggled the back door, checking the lock, and poured myself a glass of water. I glanced at my reflection in the window over the sink. And lurched back in horror.

Behind me loomed the ghostly outline of a dog-faced demon. His eyes resembled hot coals that burned with the same evil and hatred I'd seen on Becky's face. My heart was beating so fast I thought I might faint. I whirled around, closed my eyes, burying them in my fists, and shouted, "Jesus! Jesus, please help me!"

To my amazement the atmosphere in the room began to change. The haunted room became my ordinary kitchen – the eerie coldness was gone. I checked the window and saw only my own reflection. My heart rate gradually slowed down and by the time I cleaned up the broken lamp upstairs I felt foolish. After that the terror stopped for several days.

Will dropped in regularly to keep me posted on the murder and firebombing investigations. He had stepped up efforts to find Cindy Dare, and found out she had attended several months of beauty school while living in Halifax. He was trying to find out if she'd taken a job in one of Nova Scotia's many salons. He'd requested help from other detachments, but everyone was busy. So was he. One positive development – ballistics experts in Halifax had finally begun tests comparing the shells with the firing pins of the shotguns retrieved from South Dare.

I could bear Will's company in small doses. He would sprawl at my kitchen table, his big hand circling the mug of tea, watching me, his eyes friendly. He kept the conversation light and didn't try to crowd me. Though one night, after he'd laced up his boots, he leaned against the door frame and waited until I lifted my eyes to his. He told me I was looking a lot better. I shrugged. Then he hugged me, a big bear hug like he'd given David the last time he was here. "I was worried about you."

I didn't try to wriggle away from him, though I wanted to. I could smell tobacco and machine oil on his dark blue parka.

I gently pushed him away. "Thanks. I do feel a lot better. I should be back at work soon."

Will drove off and I wondered if maybe that were true. I was getting better. The fact I could bear having him hug me without recoiling or wanting to bite his head off was a good sign.

When I wasn't exercising or renovating I hung out with Edna and Grace during the day, Catherine in the evenings. Catherine and I drew close again. I felt more relaxed knowing Rafe wasn't likely to pop in and Catherine was relieved to have company. She also made sure I ate right. I was getting stronger. We began to plan our joint Christmas celebration.

A few days before Christmas I headed south to Lunenburg to pick up Veronica. As I passed through Cornwallis Cove, smoke from chimneys hung suspended over houses and exhaust from cars formed an icy fog under a cold blue sky. Dirty snowdrifts lined the bare salt-streaked asphalt. I usually enjoyed driving, but as I got out of the village I began to feel anxious and imagined my bloody body lying beside the mangled wreckage of my Jeep. I felt a palpable pull on the steering wheel to veer into oncoming traffic. I swerved onto the shoulder and rumbled to a stop. My heart thudded against my ribs. The terror was back. I tried deep breathing and focusing my concentration. I slowly drove forward. A car roared past, unnerving me.

"God, please help me!" I cried. This time, nothing happened. *That was just a coincidence last time. There is no God.* I drove slowly along the gravel shoulder, trembling, my palms wetting the steering wheel. Finally, the Jeep lurched onto the pavement and I drove, terrified, to a nearby family restaurant with a couple of old-fashioned gas pumps out front. I went inside to ask if I could use their phone. I called Catherine. Got her answering machine. Tried her office. Voice mail. Tried Will at the detachment. It was his day off.

The only other customer was a fat truck driver who sat with the waitress at a table by the door to the kitchen. I dialled Will at his number in Cornwallis Cove. He answered after about six rings. I was tongue-tied with embarrassment.

"Are you alright?"

"I'm a little freaked out." I tried to sound as calm as possible. I told him where I was.

"I'll be right there."

It took him nearly forty-five minutes. By that time I felt foolish and thought I could make it to Lunenburg by myself.

Will pulled up in his battered truck wearing jeans and a beige parka with a fur-trimmed hood, a reindeer sweater underneath. One look and I realized what had taken him so long. He had showered and shaved because his face had a fresh, bare look to it, and his hair was a little damp around the ears.

I explained that I was now alright and that maybe I would return home. He asked where I was going. I told him. He insisted on driving me there.

Though it was strange having Will drive my Jeep, I did feel more secure with him driving. Maybe I should have started that medication the doctor had prescribed. I kept chattering about the cold weather, my house renovations, anything to keep myself distracted. I didn't like the frantic edge in my voice. Out of the corner of my eye I caught him glancing at me a couple of times. Then he reached over and took my hand and squeezed it. I jerked my hand away.

Will's large fist rested on the cup holders between the seats. "Sorry. I should have asked you first."

"I don't want you to hold my hand," I said irritably.

"That's my Linda."

"Cut it out. I mean it."

"I feel better when you're like this. I really do."

When I glanced at him he was smiling to himself. Gosh, he annoyed me. Soon, though, the horrendous images – and the anxiety they created – crept back. I hunched in the seat, my body leaning away from him. My forehead rested on the cool glass. I closed my eyes and wished I hadn't called him. I hated him seeing me so weak.

"Don't." Will shook my shoulder. "Don't withdraw. Don't get pulled under. Here." He offered me his hand, resting it palm up on my knee.

"No."

"I'm not making a pass at you. I know that if you take my hand it doesn't mean anything beyond friends. I just don't want you going catatonic on me."

Despite my misgivings I gingerly placed my hand in his. It felt huge and warm, reminding me of Dad's. Pain and regret passed through me.

Several moments later we exchanged a glance and his eyes, his face, said, "I love you." *How can he look at me that way? What can he possibly see in me after I've fallen apart like this?* But somehow I felt safe in his firm grip. I hated feeling like I needed anyone, especially Will, but I was sinking. He was the only thing keeping me from going under. I hated even more that he seemed to know it.

Lunenburg's grey, yellow, and blue clapboard houses squeezed together on a hill overlooking Mahone Bay. The town's beauty did nothing to take the bite out of the wind blowing uphill from the Atlantic. Grey snow formed low dirty drifts along the gutters and pewter-coloured ice coated the sidewalks. The wind pelted the Jeep with sand and road salt whipped off the streets. Veronica occupied the apartment above the gallery where, from her living room overlooking the harbour, she and Dad used to watch the fishing boats come and go from the public dock. I felt a pang of grief.

A handwritten sign in the gallery window said: Closed for the holidays. A smaller note in Veronica's artsy handwriting said: Linda, I'm next door at the salon.

I walked a few steps and peered through the glass windows into Brenda's Shear Heaven. Bells tinkled as I entered. The smell of perm solution filled the air as a heavy-set woman squirted the contents of a plastic bottle onto the curlers of an even heavier woman. The fixtures were old, the counters chipped, the mirrors foggy. I looked around for Veronica. A thin woman with about a quarter inch of grey hair sprouting on her round head waved at me as she tilted up an old-fashioned overhead dryer. Veronica remained seated, but lifted her arms to hug me. I leaned over stiffly to receive her hug and told her Will was outside.

"Oh, really?" She smiled knowingly.

"It's not like that. He's just a friend."

Brenda met us at the counter, her bulky frame swishing under her shiny black smock. They started haggling about the price because Veronica thought Brenda was undercharging her.

"Since when does anything to do with my hair cost five dollars? Here's twenty," Veronica said as she put on a light blue fleece turban.

"You don't have any hair, my dear." Brenda pushed the money back.

"Okay. Give this to the young lady who washed my head." Veronica pushed the twenty toward Brenda. "It's Christmas."

"Hey, Kelly!" Brenda's voice boomed over the chatter and *Rockin' Around the Christmas Tree* playing on the radio.

A young woman emerged from the shadows in the back of the shop carrying a broom. Her stylish tightly cropped hair flattered her small face, pointed nose, and dark deep-set eyes. She looked familiar, but I couldn't place her. She jumped when she saw me. Brenda gave her the tip and explained who it was from.

"Thanks!" Kelly gave Veronica a fleeting smile, then nervously excused herself and began sweeping at the back of the room. As I helped Veronica on with her coat Will walked through the door. I glanced at the back of the room, but Kelly was gone. Then, while he and Veronica greeted each other, it dawned on me.

I took his arm and whispered in his ear. "There's a woman here who looks like Cindy Dare."

I moved over to Brenda. "Mind if we talk to Kelly for a minute?"

"Yeah, sure," Brenda shrugged. "She's probably having a smoke outside."

Will and I wove among the chairs to the back room. A clothes dryer spun around, the smocks' metal snaps hitting the metal drum, making a clicking sound. The back door opened to a small courtyard. A flight of worn stone steps led down behind the building to another street closer to the harbour. Will leapt down the steps and ran out of sight. I stood at the back door, uncertain what do to because Veronica was waiting for us.

About two minutes later Will ran back up the steps. "She's vanished."

"It must have been Cindy," I said. "Didn't you say she might be working in a place like this?"

We rushed back inside. The conversation stopped. Everyone's eyes were on us.

"What's wrong? Has Kelly done something?" Brenda asked.

We assured her she hadn't, just that we wanted to ask her some questions. Brenda gave us Kelly's address. Will, Veronica, and I piled into the Jeep. I insisted Veronica sit in the front.

Veronica wrapped a purple scarf carefully around her neck and arranged her light blue down coat under the shoulder belt. "Oh, dear. I've left my suitcase behind Brenda's counter." I went and grabbed it and shoved it in the back.

Will drove slowly through the narrow streets, peering down alleyways. Veronica directed us to the address.

"She won't come here," I said as we slowed in front of an old brown three-storey house that had a Rooms for Rent sign in the window.

"Let's take a look." Will jumped out, leaving the engine running. I jumped out too, glad for the first time I'd invested in a four-door Cherokee. We ran up the steps to the front door. He pulled it open and we stepped into a hallway smelling of cat urine. I moved a child's pink big wheel tricycle out of our way. We had no idea which room was Cindy's, so we knocked on them all. No one answered.

We decided to take Veronica back to her apartment so we could search some more. As we headed back in that direction Will suddenly slammed on the brakes and we all lurched forward.

"There she is!" Will burst out the driver's door and sprinted after Cindy who darted across the street. I followed. Will was gaining on her until his feet hit some ice and he slipped and fell. He waved me on. Cindy could run like a deer.

Just as I cut across the street Will shouted, "Linda! Watch out!"

A black sedan with tinted glass roared toward me and nearly hit me. I dodged it, then froze in horror as the car hit Cindy. Time seemed to slow down. She glanced off the hood, slammed into the windshield, then thudded into the icy drift on the side of the road.

Then the car sped off.

the Freedom

I darted to Cindy and found her unconscious, the side of her face scraped and bleeding. She wasn't breathing, so I gingerly moved her tongue from her airway, pinched her nostrils, and breathed into her open mouth. She smelled of blood and the herbal scent of shampoo.

Will limped over and tossed his parka over her. "I got the plate number."

Cindy began breathing almost immediately. My professional training kicked in and I worked like a robot. I didn't dare move her in case of a spinal injury, even though she was lying on an icy snowdrift. Will used his cell to call an ambulance and the police.

The ambulance arrived in seven minutes. Attendants carefully loaded a pale and broken-looking Cindy onto a stretcher and covered her with warm blankets. The local Mounties arrived in two police cars just as the ambulance left. I left Will to deal with our Lunenburg-based RCMP colleagues so I could drive Veronica home, and then returned.

After we made our statements Will and I drove to the hospital in Halifax where Cindy was in Intensive Care, still unconscious. Oxygen tubes snaked up her nostrils. Yellow antiseptic smeared the abrasions on her swollen face.

"Has she said anything?" Will asked the doctor, a dark-haired woman with a Dutch boy haircut and small round glasses.

"No. I have no idea when she might regain consciousness. She has a concussion and a broken hip. But there's every indication she's going to survive, though we won't know if there's any permanent brain damage for some time."

Will and I took turns at the chair next to Cindy's bed. During my watch I studied her face, wondering if she had in fact killed Rex Dare. I now found it hard to muster up the certainty that David had murdered him. *Are we ever going to solve this mystery?*

When I returned to the little waiting area I discovered Will was talking on the pay phone. My heart sped up when I heard him say a woman's name.

"Hi Suzanne, I'm in Halifax. At least until tomorrow." Then after a pause he asked, "How are the boys? Good, tell them I miss them. See you later. Bye."

Then he must have called the detachment in Sterling because he asked for Karen. I could tell she was giving him a hard time by the way he kept stopping in mid-sentence. Then he made a third call, to David Jordan. He muffled the conversation, so my attention drifted away.

So, Will had kids. *Is he separated from the mother, or what?* I stifled a pang of jealousy, which shocked me because I thought I'd feel relieved he was still involved with someone, had a family even. I refused to care.

Will sat down next to me. "Karen wants us to stay in case Cindy wakes up. The Halifax detachment should be able to find someone to relieve us tomorrow."

I called the Lunenburg detachment at 7:58 p.m., but they hadn't found the black sedan in question. They had traced the plates to a dealership in downtown Montréal, a franchise that sold and leased second-hand vehicles. The sedan had been rented under a stolen VISA and Georgia license. The investigators faxed a picture, but we didn't recognize the man. The beard, moustache, and glasses could have been a disguise. It was hard to make out the grainy details. The Montréal connection convinced me the Rex Dare murder was part of something much bigger than just South Dare.

Will held some ice over his knee to ease the swelling from his fall. I sat in a hospital-issue armchair with stiff vinyl upholstery and wooden armrests observing Cindy who lay helplessly except for the occasional twitch. Her eyes moved under her eyelids as if she were dreaming.

I leaned over her. "Cindy! Cindy, do you hear me?"

No reaction. I sat down, anxious again. The lights were low and weird vaporous shapes formed out of the corner of my eye. I paced back and forth in the hall between the waiting room where Will had fallen asleep and ICU. Then I saw David Jordan coming down the hall. Behind him was his ex-wife Barbara.

Blood rushed up my face in an intense blush. She had probably told him about our conversation. Then, as if reading my mind, he said, "I know Linda has had concerns about me. She was just doing her job." They stopped in front of me.

Barbara nodded without looking at me. I relayed what the doctor had said about Cindy's condition.

"I used to resent all the attention you paid to Cindy, and now, here I am, praying for her in the middle of the night," Barbara said as she and David walked toward ICU.

"I'm so sorry, Barbara," David said.

She waved her hand at him dismissively. "It's nothing. I was only noting the irony, that's all."

The nurse on duty, a wide-hipped middle-aged woman with a cap of grey hair, was concerned about the excess visitors, but when she found out David was a clergyman she allowed all three of us to go in. We sat on chairs among the tubes and intensive care equipment around Cindy's bed. David pulled his chair up close to Cindy's right side and took her hand.

"Hi, Cindy. David and Barbara are here. Lots of people are praying for you. You're going to be fine."

He closed his eyes, still holding her hand, and began to pray. The prayers heightened my anxiety. My legs trembled. I got up and tiptoed back into the room where Will slept. He looked vulnerable and boyish sprawled on the couch, one arm slung over his head. I chided myself for how my feelings toward him were softening. He belonged to someone else and I wasn't sure I could trust anyone. Loneliness overwhelmed me.

I sat on a nearby chair and the window drew my attention. I stepped over and gazed at the icy pavement six storeys below. *Open the window. Jump. Find the peace you've been looking for.* I jimmied the window. Then I banged it with my fist, trying to break the glass. Suddenly, Will bolted to my side and turned me around. I burst into tears. He hugged me.

"Let go of me." I tried to loosen his grip. He held me tight until my sobbing subsided.

"Something got into me from Becky," I whispered, my lips pressed against his wool sweater.

"I know."

"Everything's so hopeless. So dark."

"It's not hopeless." He stroked my hair.

When David and Barbara came into the lounge Will asked them to pray for me. We made our way to a little chapel at the end of the hall. They sat on either side of me on the couch.

"Barbara and I are going to pray for deliverance," David said. "Demonic spirits can play a lot of tricks with your imagination. You may feel what they feel and mistake their feelings for your own."

"Am I going to roll around on the floor like Becky?" I felt a sheen of nervous sweat break out on my forehead and my hands grew clammy.

"No. Becky didn't have to do that either. But she's a little girl and more vulnerable to believing their lies."

Fear stabbed my heart.

"Try to separate yourself from what you're feeling, especially fear or anxiety," David said as if reading my mind. "You may think it's your fear, but it's really theirs. They quake at the Name of Jesus Christ, but you may feel like you're the one quaking. Just observe the fear and don't be afraid of it."

"Don't fear my fear," I said.

"That's right. They are condemned, not you. Christ has paid the price for your soul."

"I want to believe in Jesus, but I can't," I mumbled. My nose ran and tears plunked onto my fists balled in my lap. Barbara handed me a tissue.

"Spirit of fear! I rebuke you in the Name of Jesus Christ!" David said. Though his voice was soft, it was full of authority. The fear built to where I almost couldn't bear it. I caught gulps of air and stifled a whimper. David and Barbara placed their hands on me, and peace like warm liquid gold flowed from their touch. The fear vanished.

David alternated between praying for me silently and making stern commands. He seemed to discern exactly what tormented me, addressing various feelings and thoughts by name – suicide, condemnation, derision, unbelief – there were a bunch of them. My face grimaced a few times as if some spiritual force were pushing my features as it left. The oppressive anxiety and dread disappeared.

When David prayed against unbelief a gauze blindfold seemed to slip off my eyes. It suddenly felt easy to believe that Jesus was the Son of God. Childhood memories of Sunday school, Catechism classes, and my first Holy Communion flooded back with a warmth and vitality that astonished me. All these words I committed to memory and learned by rote for my confirmation now came to life – without Ron's interpretation. Not only that, I could feel Christ's love for me. Could actually feel a sweet sorrow wash over me as if my tears were baptizing me all over again.

I felt a joy and a peace I'd never felt before. When David discerned the demonic spirits were gone I prayed the same prayer Will had prayed in my kitchen the other day, confessing I was a sinner and asking Jesus to come into my heart and transform my life.

"Linda, I want you to renounce each spirit out loud and command each one to leave in the Name of Jesus," David said.

"I can't."

"Yes, you can. I want you to do it so you can see for yourself the authority you have in Christ. It's His power operating here. It has nothing to do with Barbara or me. And now that you've received Him, He's living inside you too."

My knees knocked. Fighting embarrassment, I asked him where I should start.

"Start with unbelief. Spirit of unbelief, I renounce you in the Name of Jesus Christ," David said. I repeated what he said. I felt my faith grow a little stronger.

I did the same thing for suicide, condemnation, anxiety, all the spirits David had named. David added pride to the list, and we all laughed.

"You're going to be okay," David whispered. "Let's just pray a while longer. Thank you, Lord."

He told me to remember the authority I had in Christ anytime evil spirits tried to tempt or harass me. "Stronger is He who is in you than he who is in the world," he said.

Suddenly, I felt completely secure in Jesus, enveloped in His love and peace. The lightness, the joy, was indescribable. Will emerged from Cindy's room just as the sun was coming up and the four of us went over to the window to watch the tinge of red on the horizon. The joy was contagious, and so was the love. I loved Will. I loved David and Barbara, and clearly, deeply, they seemed to love me.

We left Cindy in the hands of an officer from Halifax who showed up later that morning. As Will and I headed back to pick up Veronica his cell rang. It was Karen.

It appeared members from the Lunenburg detachment believed they had found the hit-and-run car.

the Card

Will and I took the coast road that wound along the shores of St. Margaret's Bay to where the car had been located in Boutilier's Point. Wind buffeted the Jeep and whipped the water of the bay into whitecaps. I drank in the sights, the sounds, my mind at rest. Everything seemed bolder, brighter, as if I'd switched from black and white to technicolour. I drove, confident the fears and craziness were gone for good.

We turned left onto a short dirt laneway leading to a rocky beach, past some boarded-up cottages that might have once been part of a motel.

On the beach the wind was so strong it almost took my breath away. Two police cars parked nearby and some members in uniform worked around a black Camry. It was partially covered by a tarp beating in the wind. The tires were gone and so were the license plates. The cottages shielded the car from the road. An area of small cracks indented in a shape the size of a cantaloupe indicated where Cindy's head had hit the windshield. I winced. Corporal Randy Cohen from Ident dusted the doorway and handles for prints.

I made a cursory check of the interior, which stank of cigarettes and deodorizer. Someone had wiped the ashtray clean. A crumpled wet piece of paper – a business card – stuck to the inside of the passenger door. I pointed it out to Jimmy who picked it up with a pair of tweezers and put it in a plastic envelope. I wrote down the information: "Virtuality. Videos, DVDs, CDs, Wholesale prices." And a Miami address.

Randy asked us to interview the residents of two dwellings across the highway from the abandoned cottages.

The wind almost pushed us up the hill. Will headed to a blue house, not much more than a shack. Gusts of wind whipped smoke coming from its metal chimney. I knocked on the door of a tidy yellow bungalow. An elderly woman wearing bifocals and a housedress answered.

"Yes. I seen a white pickup truck go in there yesterday about this time," she said. "A black car was right behind it. Then I seen a man get out of the white truck and into the black car. Then I seen the car drive out, heading west."

"Did you recognize the man who got out?"

"No one from 'round these parts. Nope. He was a young man. Dark hair. Thick around the middle. Can't say as I can tell you more than that. He was wearin' a black parka with red swatches around the shoulders. They was gone in a flash. But I seen him good because I got binoculars."

I calculated it would have taken them an hour to get to Lunenburg from here, maybe less if they used the highway. Whoever was responsible might have been stalking Cindy for hours before they ran her down. I felt a chill.

"Did you see the black car return?"

"I ain't seen it, nope. But I seen the white truck leavin'. Went east. I was just getting ready to watch my story on TV so it was almost two o'clock. I seen the truck leavin' and the same man driving because I seen the red on his jacket. There was two of them in the truck. I didn't see much of the other man, except he had dark hair too."

"Beard? Glasses?"

"Nope, neither of them had no beard."

I said goodbye and met Will as he was coming from the blue shack. He said the middle-aged couple living there were hostile and told him nothing except their names.

Will and I arrived at Veronica's apartment before noon. Will had to return to Sterling so he drove my Jeep back. I planned to drive Veronica in her car the next day.

I felt tired, so Veronica suggested I take a nap while she called her neighbourhood grocery store to deliver some food.

I lay down on the single bed in the room that had been my father's den. It still contained his plaques and karate trophies. I drifted off to sleep again and had a troubling dream. Dad was holding Grace's hand, telling me he was going to give her up for adoption. I started screaming, "No, no, please don't! I *do* want her! I *do* want her!"

"She wants to kill her baby," he said to Veronica.

I grabbed Veronica and shook her, but my arms were like spaghetti. Veronica morphed into Ron. My desperation turned to hatred and impotent rage. I pummelled his face with noodle fists. "It's all *your* fault! It's all *your* fault!" But my voice was too weak. I awoke to the sound of my real voice croaking.

Shaken, I freshened up and found Veronica dozing on her living room couch, lights on, with a blue and purple afghan covering her. I tiptoed in and she woke up. We prepared supper from food her grocer had delivered. After we ate I worked up my courage.

"Veronica?" I paused.

"Yes."

I took a deep breath. She looked at me, wondering.

"Do you know where my daughter is?"

Her eyes met mine.

"Yes."

Another pause.

"Does she know about me?"

"She knows she's adopted. I think her parents are waiting for her to ask. And I've been waiting for you to do the same thing."

Veronica asked me to reach for an album she kept on top of the upright piano. We sat together on the couch and leafed through pictures of my daughter from newborn baby, to tow-headed toddler, to kindergartner, on up to a tall skinny high school girl with a heart-shaped face and streaked blonde hair, lighter than mine. I could hardly see through my tears. Luckily Veronica had a box of tissues on the coffee table. I felt a terrible lump in my throat melt. I sniffed. "I don't even know her name."

"Her name is Meredith. We first met her when she was six and again two years later. She was twelve the last time I saw her. She's fifteen now. Her parents don't get to Lunenburg often, but they did visit with us. She's a beautiful girl, isn't she?"

I nodded. "Dad met her too?"

"She loved your dad. She didn't know we were her grandparents. That was a little hard for us because we had to be more restrained than we would have been otherwise. But she's well loved. I think you'd like Jeri and Wayne very much."

The last picture showed Meredith at her junior high school graduation. She'd signed the photograph: To Aunt Veronica with love, Meredith.

She looked like me, only thinner, and in the more recent photos, blonder. She didn't resemble Ron at all, to my great relief, except for the ice blue eyes. I smiled and wiped away more tears at the same time.

"Take that with you. I kept it for you. I knew one day you'd ask."

We hugged and I held her tight. "I never, ever thought I'd say this. But thank you. Thank you for not letting me go through with..."

"All things work together for good, don't they? I wish I could say my motives were pure at the time." Veronica squeezed my hand.

On Christmas Eve day I drove Veronica up to Cornwallis Cove in her car. Will had left my Jeep in the laneway and my keys at Catherine's. A Christmas tree filled the bay window in Catherine's living room. Grace thumped down the stairs two at a time wearing her snow pants and a quilted long-sleeved undershirt. She hugged me and wouldn't let me go. I noticed a stack of photos of Rafe on the counter. When I could I slipped one inside my parka hanging in the mud room.

Veronica unpacked her bags in the den on Catherine's first floor. It had a pullout couch and a small bathroom nearby, and she'd have fewer steps to negotiate than if she stayed at my house.

I phoned the detachment to try and reach Will. He called back about twenty minutes later and told me the couple in the blue shack he had questioned were Rex Dare's relatives. He also told me Cindy had regained consciousness, but she seemed to be in a lot of pain and unable to speak. Then he asked if he could drop by.

Within half an hour he was stomping snow off his boots outside Catherine's kitchen door. When he came into the kitchen wearing his uniform and flashed his broad, slightly crooked smile at me, his warmth and tenderness nearly made me swoon, to my surprise. He greeted Veronica, and I introduced him to Edna and Grace who were seated around the kitchen table. He took off his parka and threw it over the back of the chair. Edna brought him a cup of tea. The charge in the air was contagious. Everyone seemed brighter, livelier, happier than usual. A brass version of *Hark! The Herald Angels Sing* played on a CD.

"What are your plans for tonight?" Will asked.

"I don't know for sure. Catherine's got our next few days organized for us."

"We're having dinner here and then going to church," Grace chimed in.

"Cornwallis Cove? I'm going there too. I'll see you," Will said. He touched Grace's chin affectionately and she grabbed his finger, giggled, and tried to keep him from getting up.

He put on his parka and I saw him to the door. He gazed at me for several moments, his eyes soft, a hint of a smile playing on his face, and brushed my cheek with his knuckle before he slipped out the door.

"I'd say the man's in love, wouldn't you?" Edna clucked, raising her eyebrows at Veronica when I returned to the table.

"What do you mean?" I blushed.

"You too," Edna said.

I shook my head and grimaced. Will and I were just friends. He'd said he wanted more and he was acting like he cared for me. Maybe he wasn't with his girlfriend anymore. I tried to persuade myself I didn't care one way or the other, but I couldn't keep from hoping.

I realized I couldn't wait to see him again.

the Betrayal

When Catherine came home with her arms full of packages I realized I had no gifts. I jumped into the Jeep and headed to the village craft store, bought presents for Grace, Veronica and Catherine, and had the clerk wrap them in shiny blue and gold paper. Big snowflakes were drifting down as the last-minute shoppers all wished each other a Merry Christmas. The Christmas lights strung between the streetlights glowed. Filled with Christmas spirit I anticipated the next few days with great joy. I debated whether to buy Will something, but decided to wait and see if he gave me anything first.

When I drove past Catherine's laneway I saw a rental car parked there. Dismay knocked the Christmas cheer right out of me.

Rafe was back.

Frowning, I continued to my place, took a shower, washed and dried my hair, and put on the black dress with the red flowers. Then I knelt by my bed on my cold wooden floor and prayed to God to not let Rafe ruin Christmas. I stood up feeling a little awkward. I wasn't used to this prayer stuff at all. Not free-form prayers anyway.

Standing in front of the mirror in the bathroom I smoothed some moisturizer on my face. I remembered how Will looked at me only a short time ago at Catherine's. I watched my expression in the mirror soften and I smiled, wondering if this was what being in love felt like. I immediately squelched those thoughts. If he was in a relationship with someone, then I had to stop thinking like this. *He loves me, he loves me not. Stop it!*

When I stepped into Catherine's warm kitchen wearing a dress and carrying my bag of gifts Rafe's tanned hands gripped Catherine's upper arms. When Catherine turned to me her radiant expression made me feel guilty for detesting Rafe so much. I made an effort to be friendly. To my surprise, so did he.

He looked me up and down and told me I looked terrific. *Ugh!* He offered me a glass of sherry.

Glass in hand, I followed Catherine into the living room, where Grace sat in front of a roaring fire and Veronica reclined on the couch under the afghan. The Christmas tree filled the room with the scent of balsam fir. Instead of multicoloured lights, Catherine had strung the tree with tiny white lights, silver balls and white ribbons. Rafe brought me a glass of sweet sherry in a small glass of heavy leaded crystal. Catherine laid my gifts under the tree.

Shortly after I arrived, Edna and her husband Delbert, a little round man a good half a head shorter than his wife, came over. Catherine and Edna set out plates of crackers and a nippy cheese log rolled in walnuts. While everyone chatted Rafe tended the fire in the fireplace and made sure everyone's drink was replenished. He patted Grace's head whenever she scampered by him or winked at her from across the room. Grace shrank from him. She needed time to warm to people and he was coming on too strong. I decided to give Catherine a hand with the food.

In the kitchen Catherine was removing a roast leg of lamb from the wood stove oven. The fat crackled. She added some boiled potatoes to the pan drippings around the roast. I helped her and Edna with the final dinner preparations.

We laid the table in Catherine's dining room with an embroidered white tablecloth and Catherine's grey-blue and dark purple plates. A couple of white candles amid some pine boughs formed a centrepiece. Rafe poured rosé wine into long-stemmed glasses. Soon dinner was served and we gathered around the table.

"Grace, honey, you say the blessing," Edna said. We all bowed our heads. I heard the CD of a brass quartet playing *O Come, All Ye Faithful* and lifted my heart to God with thanksgiving.

"Thank you, God, for this food," Grace said, then paused. "Amen!"

We laughed and passed the bowls of food around. Rafe carved up the lamb roast. The wine was tart, the squash sweet, the lamb pink and tender. The smell of brewing coffee wafted in from the kitchen. For dessert Catherine brought in one of Edna's homemade fruitcakes and a tureen of hard sauce.

Before long Edna began carrying dirty dishes to the kitchen, warning us that the church filled up quickly on Christmas Eve. Rafe volunteered to stay behind and clean up. I found it annoying that Catherine changed her mind and decided to stay behind with him.

"Mommy!" Grace pouted and started twisting her body from side to side. "I want you to go to church with me."

"It's okay, sweetheart. You can go with Auntie Linda. Auntie Veronica and Auntie Edna are going too." Catherine smiled, her hand gripping Rafe's across the table. Grace looked so disappointed I gathered her into my lap and hugged her.

"Delbert's going too," Edna said, proudly.

"I'm one of those twice a year folks she complains about," Delbert said. He chuckled.

Inside the packed foyer at Cornwallis Cove Baptist, an usher handed us programs and directed Grace and me to some seats near the front where we sat next to Edna and Delbert. Soon we saw David and some other men setting up extra chairs at the back. I glanced around the austere Baptist sanctuary, the wood panelling and clear windows decorated with balsam wreaths and red poinsettias, hoping to catch a glimpse of Will. Dad and I used to go to midnight Mass at Holy Child on Christmas Eve with Gran, Aunt Gladys, Uncle Fred and my cousins. I longed for those days when I knelt next to Dad and genuflected the way he did before we went forward to receive the Blessed Sacrament.

The lights dimmed, leaving a glow of candlelight and the smell of burning beeswax. We sang carols, prayed, and Pastor Don Harwood gave a short sermon.

"Tonight we celebrate a special time in history. We celebrate the birth of our Lord, Jesus Christ. We celebrate that moment in time when God became man and dwelt among us. Jesus was conceived by the Holy Ghost and born of the Virgin Mary. God the Son took everything of our human nature upon Himself, except He was without sin. He became so vulnerable for our sakes that He was born a helpless infant. His mother Mary wrapped our Lord in swaddling clothes and placed Him in a manger. A manger, the place where some of you farmers place hay for your cows. But it's not only a moment in history that we celebrate. We also celebrate the new life that we can all have in Jesus. Whenever someone accepts Christ into his or her heart it's Christmas no matter what day of the year. Because when you ask Jesus to come in the infant Emmanuel is born again in your heart. He gives us a new nature. And, for all of us sinners, our hearts are the most humble of all circumstances. Our hearts are like that manger, and our minds are like that stable. Sometimes those stables need a good mucking out."

The congregation laughed softly. Later, as David Jordan prayed at the end of the service, you could have heard a pin drop. Even the babies were quiet.

"I know we don't ordinarily do this on Christmas Eve," David said, "but some of you may have been touched by Pastor Don's sermon tonight. If you believe in your heart that Jesus Christ is the Son of God, and you wish to invite Him to come and live in your heart, then please come forward and we will pray with you. If you have already accepted Christ, you may want to take this opportunity to make your confession public. If you want to renew your commitment to Jesus, please come forward and we will pray with you. And anyone who needs healing, who needs wisdom, who needs a special touch from God tonight, please come forward and let us pray with you. The service is over now, and those who wish may exit quietly as we sing our last carol. If you feel God calling you, please come forward."

The choir sang *Silent Night* as I edged in front of Edna to go forward. Grace smiled at me. Veronica took my hand and squeezed it. Then I noticed she was standing and heading up front too.

About forty people crowded near the pulpit. Some of them stood with their eyes closed and their hands lifted high above their heads. Others stood with their hands clasped together. I noticed a few men and women in the pews scowling at the people who had gone forward.

David came over to me and placed his hands on my head and prayed for me. I closed my eyes, and felt an energy flowing out of his hands that made me feel so peaceful and relaxed I almost drifted to the floor, light as a feather. I locked my knees so I wouldn't lose my balance.

I introduced David to Veronica who then whispered in his ear for several seconds. Then he and a couple of elders laid hands on her and started praying. I closed my eyes and prayed too.

I felt someone's arm around me and knew it was Will. My grin was so wide I thought my face would break.

"What a Christmas," he said and hugged me to his side. My knees almost buckled again. Someone started singing *O Holy Night* and Will and others joined in when someone passed us a song sheet.

Just then, a dirty disheveled man lunged through the crowd. I recognized Stan, the drunk from the waterfront coffee shop. He brushed past us, cursing under his breath. An usher pushed through the crowd behind him.

"Help me, Jesus!" Stan hollered. "Please help me!"

Then he started shouting obscenities and staggered toward the simple wooden table at the front of the church. A hush fell on the room. The usher grabbed his shoulder but he shook it off. David and Pastor Don waded through the crowd toward him. When David reached Stan he threw his arm over his shoulders. Then they both laid hands on him and started praying. After a few moments he fell to the ground, writhing and groaning, but David and Don continued to pray for him, their eyes shut, lips moving. Soon Stan was quiet, lying face down.

Some stood and stared. Others began quietly leaving the church. Will had slipped away. I helped Veronica up and we headed back to our seats where Grace, Edna, and Delbert sat waiting. People crowded the aisles as they made their way out the door. As we joined the throng making its way to the foyer I saw Will helping a tall blonde woman with her winter coat. Beside her were two boys, one of them about Grace's age, the other a couple of years older, both little images of their father. The sight of the family tableau hurt so much I couldn't breathe. He was not separated. He just wanted a dirty affair.

Another hypocrite Christian.

the **Nightgown**

"Will's waving at you," Veronica said.

"Let's go." I helped Grace into her dark green coat.

"Yes, let's go." From her sympathetic tone of voice I knew Veronica had noticed Will's family. The three of us headed out the front door.

Back at Catherine's I pretended to be festive. Veronica, face glowing, sat next to me on the couch and Grace curled up on my other side, wearing her pajamas. We watched the fire, ate fruitcake and chocolate truffles, and listened to Christmas music. Catherine nestled at Rafe's feet while he played absentmindedly with her hair. When I couldn't hide my hurt and loneliness any longer I excused myself and went home.

The next morning I awoke while it was still dark, did my exercise routine, showered, and dressed in jeans and a red sweater. Then I headed to Catherine's to watch Grace open her Christmas stocking, determined to enjoy myself. A brisk wind whipped the previous day's snow across the road while a pale sun glowed through thin clouds. I trudged through the snow between our houses and then removed my boots in Catherine's mud room.

Catherine was setting out a buffet of rolls, muffins, Christmas stollen, and slices of ham, cheese, and cantaloupe on the kitchen table. Veronica sat in the rocking chair by the wood stove wearing a fleecy raspberry-coloured outfit. Grace scampered into the room. We all wished each other Merry Christmas and exchanged embraces.

I turned, and there was Rafe holding his arms wide. I pretended not to see him. From the corner of my eye I saw him shrug and exchange glances with Catherine.

After we ate, Grace cuddled with me on the living room couch while Rafe stuffed wadded newspaper into the fireplace.

"Grace, would you like to help me light the fire?" Rafe asked.

"No thank you," she said.

He stacked some kindling over the newspaper. "Come on, sweetheart."

Grace climbed off the couch and edged toward him. He hauled her close, hugging her. She squirmed out of his embrace and darted back to me. *Why doesn't he let her be?* He placed some logs over the kindling, then shoved some more crumpled newspaper under them.

When it came time to open her stocking, we enjoyed Grace's delight as she pulled out a Beanie Baby moose, a net bag full of chocolate coins, a small teddy bear wearing a yellow raincoat and boots, and a set of coloured markers. Grace darted over to the tree to help Catherine pass gifts around. Rafe cleared his throat and squatted next to the tree. *Why does he have to be the centre of attention?*

He patted Grace's head and then reached for two boxes wrapped in fancy silver paper, gold ribbon, and sprigs of holly. He handed one box to Catherine and the other to Grace. "Open these now so I can take pictures," he said, taking a digital camera off his belt.

Catherine opened her box carefully, trying to preserve the wrappings. From the soft white tissue paper inside she lifted a silk nightgown with blue piping around the neck and sleeves. An exquisite designer-quality piece of lingerie, the kind of tasteful romantic nightwear you'd see in an ad in an upscale women's magazine.

"Oh Rafe, it's beautiful!" Catherine said. Rafe's flash went off.

Grace tore the wrapping off her box and opened it. Inside was a smaller but otherwise identical nightgown. The flash went off again and again and again.

"It's just like your mommy's," Rafe pointed out.

"Isn't it beautiful, Grace?" Catherine asked. "Say thank you, honey."

"Thank you," Grace mumbled as she carefully put the nightgown back into the box.

"Gracie, how about giving me a kiss?" Rafe beamed at her.

Grace stood up, solemn-faced, her shoulders slumped.

"Grace doesn't feel like kissing you," I said. "Let her be."

"Lady, I don't know *what* your problem is," Rafe said.

"Come on, please. It's Christmas," Catherine pleaded.

"I don't need this." Rafe stood and brushed the wood chips off his jeans. He thumped out of the room.

"Rafe, please don't go. Linda didn't mean anything by that, did you, Linda?" Catherine ran after him out of the room.

Tears welled in Grace's eyes. "I don't like him." She slid her cool small hand into mine. "But Mommy likes him a lot."

I turned to Veronica. "Do you think it's appropriate for a grown man to give a little girl a nightgown like that?"

"No, I don't. But I'm not sure now was the time to bring it up, dear."

I walked into the kitchen debating whether to apologize or tell him off some more. Rafe had his leather coat on and Catherine clung to his arm, imploring him to stay.

He pointed a black-gloved finger at me. "You've got big problems. Catherine shouldn't allow you around Grace."

Catherine tilted her head up. "Rafe, please. It's Christmas. Let's try to – "

"No. I can't keep quiet about this any longer." He shook Catherine loose and stepped close enough to shove his finger inches from my nose. "Look, you lesbo pervert. You can't bear anyone being affectionate with Grace because you want her for yourself."

My mouth fell open.

"Catherine's too naive to see through you, but I do, you bulldyke," he hissed. He twisted and cocked his finger at Catherine. "Baby, if you want me in your life, you have to choose between your lesbo friend here, and me. Merry Christmas." Rafe plunked on a fur hat and stormed out the door.

"Why did you do that?" Catherine shouted at me. "You've ruined Christmas!"

"He's the one who's behaving inappropriately, not me!" I shouted back. "You don't have a problem with him giving Grace a nightgown like that?"

Veronica stood at the kitchen doorway with Grace. "Linda, I think we'd better leave."

"Why don't you run after Rafe and tell him *we're* leaving!" I felt like my cheeks were on fire.

"Auntie Linda, you haven't opened your gifts yet!" Grace cried as she watched me help Veronica pack her suitcase in the den.

I hated to leave her, but I was so angry I thought I might start breaking things.

Several minutes later, as I helped Veronica up the steps to my back door, I saw Catherine and Rafe go back inside her house, arm in arm. I felt utterly defeated. What a bleak Christmas this was turning out to be. Poor little Grace. I lugged Veronica's suitcase into my cold kitchen.

She asked me to take her to a Catholic Mass for Christmas Day. We went to Our Lady of Sorrows in Sterling. I wished I could have paid attention because the parts I *did* hear were beautiful. I wasn't sure I'd be allowed to take the Blessed Sacrament, so I waited while Veronica went forward to receive.

After Mass, Veronica and I joined some lonely diners at the resort hotel on the outskirts of Sterling. Later that day I packed some clothes, then hopped in the Jeep and followed her car to Lunenburg where I spent a few days away from my problems, and returned to my old habit of focusing on the present so I didn't have to feel hurt or angry.

the Resignation

Once back from Lunenburg after Christmas I fast-forwarded through several messages Will had left on my answering machine, and discovered one from Karen inviting me to a staff party at her place. I checked my watch. The party was already underway.

I slid into the slinky black dress Veronica had given me for Christmas, along with my mother's cultured pearl necklace. Veronica had treated me to a haircut and highlighting at Brenda's Shear Heaven. This had nothing to do with Will, I told myself.

The living room of Karen's three-storey Victorian house was packed. Will wasn't there, putting me on an emotional seesaw of relief and disappointment. To stop the inner turmoil I tried to make small talk, but the men's stares and the wives' unfriendliness made me self-conscious. The carpeted stairs leading to the second floor made a good place to retreat with a paper plate of egg salad sandwich quarters and a pile of veggies with dip.

Then I heard Will's voice greeting someone.

"Hey! It's the Incest Kid," said a voice I recognized as Bob's.

Will laughed. "Shut up, man. Don't call me that."

"Hey, he's not the Incest Kid anymore," another male voice said. "He's got the hots for Donner!" He sounded like Eddie.

"Donner? Are you crazy? My friend, you have tragic taste in women," Bob said.

I had heard other members call Will the Incest Kid before, and figured it was a nickname from his obsessive investigation into the original charges against Rex Dare.

"Donner's a lesbian, Bright," Eddie said. "You don't stand a chance. That's because Karen's zoomed in on her."

There was that label again. *Lesbian*.

Will, wearing his uniform, brushed past Bob and Eddie to the foot of the stairs. I thought of slipping upstairs, but I knew he'd see me if I moved. Then he looked up. Bob and Eddie had followed him and gawked. Eddie laughed as Bob tried to herd him back into the other room.

Will asked me to come outside and talk to him. I shrugged and reached for my ski jacket off the banister, self-conscious of my swinging honey-blonde hair, clinging black dress and made-up eyes. I threw my parka over the dress and followed him outside to the police car.

"You look beautiful," he said as he opened the passenger door for me.

I looked away, embarrassed. When I sat down I pulled the dress over my knees.

"Have I done something to offend you?" he asked as he sat next to me.

"No."

"Why didn't you stop on Christmas Eve? I know you saw me."

I shrugged.

"How come you haven't returned any of my calls?"

"I've been in Lunenburg with Veronica. I only got back this afternoon."

"Oh." He looked away. "Did you have a good Christmas?"

"Oh, yeah. It was great. You?" My voice sounded mechanical.

"Not as good as it could have been."

I felt uncomfortable and said nothing.

"Something's changed. It feels like you're angry with me." He turned toward me, his face earnest and open. "Our friendship is important to me."

"I'm not angry. Nothing's changed as far as I'm concerned." My icy tone cut him. I could see hurt spread across his face. I didn't dare remain alone with him much longer or my facade would crack. He had led me on to think he was romantically interested in me when he really had a family. *Maybe he was still looking for a little action on the side.* I ground my teeth and opened the door. I wished him a Happy New Year, told him I'd be back at work the following week and I'd see him around.

Back inside the kitchen I tried to engage Karen in a conversation about Rex's murder.

"You don't want to talk about work now, do you?" Karen smiled as she took a stainless steel mould in the shape of a wreath out of the freezer. She held the frozen fruit inside the mould over the punch bowl.

"You look great, by the way. Fabulous haircut."

She'd shed her crisp staff sergeant personality for a gushy motherly one. It scared me to death.

Then George entered the kitchen, beard perfectly groomed, capped teeth almost bluish white. He wore a black suit and a yellow and grey silk tie. We said hello and he exchanged showy air kisses with Karen.

"Have some punch, Linda?" Karen handed me a glass.

"How's your project going with Rafe?" I asked George.

He grinned. "Rafe's a character. I like him very much. But, don't ever hire a friend!"

"What do you mean?" I smiled a little to encourage him.

"I hired him to do a promotional video for my company and some Web pages. I needed them right away. Well, he kept being called away to do other things. We did a little work when he was here in November, but otherwise the project hardly got off the ground. I guess he figured I wouldn't mind waiting because we're friends. I cancelled the job."

"He musn't be too happy about that."

"He wasn't. Either was I, frankly." George laughed. "Maybe that's why he hasn't called me to tell me he's in Sterling for the holidays."

"Well, I hope the friendship isn't permanently damaged." I smiled my professional false smile.

"Oh, I'm sure it won't be. By the way, anything new on the Rex Dare investigation?"

I shook my head.

"Too bad. I hear Cindy Dare's unable to speak."

I shrugged. He excused himself and headed into the living room. Then some of the members' wives migrated to the kitchen and appeared to make a point of ignoring me, so I said goodnight to Karen and went home.

One of my New Year's resolutions was to attend church regularly. I chose the Sunday evening service in Cornwallis Cove, hoping Will had attended the morning one. When I entered the church that night people crammed the foyer and the conversation din was louder and more animated than usual. Inside, parishioners jammed the pews, many wearing angry expressions. I searched for Edna and squeezed in next to her.

The service was uneventful. Pastor Don spoke about the Body of Christ, how we all form different parts, and how we need to act as one. David sat near the front with his family. At the end of the service Pastor Don said members of the congregation were invited to stay for an important business meeting. No one budged. A balding middle-aged man with large glasses strutted to the podium.

"I'm Bob Oickle, head of the deacons. I've called this meeting with a majority backing from the members. I'd appreciate it if those who are not on the rolls would leave now. This is a private meeting."

Something ominous was in the air and I had to find out what was going on. The door to the foyer swung open, and Catherine swept inside with her notebook in hand and camera dangling from her wrist.

"Pastor Don, if you don't have these people leave, then we'll have to vote by secret ballot. We can't have people voting here who are not members," Oickle said.

"Let's get this over with," Pastor Don said.

"Okay, I recognize John Potter. You have a motion to bring forward?"

"Thank you, Bob. This is a motion to ask for the resignation of David Jordan from Cornwallis Cove Baptist Church and her sister churches, effective immediately."

An angry buzz of conversation and audible gasps made Bob tap the microphone several times.

"Quiet please! Do we have a seconder?"

"I second the motion!" Someone shouted from the back.

"I'd like to speak to the motion, if I may," Potter said.

A balding man with an ample pot-belly straining the buttons on his sports jacket, Potter read from a piece of paper. "Pastor Jordan has entered into unauthorized ministries. He's introducing activities into this church that we think are demonic. And we believe he's bringing Cornwallis Cove Baptist Church into disrepute."

A woman stood. "I was appalled at the display on Christmas Eve," she said. "This is a family church and my kids had bad dreams after that night. We can't have that kind of carrying on in here. It's devilish, and unseemly."

Several more people spoke against David until a woman with deep lines etching her face stood.

"Please, sit down, ma'am. You're not a member of this church," Oickle said.

The woman refused to sit down. A plastic barrette kept her limp brown hair from falling across her face. "You all knew Stan MacIsaac as the town drunk. After Christmas Eve he came home a changed man. He has not had a drop to drink since. Pastor David saved his life." She sat down.

"Pastor David is a divorced man!" a man shouted. "He should not be in leadership, let alone pastoring a church."

Edna arose and shouted, "He's divorced because his first wife left him for another man!"

"He doesn't have a good relationship with his present wife," another man said. "Scripture says we should have leaders whose families respect them."

Anne Jordan stepped to a microphone, elbows trembling. "Please don't judge David because I have struggled with depression and other problems. It's my lack of faith. My fault, not his. David is a godly man."

The meeting continued, heated and contentious. Despite several impassioned arguments to keep David, including one from Pastor Don Harwood himself, I had a bad feeling. The deacons handed out ballots to members. The motion carried.

David made his way to the microphone. Oickle stepped aside. David paused, shoulders heavy, and said, "It's the wish of this church body that I resign. I will hand in a written resignation tomorrow."

Pastor Harwood reached for the microphone. "Then I will hand in my resignation as well."

A collective gasp rose up. Then the two pastors, their wives, and their supporters filed outside. In the foyer Catherine's camera flash flickered like a strobe light.

Out on the sidewalk David's arm encircled Anne's shoulders. Bob Oickle pushed through the crowd toward them and reached the couple the same time I did.

"The Potters have asked me to tell you they'd prefer you moved out of their rental property as soon as possible," Oickle said, his eyes shifting from side to side. "They want to reserve it for the new pastor. We'll pay for you to stay in a motel until you find your own place."

Anne gaped at Oickle in disbelief. David declined his offer.

Oickle glanced at him, started to say something, then shuffled off.

"Come and stay with me," I blurted out.

"Oh no, we couldn't impose on you like that," Anne said.

"No imposition at all!" I insisted. "I'd love to have you. I have a huge house. Please come."

"Thank you, Linda," David said. "Anne and I should pray about this first. We'll let you know tomorrow."

I needed them to come stay with me. They would be doing me a favour.

the **Reconciliation**

Two days after the blowout at Cornwallis Cove Baptist I returned to work, arriving an hour before my shift started so I could catch up on the Rex Dare case. In the file I saw no new entries since I'd gone on stress leave. The investigation had ground to a halt. I looked for the file Will had started on Cindy Dare's hit and run.

Will had compiled a list of all the white pickups in Sterling County. He had circled a few and written South Dare next to them, but nothing more. He hadn't explored the connection between the couple in the blue shack and South Dare. I looked to see what information had been uncovered about the Virtuality XXX business in Miami. Will logged that he had tried the phone number in Miami, but it was out of service. *That's it?*

At my desk I called information in Miami and asked for the police department's number. I left a voice mail with someone in Vice. I figured I'd probably have to wait until evening before I'd be able to talk to a real person since Vice Squad members usually worked nights.

When Will came in carrying a large Tim Horton's coffee I jumped up, feeling the blood rise to my face. I decided to be strictly businesslike with him. "How come nothing's been done on the Rex Dare file?"

"Back to your old self, I see," Will teased. "I did what I could, but it's been crazy over the holidays. Domestic violence, car accidents, you name it." He sat in the desk chair belonging to the cubicle across from me. "There's another reason why I didn't finish checking the leads. The DEA has informed Karen there's a huge drug deal going down. A mother ship's going to download a cargo of cocaine and heroin onto fishing boats from Sterling County. Of course they don't know which village these boats are coming from."

I sank back in my chair, grimacing. "Oh, that's just great."

"We're supposed to poke around Cape Sterling, looking for strangers carrying cellphones and flashing lots of US cash."

"Sounds like George's buddy Rafe Lupien. Catherine's boyfriend."

"The dark-haired guy with the tan and the sunglasses?" Will stretched. "I told our DEA contacts about your suspicions and they don't seem too interested."

"What about George?"

"He's putting lots of political pressure on us." Will walked over to the file cabinet and retrieved a manila folder. He threw it on my desk. "Here. Get acquainted with this since you're joining this wild goose chase too."

"How's Cindy?"

"Still not talking. Her doctor says there doesn't seem to be any neurological damage, though. Her hip is healing and she doesn't seem to be in much pain." He sipped his coffee. Then he told me she was going to be moved to a Sterling nursing home as soon as a bed was available.

I jumped up. "How are we going to keep a 24-hour guard on her?"

"We can't." Will stuffed his empty coffee cup into the wastebasket. "GIS used up all the overtime, according to Karen."

"This is nuts! Cindy's toast if she's brought back here and left unguarded for five minutes!"

"You're preaching to the converted. But Halifax has cutbacks too." Will grabbed his parka and slipped it on. "I've got to run. Karen will explain everything."

After meeting with Karen I spent the morning filling out paperwork and familiarizing myself with the drug smuggling file.

That afternoon I scouted around a couple of remote communities along Cape Sterling. The tedious work in the bone-chillingly damp wind produced no leads. Many residents poached lobster, jacked deer, made homebrew alcohol, and stole wood from crown land. They weren't exactly forthcoming when I tried to get information out of them.

On the way home I stopped at Sobeys to buy groceries. The Jordans told me the previous day they'd accept my offer to stay with me for a while. That delighted me. I pushed my grocery cart around the supermarket, looking forward to their arrival, hoping David would reawaken my spiritual life. I looked forward to getting to know Anne better. I got stuck in the crowded aisle behind a woman who was taking her sweet time examining the prices on tomato paste. She pushed her strawberry-blonde hair back and my heart started racing. It was the same woman I'd seen with Will on Christmas Eve. She recognized me and grinned. "Hello! You're Linda Donner, aren't you?"

"Yes, I am." I wished I could slink away.

"Will's told me a lot about you," she said, beaming.

A little boy about seven ran up and dropped a box of corn flakes into her cart.

"This is my son Aaron. The other one's around here someplace."

"Hi, Aaron." I hoped my face wasn't too red. Aaron, who looked like Will, shrugged and shyly leaned against the woman's leg. I felt like hands were wringing my heart like a dishrag.

"My name is Suzanne." She extended her hand and we shook. "I hope Will invites you to come and see us sometime soon." She had pale freckles and blue eyes. Will's taste in women seemed to be toward tall blondes, though Suzanne was fairer and heavier than I was. I was surprised she knew about me. Perhaps I'd misread Will's signals and he really only ever saw me as a friend. No. He'd told me he wanted more than friendship.

Suzanne and I said polite see-you-laters and then went our separate ways. I was furious Will would tell Suzanne about me, but not me about her.

As I pulled into my laneway I noticed a satellite van from a Halifax TV station parked in Catherine's, but didn't think much of it. The prime minister had held a news conference in Yarmouth earlier that day, so I figured the news crew members were friends of Catherine's, stopping by for a visit on the way back to Halifax.

I put the groceries away, filling the fridge and empty pantry shelves. I turned the furnace on and opened the registers in the other two bedrooms upstairs. After I changed into jeans and a turquoise sweatshirt I raced through the bedrooms with a dust mop and wiped down the windowsills. The warm air from the heating ducts smelled like hot dust.

When the Jordans arrived about an hour later little Joy and the toddler Samuel's eyes drooped with fatigue. The family had already eaten supper so I offered my bedroom so the children could lie down. David told me Will would be bringing their beds and a futon later that evening.

Anne and I shooed the children upstairs. After they'd put on their pajamas and brushed their teeth they lay down on my bed under the down duvet. They looked so sweet, my heart overflowed. Will arrived soon after, and he and David whisked the beds upstairs. They set up the futon in the second bedroom. I had insisted Anne and David take my bedroom, but they had refused.

My kitchen was toasty warm and I was self-conscious about how my hat had flattened my hair. *Since when had I ever cared about stupid things like that?* I decided to make some chili, so I chopped onions while David and Will chatted at the table and Anne rested upstairs.

When everything was simmering in the pot I covered it and sat down to drink some tea, which was always brewing whenever the oil stove was on. David excused himself to see how Anne was doing.

Will and I sat diagonally from each other, sipping our tea. I felt awkward and angry at the memory of Suzanne and the boys.

"I ran into Suzanne at the mall," I said. "And Aaron and Jason. They look just like you."

"Yeah, there's a family resemblance."

"What is she then, your girlfriend or your wife?"

He looked at me and smiled. "Now I get it." He rocked back in his chair. "Now I understand why you've been so cold."

"I don't know what you're talking about."

"Suzanne's my sister. Aaron and Jason are my nephews."

"Your sister?" Flabbergasted and embarrassed, I realized how much I had given away about my feelings for him.

"I thought you knew! Why do you think they call me the Incest Kid? My sister and her kids moved in with me almost three years ago after her husband beat her up. Oh, Linda." His grin stretched across his face.

"Why do you think this is so funny? Did you think you were so important to me that I was going to ask about your marital status?" I clenched my fists, digging my nails into my palms and hoping my jaw wouldn't start quivering.

"I don't think *it's* funny. I think *you're* funny." He reached for my fist and I nearly upset my mug drawing it away from him.

"Linda loves me." He bent forward and peered at my face, eyes shining with love.

"I do not."

Then all the feelings I'd been pressing down bubbled up to the surface. I burst into tears. I could have died of shame. I hunched over my mug, face in my hands, and sobbed. I could hear his chair creaking.

"I'm real sorry, Linda. It never occurred to me you'd think I had a girlfriend."

I squelched the sobs and sniffed. I wiped my eyes and tried to appear as unfazed as I could. "You told me you had a girlfriend."

"I couldn't have."

"You implied you did."

"Oh, so you can read minds, eh?" He grinned at me, but his smile faded, probably because I was trembling. "I haven't had a girlfriend in three years. I thought everyone knew that. I've been cautious about getting involved. Until now."

"Well, forget it." I hid my face in my hands again.

His chair creaked again. He was tilting back on it. I peeked at him through my fingers to see if he was still smiling at me.

"She loves me," he said.

I jumped up and tried to push him backward onto the floor, but he righted the chair and grabbed my arms. I tried to pull away, but he was too strong. When he let go I had to lean a hand on the table to keep my balance. He stood and edged around the table. He pulled me gently to him and hugged me close. I must have felt like a statue, my muscles were so tensed. I reached out a hand and grabbed a stack of napkins to wipe my eyes and blow my nose. My head ached. I didn't want him to see my face.

"Hey." He stepped back and gently pushed the bangs from my eyes. I glanced at his freckled face, open and innocent, a slight smile showing his beautiful teeth. "Linda loves me."

But he was really saying "I love *you.*"

the **Newscast**

While Will held me close, the stairs creaked. I broke away from his embrace just before David treaded into the kitchen on sock feet. I hoped my eyes weren't red from crying.

"Something's going on outside," David said.

The three of us darted into the darkened living room. From the window we saw the TV van all lit up, its satellite dish raised on a retractable post. A man in a dark blue parka ran cable from the truck toward my place.

"Looks like we're going to be on the news," David said.

Someone banged on the back door. I closed the kitchen door and stood in the darkened mud room to compose myself before I opened the back door. When I did, I found Heather Franklin on the doorstep.

"Hello, Constable Donner. You remember me?" Heather's voice oozed fake friendliness.

A man with a camera on his shoulder turned on a bright light and aimed it at my face, nearly blinding me. I could barely see Heather through the glare.

"We'd like to talk with David Jordan," Heather said into her microphone. "I understand he's staying with you."

"Get off my property or I'll arrest you for trespassing."

"We'd better get off," I heard the cameraman say. "They could confiscate our tapes." When I was satisfied they were leaving my yard I stomped back into the kitchen.

David, Will, and I stood in the dark in the living room and watched as the news crew picked its way across the frozen scrub to Catherine's. Anne joined us. One of the men fired up a huge spotlight next to the van and aimed it at my house.

We had a while to go before the news came on, so I served chili, fresh Sobeys bakery whole wheat bread, salad and hot tea. We all sensed something ominous brewing outdoors, so after supper we moved the TV and VCR into the kitchen and arranged the chairs so we could all watch. I had no curtains in the living room and didn't want the news crew to see us inside.

I flicked on the TV just as the music and opening animation started. Then over pictures of Cornwallis Cove a male announcer read the headlines: "Devil hysteria: A Nova Scotian community ripped apart. Is this a new cult in the making?"

Though Cornwallis Cove had made the headlines, the story we dreaded wasn't first in the lineup. We had to wait as several international and national news stories went by. I began to grow increasingly anxious. Then the male anchor began to read the introduction to Heather Franklin's story.

"In Cornwallis Cove a charismatic and controversial religious leader who says he can exorcise demons has blown apart this tiny Nova Scotian community. He has whipped up hysteria, splitting families and dividing churches. Some say that a new religious cult is in the making. But, as our reporter Heather Franklin has discovered, some people are ready to exorcise the community of this man with the strange ideas, and an even stranger past."

"Hello, Heather. What's the latest development in Cornwallis Cove?" the announcer asked. Heather's picture popped up side by side with his.

"Hello, Frank. I'm standing outside the home where David Jordan, his wife Anne, and their two children are living under police guard."

"Police guard?" I snorted. "I oughta put a round or two into that spotlight."

The video then moved to the footage of David protesting in front of the abortion clinic and getting arrested.

"David Jordan has left controversy and division behind him every place he's gone," Heather's voice-over said. "He was once a leader in the anti-abortion movement who faced arrest numerous times. This arrest four years ago landed him a month-long jail term.

"That same year, after his release from prison, someone firebombed the abortion clinic in Halifax. Police charged Jordan with arson, but dropped the charges after other anti-abortion activists vouched for his whereabouts. No one was injured in that fire, but the clinic was closed for several weeks.

"Then he surfaced in Sterling County. Last November someone firebombed his home under circumstances quite similar to that of the clinic bombing in Halifax," she said. The TV showed pictures of his burned-out house in South Dare.

"She's insinuating you bombed the clinic and your own house," Will said. Dread ached like frostbite in my gut. I'd helped build that case against David.

"Of course she's staying within legal bounds," I said. David had turned pale.

The report continued. "Shortly after the firebombing of the Jordan house, this man, Reginald Dare, was found dead in the woods behind Jordan's latest church. He'd been shot point-blank with a shotgun blast to the chest."

The screen showed a grainy snapshot of Rex Dare in a work shirt similar to the one he was wearing when he died.

"It wasn't point-blank," Will said. "Don't let the facts get in the way of a good story."

"Tonight in Sterling County police officers told reporters they have found the murder weapon in the Rex Dare case."

Will and I looked at each other, our jaws hanging open. Karen appeared on the screen.

"Ballistics tests show one of the weapons we confiscated is the murder weapon. We have lifted fingerprints from the firearm, and expect to be laying charges tomorrow," she said.

"Three years ago Rex Dare was charged with sexually abusing several children in the community of South Dare, some of them his own," the voice-over continued. "The judge threw the case out of court. But rumours have persisted in the community that Dare was the leader of a satanic cult. David Jordan allegedly tried to stop the cult and exorcise the demons from the children whom he believed the cult had victimized."

The TV showed Bob Oickle standing by the sign outside Cornwallis Cove Baptist Church. "David Jordan has whipped people here into hysteria. It's like the Salem witch trials. He's a dangerous man."

Heather's voice-over continued over a two-shot of her talking with Bob Oickle. "At a special business meeting of the Cornwallis Cove Baptist Church on Sunday the elders and deacons unanimously demanded Pastor Jordan's resignation."

"It was far from unanimous," David said.

"He was hypnotizing people," Oickle fumed. "Causing them to roll around on the floor and bark like dogs. We had to take a stand."

"David Jordan practises medicine without a license," said the chief social worker at the Sterling Department of Mental Health. "We're investigating to see whether charges can be laid against him. The charges relate to a so-called exorcism on a child we cannot identify for reasons of confidentiality. This child is now in the custody of Children's Aid. Her personality has been totally changed. She's no longer recognizable as the child she once was."

Heather's voice-over continued. "Not everyone holds a negative view of David Jordan. In fact, he's attained a level of popularity in Sterling County some officials find disturbing. Experts say hard economic times in Sterling County could lead to a susceptibility to hysteria about devil worship and witchcraft. But, those who support Jordan dismiss charges that he's a demagogue."

The news item cut to a picture of a sober Stan MacIsaac, clean shaven, pressed plaid shirt, and slicked-back hair. "He saved my life. He set me free from the demon of alcohol," Stan said. Then a picture of Heather standing with Pastor Don Harwood appeared on the screen.

"The former senior pastor of Cornwallis Cove Baptist, Don Harwood, resigned when his protégé was forced out," Heather reported.

"I think it's a tragedy," Don Harwood said. "David Jordan is one of the most spiritually gifted men I've ever met. God has used him to heal and deliver people."

"Why did you resign?" Heather asked.

"David has a love for the lost and the unlovely that puts me to shame," Harwood continued. "I'm disappointed that so many in my former congregation would rather stay comfortable than radically trust in a supernatural God. I'm sorry they want to quibble about mistakes in David's past. I'm reminded of the Scripture that says 'The upright man is laughed to scorn.'"

Then Catherine was on-camera.

"Catherine Ross is the editor of the local *Sterling Spectator*."

"Families are divided," Catherine said. "Churches are divided. It's hard to be neutral about David Jordan. People either love him or hate him."

Then Heather spoke directly to the camera.

"Now that David Jordan has been cut off from his source of livelihood at the Cornwallis Cove Baptist Church, some predict he will start up his own ministry and live off donations from the many followers who are only too willing to believe in the power of demonic forces, and in a man who says he can set them free. Frank?"

"Thank you, Heather. When do you expect charges will be laid in the Reginald Dare murder?"

"Frank, we may hear as early as tomorrow. Staff Sergeant Karen Ramsay expects to hold a news conference when the fingerprint tests are complete. We'll be there."

David asked me to turn off the TV. We sat in stunned silence until the phone hanging on the kitchen wall began to warble. I picked up the receiver.

Karen was on the line asking why I told the media the Jordans were under police protection.

"I said nothing to them, except to get off my property."

"Are the Jordans at your house now?"

"Yes."

"Find them another place to stay. Immediately. Check them into a motel in Sterling. You cannot contaminate the arm's-length relationship we must have with people under criminal investigation."

I took a deep breath, stepped into the mud room, and closed the door over the phone cord. I muffled my voice. "What criminal investigation?"

"We're about to charge David Jordan with Rex Dare's murder."

"You're what?"

"His fingerprints are all over the murder weapon. Get him out of your house. That's an order."

"Take your orders and stick them."

"I will pretend you didn't say that."

"I'll have my letter of resignation on your desk tomorrow."

"Don't be foolish. Get those people out of your house. Now! You're tarnishing the reputation of the RCMP if you keep them there." She slammed the phone down.

I opened the mud room door and Will, David, and Anne looked at me in horrified silence.

"What's going on?" Will asked.

"I can't talk about it right now. I can't think straight." I hung up the phone, rubbed my forehead, then paced into the living room and back again.

"Your boss doesn't want us staying here," David said. "We'll leave. You shouldn't jeopardize your career on our account."

"I insist you stay here. This is a matter of principle. I didn't sell my soul to the Mounties when I signed up."

After the Jordans had gone to bed I told Will what Karen had said.

"The tests aren't going to be conclusive," I said.

"What if they are?"

"What do you mean by that?"

"Just what I said. I'm not saying David's guilty. But be prepared that they have some hard evidence." Will pulled a toque over his head and closed the door behind him.

the Charges

When I returned from my run early the next morning the satellite truck was gone and Anne was frying bacon and eggs. I couldn't bear to tell her about the impending charges, not in front of the children, so I rushed upstairs to shower and change into my dress uniform because I had a court appearance later that morning. When I came downstairs wearing my red serge tunic and breeches Catherine was sitting with David and Anne at the kitchen table.

"Heather's pretty sure they're going to charge you with murder today," Catherine said.

"Linda, did you hear that?" David asked.

"Yeah, I did." I wished I'd told them before Catherine had, but now it was too late. "You better call a lawyer. I've got to get to the detachment to see if I can find a way to stop them."

I slipped outside, feeling anguished for the Jordans. Heavy layers of grey clouds hung low in the sky as snow flurries drifted down. Inside my Jeep I tuned the radio to the local station and the DJ warned a blizzard was going to hit Sterling County by nightfall. I mentally catalogued the so-called evidence I had once compiled against David when I was so sure he was the murderer – and a child abuser to boot – and expected to find out somehow his prints were on the murder weapon. I wracked my brain for a possible explanation.

At the detachment Will told me Karen wanted to see us. Instead I sat at the computer and wrote my letter of resignation. Karen appeared in the doorway just as I'd finished printing.

"Donner, I want you in my office," she ordered.

Soon Will, Bob, Eddie, François, and I were seated across from Karen who occupied the chair behind her desk.

"The ballistics results showed the gun you and Will seized from Alan Dare is the murder weapon."

I opened my mouth to speak.

"Quiet! David Jordan's fingerprints are all over that gun. Alan Dare's prints are also there."

I perched on the edge of the chair. "So, why not charge Alan?"

"He said he had lent the shotgun to Cindy," Bob said. "We have other witnesses who say David regularly spent time at Cindy's cabin. Some say they witnessed them involved in sexual activities. As for Rex's murder, David had the motive and the opportunity."

My bowels turned to water. I remembered I had used the exact arguments I was hearing now. "How did the murder weapon end up back at Alan's cabin?"

"He says he found it in the bushes near where the shells were discovered. He recognized it was his and took it home," Bob said. "Besides, Alan didn't have a motive for killing Rex."

"Yes, he did," Will said. "Alan had a crush on Cindy. He might have killed Rex because Rex threatened her. That's a much more plausible scenario to me."

"Alan told us he knew nothing about the Rex Dare murder," I said, hotly. "Yet, you're saying he picked up the shotgun within a rock's throw of where the body was found and brought it home. Why didn't he say anything before now?"

"Well, Alan's a bit slow," Bob said.

"Why didn't you tell us before now that David's prints were on the murder weapon?" Will asked.

"You don't exactly have a lot of objectivity in this, my man," Bob said.

"Why didn't you tell us David was even a suspect?" Will asked Karen.

"You and Donner are under his spell," Eddie said. "You both received his personal blessing on Christmas Eve. And you both took part in an exorcism the same night your car got blown up."

"That's an outright lie," I said. "We were not taking part in it at all."

"Hey, Donner, you did some really good police work in the beginning," Bob said. "Your original notes were great. But then you lost your professional distance."

"If he were the murderer, why would he be so stupid as to throw a gun in the bush that had his fingerprints on it?" I argued. "Whoever left that gun there intended for it to be found, and intended for Cindy or anyone else who'd handled it to get blamed."

"Why don't you go back on stress leave?" Eddie said.

"That's enough, Eddie," Karen said. "Linda, you and Will are too close to this. I'm appalled David Jordan is staying with you, but it won't be for long. He is being arrested as we speak."

My chest felt like it was going to cave in at the thought of David being arrested. The wind beat the branches of a spruce tree against Karen's window.

After the men left her office I handed her my letter.

Karen glanced at the letter and tore it up. "I expect you to go to court today and testify. Then you're going back on stress leave until you snap out of this. You can turn in your gun when you return from court." She tossed the pieces in the trash.

I marched out, sick at heart. I put on my parka and traipsed over to the courthouse, hoping the ten minute outdoor trek would calm me down.

Inside the courtroom I found it hard to pay attention. The hot stuffy room, hard wooden benches, the low-lifes and their hopeless lives made it feel like the waiting room to hell. A massive sense of guilt twisted my gut, forcing me to make several trips to the bathroom.

Michael Ross came in wearing a black robe for his role as Crown prosecutor. Then I felt someone nudge me. Grace had slid onto the bench next to me.

I could feel my face brighten. "What are you doing here, pumpkin?"

"I'm staying with Daddy. Mommy just dropped me off here because she's going to Florida," she whispered.

So, Rafe had persuaded her to go with him. Showed what her priorities were, even on a big news day like this with David being arrested and all. But she'd shown no regard for me or Grace when it came to this sick relationship with Rafe. She was addicted and her weakness repulsed me.

I put my finger over my lips because the judge was peering at us over his reading glasses. Then the clerk called me to testify. Grace beamed with pride as I stood and squeezed past her in my dress uniform.

As I left the stand I mouthed a silent "See you later" to her and left the courtroom.

Through the exterior glass doors I saw Heather standing between two technicians under the building's overhang. Heather held her cell to her ear, her fine straight chin-length hair falling like a curtain in front of her face. A satellite truck was parked on the street and thick blue electrical cables ran up the courthouse steps and into the foyer. I stepped over them, walked over to the clerk's office, and asked to use the phone there. I called home and Anne answered. She told me about the arrest and assured me she was okay. Earl Broadfoot and his wife had arrived to keep her company.

As I put down the phone Bob Morin was leading David Jordan into the clerk's office in handcuffs and leg irons. The sight crushed me.

"Get those leg irons off him," I insisted. "This is ridiculous."

"We always do this with murder suspects. You know that," Bob said.

Inside the court the clerk read out the charges against David who stood alone, his cheap black suit shiny from too many iron-ings, and his greying bushed-out hair with visible comb marks running through it. I felt as guilty as if I had fastened the leg irons myself and was helpless to get them off. *How could I ever have hated this man?* He looked so humble and ordinary. His pant cuffs were salt stained and his heels worn, his shoulders wide but too lean. My throat grew tight and tears burned my eyes. When he turned around his eyes settled on mine and seemed to be full of concern for me. *For me!* And here he was, in leg irons, standing before a judge. David had no lawyer with him. The judge ordered him to be held without bail.

I accompanied him as he shuffled in the leg irons downstairs to the courthouse lock-up, a barred cage housing a couple sets of bunk beds. The custodian unlocked the door and David went inside. Bob unlocked the cuffs and irons. Then, once Bob was outside the cell, the custodian locked the door.

I pressed against the bars. "David, I'm so, so sorry." I wished I could trade places with him. "Can I get you anything?"

"Don't worry, Linda. I'll be fine. Please take care of Anne and the children." He rubbed his wrist. "You could get me a Bible."

I leaned close to the bars. "They found your fingerprints on the shotgun that killed Rex." I knew I might have crossed a professional line by revealing that to him, but heck, his attorney – when he found one – would know that soon enough.

David looked down, his fingers clutching the bars as if deep in thought. "Cindy Dare had a shotgun in her cabin." David locked eyes with me. "Alan had given it to her because she was terrified of the bear. I tried to persuade her to come and stay with Anne and me, but she wouldn't. So I tried to show her how to use the gun safely."

"How come you never told me any of this before?" I asked.

"Never thought it was important."

I gripped the bars and gazed at my boots, feeling hopeless.

"Look at me, Linda. This will all work out. I'll be out of here soon." The bars made shadowy vertical lines on his face.

"This is all my fault."

"You were doing your job. God is in control. He's allowed this to happen for a reason."

When I left the lock-up area I saw a makeshift table had been set up in the foyer. Karen and Michael, still in his black gown, sat behind the table before microphones from several radio and TV stations. A technician fired up powerful lights. Heather stood to the side, glancing into the mirror of a small compact. I pulled the brim of my Stetson low so she wouldn't catch my eye.

Then a tap on my shoulder. Will leaned down close to my ear. "They're bringing Cindy Dare to the nursing home today. She could be here in an hour."

I whirled around, my mouth open, aghast. "No. Please tell me this is a joke."

In a quiet corner of the courthouse hallway I told Will what David had said about how his fingerprints got on the shotgun. Then we agreed to meet later that afternoon at the nursing home when Cindy was scheduled to arrive.

Back at the detachment I wrote up a report of my conversation with David, hoping it might spring him from jail. When I handed it to François he listened politely to what I said, his brown face backlit by the outdoor light from the window behind him. The flurries had stopped, but the skies were still overcast.

"I'll make sure everyone working on this file knows about this," he said. "But this isn't enough to stay the charges."

Then I turned in my gun and asked Debbie to store my personal files. I drove downtown and bought a cup of coffee and a slice of pizza at a café on the waterfront. Sitting in the back I watched the seagulls riding the wind near the outside deck's railing. Even through the plate glass I could hear them keening as if at a funeral. The tide was out and all the fishing boats banged against the public dock's pilings nearly thirty feet below its surface. I felt like a steam shovel had scooped out my insides and my ribcage was caving in. The pizza tasted like ketchup-covered cardboard. I had to make things right and get David out of jail. I had to find the real killer.

At the nursing home, when Cindy's ambulance arrived, Will and I stood in the cold wind as the attendant prepared to move Cindy inside. White blankets covered her up to her chin. She had her eyes screwed shut. *If only she'd talk.*

"They haven't cleaned out Cindy's room yet," Will told me. "The old lady who died is from South Dare. Her name is Ellie. Her son Glendon committed suicide a few years back. They don't know what to do with her personal effects. Why don't *you* take them? We can find out later if there's any next of kin."

Inside, the nursing home smelled of urine, pine disinfectant and steamed carrots. A nervous woman with a plastic name tag that read Dina took me to the room. The bed was stripped to the bare mattress. In the other bed a bald woman with a sunken mouth twitched in her sleep.

Dina rushed out, then came back with some sheets and a plastic cover for the mattress.

When I helped her make the bed her thin face brightened with gratitude.

"This room hasn't been cleaned out properly." Dina smoothed the blanket on the bed. "No close relatives that we know of."

"I'll gather her things together."

Dina thanked me and rushed out again.

I opened one of the dresser drawers and found a flyspecked diary with a blue vinyl cover held closed by a little lock. Underneath was a parcel wrapped in a plastic Sobeys bag. I found a video inside. In the closet I tore a sweater and a couple of housedresses off the clanging hangers. One of the other drawers contained some of Ellie's underwear and socks. I stuffed them into the bag.

"What was the dead lady's name again?" I asked Dina.

"Ellie Dare. I can give you the paperwork we had on her. Maybe you'll find a relative who'd want her things." She pointed to the nightstand and a cheap studio portrait of a handsome but vacant looking young man. "That's her son. You should take that too."

I picked up the photo, also flyspecked and greasy to the touch, and placed it into the now bulging bag. I walked over to the windows and inspected the cheesy vinyl sliders and flimsy locks. The room faced east toward a residential neighbourhood of small bungalows. A small hedge, barren of any leaves, crushed by ice and old snow, edged the parking lot. Snow flurries whirled under a dark grey sky.

The ambulance attendants rolled Cindy down the hall. Her face grimaced in pain and her eyes darted from face to face. Then she clamped them shut. She groaned as the attendants moved her from the gurney to the bed. Dina arranged her bedclothes and cranked the bed up slightly, murmuring words of comfort.

Will lumbered into Cindy's room and sat on a chair next to her bed. "Cindy, Linda and I are your friends. We're friends of Pastor David's too. You can trust us."

Cindy averted her eyes, her chest heaving.

I looked at Will and mouthed, "Does she understand us?"

He shrugged.

I lifted the shopping bag up a little and said to him, "Tell me about Ellie and Glendon. What should I do with her stuff?"

"I found Ellie after her son shot himself in the face with a sawed-off shotgun. She'd been lying in her soiled bedclothes for days. Maggots were all over the sores on her legs. Some things...,"

"There's a diary and a video in here," I said.

"Keep it. We can examine them later. "

Cindy began to wail. She did understand us, or so it seemed. But she would not answer any questions. A nurse burst in, alarmed at her crying, and sedated her.

I spent the rest of the afternoon at the nursing home. Cindy fell into a drugged sleep. The sickly sweet smell of the old lady in the next bed nauseated me. Her meal sat uneaten under the metal covers while the wind howled outside and snow pelted the window.

the Video

I ran to my Jeep with the plastic bag containing Ellie's personal effects. The wind tore at my coat and the icy snowflakes felt like needles on my face. On my way home I detoured by the former Pizza House where Rex Dare's alleged ritual sexual abuse had taken place. Someone had replaced the plywood covering the Quonset hut's front windows with new plate glass. Open Soon! Farm and Garden Supplies. Big Savings! announced posters pasted inside the windows. I'd often driven by here hoping for some inspiration, some clue, and toured the inside several times and came up with nothing. Same thing this trip. The wind blew the snow sideways and the streetlights came on.

It took three times longer than usual to get home. Anne sat at the kitchen table with Earl Broadfoot and his wife Joyce, a tall athletic looking woman with a long face. Donated loaves of homemade bread, muffins, and casseroles covered the counters and filled the fridge.

Anne fixed me a plate and poured me a mug of tea while I brought them up to date on Cindy's arrival in Sterling and what I knew about Ellie. After I ate I took the video and Ellie's son's diary out of the plastic bag. The blizzard howled and moaned outside.

I turned the locked diary over in my hands. "How do I open this?"

Earl produced a Swiss Army knife from his pocket and picked the lock.

Glendon had written his name inside the vinyl cover in childish handwriting. Glendon Dare. As I began reading I found his spelling was terrible but phonetic enough for me to get the gist of what he was saying. From what I read Glendon had fantasies of making big bucks as a Hollywood movie star. The last few pages sickened me. Them movys wernt what I thot. Rex made me hert them kids. He made me do bad bad things. He made me dress like the devil. I spat on his mony.

I passed the entry over to Earl. As he read his cheeks turned a mottled crimson. "Earl, perhaps we should watch the tape alone." I'd moved the TV back into the living room, so he and I headed there. The ladies stayed in the kitchen.

I brought an extra chair in and gestured for Earl to take the recliner. I shoved the tape into the VCR and flicked the remote control. The tape was grainy, badly lit, and showed several men and one woman dressed in animal costumes and devil suits torturing and sexually abusing a group of children. I fought nausea as I strained to recognize anyone. One of the children was Becky Dare. The woman's thick body resembled Dawn's.

My stomach heaved during a scene where a costumed man stabbed a baby with a lance and threw the infant into a fire. I rewound the tape and watched it again. Maybe the baby was a doll, a prop. But terrifying the children with such a scene was grotesque, even if the baby wasn't real.

"If only we'd had this video when Rex went to trial." Earl wrung his hands, then started pulling on the edge of his moustache.

"I don't recognize most of the children in that video," I said. "Where are they now?"

"Some of them were Dawn's kids. They were taken by Children's Aid and have been adopted out of the province," Earl said.

Later that evening in my bedroom I changed into long underwear, jeans, and thick wool socks. I pulled a green wool sweater over a turtleneck, grabbed my sleeping bag and an extra pair of gloves, then headed into the storm to stand watch at the nursing home.

Because of the wind and blinding snow it took me nearly an hour and a half to get back to Sterling. No vehicles except for a solitary yellow snowplough on the highway. Inside the nursing home Will leaned against the wall in Cindy's room as two nurses moved her sunken-mouthed roommate onto a stretcher. They covered the old woman's face.

"You'll have a bed tonight," Will joked, gesturing toward the now vacated bed.

"I've got something to show you." I handed him the video. "If they don't have a VCR here, maybe you should take this back to the detachment."

Cindy lay on the bed, eyes glazed.

"Rex Dare had Glendon abusing children and filmed it," I said to Will. "That tape shows a bunch of people in animal costumes and devil suits torturing children. One of them is Becky. In the diary Glendon says he took part. Your satanic ritual abuse was a porn flick!"

I took the vinyl book out of the plastic bag.

Will shook his head and handed back the tape. "I'll take your word for it."

"Do you think the child pornography is still going on?"

"In South Dare, anything's possible."

Tears rolled down Cindy's cheeks, though her eyes were fixed on a spot on the wall. I whispered for Will to take a look at her.

"Remember that business card we found in the car that hit Cindy? Maybe Virtuality is an outlet to sell this garbage," I said.

"That card could have been there from a previous renter, though. Lots of Quebeckers vacation in Florida."

"You know, if David did kill Rex, I wouldn't blame him. Not after seeing that tape. I wish I could kill him a second time."

"I hear you."

I studied Cindy's face. Her eyes were closed and her fingers clutched the blanket covering her chest. "So, who ran her down?"

"Lonnie. Of course he denies it. And he has about forty people in South Dare willing to say he was home that day." Will sat down on the other side of Cindy's bed. "And Cindy won't talk to us."

I told Will what Dot had sent me about Rafe having once been charged with prostitution-related offences. Will shrugged and suggested I contact Miami Vice. I borrowed his cell and slipped into the hall. I called one of my contacts in the States, someone I'd worked with on an international Internet child porn sting. I was surprised and relieved to find him at home. After a minimal amount of small talk I asked him if he had any contacts in Miami who might help me. He gave me the name of Detective Alberto Rodriguez on the Vice Squad of the Miami PD, his direct phone line, cell and home phone number. *Why hadn't I thought of this sooner?*

I called the office first. The phone rang and rang. I was just about to press end when a man with a high hoarse voice answered.

"Vice. Detective Rodriguez."

I told him who I was and why I was calling.

"What do you know about Virtuality XXX?" I had my pen poised over a notebook.

"Oh, yeah. They sold pornographic videos, DVDs and CDs, interactive stuff for the high-tech types."

"Any child porn?"

"Not that I know of. I hate to say it, but the kind of garbage they sold happens to be legal. But the business folded, or moved on," he said.

I explained to him about the video, the business card, the sexually abused children in South Dare, and my concerns there might be a Florida connection.

"Would you be willing to find out where the owner of Virtuality has moved to?"

"If those scumbags are selling kiddy porn, then I'd love an excuse to nail them," he said.

Then I asked him about Rafe Lupien. Rodriguez said the name wasn't familiar. He couldn't remember the Virtuality owner's name, but he was sure it wasn't that.

I gave Rodriguez Rafe's Florida driver's license number and told him to expect an e-mail from Will the next day with Rafe's photo attached. I knew the photo I'd taken from Catherine's would be useful. Rodriguez promised to check out both Rafe and the former porn company.

Back inside Cindy's room I handed Will his cell, feeling I was finally making some progress. Then I heard the sound of boots pounding the hallway outside. Bob and Eddie stomped the snow off as they entered Cindy's room, their hats and shoulders white with snow.

"Cindy's not supposed to have any visitors," Eddie said. "Get lost, Donner, you're interfering with an investigation."

"Has she said anything?" Bob asked Will.

"No," Will said, standing up.

Bob took the seat next to her bed. "Mrs. Dare!" Bob shouted. "Can you hear me?"

"She's not deaf," I said, standing at the foot of her bed next to Will.

"Shut up!" Eddie said.

Bob glowered at me. "Get lost, Donner. Seriously."

"Cindy, did you know that David Jordan has been charged with the murder of your – of Rex Dare?" Bob shouted again.

No response.

"We suspect you may have been an accessory to the crime!" Bob shouted again.

Eddie moved to the head of the bed on the other side. "We know you're a witness," he said, softly. "We can protect you. Tell us, Cindy, was David Jordan the man who tried to run you over in Lunenburg?"

"Oh, come on!" I said.

"Get out of here, Donner!" Bob shouted.

Will took me by the elbow and led me out of the room. I watched Cindy's eyes follow us. She was terrified – the same haunting fear I remembered when I surprised her outside the church the day Rex was killed. As soon as Will and I were outside the door she began to scream in a high-pitched wail.

A nurse barged past us as Cindy's wail continued. Will and I edged back to the door. Her crying was even more hysterical than it had been earlier.

"Hush, hush," the nurse said. She was a woman about my age with long brown hair pinned at the nape of her neck. She had freckles, hazel eyes, and a long pointed nose. "We can't have you upsetting her like this," she said to Bob and Eddie. "She's going to disturb all the other patients in here. I think all of you should leave."

"This is a police investigation," Bob said.

"I'll have to call the doctor," the nurse said. "Please leave. I'll call your superior if you don't. She could go into shock."

Outside, the four of us crowded under the overhang at the front door. Howling winds drove the snow against our faces, making us squint and pull up our collars.

"Donner, I don't want you anywhere near her!" Bob shouted over the wind.

We scraped off our vehicles while the wind whistled around us. Bob and Eddie left in separate cars. I removed Rafe's photo from the back of my Jeep, slipped it under my parka, then climbed into Will's truck. After reassuring me he'd scan and e-mail it to Rodriguez in Miami he placed it on the seat between us and looked at me wistfully. Feeling awkward I took out my notebook and gave him Rodriguez's e-mail address a second time. Then I told him I'd sneak back to the nursing home as soon as I knew Bob and Eddie were off duty.

By the time it was safe to return to the nursing home several more inches had accumulated and the wind was whipping the snow into drifts. I positioned my Jeep where I could see Cindy's window and the back entrance. The wind sculpted the snow-covered cars into weird shapes like great white sharks. I hunkered into my parka, turning the heat on every now and then to take the edge off the chill. I frequently had to get out to stretch my legs and clear the windshield.

Periodically I tested all the nursing home's exterior doors to make sure they were locked. The wind tried to rip my hood off my head. Already snow had drifted a couple of feet deep in places. I trudged back to my Jeep and once inside I unrolled my sleeping bag, pulled it up over my feet, reclined my seat, and listened to the radio. I found a Christian station from the States.

A male announcer with a Southern twang said, "God says in the Book of Ezekiel 'A new heart also will I give you, and a new spirit will I put within you; and I will take away the stony heart out of your flesh, and I will give you a heart of flesh.'"

I reached forward and turned the volume down, then leaned back against the seat, my arms across my chest. I felt like I had a heart of flesh just out of the freezer that hadn't entirely thawed yet. Snow pelted the windows as I snuggled into the sleeping bag.

At 6:07 a.m. I waded through the snow across the darkened parking lot to test the front door again. It was still locked. The nurse who'd ordered us to leave the previous night saw me and unlocked the door. She asked me what I was doing. When I told her my name she grinned and invited me to come in for a coffee.

I was surprised at the sudden change in her attitude. I told her I had to go shut off my Jeep and I'd be right in.

We sat down behind the counter overlooking the entrance hall and she brought me a mug of coffee. Her hair was coming loose, and while most of it was still clasped to the back of her head, some longish strands framed her freckled face. Her pointed nose and chin made her look regal and haughty, though when she smiled her face was radiant.

"I've heard about you. I know David and Anne Jordan. I support the work he's doing. My name is Jessica. Jessica Vandergrift."

She told me her husband had been present for Becky's exorcism.

"We've located Becky. She's fine. She's with a Christian foster family, isn't that amazing? We're trying to arrange to bring her to see her mother. It might help Cindy come out of the trance she's in. No one's been able to reach her. But when I told Cindy her daughter was safe she seemed to respond."

I nodded. "Yeah, I get the impression she's taking in what's being said. At least some of the time."

When I stepped outside into the morning darkness the wind had died down, but the temperature had dropped. A tractor had cleared a patch in the parking lot. My heart then sank as an immense municipal snowplough came along and swept a massive drift across the lot's entrance. I shovelled as many of the big snow chunks aside as I could.

Then I scraped and shovelled to free my snow-covered Jeep. Once I had the windows cleared off and the interior warm I fastened my seatbelt and tried to plough through the remaining drift to the road, wincing as the Jeep bumped against some remaining icy chunks. I got stuck and had to shovel some more to get clear.

I stayed on the highway's single ploughed lane, but the road along the cove was pure white. Not a tire track. I stopped, uncertain whether I could make it because of the drifts. Then I noticed a huge yellow snowplough looming up behind me, yellow lights flashing. I got out of my Jeep and asked the driver if he could also plough the sideroad up past my house. I followed the plough as it threw curtains of snow onto the shoulder.

I parked on the road and waded through two-foot drifts to my back door. Inside the kitchen I told Anne about the latest developments at the nursing home.

"That's wonderful about Becky," Anne said. "But I don't trust Cindy. You know that back in Halifax she turned against David and lied about him."

"Yes, I know. Why? Do you have any idea?"

"David thought Rex forced her to. Rex had Becky with him and wouldn't let Cindy see her. Cindy didn't seem so innocent to me. I used to think David was too naive to see how manipulative and attention seeking she was. But then I realized he did see it, but he saw past it, to Christ in her. I'm not able to do that with people the way David does."

"Your faith right now is amazing."

"I've had to choose faith because I would find all this unbearable otherwise. But you know what? God has never been more real to me."

I climbed upstairs and tried to get a few hours sleep. *Would He ever be as real to me?*

the Seduction

Later that morning sun streamed in despite my window blinds. The bedroom door squeaked open a crack, then closed. I heard children giggling. I smiled, stretched, and looked at my alarm clock. *What day is it?* It was 11:47. Then the door opened again and Joy peeked in, her chubby little hand on the doorknob, her smile showing neat little rows of baby teeth.

"Hi, Joy. Come on in. Where's Samuel?"

Joy shut the door and her feet pattered away down the hall. I could hear Anne gently rebuking her children for bothering me. The phone rang. I reached over to my nightstand and picked up the receiver. It was Will. He told me he was out on Cape Sterling trying to find out where and when the big shipload of drugs was coming in. Then reality dropped on me like a load of wet cement. David was in prison and no one was guarding Cindy.

"Linda, they're bringing David to court this afternoon for a plea and then they're taking him down to Sackville, to the correctional centre."

I swung my feet off the bed and sat up straight, my stomach wrenching. "Today? The regular plea day is Monday. The roads aren't even cleared yet."

"You should see the angry crowds already hanging around the courthouse. The powers that be want David out of town as soon as possible."

"I'll be right in. I'll bring Anne and the kids." I raked my fingers through my matted hair.

I told Will the latest news about Becky. He assured me he'd sent Rafe's picture to Rodriguez in Miami.

Downstairs, after I showered and dressed in some pressed jeans and my red sweater, I wolfed down a fried egg sandwich while Anne got the kids into their snowsuits and boots.

Outside, the sun was blinding, glancing off the fresh snow. A snowplough had been through and left a trail of sand on the white road. Once we were on our way in my Jeep little Samuel fell asleep, while Joy pointed out the window and chattered about what she saw. Anne wrung her hands in her lap. The bright sunlight was harsh and provided no warmth in the frigid air.

At the courthouse, cars lined the side streets up against the three-foot snow banks. I dropped Anne and the children off. They waddled in their padded snowsuits and Samuel had to climb slowly, one step at a time. I parked at the detachment several blocks away, then sprinted through the snow back to the courthouse, the powdery snow filtering over my boots and down into my socks. I bounded up the steps into the lobby now packed with people. Catherine was missing Sterling's story of the year to be with Rafe in Florida.

The bailiff tried to bar my entrance, but stepped aside when he recognized me. Just as I entered, the clerk had asked everyone to rise for the judge. I couldn't see Anne, so I squeezed in near the back.

The proceedings were over in a matter of seconds. Michael Ross stood before the judge's bench wearing a long black legal gown. David Jordan, wearing the same shiny black suit, stood next to his new lawyer, Claire Lauren, a short wide woman with bright red hair.

David pleaded not guilty and asked to be tried in Supreme Court with a judge and jury. The judge denied the request for bail. Then the sheriff accompanied David out of the courtroom and back to the lock-up. I winced when I saw the leg irons again and the way they made David shuffle and stoop. Finally, the clerk asked us to rise as the judge left the courtroom. I pressed through the crowd to find Anne weeping, Samuel's little face red and solemn, and Joy, her rounded brow puckered with worry, patting her mother on the back. Soon women from Cornwallis Cove Baptist surrounded Anne and began to comfort her. Knowing she was in good hands I left the courtroom to find Michael.

He was at the top of the courthouse steps, still wearing his black legal gown, smoking.

"Why have you charged him?" I said. "You have no case."

"Constable Donner!" He grinned, then blew smoke out the side of his mouth. "Thanks to you, I think we do."

I told him how David's fingerprints came to be on the murder weapon.

"Your corporal passed that along to me. The fingerprints are only part of the case we have against him. As you know."

"I was wrong."

"Why don't you come by and see me at my office? I'd be happy to listen. But I don't promise to be convinced." Then he winked.

Then I asked him if I could see Grace.

"Sure. Tomorrow after school is probably okay. Just let me check first to see if she has piano lessons or something like that. I guess you've got plenty of time now that you're on stress leave."

I was taken aback, amazed at how fast the news had travelled.

Michael crushed the cigarette butt against the marble step with his shiny black shoe. "Talk to you tomorrow, okay?"

When I returned home with Anne and the children the sun was slipping behind the line of trees at the edge of the pasture behind my house. After supper Anne did the dishes and I went up to my bedroom and phoned Rodriguez in Miami. He told me he did know of Rafe Lupien – under the name Ralph Eddine.

"A rap sheet?" I held the receiver to my ear with my shoulder while I found a pen in the drawer and opened a notebook.

"No. We couldn't make the prostitution-related charges stick. None of the women working for him would testify. He had a hypnotic power over them."

"He's a handsome fellow," I said, unable to keep the disgust out of my voice.

"Well, that ain't his real honker. It's a nose job. He had his chin rebuilt too."

"Any connections to the porn industry?"

"Nothing I know of. He has connections with all the big-time scum in Miami, though. We've seen Ralph hanging out with the drug lords, the kingpins in prostitution and other rackets. He had a travel business for a while and also owned some nice yachts he hired out, so we suspected drug smuggling. His businesses smelled to high heaven, but he's one smart cookie. He's not like most of the dregs we deal with because he doesn't have a secret wish to get caught."

I tugged at my hair until my scalp hurt. "He says now he's got some kind of video production business and does some computer-related stuff. I thought he was smuggling drugs. But maybe the video business is porn related."

"He has the right contacts for both. If his computer business is legit, maybe that's why I don't know about it. If he's dealing large quantities of drugs, or into child porn, I can find out."

Rodriguez said he hadn't had a chance to look into what had become of Virtuality XXX, but he'd go check it out the next day.

Through the window I saw headlights turning into my laneway and recognized Will's truck. I ran my fingers through my hair as I went downstairs and heard him stomping the snow off his boots in the mud room. When he entered the kitchen Anne welcomed him with a hug. He smiled at me over her shoulder. Then he greeted the kids, sat on the daybed, and roughhoused with them for a while. Samuel and Joy were soon laughing and climbing all over him. He tried to keep them from grabbing a large manila envelope, which he eventually handed to me.

Anne took the children upstairs to get them ready for bed. Will joined me at the kitchen table. I opened the envelope and pulled out the picture of Rafe I'd removed from Catherine's house. "He had a nose job." Then I told him what Rodriguez had said.

Will picked up the pepper shaker and rolled it in his hands. "Linda."

"Is George Hall involved in any this?"

Will shrugged. "I don't know. If I were to suspect George of anything, it would be drug smuggling because he's the only one with the bankroll, and the brains."

Will pushed the pepper shaker to the centre of the table. "I need to talk to you."

"What?" I glanced at him, my train of thought broken.

He sat kitty-corner to me at the table. His eyes looked tired and his expression serious. "Can you stop thinking about work for a minute?"

I immediately felt tense and self-conscious. I stood up. "I'll make some tea."

"I don't need any tea. Do you?"

I didn't know whether to sit or stand. He took my hand and gently pulled me down onto my chair. I withdrew it and busied myself, moving the chair closer to the table. My heart thudded and my face grew warm.

"Why do you treat me like a stranger?"

"I don't know what you're talking about."

"When we're alone all you do is talk about David or Cindy or Rex."

"Don't you think it's important?"

"Of course. But what about us?"

"There's an us? How come I don't know about it?" I quipped, smiling. The hurt look on his face made me wish I'd kept my mouth shut.

"Why are you brushing me off?"

I silently squirmed. "Maybe I'm not ready for what you're looking for."

"What do you think I'm looking for?" His expression was serious, but his eyes shone with love and concern. He took my hand, which was as tense as a lobster claw. His was big and warm. I averted my eyes.

"I don't know."

"I love you, Linda."

I glanced at his face quickly again.

He let go of my hand. "I'm sorry. I'm scaring you to death."

I felt a smile flicker on my lips. "That's an understatement."

"Me too. Look at me. I'm shaking."

He looked calm and solid as he always did.

"You want a girlfriend? A lover? What do you want from me?"

"I want you to love me."

Right at that moment I felt nothing for him. Just frozen. Numb. "I thought you knew how I felt about you." I clacked the salt and pepper together.

"I thought I did. But you've been so cold."

My chest tightened. "All I can think about is getting David out of jail. I don't think I can handle any extra emotional demands right now."

"We could do that as a team. You don't have to shut me out, Linda."

I shrugged.

"Maybe you have other reasons for shutting me out..."

"Maybe because I'm a *lesbian*?" I cringed as soon as I blurted out the words. A wave of pain surged through me. All the hurt I'd pressed down after Rafe and Catherine's accusations and the taunts from colleagues at work. But even deeper than that, I realized I was unable to respond to Will the way I wanted to. Especially when I was with him. I loved him when he wasn't around, and yearned for him, but when he was present, most of the time I felt frozen.

"A lesbian? No, that's not what I was thinking."

Tears spilled out of my eyes. I pinched them shut, trying to hold them back. My nose ran. I longed to be able to tell Will I loved him. That he was my best friend. But every time I thought about physical contact with him, even a hug, something in me resisted and shut down.

"Is that what you're afraid of? That you're a lesbian?"

"I don't know what I'm afraid of," I whispered and began to sob, big chest-heaving sobs. Will grabbed some paper towels for me. I wiped my face.

"Do you think that even if you were a lesbian that would change how I feel about you? I'd still want us to be friends. Close friends." He stood up again and stretched.

"Please, don't go," I said.

"I'm not leaving. The chair's uncomfortable and I'm beat. Maybe I will have some tea. I'll make it." He filled the kettle with water and set it over the hot part of the stove. Then he took off his Sam Browne and carefully laid it on the floor, his pistol still in the holster. I heard the springs on the daybed groan as he sat back against the pillows. I remained at the table, trying to regain my composure.

When the kettle boiled I made tea and brought him a mug. He now sat on the edge of the bed, so I sat next to him, close enough to feel the warmth of his body. He gently brushed the hair away from my face, and brushed my cheek with the back of his hand.

"Do you feel attracted to women?"

I shook my head.

"You're probably not a lesbian, then."

"Maybe I haven't met the right woman yet."

We both laughed. But that pain inside me was radiating in waves, and soon I was laughing and crying at the same time. I suspected my possessiveness about Grace and Catherine had been inappropriate, but the feelings were never sexual.

"Are you attracted to men?"

"I haven't been attracted to men in a long time," I said, anxiety building again. I didn't tell him I'd had a couple of boyfriends, and had even lived with a guy for a year, but felt nothing for them. I went through the motions, that's all.

Father Ron's face then swam by in my mind, his hypnotic ice blue eyes and his white clerical collar.

"What's happening, Linda? You're drifting away."

"I was in love with a man once," I said, choking on the words. "I was thirteen."

"That's awfully young."

I forced out the words: "He was a priest."

"Did I hear you right? A priest?"

I nodded.

"A Catholic priest?"

I buried my head in my hands.

"I'm not sure I understand." Will put his arm across my back and drew me close. I pressed my wet face against his shoulder.

"His name was Ron. He seduced me and several other girls at my school. Got me doing things that made me so uncomfortable, but I couldn't say no to him." I took a breath. "Then one day, he raped me. But even after that he had an awful hold on me. I kept on meeting him. We had intercourse maybe three or four times. I got pregnant." My voice sounded like a forlorn thirteen-year-old girl. I could hardly talk.

"When I told him I was pregnant, he said it wasn't his." I sobbed. "He called me a 'habitual liar.' Then a day later I stumbled across him at the Arboretum, this park he used to take me to. He had Tammy Moriarty down on her knees."

Will groaned in disgust. Then he hugged me tight.

"Ron seduced five other girls in my class. Two of them while he was also seducing me.

"The most sordid thing in my life was the trial. I had to sit there, my stomach the size of a beach ball, and testify against Ron while his lawyer tried to blame me for what happened. I could feel the baby kicking.

"Then I had to listen to five other girls tell almost the same story. He made us all feel special, but none of us were. Dad wept when I was on the stand. It was unbearable."

"What happened to the baby?"

"I gave her up for adoption. I've felt guilty ever since."

Will put his arm across my shoulder and pulled me close while I sobbed, still burying my face in my hands.

"You and Veronica are the only ones who know. I've carried this knot of hatred more than half my life. I know I'm supposed to forgive him, but I can't."

Will held me for several minutes until I stopped crying.

"I made a vow to myself that I would never allow someone to hurt me again. I've been emotionally numb ever since. I want to let people in, but I can't. Not the way I'd like to."

"Maybe you're punishing yourself." Will stroked my hair. "Maybe it's time to forgive *you*."

"I don't understand." I felt a wave of resentment and disentangled myself from his arms. "Why would I need to forgive myself?"

"Maybe you blame yourself for the feelings you had."

I stood up. "Are you saying I brought this on myself? That I asked for it?"

"Of course not! Linda, please sit down."

"I didn't pour out my life story to get a lecture. And I don't like hearing you talk like Ron's lawyer. He tried to make me and the other girls out to be a bunch of whores."

"That's not what I said. Linda, I'm sorry if I didn't put it right." He took my hand and pulled me down next to him.

"You invited him to your bedroom, didn't you?" Ron's lawyer had said, pointing his finger at me during cross-examination. "This wasn't rape. This wasn't even seduction. Your Honour, this was a sexually precocious young woman eager to manipulate and ensnare this emotionally vulnerable young man."

Will's voice snapped me back to the present. "Linda, what this man did to you was criminal. I've read that girls and boys who have been abused by people in positions of trust sometimes feel betrayed by their own bodies. You couldn't help the way you responded. Seducers like this priest know how to manipulate the feelings of their victims, to groom them. These predators can draw up emotional cravings and sexual feelings in their victims. You know that."

I removed my hand as if his had suddenly turned red hot. "I didn't enjoy the sex with him, Will. I find it totally offensive that you would even assume that. Every child molester fantasizes children enjoy what they do to them."

"I'm not assuming anything. I'm sorry if I said the wrong thing. Please forgive me." He put his arms around me. I shook myself loose.

"I was a virgin. He raped me. It hurt, for crying out loud. Other stuff he did to me repulsed me. I knew it was wrong. But he was a priest. I was raised to put priests on a pedestal. He told me I had to learn to surrender to God. The creep."

Will hugged me to him. My face was crushed against his grey shirt.

"Since Ron, I haven't been able to enjoy affection either. I don't need you to hold me."

Will let go of me and lay back against the pillows. "Can I do it anyway?"

He gently pulled me down so my head rested on his chest.

"Don't worry, I'm not going to take advantage of you. I'd never do that." He slipped one of his hands over mine.

"As if you could."

He stroked my hair, and I relaxed. In a few minutes he was breathing slowly and steadily and I realized he was asleep. I disentangled myself from him and looked at his broad forehead, freckled face and reddish eyebrows. I was tired too and wanted to rest next to him, but had to go to the nursing home to keep watch over Cindy.

Sitting on the edge of the daybed I shook him awake just before I left. Still lying against the pillows he studied my face, his eyes shining with love. "You feeling better?"

"Yes. Thanks for being my friend." I melted into his arms. *I love you, Will.*

I didn't want to let go.

Then the old feelings began to frighten me again, so I did.

the **Forgiveness**

A few minutes later Will was driving home and I was on my way to the nursing home.

When I arrived Jessica, the night nurse, accompanied me down the darkened hallway to Cindy's room. She was sleeping and a new roommate occupied the next bed. I opened the curtains to scan the parking lot. Nothing unusual. Then I checked all the exits and found them secure.

Jessica told me I could rest in the lounge, which was about halfway down the hall and on the same side of the building as Cindy's room. My bunched-up parka made a half-decent pillow on the vinyl couch.

"A new heart also will I give you...." I could feel. My heart felt new and fresh, thawed and vibrant with feeling. My love for Grace had been a forerunner to this pulsing, overflowing sense of being alive, awake and whole.

I pushed the table aside and got down on my knees. *Thank you, Lord. Thank you for Will.* My heart was full of praise and thanksgiving, but soon the room grew strangely quiet. I heard the old man snoring in the room across the hall and the *tick, tick, tick* as the wall clock's second hand moved. In the stillness I became aware of the toxic hatred I still felt for Ron. I could feel it burning like smouldering coals ready to ignite. Then a strong impression came over me that stopped me short. *You must forgive him.* It was not an ordinary thought. It was a command, and not exactly in words – but in feeling – and the meaning was clear.

Something inside me began to writhe and squirm. I felt like part of me was shaking my fist at the sky saying, *I won't forgive Ron. I hate him. Look what he did to me.* I recognized part of me thrived on hating and judging others, as well as hating God. I didn't want to feed that part of me anymore, but because I'd identified with her for so long, I felt like I was dying. Yet somehow I knew my new spiritual life depended on resisting her.

"Jesus, I choose to obey you," I said out loud, even though sweat had broken out on my forehead. "I forgive Ron. But please, help me, because I hate him so much." My breathing was slow and heavy, and hot tears rolled down my cheeks and spilled onto the vinyl couch. I wiped my nose with the woollen sleeve of my sweater. I kept on resisting the feelings of hatred, and prayed with deep longing beyond words until the hatred changed into a feeling of deep hurt. "I forgive him for hurting me," I said. *You must forgive yourself as well. Give yourself permission to feel again.*

After several moments the hurt faded into a sorrow so sweet my tears mingled with joy. *Lord, I choose to forgive myself. Please help me.* I realized what comfort and joy I'd been missing for so long by shutting God out of my life, by dismissing the faith I'd grown up with, and holding onto hatred and grudges instead.

The time of deep spiritual communion ended when I heard the phone ringing out at the front desk. *That's odd. Who would be calling at this time of night?* A few minutes later it rang again. Then again. I crept down the hall, carrying my flashlight. At the front desk Jessica's forehead was creased with worry.

"What's going on?"

"I don't know. The phone keeps ringing and each time I pick it up there's nobody there."

Suddenly, a blast of cold air blew down the hallway. Someone had opened the back door. The phone calls had been a diversion.

"Pull the fire alarm! Call the police!" I shouted as I ran down the hallway toward Cindy's room. The lights went off, leaving only low emergency lights near the exits. The other two nursing assistants raced past me to the front desk.

At the end of the hall a shovel propped the back door open. I had no gun, but decided to pretend I did. When I reached Cindy's room I flicked on the flashlight, swept the room with its beam, and hollered, "Freeze!" A man wearing pantyhose over his head was holding a pillow over Cindy's face.

Suddenly, the fire alarm began to clang, making a jarring sound so loud my ears hurt. Someone hit me from behind and I fell against the wall, nearly losing consciousness. But I sensed the man at Cindy's bedside rush past me and outside. I staggered after the fleeing men until I was sure they'd left the building. The back door was closed now, but still unlocked. I twisted the deadbolt into position, then raced back over to Cindy's bedside. She was gasping for air. When I made sure she could breathe I tried to reassure her she'd be okay.

I rushed to her window and watched a white pickup barrel out of the parking lot with its lights off. The fire alarm made my head throb. When I reached up to feel the goose egg on the back of my head my hand came away sticky and wet with blood.

The firefighters soon arrived, shut off the alarm, and gave Cindy some oxygen. They helped me inspect the entire home to make sure all the intruders were gone. Ten minutes later Bob arrived.

I couldn't resist reminding him that Cindy would be dead now if I hadn't defied his orders.

Jessica led me into a bathroom and washed the blood off my head, face and hands. My scalp burned when the cool water ran over it. I watched the pink blood-tinged water whirl down the drain. She gave me a large gauze pad, ice bag, and white towel to hold against the back of my head. Then we went into Cindy's room where one of the nursing assistants was sponging her forehead with a washcloth. Jessica sat next to her bed and took Cindy's limp hand in hers. The old woman in the next bed snored and wheezed. Bob stood behind me at the foot of the bed.

"Cindy, do you know who tried to kill you just now?" I asked.

She shook her head.

Astonished she actually responded I leaned over her. "Do you know how Rex Dare died?"

She looked straight ahead, paralyzed with fear. I was tired, cranky, and my head was throbbing. I tapped Jessica on the shoulder and asked if I could take her seat.

I sat down. "Listen, Cindy," I said. "Someone dear to both of us could go to jail for the rest of his life if you don't tell us what you know. Do you want David Jordan to go to prison for something he didn't do?"

"Don't put words in her mouth!" Bob said.

"I know what I'm doing," I snapped. I turned toward her again. "This man here, this police officer, is convinced David Jordan killed Rex Dare," I told her. "Is he right?"

Cindy began to tremble. I put the towel, bloody gauze pad, and ice pack on my lap to free both my hands. Leaning forward I clapped my hands in front of Cindy's face. She jumped.

"Snap out of it!" I yelled.

"Cut it out, Donner." Bob grabbed my shoulder.

I shook his hand off. "I'm not leaving until she tells us the truth." I picked up the towel, ice pack, and gauze again and held it against my sore head. "For crying out loud, Cindy! Talk to me." My voice cracked. "You can help David if you want to."

"Come on, Linda, someone just tried to kill her," Bob said. "And you need stitches. You may have a concussion."

Bob's professional manner persuaded me to get up, reluctantly. Cindy still trembled, but now she was looking at me instead of looking hypnotized.

"Cindy. Are you going to let David Jordan – "

Bob yanked my shoulder. "Come on. You're badgering her. Let's go!"

As he prodded me into the hall Jessica shot me a look of sympathy. Then I heard Cindy mumble something. I froze. Bob and I traded glances and we headed back into her room.

"What did you say?" Jessica was seated next to Cindy and leaning close to her, holding her hand. Bob and I stood on either side of her bed.

"I..." Cindy paused and bit her lip. "I killed Rex," she whispered.

"Look Cindy," Bob said, "Don't tell us something that isn't true just because – "

"I killed Rex," she said, more loudly this time. "I killed him. I shot him with Alan's shotgun." Cindy's teeth chattered. Her skin had turned a blotchy pink and white and her lips were bluish.

"You aren't saying this because you want to protect David Jordan?" Bob said.

"No. I want to stop hiding. I killed him," she said.

Bob sighed and flipped open his notebook. "Would you like to make a statement?"

He advised her of her rights, including her right to have a lawyer. Cindy said she didn't want one.

"Why did you kill him?" Bob asked.

"Because he wanted to keep using Becky," Cindy said. "Because I was tired of living afraid all the time. Because he was evil."

During the interview it was clear she knew specific details that only someone at the murder scene could have known. She described how Rex had been smoking a cigarette when she shot him. How she'd called his name and he'd faced her. When Bob finished taking her statement he accompanied me to the nursing station near the front door.

"So what, she confessed," Bob said. "That still doesn't rule David Jordan out."

I held the ice pack to my head. "I disagree. You've got to let David go now."

"I'll drive you to the hospital," Bob said.

"Nah, I can drive. I'm okay," I said. *Why would I accept help from him?* He was still bent on proving David guilty, despite what Cindy said.

Outside, Bob and I discovered someone had bashed in the windshield of my Jeep and slashed the tires. So I returned inside the nursing home to rest in the lounge while Bob waited in the foyer for IDENT.

I phoned Will and filled him in. He rushed over. When he arrived I got up, still holding the ice bag against my head, and let him hold me. It felt so good to lean against him and I didn't care if Bob saw us.

While Bob continued to wait for IDENT Will phoned the detachment and told Karen. She told him to bring me to an 11 a.m. meeting at the Crown prosecutor's office.

Will drove me home so I could shower and change. At home I told Anne about Cindy's confession. Her tense shoulders dropped about three inches.

By 11 a.m. I was back in uniform, sitting in Crown Prosecutor Michael Ross's office with Eddie, Bob, François and Karen. I even had my gun back. Will had returned to the nursing home to keep watch over Cindy.

The meeting wasn't going well, though. I found myself getting impatient.

"She confessed after you badgered her," Bob said.

"How did she know Alan's shotgun was the murder weapon?" I asked.

"Because you told her?" Bob said.

"I never said a word to her," I said. "David Jordan showed Cindy how to use Alan's gun. That explains his fingerprints being there."

"I don't believe Cindy," Bob said. "She's never had one iota of credibility."

The goose egg throbbed and my scalp hurt. "But she mentioned the cigarette," I said. "That's the key. Only the murderer knew Rex was smoking a cigarette when he got shot and that he turned to face the shooter."

"Unless someone privy to the investigation is blabbing about the evidence," Eddie said.

Michael looked puffy and hungover. "This is a mess." He locked eyes with Karen.

She nodded slowly. "With Cindy's track record we run the risk of releasing David, then having Cindy recant her confession."

"What about a polygraph test?" I said.

"What good will that do?" Bob said.

"We'll at least have a better idea of whether she's lying or not."

Michael rubbed his eyes. "I don't know what to do. We try David and his defence lawyer trots out Cindy Dare who says she did it. So, I rip her credibility to shreds with your help. But then the jury sympathizes with her because we're beating up on the poor thing."

"Cindy's prints weren't even on the gun." Eddie said.

"Ever hear of gloves?" I shot back.

"Does Cindy have a lawyer yet?" Karen asked.

"No. She waived an attorney. There's always the risk her confession could be ruled inadmissible," Bob said. "If she goes back into one of her mysterious silences, then where are we?"

"If we drop the charges against Jordan and charge Cindy instead, any of the criminal lawyers will use the battered wife's defence." Michael massaged his forehead. "We've got to disclose this to David's lawyer – Claire."

We didn't reach any conclusions. To my frustration Michael and Karen thought it would be wise to wait and not release David. They arranged for Claire to interview Cindy at the nursing home.

Karen insisted I see a doctor to make sure I didn't have a concussion. At the clinic the doctor stitched up my scalp, examined the goose egg, and told me to take it easy for a couple of days. From the hospital I called a cab to take me back to the nursing home so I could bring Will up to date.

Though Cindy's confession was good news for David, both of us were discouraged that our colleagues still saw him as a suspect. We were both starved, so we sent out for fried scallops and chips and ate them in the lounge off Cindy's room. A group of patients in wheelchairs clustered by the TV, watching a game show. Will and I sat side by side on a couch along the back wall.

He squeezed my hand. "I don't think I could handle it if anything happened to you."

My fingers flew up to the goose egg hidden by my hair. "I'm fine. It wasn't anything, really."

He tugged at my hand. "That's not what I meant. Look at me."

I did. I looked at his intense blue eyes, his reddish hair swept back off his forehead, his pale eyebrows, his freckles, his clean shave and his square jaw. I could hear the TV blaring in the room, but time slowed and I didn't know if I was still breathing. I was between breaths. *I love you. Is that what you mean?*

I dropped my eyes. "People are looking at us."

"They can't see this far." He tipped my chin, a half smile on his face, and gazed at me for a few moments, his eyes shining with love. He was the most beautiful man I'd ever met. Then he leaned over and kissed my lips. His were cool, and soft. His gentle kiss stirred feelings I thought I was no longer capable of. He was gazing at me again, and the best I could do was not pull away. Not hide. He touched my cheek and stroked my hair. I snuggled into him, grateful for this soft place in my life where it was okay to fall.

After a while I looked at my watch. One twenty-seven p.m. I hoped to see Grace that afternoon after school, so I excused myself and used the front desk phone to call Michael. First, I argued with him some more about releasing David and that irritated him.

Then he told me to call Margo at his home number to arrange to see Grace.

"What time does Grace get out of school?"

"Hell if I know," he said irritably. "Ask Margo. Bye."

What a creep! I hung up the phone, then tried his home number. The phone rang and rang. Then a woman answered. She was out of breath. Loud music pounded in the background. I told her who I was.

"Michael said I could see Grace after school today. Maybe I could take her out for hot chocolate or something."

"If Michael says it's okay, it's fine with me."

"What time does she get home?"

"I don't know. Around 3:30, I think."

"You don't meet her at the school?"

"We're only six blocks away."

Most parents hadn't let their kids walk alone to and from school since the first rumours of satanic ritual abuse years earlier. Grace usually took the school bus to and from Catherine's.

"Why don't you come by at 3:45?" Margo said. "That'll give her a chance to change her clothes."

At 3:35, because my Jeep had been towed to the shop for new tires and a new windshield, I took a cab to Michael's Victorian house, which was built into the hillside overlooking Sterling Harbour. With fancy gingerbread trim and a widow's walk on the top it reminded me of the tiers on a wedding cake. Snow covered the porch railings and the roof like frosting. Christmas lights glimmered like gumdrops underneath the snow-covered shrubs in front. *Kind of wasteful to leave them on all day.*

Someone had done a hasty job of shovelling the front walk. On the wide porch I waited a long time after I pressed the doorbell. I twisted the brass doorknob and found it locked. I rang the doorbell again and this time I leaned on it a few times. *Ding dong, ding dong, ding dong.* Finally, the door opened and a woman with her head wrapped in a towel opened the door. She wore a thick terry cloth robe.

"I was taking a shower." She drew a pack of cigarettes out of her pocket and lit one. She seemed a little older than me, maybe thirty, and had narrowly plucked eyebrows, huge brown eyes and high cheekbones. She sucked on her cigarette and her breath smelled of alcohol. *Was this Margo? Was she the one who'd once been Will's fiancée?* I felt a pang of jealousy. When she invited me in I figured Grace was already home.

I followed her into a room with a marble fireplace, high ceiling and expensive furniture. Newspapers, ashtrays, magazines, dirty clothes, CD cases, and dumbbells spread across every surface. It smelled of cat litter in the hallway. I sat down on the couch. Michael should hire a cleaning lady. He could afford it. They treated this grand old home like a dump.

"Is Grace home yet?"

Margo got up and hollered up the stairs. "Grace? Grace!"

"I guess she's not," she yawned, holding her burning cigarette in her right hand, which she held palm up.

"You mean you don't know? Maybe you locked her out!" I detested her. It wrenched me to think Will had once made love to her.

"Grace has a key. Look, you're welcome to wait here for her. I've got to get dressed." She glided out of the room.

I paced in and out of the living room, frequently looking out the front windows for signs of Grace. I should have met her at school. *Should I go meet her now?* But there were several routes she could take home. Margo returned to the room wearing skin-tight jeans, a fluffy yellow sweater, her blonde hair set in curls by a curling iron, but not brushed out.

"Maybe she stopped to visit some friends," she said.

"I'm going to walk up to the school and see if I can meet her." I laced up my boots. "Please search the house. Every closet. The basement. Everything."

Margo agreed.

Before trudging up the hill I stomped through the snow around the house to see if Grace had fallen while trying to reach the back door.

The snow was pristine, untouched by footprints except my own.

the **Kidnapping**

As I ran toward Grace's school snow had started falling again, the temperature had plummeted, and the wind had picked up. My head and ears were freezing, but I couldn't wear a hat over my injured scalp. I wasn't sure which route Grace would take from school, so I followed my intuition.

When I reached the school first stop was the principal's office. He informed me Grace had left at 3:20 p.m. I asked for the names of her classmates and their phone numbers. The secretary spent a few moments at the copier, then handed me the list. Maybe Grace had gone to visit a friend after school. Maybe she had tried to call Margo while she was in the shower. When I phoned Margo from the school she assured me she had even checked the attic. Apparently Michael hadn't heard from Grace either. It was now 4:33.

By the time I sprinted back to Michael's the sun had set and the driving snow made seeing more than ten feet ahead almost impossible. Wind whistled through the trees, rattling the branches and howling around the houses. My head throbbed as my boots hit the packed snow on the road. I carried all the school information in a manila envelope clasped to my chest.

The porch light was off, but the Christmas lights strewn over the shrubs glowed under the snow. Margo was in the living room, straightening up. She answered the door and wordlessly stepped aside, cigarette burning in her hand.

I looked for the switch to the porch light and flicked it on. "No word?"

"No." Margo checked her watch, then shrugged. "I hope she's okay."

She offered me a drink, but I declined. She poured herself a whiskey on the rocks, and drank it as she stacked books and magazines and emptied the smaller ashtrays into a bigger one. I started phoning the parents of each child in Grace's classroom in turn. None had seen her.

I phoned my house just in case Grace had taken her usual bus to her mom's, found her own home locked, and gone over to my place. I called Edna just in case she was with her. Edna became alarmed as well.

At 6:30 there was no still no sign of her. I left a message for Will at the detachment. Then I heard footsteps stomping on the porch. Margo rushed to the door and opened it to reveal Michael whose shoulders and fur hat were covered with snow. In the foyer he shook off his hat and coat and slipped off his snowy boots.

Margo lifted her glass and raised her eyebrows as if to ask Michael if he wanted a drink too. He must have nodded yes because she left for the kitchen and soon I heard ice cubes tinkling. Their nonchalance appalled me.

"Did she go home with one of her classmates?" he asked.

"I've called most of them and no one has seen her since school finished."

Michael sank into the couch. "There's probably some simple explanation."

Margo handed him a drink that looked like about four fingers of straight whiskey over some ice cubes. He lifted the glass to me. "Did Margo offer you anything? I gotta make sure she's trained right," he winked.

"Your daughter could be dead. Or kidnapped. How can you treat this like happy hour?"

"Grace ran away when Catherine and I got divorced." Michael gulped some whiskey and grimaced. "She hid in her babysitter's closet. Maybe she's hiding at the school."

I noticed his hand was shaking. *Is it the alcohol or concern for your daughter?*

I grabbed the phone, called Will's cell, and asked him to pick me up. Ten minutes later I heard his boots on the porch. The bell rang and Margo and I both raced for the door. She opened it.

"Hi, Will," Margo said coyly. "How are you? Long time no see."

Will nodded politely, peered around Margo, and asked me, "Any sign of Grace?"

I shook my head and bit my lip, almost frantic with anxiety as I laced up my boots and threw on my parka.

"Why don't you come in?" Margo jutted her breasts out under her fuzzy sweater. Her voice had a throaty purr.

Will ignored her. I bumped her aside to get outdoors.

Out on the porch snow blew like thick smoke and stung my cheeks. Another howling blizzard. Grace could die in this weather. Will and I ducked our heads and made a dash for his truck.

"Margo should have met Grace at the school and never let her walk home alone," I said as I fastened my seatbelt. "If something's happened to her, I'll never forgive her."

"We'll find her," he said.

"Even though Grace is missing, Margo acts like she wants a roll in the hay with you." Jealousy stabbed my heart. "What did you ever see in her?"

"I had this thing about trying to fix wounded people." Will backed his truck out of the parking spot in front of Michael's house. "Tell me everything you know so far about Grace," he said, changing the subject.

We chugged up the hill in four-wheel drive to Sterling Elementary and found the school locked. Will and I searched the perimeter of the building and finally caught the attention of a janitor who let us in. We did a systematic search. No sign of Grace.

We drove back to Michael's. The snow made driving treacherous.

"At least I don't have to worry about Rafe." I bent forward with anxiety, my stomach cramping. "Catherine's with him in Florida."

Will peered intently over the steering wheel at the white flakes swirling in front of the headlights. "What do you think of Michael's theory? You think she ran away because she's mad at her mother for leaving her behind?"

"I don't think she'd run away. My gut tells me something awful has happened."

Will pulled up alongside the drift in front of Michael's house. We stomped inside to see if they'd had any word. It was now 8:03 p.m.

Michael was slightly drunk. A phony sentimentality overlaid his concern for Grace. I made a mental note to consider both him and Margo suspects.

At Michael's Will and I phoned the rest of Grace's classmates. Finally, I reached someone with some information, but not what I'd hoped to hear. Kara was asleep, but her parents woke her up. She told me she'd seen a dark purplish car pull up alongside Grace as she was walking home. When the car door swung open Grace spoke to the driver whom Kara couldn't see. Then she got inside the car and it drove away.

Michael's reaction to this news was more in keeping with that of an anguished father. He started tearing at his wavy hair, then dug his fists into his eyes. He was wracking his brain, trying to figure out who might have picked her up. He and Margo couldn't think of anyone.

Whoever did so wasn't a stranger. *Who could it be?* George Hall's name popped into mind, so Will and I headed for his mansion overlooking the cliffs of Sterling Bay. We fishtailed up the steep hill toward his posh neighbourhood and found a couple of snow-covered limousines and several expensive rental cars filling his circular drive.

We fought the wind and driving snow to the front door. After we pressed the bell a man wearing a tuxedo answered. Beyond him I saw George standing with several men on the edge of the immense marble foyer. When he saw us he excused himself, waddled over, and invited us in. We tracked snow onto his shining floor. I told him we were looking for Grace Ross.

"Someone driving a purplish car picked Grace up at school. Could any of your visitors have picked her up?" I asked.

"You're welcome to ask." George made a sweeping gesture with his hand.

"Has Grace ever been here?" Will asked. "Could she be hiding here without your knowing it?"

"She's never been here. I hardly know her. I met her for the first time that day I met you at the restaurant in Annapolis Royal," George said to me.

He seemed sincere and genuinely concerned. "May I offer you something to eat? Some coffee? I have some friends visiting from out of town and we've got a buffet in the dining room. You're welcome to join us. Your staff sergeant is here. So are the mayor and the county warden."

Karen came out dressed in black velveteen slacks and a matching tunic woven with sparkling gold thread. She wore eyeshadow and had loosened her burgundy-tinted hair. I explained that Grace was missing and asked what resources we could put into searching for her.

"It's still a little early to pull out all the stops, isn't it?" Karen said. "Maybe her mother came back and hasn't gotten around to calling her dad."

"I doubt it. There's no one home at Catherine's," I said.

"Do the usual. Put her name on the computer. Do whatever checks you think are necessary. I'll assign the members on duty tonight to help you. Call Search and Rescue. I'll figure out tomorrow morning if we need to add more resources than that."

George Hall had rejoined us for the last part of our conversation. "I'd be happy to bring my company helicopter in from Halifax to aid in any search, but the weather's too bad right now. We're supposed to get snow all night and most of tomorrow."

George then herded his guests into the foyer so we could question them. Nothing. No one had seen Grace. Anxiety gnawed at my gut like hyenas on a carcass. I called Search and Rescue and asked the co-ordinator to meet us at Michael's.

When Will and I returned to Michael's he was pacing and clutching fistfuls of hair. "I've been trying to reach Catherine in Florida. She hasn't returned any of my calls."

"Is it possible she came back and picked up Grace herself?" Will asked.

Michael shook his head. "I doubt it. It's not like Catherine to be so hard to reach. I've tried her hotel and her cell. Usually she would have called me by now to see how Grace is doing."

I clutched my stomach and broke out in a cold sweat. When a three-man team from the volunteer Search and Rescue team arrived, I filled them in on the details of the investigation so far, and left them with Michael to get photographs and any other information that might help them in their search.

As Will and I drove back to the detachment his truck could barely make it up the hill. The snow was falling so fast the ploughs couldn't keep up. Heartsick, I hoped Grace was at least indoors.

Michael had given us a recent photo of her, and when we made it to the detachment we scanned it into the nationwide police computer. We also sent it to the police computer network in the States. We briefed the members on duty that night and the Search and Rescue team volunteers. I called Catherine's hotel in Florida several times, leaving messages. Her voice mail was full.

As we bundled up to head home I slipped Grace's photo in the inner pocket of my parka. Will's calm and professional demeanour reassured me. I had to hope we could find her. I silently kept pleading with God for Grace's protection.

On the ride to Cornwallis Cove wind whipped the snow against the truck and rocked the cab. In places the drifts were four feet deep and we had to drive around them. A wrong turn would have landed us in the ditch or trapped us in the snow.

We finally made it to my place to find Edna's pickup parked in my laneway. Inside, Anne and Edna were praying at the kitchen table, keeping each other company and anxiously awaiting any news. Catherine had not called.

"Do you think Grace is mad that Catherine went to Florida with Rafe?" I asked.

"Do you blame her?" Edna said.

"How does Grace get along with her dad?"

"Okay, I guess." Edna dabbed her eyes with a tissue. "I think she's kind of indifferent to him. He buys her lots of gifts but doesn't spend much quality time with her, if you know what I mean."

Edna and Anne served Will and me soup and oatmeal bread. Anne asked when David might be released seeing as Cindy had confessed. We had to tell her the confession wasn't enough. Gloom and dread settled over all of us.

I forced myself to eat. Then all that night and early morning, still dressed in my uniform, I continued to call Catherine's hotel. By 4:07 a.m. she still hadn't returned to her room. Anne had gone to bed hours earlier, Will had fallen asleep on the daybed in the kitchen, and Edna was asleep in the reclining chair in the living room. They snored softly in counterpoint.

For the umpteenth time I called the hotel's front desk and asked if the clerk would send someone upstairs to check Catherine's room. She said they had no one on staff who could inspect the room at that hour of the morning. I tried Rodriguez, but got his voice mail every number I tried.

I called Michael at 7:03 a.m. His voice was hoarse from lack of sleep. Catherine had not returned any of his calls either. I tiptoed past Edna who was still asleep in the living room. Frost crystals lined the bottom of the windows. Outside in the dawning light I could see the snow had stopped, but it was now more than three feet deep and heavily drifted. *How are we going to get into town?* Then powerful headlights illuminated the front of my house and what looked like a four-wheeled tractor with a plough scraping the road turned into my laneway. It cut through the drifts with ease.

I darted through the kitchen, stuck my head out the back door, and waved. It was Delbert driving a super-sized tractor called a tree farmer. He hollered, "I'll plough all the way to the highway if I have to!"

Will was stirring on the daybed, so I sat next to him and told him about my phone calls. I felt waves of exhaustion and anguish. Will had slept in his uniform and his hair swirled into a bird's nest in the back.

"Linda, get some sleep." Will buckled his utility belt. "You'll be no good to anyone if you don't. I'll interview Grace's classmate and check in with the search teams."

I helped Will shovel out his truck, then watched as he followed Delbert's tree farmer to the highway.

Upstairs, I threw myself on my bed. I don't think I slept, but at least my body was resting and my eyes were closed. Soon I could hear the Jordan children's lighthearted voices and their scampering feet. All I could think about was Grace and her safety. I knew volunteers had been out all night tramping the snow in an ever-widening grid around the school.

A couple of hours later I shook off the comforter, peeled off my sweats, and headed for a bracing shower. My head felt a lot better.

The throbbing was gone, but my scalp was sore and the goose egg hurt if I probed it. I couldn't sleep while Grace was missing. I threw on a fresh uniform.

Anne had prepared a fresh pot of coffee. I nodded good morning and poured myself a mug. I popped a piece of Edna's oatmeal bread into the toaster. My stomach was in a knot, but I had to keep my energy up. Just as I lifted the mug to my lips the phone rang. It was Will. I didn't like the sound of his voice. "What's up?"

"An ambulance picked up a little girl near South Dare. Severe hypothermia. You better get in to the hospital in case it's Grace."

South Dare? What was Grace doing in South Dare? I felt sick to my stomach. "Is she going to make it?"

"I don't know," Will said. "It doesn't sound good. Can you drive okay? The roads are pretty bad."

"I'll make it."

I hung up the phone, and nearly doubled over with cramps at the thought of Grace lying half frozen in the snow. I told Anne what Will had said, and she tugged on my arm.

"No situation is hopeless," she said, her eyes brimming with tears. "I'll call the Broadfoots. We've been praying she'd be found. We'll start praying she'll survive."

"I've gotta run." I pulled myself up straight and wiped my wet cheeks with a paper towel. Anne handed me her car keys.

Outside, the Jordans' car was hidden under an igloo-shaped pile of snow. I dug for the door handle, pulled the door open, and started the engine. I frantically swept the snow off the car. Then I had to shovel the drift Delbert's tree farmer had made around the car when he ploughed the laneway. I'd worked up a sweat by the time I got into the driver's seat. I rocked the car back and forth, tires spinning, until I had enough momentum to smash through the remaining snowdrift onto the ploughed part of the laneway. Then I followed the tree farmer's narrow track all the way to the highway.

The highway was in good shape, ploughed and salted, so I sped into Sterling. Just as I was passing the tavern a dull brown pickup truck coming in the opposite direction skidded into a left turn, cutting right in front of me. I slammed on the brakes and skidded into the opposite lane. Luckily there wasn't any oncoming traffic. I made an angry gesture at the driver, whom I recognized as Lonnie Dare. My eyes widened as I caught a glimpse of his parka.

It was black, with a red triangular patch at the shoulder. I debated whether to bang a U-turn and skid into the tavern parking lot, but meeting Grace at the hospital was my priority. I silently filed the information for later.

I sped down the snow-covered road to Sterling General. I parked next to a six-foot snowdrift and ran to the ambulance parked by the emergency entrance. The paramedics were unloading an elderly woman. *Was Grace here already?*

In the waiting room a mother cradled a feverish-looking toddler. A bald man rested his bloody forearm on his knee, and a fat elderly woman wheezed, her face bright pink. I bounded to the reception area and asked if an ambulance had brought in a hypothermic little girl. The receptionist said the child was inside the first room to the left.

A team of people surrounded a small form on the bed, blocking my view except for a small white foot, unearthly pale, extending from under the white sheet. I could hardly breathe.

"We need more warm blankets!" shouted a young woman in a white coat. "Heated blankets. She's got hypothermia. Bad frostbite on both her feet and hands!" The woman leaned over and listened to the little girl's heartbeat with her stethoscope. I squeezed in to get a closer look. When I saw the small form surrounded by the emergency room team I gasped in shock.

A beautiful ghostly-white little girl lay on the gurney. I didn't know whether to rejoice or despair.

It wasn't Grace.

the Defiler

The doctors didn't know if the little girl would live. A man who lived on the outskirts of South Dare had found her lying unconscious on the settlement's back road. He had nearly run her over on his snowmobile. A county plough had to clear the road so an ambulance could pick her up. I checked the labels on the child's clothes. They were in French. *Where was she from? Québec? France? Belgium?*

Back at the detachment I called Catherine's hotel in Miami.

"Catherine Ross, please."

"I'm sorry, she checked out," a female voice said.

"Checked out! Did she get my messages? This is the Royal Canadian Mounted Police calling from Nova Scotia. There's a family emergency."

"Here's my manager," the voice said.

"Hello, Irving Grant here," said a deep raspy voice.

"I've been trying to reach Catherine Ross all night. Now your desk tells me she's checked out. It's extremely urgent that I reach her."

"She didn't exactly check out. We had her arrested for credit card fraud."

"You what?"

"She's with the Miami Police Department as we speak."

"Credit card fraud?"

"You heard me."

"What about Rafe Lupien?"

"Who?"

"Raphael Lupien. The man she was with. He sometimes goes by the name Ralph Eddine."

"She booked the suite in her name."

"Who's the arresting officer?"

"How am I supposed to know, lady?"

I slammed down the phone, then picked up the receiver and called the Miami Police Department. I ended up in voice mail hell. *Lord, please help me.* Then it occurred to me to call Rodriguez at home again. I raced to my desk and found the number. His high voice sounded groggy and huskier than usual.

"Hello, Detective Rodriguez? It's Constable Linda Donner from Nova Scotia."

"Got your messages. Going to call you today," he said. "Got new information for you."

"I need your help. A little girl has been kidnapped. I've been trying to reach her mother who's in Miami right now. I've been told she's at the police station, under arrest for credit card fraud. She's down there on vacation with Rafe Lupien, a.k.a. Ralph Eddine. She doesn't know her child is missing. I can't get through to anyone who knows anything."

"Does she have any idea what a scumbag her boyfriend is?" Rodriguez said. "We paid Virtuality's new office a surprise visit last night and picked up boxes of CDs, DVDs, and videos of kiddie porn. We have evidence Eddine produced them."

His words hit me like a punch in the stomach. *What kind of access has Rafe already had to Grace?* If Rafe wasn't with Catherine, maybe he was back in Nova Scotia. *Lord, please keep Grace safe.*

I gave Rodriguez Catherine's name and he promised to go to the police station right away to find her.

I called Michael who was stunned by the credit card allegations and Rafe's involvement in child porn.

"Catherine and I have had our differences, but she's never done anything dishonest in her life. What's this creep got her into?" His voice shook. "Child pornography! How could Catherine get involved with someone like that? Is Rafe with her?"

"Doesn't sound like it." I held my left arm across my gut, feeling nauseous with anxiety.

In less than an hour the phone on my desk rang. I darted over and grabbed the receiver, my knees trembling. It was Rodriguez.

"I found Catherine Ross," he said.

"Did you tell Catherine her daughter is missing?" I gestured frantically for Will's attention. He was searching European missing persons databases on the computer. Finally, he noticed my waving arms.

"I haven't had a chance to talk to her. From what the arresting officer tells me her boyfriend left her high and dry with a bill she couldn't pay. She gave her credit card when they checked in, but when it was time to pay the bill, it was maxed out. She says he told her he'd pay. But he disappeared the day before yesterday."

"Two days ago?" I had to steady myself by bracing my hand on my desk.

Will strode over. "What's going on?" he asked.

"She got back to her hotel room late last night," Rodriguez continued. "Like 4 a.m. She says she was looking for him at the clubs she knew he liked. When she got back to her room someone had trashed it – slashed the couch and chair with a box cutter. Yanked the phone cord from the wall."

"May I speak with her?" I straightened and turned to look at Will.

"I don't know. She's pretty upset. I think she's going to need a doctor or something. And no one's told her about the child porn or her missing daughter."

"I've got to talk with her. Are they going to book her?"

"Nah. Looks like she got burned by her boyfriend. But the officers tell me she's having a hard time believing he put the screws to her. She's convinced something bad has happened to him."

"Can you take her for a coffee or something? Calm her down a bit? I've got to see if there's any way Lupien, I mean Eddine, could have come back to Nova Scotia."

"Well, she's got no cash, just a plane ticket back home. Maybe if I offer a ride to the airport she'll talk with me."

I stayed at the detachment to wait for Rodriguez to call again while Will went to interview Grace's classmate Kara and her family. When he returned he said Kara couldn't add anything new to the description we already had of a dark purplish car whose driver had a short conversation with Grace before she hopped inside. The thought it might be Rafe sickened me. *Where is he?*

Rodriguez called back. He cleared his throat. "Catherine wants to speak with you. Hold on." I heard the sound of a chair scraping and footsteps.

"Well, Linda, I bet you're just aching to tell me 'I told you so,'" Catherine's voice quavered.

That was the last thing I was thinking. I dreaded having to tell her more bad news. I mustered as much calm professionalism as I could. "Catherine...Grace is missing."

The silence made me wonder if the line had gone dead.

Then, "I don't understand." Catherine's voice sounded small.

"Grace never came home from school yesterday. One of her schoolmates saw her get into a purplish car, probably a rental."

I heard Rodriguez's voice in the background asking Catherine to sit down.

"She's not with Michael? Didn't Margo go meet her at the school like I asked her to?" Catherine's voice rose in pitch and volume.

"Who does Grace know well enough to willingly get into a car with?"

"David Jordan? Pastor Don Harwood? Edna or Delbert?"

"George Hall?"

"She only met George once." Catherine's voice grew shrill with fear. "I don't think so. Grace has always been cautious."

"Could she be with Rafe?"

"Why would she be with Rafe?"

"Catherine, did Rafe have time to get back here?"

"I haven't seen Rafe since the day before yesterday. We had plans and he never showed up."

"Then Rafe could have picked her up. He had time to get back to Nova Scotia?"

"Why do you think he's responsible?" She was getting snippy.

I told her to ask Rodriguez about the child porn bust. The receiver fell to the floor. I heard the mumble of their voices, then a plaintive wail from Catherine that cut me to the marrow. She was expressing exactly how I felt. I heard a fumbling noise, then sobbing sounds.

Rodriguez came back on the line, his voice tight with anger.

"Remember those DVDs I told you about? Guess whose picture is on the cover."

"Oh, Lord God. Tell me it's not Grace." I could barely breathe.

"Sorry. These DVDs are grotesque. The little girl's picture is right there on the cover, advertising this filth."

I gasped.

"It doesn't look like she's in any of the porn on the DVD itself, though," Rodriguez said.

"Oh, thank God."

Rodriguez muffled the receiver. A few seconds later he said, "Hold on, Catherine wants to talk to you."

"Oh my God. My God!" Catherine cried. "How could I have been such a fool! Oh my God. Oh Grace." I heard her crying out loud. "Remember that silk nightgown Rafe gave Grace for Christmas? He took pictures of her wearing it, surrounded by her stuffed animals and dolls."

"That's on the DVD?" I asked, outraged.

"Detective Rodriguez says she's only on the cover. He says the stuff inside is unbearable to watch. Hideous."

"He was using Grace's innocence as an advertisement."

"I can't handle this," Catherine said, her voice tiny and trembling. She put Rodriguez back on the phone.

"Linda? I'll have Catherine on the next flight to Halifax."

We had to find Rafe.

the Informant

After my conversation with Catherine I phoned George Hall, both at his home and his office. His secretary told me I might find him at his Sterling fish plant. When no one answered the phone there Will and I raced outside to a police car.

Will drove through the snow-packed streets downtown to Water Street, wending his way between the towering drifts looming on both sides of the road. The early afternoon sun shone through a break in the mushrooming grey clouds.

George Hall's fish plant took up an entire wharf in the industrial end of town. The old wooden building, painted white, jutted out over the harbour on thick wooden pilings smelling of creosote. About forty people milled about in the loading area where normally one or two of Hall's tractor-trailers would have been parked. Huge snowdrifts had been ploughed up at one end of the parking lot.

I noticed a big red and white For Sale sign on the building. "That's new. When did George put this place up for sale?"

"Beats me," Will said, peering through the windshield. "What's going on here?"

As we pulled up, a man banged the hood of the car with his fist. Someone picked up a brick and threw it at one of the plant's windows. The crowd cheered when the glass shattered. Our car began to rock. Turning around I saw some men pushing the rear of the car up and down. Then a stone hit the rear passenger window and cracked it. I radioed Dispatch for reinforcements.

"Armegeddon outta here." Will revved the engine and backed up slowly. Hostile men's faces pressed in around the car, fists pounding the windows. We made it to the street as the crowd jeered and several men kicked our car. He parked further down the street where we would be less of a provocation, and we waited for backup.

Soon two more police cars pulled up. Bob and Eddie jumped out.

Will and I walked over to a man standing on the sidelines dressed in a green camouflage-print parka and asked him what was going on. The man waved his arm angrily at the For Sale sign.

"George Hall is putting us out of work!" he shouted.

"We don't have enough weeks to qualify for unemployment insurance!" another man shouted. "There's enough fish! He could keep the plant running while he looks for a buyer!"

"What a powder keg," Eddie said, his double chin quivering. "Wouldn't take much to set this crowd off."

"They almost rolled our car," I said.

Eddie snorted. "You can take the people out of South Dare..."

A truck squeezed past the police cars – the same brown pickup Lonnie Dare had been driving, but this time Gordon was at the wheel. *Did they paint the white pickup?* He climbed out and, with the help of some of the protestors, rolled a black oil barrel off the truck's back and unloaded some discarded lumber studded with old nails. Within minutes a fire blazed in the barrel. Some of the men marched around with hand-lettered signs demanding the plant stay open. Will and I waded through the crowd to the main office. A young woman looked through the glass after we knocked, then opened the door.

"Get your coat," I said to her. "We'll escort you out. Is anyone else in there? Is George Hall here?"

"No, Mr. Hall's in Halifax, I think. The electrician is here working on the freezers. And the assistant manager is in the office."

Dismayed, I grabbed Will's arm. "I've got to get out of here. I can't stop looking for Grace now."

"Let's escort these people through the crowd, then we'll go," he said.

Two more police cars pulled up. With so many members present the crowd had become more subdued. Besides, the fire in the barrel gave them a hub to revolve around. When the assistant manager, a stocky white-haired man with small black-rimmed glasses, came out, the crowd roared. Above his head an egg splattered against the shingled wall.

"Hey, I'm going to lose my job too! I'm on your side!" he shouted.

He told us he was going to stay and help keep the protest from getting out of control. He stepped into the crowd. Someone shoved him, but he didn't flinch. Soon he was indistinguishable from the rest of the angry men and women.

Will and I escorted the secretary to her car and the electrician to his van. Then we left the other Mounties to do crowd control and headed back to the detachment.

Karen was pacing outside her office, listening to the crosstalk on her walkie-talkie. She ordered us to get back to the fish plant to help secure the downtown. She told us she'd called the Emergency Response team, or ERT, but it could take them more than two hours to get there from Halifax. She wanted us to join the other members to prevent the picketers from rioting and destroying Sterling's commercial district.

"Karen, I've got to talk to you about the missing girl," I said.

"Make it quick."

"Catherine Ross, Grace's mother, had a boyfriend from Florida. We think now that *he* kidnapped the girl."

Will handed me his cell and the keys to his truck. "Don't go to South Dare alone. Call Earl. I want to be able to reach you. The phone is on vibrate – "

Karen stepped between us. "Linda's not going to South Dare. Grab a shotgun and a helmet and get downtown."

Will squeezed my shoulder, then walked down the hall.

I spread Catherine's picture and the blown-up copy of Rafe's driver's license on a desk. "This is Raphael Lupien. He's Catherine Ross' boyfriend. He's also a friend of George Hall's."

Karen's husky laugh rang out. "Rafe?"

Her casual laughter stunned me. I gaped at her. "His real name is Ralph Eddine."

"Linda, you're barking up the wrong tree."

"You know him?"

"He's the wrong guy. Trust me. Get downtown. Now! " She spun around and strode away.

I followed her. "Rafe is making child porn." My voice rose. "A Miami police detective says he found porn – CDs, videos and DVDs – in one of Rafe's Miami businesses. There's a picture of the missing girl on the cover of one of the DVDs."

Karen spun around. The veins popped out of her neck and her eyes bulged. "You back off Rafe Lupien, do you understand? How dare you sic unauthorized police contacts on him! You have no idea what you're doing. You drop this!"

"Catherine Ross is sure Rafe has kidnapped her daughter!" I shouted back. "Grace is the Crown prosecutor's little girl!"

"Rafe is in Florida." She turned her back on me and marched into her office.

My mouth hung open for a second or two, then I dogged Karen's heels into her office. "He *was* in Florida. He was with Catherine down there, but she hasn't seen him in almost two days."

"You've got the wrong man. Get downtown." She picked up her phone and dialled. "Hello, Craig. Karen Ramsay here," she said. "When's the last time you talked to Rafe?"

She nodded her head, the receiver pressed to her ear, and sank into her swivel chair. "Everything still according to plan?"

"What's going on?" I demanded.

"No, nothing's wrong on this end. I just have an overzealous constable here who thinks Rafe is responsible for kidnapping a little girl here in Nova Scotia."

Karen's whisky laugh rang out. "She says a Miami Vice detective has evidence Rafe is trafficking kiddie porn."

I leaned over her desk. "It's Rodriguez, Detective Alberto Rodriguez, Miami Vice." Karen's strange behaviour shocked and disturbed me.

"Maybe you should tell this Miami detective to back off," she said into the receiver.

Then she asked me for Rodriguez's name again. I repeated it, and she passed the name onto Craig. She hung up and leaned forward.

"Listen carefully, Linda. Rafe Lupien is a DEA informant. Only a handful of people know that. I was told only as a courtesy. I don't want you telling anyone, not Will, not anyone, you hear? Not even François knows."

I froze in stunned silence while her words sank in. "I don't care if Rafe *is* a DEA informant," I said. "The guy's making kiddie porn and he could be in South Dare right now with Grace Ross. Do you have a way of reaching him? A cell number?"

She clenched her teeth. "You don't get it, Donner."

Karen jumped out of her chair and leaned over her desk. "You've been acting like you've got some screws loose ever since you got here. I've been protecting you, nursing you along, giving you stress leave, defending your backside, and all you've done is buck orders, do your own thing, and land yourself in deeper and deeper trouble." She wagged her finger at me. "I'll make sure you're finished as a member. You don't have what it takes!"

I felt like her blast had just singed off my hair. I desperately tried to lower the hostility level. If I wanted to find Grace, I needed Karen's co-operation.

"I'm sorry. I was disrespectful. May I please go to South Dare –"

"No. Get youself downtown!" she barked.

"What's the DEA connection? Please tell me what's going on," I pleaded, tears in my voice.

Karen looked at her fingers splayed on the surface of the desk, sighed, softened somewhat, and then straightened her back.

"Rafe is involved in a massive sting operation that could bring down one of the Colombian drug cartels. The sting also involves organized crime elements in Thailand and Burma, which are shipping heroin to Colombia, then transshipping it up the Atlantic coast. When this is over it'll be the biggest drug bust in Canadian history, by far. Rafe's also working with the people from Montréal and Vancouver who are financing this massive buy. They have connections on the cape we haven't nailed down yet. What do you think you and Will have been working on?"

"What if Rafe is a sexual predator who has kidnapped Grace Ross?" My forehead felt hot, and my breath was jagged.

Karen strode toward the members' exit to the parking lot. I dogged her heels again.

"Give it a rest, Donner," she ordered. "He's got some connections with shadowy people, but he's one of the good guys. It took a long time to get this sting in operation. He's spent years positioning himself to help us out like this and only a handful of people know about it. Now you're one of them. I expect you to keep your lips sealed. Understand?" Karen zipped up her bulletproof vest and pulled on her parka.

"Let's go." She grabbed her cell and a freshly charged walkie-talkie. The door from the parking lot burst open as some auxiliary constables arrived in uniform. For a moment Karen was distracted briefing them.

I headed for the bathroom. I turned on my walkie-talkie and listened to what other members were saying as they tried to quell the riot in Sterling. Sirens were blaring in the background. I felt torn. If I went to South Dare now, I'd lose my job and access to the computer and other resources to find Grace. Then I felt a vibrating sensation in my pocket. I flipped open Will's phone.

"Where are you?" Will asked.

"The detachment." I stared at the terra cotta tiles on the bathroom floor and the black grate over the floor drain.

"Promise me you'll call Earl. He knows his way around South Dare."

"Where are you?"

"A phone booth on Water Street. We have things under control down here."

Several loud bangs like firecrackers exploding interrupted his conversation.

I heard the receiver bang against the wall of the phone booth.

"Officer down! Officer down!" a voice shouted over the walkie-talkie.

Oh Lord, please.

Don't let it be Will...

the Murderer

I drove Will's truck down the hill to the waterfront through streets resembling bobsled runs because of the high drifts on both sides. On Water Street advertising flyers and rotted food from torn garbage bags littered the packed snow. To the side of the road a pile of old boards and a broken wooden desk burned with orange flames. Another fire of gas-soaked tires gave off the stench of burning rubber and pumped black smoke into the air. In the distance I could see smoke and flames pouring from the fish plant.

Two RCMP members stood by a police car, blocking traffic. I jumped out of Will's truck just as an ambulance swerved around me to their barricade. One of the constables pointed toward the public wharf and it sped off, siren blaring. About twenty people stood behind the police line. Michael Ross was among them.

"Who got hit?" I asked one of the constables whose face was white with strain.

"Eddie Johnson."

I almost melted with relief it wasn't Will.

"How bad?"

"In the thigh."

Michael stepped forward and grabbed my shoulder. "I spoke to

Catherine!" he shouted over the din. "She's convinced her boyfriend kidnapped Grace. What's being done about it?"

"You'd better talk to Karen!" I shouted back. "I'll take you through to her, if you want."

The constable advised us to drive around to the barricade on the other side rather than through downtown in case more bullets started flying.

As Michael and I pressed through the crowd toward my truck, trying not to slip on the packed snow, the siren grew louder again. The ambulance wove among the stones and debris toward us, squeezed past the police car, and sped by on its way to the hospital.

With Michael in the passenger seat I backed out slowly, then drove up the hill, wheels slipping even in four-wheel drive. I tried to cut across town on one of the cross streets, but snowdrifts had narrowed it to only one lane and oncoming traffic blocked my way. Spectators were climbing the drifts to watch the riot from a safe distance. I could see store owners armed with deer rifles and shotguns guarding their property from their flat rooftops.

Wheels still spinning I backed out the narrow lane and fought traffic uphill. The town looked so strange hidden under the thick white blanket, and the roads were choked with cars that couldn't make the hills. I regretted we hadn't taken the Water Street route. However, *I* was wearing a bulletproof vest. Michael was not.

Finally, we reached the other end of Water Street. I waved to the auxiliaries and then drove around them to where Karen stood with Will and Bob. They all carried shotguns or riot shields.

Black smoke curled up into the white sky. Near the horizon a big orange sun peeked through the clouds. Ashes and cinders from the fire floated down with the odd snowflake. The crowd had grown to a mob of about two hundred angry shouting people, mostly men, chanting, "Kill the pigs! Kill the pigs!" I recognized many of the faces from Rex's funeral and from the taverns, pool halls, and arcades around Sterling. But I could no longer find Gordon or any other close relatives of Rex Dare in the crowd.

I made my way over to Karen and told her Michael wanted to talk with her. She said nothing for a moment, her teeth clenching and unclenching. Then she thrust her shotgun into my hands and strode over to the truck to talk with Michael. I took her place at the barricade.

About ten minutes later she returned and grabbed her shotgun back.

"Tell Search and Rescue to move into South Dare!" she shouted over the noise of the crowd. "You may go by yourself. When the ERT comes I'll send Will or Bob to assist you."

"George Hall. Does he have anything to do with this drug sting?" I asked.

"No. George is clean. Beat it." Karen wiped her face with her glove and smeared the soot on her cheek.

I told Michael I had to find out if Cindy knew Rafe. If he was linked to South Dare, that would narrow our search. We made our way to the nursing home.

When we arrived the officer who was supposed to be guarding her was nowhere in sight. Cindy slept, her covers folded neatly at her chest and her arms resting on top of the blankets.

"Cindy. Wake up!" I said.

She blinked her eyes and squinted at me. That fearful hypnotized look crossed her face.

"Cut it out!" I snapped. "We don't have time for this nonsense."

I pulled up the chair as close as I could and waved the enlarged photograph of Rafe in front of her and watched her face. "Do you know this man?"

Cindy turned pale and a sheen of sweat appeared on her forehead.

I showed her a picture of Grace. "See this little girl? Her name is Grace. I believe that man has Grace and is going to use her in a pornographic movie, just like Rex used Becky. Have you ever seen him before?" I held the picture of Rafe in front of her again.

"Why are *you* here?" Cindy asked Michael who stood at the foot of her bed. "You didn't believe us. You were on Rex's side!" she cried.

"That's not true. I tried to put Rex away," Michael pleaded. "That little girl's my daughter. If you know anything about this man, please help me."

"That's him. That's him!" she whispered, her dark eyes on the photo.

"That's who?" Michael asked.

"The man who killed Rex."

"He what?" I almost fell off the chair.

"He shot Rex. I seen him."

"Why didn't you tell us this before now?" I yelled in frustration.

"I didn't think anybody would believe me." Tears coursed down her pink and white cheeks. "They never believed me in the past. He wasn't from the mountain like us."

"You said *you* killed Rex!" I sputtered.

"Because you had Pastor David in prison. That man seen me. He was gonna kill me or get Lonnie and them to do it. I figured I'd be safer in prison and Pastor David would go free."

"Did he make the films of the orgies involving Becky and the other kids?" I asked.

"No. I ain't never seen him before the day I seen you at the church."

I let out an exasperated sigh. Precious time was ticking away. I tore my notebook out of my vest. "Tell me what you saw." Michael took a tiny voice recorder out of his pocket and started recording.

"I seen you poke your head out of the church and I took off scared to my place in the woods. I got to my cabin and somethin' didn't feel right. Then I heard voices coming from inside. One of them voices was Rex yelling."

"What was he saying?" My heart hammered with anxiety over Grace, but I knew I might never get this story out of Cindy again.

"He's saying stuff like, 'You can't do this to me,' and 'I'll ruin you and George,' and 'I want my share of the action.'"

"Okay, so?" I wrote as fast as I could, just in case Michael's recorder malfunctioned. So George *was* involved. The one place I hadn't checked was his lodge in South Dare. I had to get out there.

Cindy cleared her throat. "I hid in the bushes near the door. Then Rex and that man in your picture there, they came outside."

I nodded and wrote. "Yup, go on."

"Rex says, 'George can't cut me outta this. I've got things on him going way back. I'm warning ya,' and the other man, he says, 'Hey, Rex, if it were up to me, you'd be a key player. I'll try to get you back in, but he thinks he can do it without you this time.'"

"I seen the man put his hand out to shake Rex's hand. Then that man said, 'Where's Cindy, Rex? We can't have her out here talking to the cops and to that priest.' He called Pastor David a priest. Then I heard Rex say he thought I would be at the church. The man told Rex to go ahead and he would get the shotgun."

"The shotgun?" *Hurry up, Cindy.* "What shotgun?"

"The shotgun Alan Dare give me because I was so scared of the bear. It was hanging across some spikes on my wall. Rex said okay and he started walking down the path toward the church. As soon as Rex was down aways I made a run for it down the other path. But soon I was outta breath. I was into an area where the brush was low and you could see the other path. I didn't want Rex to see me, so I hid behind a tree. I seen Rex coming down the other path. He stops and lights a cigarette and stands there, like he's waiting for the other man to come. He's standing there, smoking and just looking around. Then I seen the other man coming down the same path that I'm on. He's carrying the shotgun and he's running funny. He's crouching low and moving really fast, like he's in the army or something. He's real quiet too. I can't scarcely hear him. He stops, just feet away from me, pops up, aims the shotgun, and shouts Rex's name. Rex turns toward him, and the man pulls the trigger, and *blam!* Rex falls down. I panic and run toward the church. I hear the man swearing and he fires shots at me. I don't know what happened after that. I didn't go back to the church. I ran through the woods and hitched rides until I got to Lunenburg, where I knew someone from hairdressing school."

I glanced at Michael whose eyes had bluish circles under them. "Was this the same man who tried to run you down?"

"No, Lonnie done that." Cindy's teeth were chattering.

"You saw him?"

"No, but Aggie come and visited me. She told me Lonnie done it 'cause they thought I killed Rex."

"Was Lonnie Dare involved in the films?"

Tears streamed down Cindy's mottled pink cheeks. "Yeah, Lonnie was."

"And George Hall too?" I asked.

"George Hall's been doing kids in South Dare since I was a baby. I don't know if he was in the films. A lot of the men had masks on."

"Michael, you've got to get David Jordan out of jail," I said.

"I'll call the judge right now." Michael lifted the phone.

He remained with Cindy to get more details and told me he'd brief Karen. I used Will's cell to contact Earl Broadfoot and asked him to meet me in South Dare. We agreed to meet at the entrance road to George's lodge if the road was ploughed that far – otherwise by the church.

The shadows lengthened as the sun slipped halfway below the horizon and gleamed hellishly red through a patch in the grey clouds. The sun's glare, even with sunglasses, made it hard to see. I had taken off my police cap and stuffed my hair under a toque I found on Will's truck bench. My goose egg was still tender.

Ploughs had only cleared one lane of the road to the settlement. Snow buried the squalor surrounding the shacks, and drifts covered some of the smaller cabins and trailers so residents had to tunnel out. On the unploughed side roads I noticed rounded humps that looked like they might have vehicles underneath. Snowmobile tracks criss-crossed the area. I turned at the road that went past the church and found the plough had continued to where I was to meet Earl.

The plough had not only passed by George's lodge, it had swept a huge drift in front of the entrance road. Earl was nowhere in sight. I climbed the drift, which was about seven feet high and fifteen feet wide at its base. At the top I discovered the road to the lodge was thick with snow so deep I couldn't tell where the ditches were. The sun had settled behind the lodge and the darkness around me deepened. I was glad I'd left the headlights on to help me see when I climbed down.

After Cindy's latest confession I had been certain Rafe and George must be hiding out at George's lodge. Now the place seemed totally snowed in. *Where has Rafe taken Grace?* Soon headlights from behind me filled the truck's cab with light. I twisted to see the outline of a pickup truck. There was barely enough room for it to pass me. *Was this Earl?* I couldn't make out who it was.

When it drew alongside I shined my flashlight inside to reveal Gordon Dare at the wheel, blinking as he rolled down the window. Alan Dare sat in the passenger seat staring at the light with glassy eyes as expressionless as a goat's. My heart felt like someone was sitting on it. I pressed the button to let the passenger window roll down partway.

Gordon beamed his flashlight back in my face. I raised my hand to block the light. He lowered it, but I kept mine shining into their cab.

"Get too hot for you in Sterling? Heh heh," Gordon chortled, that weird light in his eyes glinting as if some other entity lurked there, his crooked tartar-covered teeth bared in an unpleasant grin. "I wouldn't hang out here if I was you. You remember what happened last time."

"Is that a threat?" My heart began to pound, but my voice was hard.

"Oh no, ma'am. It ain't no threat. No threat at all."

"How come you're driving Lonnie's truck?"

"This ain't Lonnie's truck. This is Alan's mother's truck," he said gesturing toward Alan who grinned a hideous parody of a smile. He had a big gap between his front teeth.

"Well, maybe I should stay out here to escort you," Gordon leered.

"Get lost."

"I ain't doin' nothing wrong," he said.

He rolled up his window and drove off. A few moments later I saw more headlights in my rear-view mirror. The truck drew alongside and the driver flicked on his interior light. To my great relief I saw it was Earl.

He motioned for me to follow him. Earl's truck pulled a small trailer with a snowmobile on it. It fishtailed crazily over the slippery road. After about half a mile he parked and walked over to Will's truck, wearing a black snowmobile suit. I unlocked the door on the passenger side and he slid in next to me.

"Our best bet is to try to find Lonnie," Earl said. "If there's any pornographic action, he'll be in the thick of it."

"You know that airplane hangar of George's? It's a Quonset hut like the former Pizza House, but bigger. Do you think the kids confused George's hangar with it?"

"That had occurred to us too. We even checked it out. No evidence there. George had some dealings with Rex, but all legitimate. We couldn't find any connection to the sex ring."

I recapped what Cindy had told us about Rex's murder and George's role as an abuser of South Dare children.

"I wish she'd told us this about George four years ago. She

nearly drove us crazy with her constantly changing stories," Earl said.

"Michael Ross is trying to get David out of jail."

"He's out. Anne called just as I was leaving. She says David's on his way home, but it might take a couple of hours."

That little bit of good news helped me bear the strain.

We decided to go to Rex Dare's former compound first to see if we could find Lonnie. Earl led the way in his truck and I followed to a place where we could pull off the road.

In the deepening darkness I helped Earl unchain the snowmobile and get it off the trailer. He started the engine and I climbed on behind him. The machine was much quieter than I expected and powerful enough to move at a good clip. The headlight beam showed the road had been packed down by a lot of snowmobile traffic and that kept us from sinking too much. In some places the weight of the snow bent the tree branches down to form an arch over our heads. The moon, almost full, was rising. Visibility in the moonlight was relatively good.

The sparkling snow, the moonlight, and the headlight beam made everything seem eerie and magical, like an evil spell enchanting everything. Earl turned abruptly and came to a stop in a trampled area between a collection of shacks. The larger house where Rex once lived was dark. Light from a grimy shack window cast a yellowish glow on the snow.

The red tips of cigarettes moved in the dark next to silhouettes of a couple of people who stood outside one of the other shacks. I beamed my flashlight on them. Two teenagers squinted at the light.

"Where's Lonnie, Jonas?" Earl said.

"How am I supposed to know?" Jonas' voice hadn't changed yet.

I knocked on the door of the cabin with the light on inside.

Dodie LeBlanc answered. Her hair was cut less than an inch long and bleached almost white-blonde. The once bald areas had grown in. She wore thick makeup, false eyelashes, and a dingy white terry cloth robe. Her breath reeked of alcohol. I scanned the tiny kitchen for her little girl Melodie.

Dodie backed away from the door and sank onto a chrome chair. Her robe fell open revealing a red sheath dress split more than halfway up her thigh. Her broomstick-like legs and knobby knees detracted from the femme fatale she was trying to project. I felt sorry for her.

"You with Lonnie now, Dodie?" Earl asked. "Where is he?"

"How would I know?" She sneered, then took a sip from a pint bottle. "I don't keep tabs on him."

An old pot-belly stove made the shack as hot as a sauna. A kettle boiled away on top, steaming the windows. Earl edged toward the tiny bedroom.

"You look like you're all dressed up to go out on the town," Earl said from the doorway.

"Don't I, though." Dodie was nodding, she was so drunk.

"Where's your little girl?" I asked.

Dodie looked at me in an alcoholic daze. Her jaw hung open and she looked like she was trying to focus her eyes. Earl had reached the other room.

"She's in the bedroom," she said. I heard fear rising in her voice.

"There's no one in the bedroom," Earl said.

Dodie lurched to her feet and staggered past Earl into the bedroom. I followed. She tore the blankets off the bed where pillows had formed a child-sized lump. "Melodie! Melodie!" she cried. "Oh my God, oh my God! He's taken Melodie!"

"Taken Melodie where?" Earl asked.

Dodie brushed past us and ran out the door in her slippers, her bathrobe streaming behind her. She ran between the deep drifts on the footprint-packed path.

"Melodie! Melodie! Oh my God!" she screamed.

We bolted outside after her. Dodie climbed onto Earl's snowmobile, weeping and screaming.

"Where's Lonnie?" Earl asked.

Dodie tried to start the engine.

Earl and I lifted her by her bent elbows and carried her back to the shack. Her chest heaved and she retched. She kicked and struggled, but she was as weak as a bird so we subdued her easily and got her back inside.

"Is Lonnie making a movie?" I asked.

"You've got to find him. He's got my little girl."

"Dodie, are you going to be in the movie? Looks like you're all dressed up for it," Earl said.

"He told me *I* was going to be in it. Liar. Liar. Liar!" she cried.

"Where are they making it?" I asked.

"In the Pizza House."

"That's impossible."

"We was always blindfolded, but I know what the inside looks like. I'm not stupid."

She dove at a pile of clothes on the floor and pulled out a pair of worn snow pants. She hiked up her dress and pulled them on.

"He's gonna use my little girl like they used them kids last time. He promised me they wouldn't do that. Please help me find my little girl. She's only six."

"Dodie, the Pizza House is George Hall's airplane hangar, right?" Earl said.

It was like watching a light go on in Dodie's brain. Her reddened lips twisted into an angry sneer and her brown eyebrows came together. Her scalp showed through her white-blonde hair as a look of rage and betrayal spread across her face.

"Yeah. I guess it is."

the Sound Stage

We drove Earl's snowmobile back to his truck, and as we loaded it back onto its trailer I heard the faint sound of another snowmobile in the distance, barely audible over the whistling of the wind through the snow-covered balsam firs. Then I heard a helicopter's beating blades grow louder and louder. Flying low and coming toward us its searchlight swept the woods. Earl and I jumped into his truck. The helicopter hovered over us, then veered off. We climbed out and listened until we could no longer hear it.

He suggested we try to get to George Hall's lodge via a snowmobile trail. As I drove Will's truck following the red tail lights on Earl's trailer I prayed the Lord's Prayer out loud.

"Our Father, Who art in heaven. Hallowed be Thy name. Thy kingdom come."

I paused. *Thy will be done. What if it's God's will that Grace never comes home again?* My muscles tensed. The thought was unbearable. *Oh Lord, please protect Grace and let her come home unharmed. I'll give you my whole life. Please, God.*

The church parking lot hadn't been ploughed, so we pulled as close to the drifts by the roadside as we could. My boots sank in the fresh snow as I trudged on wobbly legs to Earl. A light burned over the church's front door.

"I'm terrified we won't find Grace in time." My voice was thick and shaky.

He put an arm across my shoulder and hugged me to his side. "Lord, I pray for my sister, Linda. Please comfort her and guide us. We pray for Grace's protection," he said.

Then he prayed silently for several seconds. I tried praying the Lord's Prayer again, but still balked at *Thy will be done.* Could I trust God with Grace? My emotions said no.

Then I recalled something David had said: "God doesn't care about your feelings. He cares about your will. The choice you make. He wants your will to line up with His."

Thy will be done, I said inwardly, even though I felt fear, dread and turmoil. "Thy will be done," I said out loud, resisting those feelings. *I choose your will, no matter how I feel.* Within moments I felt peace seep into my being. For several seconds I rested in that peace. I knew I had the strength to face whatever lay ahead, and God's grace to strengthen me to play my part in the unfolding of His will. I felt confident God was in control. Confident that He loved Grace too.

"You alright now?" Earl asked.

I nodded. There was something about the way the light from the church reflected in his eyes. They seemed ablaze, as if Jesus were looking at me through them.

We took the snowmobile off the trailer again, and I hopped on the back with Will's toque over my ears and my gloved hands around Earl's waist. The snowmobile bumped over an old logging trail Earl said would take us to George's lodge from the south. The snow was already packed by the tracks of several other snowmobiles.

We must have ridden through the woods for close to twenty minutes when we came to a moonlit clearing where several paths converged before Earl shut off the engine.

"We'll walk in from here," he whispered. "We're about a kilometre from the landing field behind George's lodge."

We pushed the snowmobile under some snow-laden branches. Then we followed the trail of packed snow left by previous snowmobilers. Our boots sank about a foot with each step. We trudged for about fifteen minutes under the moonlight.

Suddenly, I heard someone cough and clear his throat. I grabbed Earl's sleeve and we stopped. About fifty yards ahead a lighter flickered, partially illuminating the features of a man. The lighter clanked shut, dousing the light, and we heard the crackle of a walkie-talkie and male voices on the tinny speaker.

Then the helicopter swooped overhead. Earl and I tumbled under the heavy boughs of a large spruce. The helicopter hovered over the men we had seen, shining its searchlight on them.

"They must have lookouts posted all through the woods co-ordinated with this helicopter," Earl whispered.

I dug Will's cell out of my pocket and flipped it open. No Service. I showed Earl the glowing letters.

He leaned close and whispered, "We need to get help."

"You go. I'll keep an eye on things."

Earl shook his head. He grabbed my arm.

I leaned into his ear. "I'm staying. I won't do anything stupid."

After whispering a quick prayer for my physical and spiritual protection Earl picked his way cautiously along the edge of the trail. As soon as he was out of sight I continued ahead as softly as I could.

Snippets of the lookouts' conversation drifted over to me. They seemed oblivious to my presence. I felt like I was invisible. The thought crossed my mind I was being foolhardy, but I felt a complete calm I believed came from God. I slipped past them and could see the lights from the hangar through the trees.

Their walkie-talkies crackled. Suddenly, the helicopter roared overhead, whipping the tops of the trees. It dipped in the air and bobbed crazily like the pilot was drunk or showing off. Then it landed by the hangar, its blades whirling and its skis sinking in the snow. I stuffed my gloves into my parka pocket and reached for a lighter pair, flexible enough for me to use my gun.

"Stay here, slimebag," I heard one of the lookouts say.

"I gotta see what's going on."

"You move one step from this spot and I'll shoot you."

"What's the matter with you?" The other man shouted. He flicked on his lighter and lit another cigarette. I figured the man with his back to me was holding a gun on the man with the smoke.

"We're getting paid to stay here."

"You heard the radio, man. Someone took a shot at the helicopter. The pilot's been hit, for Pete's sake!"

"There's others attending to that. I told you, move out of here and I'll shoot your head off."

"What the hell they doin' in that hangar anyways?"

"I don't know and I don't care. Don't move."

While the men were distracted by their argument I continued to make my way forward toward the airstrip. Once off the trail packed by snowmobile traffic I sank into hip-deep snow, pushing through the trees and brush to the field. The helicopter's engine had cut out, though the blades still whirled, *chop, chop, chop.* The noise hid the sound of twigs cracking as I pushed through the undergrowth. It was tough going. Finally, I broke through the brush into the field and surveyed the scene. The helicopter's blades still spun slowly. I couldn't count how many people had gathered near the bird because the pilot's door was on the opposite side. I waded along the perimeter of the field as close to the edge as possible.

Wading through the deep snow required lots of stamina, but I made steady progress. Having circled around enough for a good view of the helicopter I saw three men lift the pilot out of the cockpit. He couldn't walk and had his arm slung over one of the men's shoulders. George's SUV drove up. I dove into the snow as its headlights illuminated the spot where I was standing.

I tunnelled to a place beyond the headlight beams and poked my head up again. George and the other men were too distracted by the wounded pilot to notice me. They eased the pilot into the truck and drove off. I continued around in an arc that took me toward the back of the hangar. Through the partly open back door dim light from inside reflected on the snow.

Even with gloves my hands were stiff and cold, so I hugged them to my body under my parka. When they had warmed enough to handle my pistol I pushed through the snow toward the open door. At the side of the hangar a generator hummed and diesel fumes penetrated the air. The snow around the door was trampled and dirty. I readied my gun as I moved to the side of the door to peek inside and found I was staring at the back of what seemed to be scenery flats.

Rough two-by-fours held the plywood panels in place. From the arched roof a lighting grid illuminated the area inside the flats. Dirty wet footprints and dozens of cigarette butts soiled the polished cement floor. The way was clear and I slipped inside.

Behind the flats a man shouted and cursed. My blood chilled when I recognized Rafe's voice. He must have been standing at the other end of the hangar, maybe seventy-five feet from me, with a lot of gear and the scenery flats between us.

"You stupid fools!" he screamed. "We're five hours behind schedule! What's the matter with you people? It's one screw-up after another!"

He laced his tirade with blasphemies and obscenities. I inwardly rejoiced. Something was fouling up Rafe's plan, impeding it. Maybe our prayers were getting in his way.

I peeked through a crack and saw three video cameras on wheels, thick cables running from them across the floor, and two men and one woman behind them. One of the flats was painted to resemble an altar, except the crucifix was upside down. The blasphemous sight deeply offended me. On the imitation altar rested an ornate chalice and a communion paten full of wafers.

About twenty people gathered near Rafe. Three of them were dressed as priests with red vestments. One wore a bishop's mitre. Six people were nearly naked except for spike collars around their necks and leather thongs. The men, whose bodies gleamed with oil, shivered from the cold. One was dressed as a satyr, with a hairy lower body padded and reshaped to look like a fat goat's. He had horns attached to his head. There were two women wearing long shining gowns with garlands of flowers in their hair.

I edged closer into an area where costumes were stored and gasped when I saw an array of animal heads – a donkey, goat, bull, gorilla and matching costumes.

Where is Grace?

I squeezed between the costume racks, trying not to knock down any props. Just ahead was a makeup area with mirrors framed by lights and counters strewn with cosmetics. A heavily tanned young woman sat at a mirror watching Rafe who was still screaming in frustration. Scanning the faces of the actors and crew

I didn't recognize any of them from Sterling or South Dare. They must have been professionals imported from somewhere else.

"Time is money!" Rafe screamed. "If there are any more screwups, it's going to come out of your pay!"

Then his voice dropped. He was arguing with someone, but I couldn't hear what he was saying.

Then, "We're going to take a fifteen minute break!" he bellowed. "There's some food and coffee down at the lodge! Then let's get this damned show on the road! Fifteen minutes, sharp!"

I sank lower among the clothes until I could see Rafe's legs and torso. Another set of legs waddled after him. They looked as if they might belong to George, but I wasn't sure until I heard his deep voice.

"This is no good," George said. "We have to pull the plug and get out of here."

"Don't worry! It's under control. The crew isn't used to this studio, that's all."

"It's not under control. Someone shot at the helicopter. Hit the pilot in the leg. He's bleeding badly. And one of the lookouts saw that woman Mountie scouting around."

"You were supposed to take care of the police."

"I did. Most of them are trying to quell the riot we started in Sterling. But without the helicopter we have no early warning system. Farmers and volunteer firefighters are gathering at the South Dare church. Most of them have rifles and snowmobiles."

Rafe started swearing and kicked a wastebasket over.

"Have your snipers hold them off."

"I will not be a party to murder."

"I didn't say murder anyone. A few shots, even into the air, should be enough to hold them off. Bring the children in now. Let's at least shoot the scene they're in before we get out of here," Rafe pleaded. He changed personalities like a model changes clothes.

"There's another problem."

"Oh, don't tell me you lost another one?"

"You can't use Catherine's daughter."

"We have to. You let that other little girl get away. We need someone totally innocent or this movie isn't going to work."

"You can make it work without her. Catherine's your girlfriend. Don't you have any sense of loyalty?"

Rafe laughed. "George, you're not thinking straight. What difference does it make?"

I moved closer to the scenery flat and peeked between the cracks to get a clear view of both Rafe and George.

"You're not using Catherine's daughter. And no one gets snuffed." George's voice was shaking. He took a gun out of his belt and pointed it at Rafe, his hand trembling.

"Hey, man. What are you doing that for? Come on, George. I'll whisk Grace back to her mom and it'll be like nothing happened."

"No, come with me. We're getting out of here."

"You've got hundreds of thousands of dollars riding on this thing," Rafe said with a fake-sounding catch in his voice. "We can't blow it now. When we finish this you'll be initiated into the occult arts as an adept. And the movie will make millions. You won't need to ever set foot in this backwater again. We can retire in Thailand and live like princes. Give me that gun, George."

George stepped backward, tripped, and dropped the gun. Rafe kicked it aside, then embraced George, whispering in his ear.

"Please, George. You gotta know I love you more than anything. You're like a father to me."

"You're going to sacrifice Catherine's little girl! I saw your script!" George cried.

"Come on, George. This is a movie! This is art. We aren't going to hurt her. We have all those guests who've paid to take part in the orgy we're going to film. We owe them the pleasure we've promised. We'll make a fortune. My DVD with Catherine's daughter on the cover is selling like hotcakes. No one wants to see corrupted little children who are really miniature adults. They want to imagine having sex with an innocent child, someone not already violated by someone else. They want to absorb that sweetness. We gotta use her, not only for the sake of the art, but for the powers we'll both gain. Supernatural powers. Then we can just get in the helicopter and disappear with the videos. Let everyone else fend for themselves. Grace is my shining star. Please, George, I gotta use her."

"I'm not even sure the helicopter's flyable." George's voice sounded choked and hoarse.

"Why don't you go outside and check it out? I'll get the children and we'll film what we need with them. Get your hired hands to keep the vigilantes at bay. No one needs to get hurt. We're all set to go. I need two hours with the children. That's all. Then we'll be home free. Go check out the bird."

George moved out of sight.

"Stupid fool," Rafe muttered. He picked up the gun, then left the makeup area and yelled at the crew who must have drifted back to the set from their break. "Time's up! Let's get this show on the road!"

I had to get to the helicopter before George did. I suspected he'd command the lookouts to shoot anyone who got too close. I worked my way backward from among the clothes, then crept along the outside of the scenery flats and out the back door.

At the helicopter I climbed up into the cockpit. Inside it smelled of fuel, burned rubber and fresh blood. I felt cold and clammy, my heart jumping in my chest and my ears ringing. *What if I guessed wrong and George wasn't coming to the helicopter?* I made a quick scan of the cockpit with my flashlight, then yanked and tore on some dangling wires until a few broke loose. I tried to smash the dials with my baton, though I barely managed to crack the glass. Then I saw the box that transmitted the signals for the walkie-talkies and turned up the dial to hear the crosstalk.

"Do you read me? Over," said a voice that, despite the static, sounded like one of the lookouts I'd passed in the woods. A red light flickered to show the sound level. I turned down the dial and searched for the wires connecting it to the battery. When I found them I yanked them until they came loose and the red light on the box went out.

Leaning back I realized I was sitting against something. I picked it up and saw it was duct tape! I laughed to myself. *God seems to be looking after every detail.* I had cuffs on my belt, but duct tape would also come in handy. I slipped behind the seat.

Within minutes George came into view carrying a red toolbox and a huge battery-operated lantern. He set the toolbox down on the snow, climbed into the pilot's seat, and surveyed the controls with the lantern. I pressed my gun to his temple.

"Shut up, or you're a dead man," I whispered. I passed him the duct tape.

"Pull off a piece of this and put it over your mouth."

He shifted in the seat and swung his legs toward the outside. Just as he was about to jump out, I bashed the gun down on his skull as hard as I could. He lifted his arm to ward off another blow and scrambled to get out. Grabbing his collar I bashed him again. He slumped into the seat. I peeled some duct tape off and wrapped it around his mouth and the back of his head. Then I handcuffed his hands behind his back and left him pitched forward, his head bleeding over the controls. I checked to make sure he could breathe and ran my fingers over the back of his skull where I'd hit him. A couple of goose eggs were swelling and his scalp bled profusely. I wiped my hands on the back of the leather seat.

Squeezing by him I climbed out of the helicopter on the side facing the woods so any lookouts at the hangar couldn't see me. After holstering my gun I scrubbed my fingers with some snow. My hands ached. If Grace was going to be part of Rafe's movie, he would bring her to the makeup room first. That meant I had to intercept her. I snuck around the helicopter and peered under the rudder, then ran through the snow toward the back door of the hangar.

the Captive

Under the hangar's back door light two men with what looked like AK-47s slung over their shoulders leaned against the corrugated metal wall, smoking cigarettes. I dropped to the snow and crawled toward the side of the building, which was in deep shadow. The roar of a generator drowned out the noise of my footsteps as I felt my way cautiously toward the front of the hanger.

A five-foot plywood fence surrounded the generator. I peeked around it toward the front of the building to see four men trudging up the hill dragging five young children by their hands. The children had to skip and trot to keep pace with the men.

I blinked. There she was, her eyes wide with fear. I had to bite my lip to keep from calling out to her, to let her know I was there, that everything would be alright.

It was Grace.

Dodie's little girl Melodie trotted alongside Lonnie who was wearing the black jacket with the red shoulder trim, his long hair streaming in the wind. The fact the children were not blindfolded made me realize Rafe didn't care what they saw, or whether they could describe their surroundings later.

Another sign he planned to kill them.

Once the men brought the children inside the hangar, I skirted the generator and sprinted along the side to the front door where I hoped no one was standing guard. Just as I came out into the open to access the door a couple of snowmobiles came up the path from the lodge. I straightened up, slowed down, and strode toward the hangar as if I belonged on the property. My toque and blue-black parka made my uniform less obvious and the deep snowdrifts hid the bright yellow stripe down the side of my slacks. To my relief the men didn't seem to notice me as I slipped inside the front door.

Once inside a small foyer the rear of a scenery flat blocked any view of the sound stage. Off to the left was the makeup area, walled off with partitions, where I assumed the men had taken the children. I heard a child crying and several voices, mostly male, speaking at once. Over to my right was a small enclosed office area. I found a door facing the flats slightly ajar. I slipped inside the office and twisted the lock.

The office walls did not extend all the way to the curved roof of the hangar. Behind me a picture window of heavily tinted glass faced outdoors. I climbed on top of the desk and peered over the partition. I could see Grace sitting in the makeup area. She still looked frightened but otherwise unharmed. Melodie leaned against Grace's chair, eyes dazed. Her long platinum-blonde hair fell to her shoulders in stiff curls.

A couple of terrified-looking little boys, about six or seven, stood behind Grace wearing navy blue shorts, long socks, white shirts, and little navy blue ties. I figured they were European school uniforms. Another little girl, shivering and sobbing, wore a frilly white dress like a wedding gown, similar to Melodie and Grace. They reminded me of the dress Gran sewed for my First Holy Communion. *How dare Rafe profane God and these children with his filth.*

Rafe stood behind Grace and looked at her reflection in the mirror. "Don't tart her up with too much makeup. I want the children to look innocent."

"It's cold in here," I heard one of the men say with a strong German accent.

"It'll be hot as Hades under the lights," Rafe said. "Nothing to hinder the free play of lust, I assure you. Aren't they beautiful?

Isn't this one especially beautiful?" He bent over so his cheek pressed against Grace's. Then he straightened up.

"Grace, you're my girl. Your mother will be so proud of you." He patted her head.

"Where is Mommy?" The mournfulness in Grace's voice wrenched my heart.

"She's on her way here right now," Rafe said.

Men crowded around him wearing the costumes I'd seen earlier. I winced with disgust when a man wearing only a thong sauntered into the makeup room.

"Lonnie, where's George?" Rafe asked. "We're going to start the orgy scene. I need him. I sent him out to check the helicopter. Get him."

Lonnie had already taken his shirt off. The way he shoved his arms into his parka showed me he was furious. I ducked so he wouldn't see me, but caught a glimpse of that black jacket with the red trim.

"Powder and some foundation is all you need," Rafe said to the men, irritated. "Why don't you guys put on your own makeup? That'll save time. Just help yourself to what you need."

Men mumbled in heavily accented English. One complained it was too cold inside the hangar. Rafe ordered them to keep their hands off the children until the cameras started rolling.

Will's phone vibrated in my pocket. I took it out and squatted on the desk behind the partition. Karen was on the line asking me where I was. I told her.

"The little girl? Is she there?"

"Yes," I whispered.

"The ERT is on its way," she said. "You were right about Rafe. Our DEA contacts checked out what you told us. It's even worse than that. He's absconded with the money we gave him for the drug sting. Is he there?"

"Yeah," I whispered.

"Hang in there, Linda. We're on our way. Will and some other members are already outside."

I closed the phone and stuffed it back into my pocket. Outside the picture window I could hear a man hollering. Then the hangar's front door banged open against the partition, making me nearly jump out of my uniform. I peeked over the wall and saw Lonnie striding up to the scenery flats. He shouted for Rafe who met him near the makeup area.

"That woman cop is here. She handcuffed George to the helicopter seat and hit him on the head. He's in pretty bad shape."

Rafe let out a string of expletives, his whole body contorting with rage. "Find her. Search everywhere."

"I gotta cut George loose," Lonnie said. "I need a hacksaw."

The doorknob to the office jiggled and someone kicked the hollow wooden door. Training my pistol on the door I heard the sound of keys jingling, then one scraping in the lock. The interior office light came on overhead.

"This wasn't locked before," Rafe said, apparently trying another key in the lock. I realized I had only moments before he saw me. *Should I shoot him?*

Then the hangar's front door banged against the partition behind me again. I nearly dropped my gun.

"Lonnie, you slimeball! Where are you, Lonnie?" a voice shrieked. It was Dodie's. "I'm going to kill you, Lonnie!"

"Come on, Dodie, sweetheart, put the gun down," Lonnie's voice pleaded. "Melodie's right here. Right behind me. See? She's fine. You don't want to kill me."

"How could you do this to my baby! You monster!" Dodie screamed. "How could you?"

Then a single, deafening blast.

Silence.

"Mommy!" Melodie screamed.

"What did you do that for?" Lonnie wailed.

"I just saved your life, you fool," Rafe said. "Bring George back here. Tell your men to find that cop. Get the little girl away from that woman. She's getting blood on her dress."

Melodie wailed.

Suddenly, the office door banged open. Two men wearing bandanas stormed in aiming shotguns at me. Behind me a voice from above the partition ordered me to drop my gun. My concentration broken, I dropped it.

Rafe swaggered in, a derisive grin on his face. "I knew you were in here." He gave one of the men a roll of blood-spattered duct tape. "Tie her to that chair." Rafe picked up my pistol.

The man stripped tape off the roll and secured my arms. I strained against the tape bound around my chest. Then he bound my legs to the chair. The man's parka smelled of spruce trees and chewing tobacco.

"This place will be overrun with police any moment now," I said.

The man tying me up started to put tape over my mouth, but Rafe shook his head.

Then Rafe slapped my face. Hard. "I've got you as insurance, princess!" Rafe sneered. "We may want to have a little action with you later. The Mountie uniform's a nice erotic touch."

I closed my eyes for a couple of seconds and breathed in slowly to control the pain. Despite it I was amazed at how free of fear I was. Or anger. *Thy will be done.*

Then George shuffled in, leaning on Lonnie who looked stunned and resentful. George's blood had dribbled all over his beige parka making a soggy maroon cape. He sat in an office chair on castors.

Rafe handed him my gun.

"Keep an eye on her, George. We're in the home stretch now, my friend. We'll use her as a hostage along with the children if the pigs show up too soon."

He turned to Lonnie. "Make sure we don't have any holes in our defences. I'm counting on you."

Lonnie's eyes glistened with hatred, but he obeyed. He and Rafe left the room.

George winced as he rested his gun hand on his knee.

"Why are you letting Rafe do this?" I said.

"Shut up."

"You don't like what he's doing. I know you don't want anyone murdered."

He waved the pistol at me. "I told you to shut up!"

"What kind of hold does Rafe have over you?"

"What kind of question is that?"

George adjusted his grip on the gun. *He's not used to handling a gun.* He gingerly touched the back of his head with his free hand. *If I can only find a way to persuade him to help me save these children.*

"Why does Rafe have so much power over you?" I repeated.

"Oh what, if you can find the source of Rafe's power, you can turn it to your advantage?" He touched his scalp again, then gazed stupidly at the blood on his fingertips.

"Yes, and the advantage of those children out there. You're not a murderer, George. You know Rafe plans to kill these children." George's eyes darted back and forth as he weighed his options.

We heard someone blow a whistle.

"I want the techs in position!" Rafe shouted on the set. "Bring the children here. Now!" I heard children whimpering and crying. My eyes filled with tears and sweat trickled down my back.

"He's not going to hurt them," George said. Using his feet he wheeled his chair backward and closed the office door.

"Just like Becky Dare wasn't hurt the last time you made one of these videos?"

"Rafe wasn't involved in that. This production will be art."

"Having an orgy between grown men and children is art? Killing children on video is art?"

"He's not going to kill them." But George's shaky voice betrayed his uncertainty. "What Rafe does is pushing the envelope, yes. But Rafe is an artist, like the Marquis de Sade."

"Artist?" I cried. "He wants to defile these children! He's a vampire stealing their innocence!" Tears rolled down my cheeks. *Lord, help me stop these men!*

"Ah, but it's what Rafe does with stolen innocence. That's where the art comes in. He defiles, yes. But it's more than that. He changes places with them. He takes their innocence, yes. He communes with it and consumes it. He becomes innocent through these children and his film will show this transformation. On a mythological level he's found the fountain of youth. That's what this is all about." George's face was enraptured by the vision Rafe had created. The hair on the back of my neck stood up.

"That's evil and you know it."

"Constable Donner, this is beyond petty man-made categories of good and evil."

"Rafe plans to kill you too George. He's using you."

"Maybe so." George let the gun rest sideways on his knee. I could have knocked it off his lap, but sensed he was softening toward me.

"You don't care?" I asked. "If you don't care, why not save the children? Do something good as your last deed."

"It's gone way too far now. Rafe has supernatural powers. He'll get his way. He always does."

I grimaced and rolled my eyes.

"Oh, you don't believe me?"

"Powers like Rex's?"

"Rex was a con artist," George said. "He pretended to have powers and for a while he had me convinced. Rafe is the real thing."

"No, George. Rafe is just a better con artist than Rex."

"I've seen him possessed by a deity," George said. "He's told me things about myself that I've never told a human soul. I've seen him bend spoons and make objects float. He can bend people to do his will."

"You are not a murderer, George. Help me save those children."

The office lights flickered, then shut off leaving the office in blackness. No light came from the sound stage beyond the flats. The children screamed. The tinted glass in the picture window prevented the moonlight from penetrating. My heart thumped with anticipation. The ERT must be outside. Rescue was at hand.

"Shut those brats up!" Rafe screamed curses in the studio area. George's chair creaked. It sounded like he stood up. I heard his feet shuffle and could barely make out a black form staggering out of the office. I struggled against the tape binding me to the chair. Then more shuffling feet, and George's chair creaked again as a shadowy form sat down again.

"George, what's going on?" Rafe shouted. It sounded like he was in the hallway outside the office. I saw a flashlight beam dancing outside the door. "We don't have enough power to run the control room or the lights!" Rafe shone the flashlight on me.

"Has anyone checked the generator? Maybe it's out of fuel," George said. I heard the scuffle of footsteps. Rafe pushed past George and pressed the cold metal of a gun against my cheek. Behind the scenery flats, in the darkness, I could hear the children whimpering in fear.

"What's going on? Was someone with you?"

"The Emergency Response team is outside. This place is surrounded."

"You think you're getting out of here alive? Keep an eye on her, George." Rafe shoved me, making my chair slide against the wall, banging my arm. Then he made his way back to the set.

"Let me loose," I pleaded with George. "If you help me rescue the children, things will go better for you." With my feet I moved my chair closer to the desk.

"Quiet," George said in a choked voice. "Don't move."

I heard Rafe shouting and within a few minutes I heard a child screaming, men swearing, and crashing sounds as if a fight had broken out on the set. I heard something like props smashing to the floor and bodies thudding against the scenery flats.

"The police are here," I said to George. "So much for Rafe's supernatural powers."

George pushed my chair away from the desk. I could barely see in the dark, but I heard a sound like a desk drawer being yanked open. His hand rattled whatever was inside. I wondered if he was looking for another gun. He pulled my chair toward him and I felt a scissor blade slip between my arm and the tape. He snipped the tape and released my arm. I shook it to restore the blood flow. He let the scissors clatter to the floor.

"You're on your own." In the dark, George felt his way toward the door and slipped away while all hell seemed to have broken loose on the set.

I found the scissors with my feet and strained to reach them with my free hand. The children's cries and screams tormented me. One of them could get killed if anyone opened fire. The shouting and crashing grew louder, more violent. I tore at the tape and finally loosened it enough to reach the scissors.

I cut the duct tape around my chest and freed my other arm, snipped through the tape around my legs, and burst out of the chair.

Carrying the scissors like a weapon I felt my way behind the scenery flats. Lantern light and flashlight beams in the studio area created shafts of light behind the scenery flats.

"Tie him up," a voice ordered. It was a familiar voice, but not one that belonged to anyone I knew from the detachment. Maybe it was an ERT member from Halifax.

"Where's that pervert George!" the voice roared.

I heard slaps, thuds and grunts. I shuddered, realizing whoever was shouting was no Mountie and the ERT was not responsible for the mayhem.

"Please, stop," Rafe pleaded. "You can have a piece of the action. Don't hurt me, please."

I heard scuffling and then a gun went off with a loud *bang!* I jumped in the opposite direction, scrambling as fast as I could.

"I got George!" a voice shouted.

I peeked through one of the cracks and saw Rafe stripped to his black thong. Two men dragged him across the floor and tied him spread-eagled to the fake altar. By the roving flashlight beams I made out Lonnie and Gordon emerging from the shadows with George whose hands were raised. I saw the backs of three or four men silhouetted by the flashlights.

"George Hall, you scumbag," the voice raged. It was Lance. "It's payback time! In a moment this place is going to look like Waco!"

Lance emerged from the dark, tossing liquid from a jerry can at the scenery flats. Soon the thick smell of gasoline filled the hangar. He hurled some over George and Rafe. The same bandana-wearing men who had been guarding the set were now marching to Lance's orders.

My pulse beat in my skull. I couldn't see the children. The half-naked men who had been ready to perform on film huddled together, shivering. One of them was crying hysterically. Lance slapped his face and splashed gasoline around his feet and those of the other men.

"Lonnie, please. Help me, man," Rafe begged. His face was covered with blood.

"You shouldn't have shot Dodie," Lonnie hissed. "You didn't even give me a chance to talk her out of it." He choked on his sobs.

"Come on, Lance. We can all be rich," George said. "We can all have powers beyond what your father ever dreamed of."

"You think this is about money?" Lance screamed, his face inches away from George's. "Or power? You destroyed my life! You thought you could use us and then toss us like garbage! You pervert!"

Lance spat in George's face. "This is payback time for all those times you did us when we was kids. It's payback time for the way you did other kids when we was too old for you to use. It's payback time for the power you held over Rex."

"You got it wrong, Lance. Rex had power over me," George pleaded.

"You killed him!" Lance screamed.

"I didn't kill him, I swear!"

"South Dare folks want to let you know what they really think of you," Lance said. "Strip him and tie him up."

George struggled against Lonnie and Gordon until Lance punched his face. When George slumped forward Lonnie tore at his shirt and used a knife to slice off his pants. In seconds George's chubby hairy body, clad only in white boxer shorts, was tied to the altar next to Rafe.

I had to find the children.

Now.

the **Battle**

A strong impression came over me. I would find the children hiding among the costumes in the makeup area. *Is God speaking to me?* The impression was wordless, but I knew exactly what I was supposed to do. I scrambled in the dark behind the scenery flats, nauseated by the smell of gasoline, terrified a stray spark would ignite a huge explosion.

I stumbled over what felt like a sack of flour. I felt it and realized it was a small child huddled in a fetal position. I heard whimpering, reached out, and felt another warm little body shrink from my touch.

"It's okay. I'm a police officer. I'm going to get you out of here," I whispered. "Where are the others?" Suddenly, I felt little arms grip my legs. *Oh, please be Grace!*

"Auntie Linda?" she sobbed.

I grabbed her and held her tight, stroking her hair. Then I told the others they needed to do exactly what I said.

I prodded her and the other two, who I guessed were the little boys, and pushed them toward the hangar's front door. The other two little girls were missing.

"Melodie!" I whispered through the darkness. "Come on, Melodie, we have to get out of here!" Once outside I raised my hands in the air just in case someone from the ERT had his sights on me. Grace shivered in the frilly white dress and clung to me.

Everything was quiet outside. The moonlight reflected on the snow. My heart hammered when I saw no sign of Will nor the other members. A snowmobile started, then several more. Then with great relief I saw Melodie and the other little girl hiding behind the tarp covering George's plane.

I herded the children toward the lodge, urging them to run. Someone with a bandana ran out of the hangar, hopped on a snowmobile, and zoomed right by me. Soon several snowmobiles whizzed past. The guards from South Dare were leaving, slipping into the woods. The front door to the lodge was ajar. I scrambled up the steps, the children behind me.

"Freeze!" Will said.

"It's me, Linda!"

"Oh, thank God!" He grabbed me with one arm and holstered his gun. My knees wobbled with relief and he kept me from falling. With his other arm he pushed the children inside.

I pulled away from his embrace. "Where's the ERT? Lance has poured gasoline all over the hangar," I said. "He says he's going to burn the place down and at least twenty people are inside."

"They're on their way from Sterling. I'll relay that info now," Will lifted a walkie-talkie.

Earl emerged from the shadows with a flashlight. "There's a wounded man in one of the bedrooms. He's unconscious. He's lost a lot of blood."

"Must be the helicopter pilot." I wiped my running nose with my sleeve. Grace clung to me. Despite the warmth inside the lodge, she shivered.

Will and Earl left to meet the ERT. I stayed behind with the children, exhausted, yet relieved. Inside a book-lined den where a fireplace contained some gleaming red coals I threw some wood on and soon a fire blazed. The children huddled on the green leather couch facing the fire, covered in a soft mohair blanket I found.

Out the window I saw the helmeted ERT members in their black suits flit through the moonlit landscape. The lights from two snowploughs lit up the laneway. Behind them shone the headlights and flashing lights of several police cars and some ambulances.

Will brought one of the ERT corporals into the lodge, introduced us, then ran back. I debriefed him on what I'd seen inside the hangar.

He took off his helmet and handed it to me. It had a small microphone jutting out and a headset inside.

"One of your members has gone into the hangar. Your staff sergeant wants you to persuade him to get out of there." *Will's inside the hangar?*

"Put this on," he said.

I slipped it onto my head.

"The actors and technicians are coming out now!" I heard Will shouting through the helmet's headset. "They are coming out now!"

"Will, come out of there! Do you hear me? Will!" I pressed the helmet against my head. "I don't think he can hear me!"

Will was yelling, "Lance, let's go! Don't throw your life away!" I visualized Will standing on the darkened set, lit only by flashlights. I imagined George and Rafe still tied spread-eagled to the altar.

"Get out of here, Will!" Lance cried. "I don't want to kill you!" I could see in my mind's eye the gun Lance waved in Will's face. *One gunshot could ignite the gas fumes.*

"Will, get out of there!" I shouted. *Lord, please make him listen!*

"We're all going to get out of here, Lance," Will said. "I'm going to cut George and Rafe loose."

My stomach lurched.

Karen's amplified voice boomed over a megaphone. "Drop your weapon, put your hands up, and come out."

"Come on, Lance, Lonnie's safe outside," Will said. "Don't let yourself become one of the bad guys."

"It's too late! I already have!" Lance cried. "I have to stop the horror. It's like a virus. It's got to be burned out. It's got to end right here," he sobbed.

"Put the lighter away, Lance. Come on. You don't want to burn us all up," Will said.

"Will, can you hear me?" I shouted. "Get out!"

I gazed at the children huddling together on the couch.

"Stay here, okay?" I said to the ERT corporal.

Without waiting for his response I bolted from the room, down the outside steps, and raced toward the hangar, helmet on. Two men on a snowmobile reached Karen at the same time I did. The driver was Earl. My heart swelled with relief when I saw that his passenger was David Jordan. *David must have gone directly to the church from prison.*

"Lance and Will are inside the hangar!" I yelled to David over the noise of the sputtering motor. "It's full of gasoline fumes. Lance is going to blow the place up."

ERT officers took up positions around the hangar. Karen put a bullhorn to her lips. "You are surrounded. Come out with your hands up. No one will get hurt. Constable Bright! Come out of there now! This is an order!" Karen's voice boomed.

"Will, can you hear me?" I said. "He can't hear me!"

"I'll go in," David said to me. "Lance will listen to me."

David and I started walking toward the hangar.

"No, you can't go in," Karen said. "No civilians."

"David can convince Lance to let everyone go, Karen. I'll take him in," I pleaded.

"I'm going to cut George loose," I heard Will say through the helmet headset. "I'm going to take George outside."

"George isn't going nowhere!" Lance screamed. "You get out of here, Will! George stays! Get out now! I'm going to light this!"

More people arrived on snowmobiles. Marie Dare was among them. She pushed toward Karen.

"That's Lance Dare's wife!" I shouted at Karen. "Maybe she can stop him!"

Karen explained to Marie what was going on and handed her the bullhorn. With Karen momentarily distracted David and I sprinted across to the hangar, now illuminated with police spotlights.

"Lance! Lance!" boomed Marie's plaintive voice. "It's me. Marie. Please come out. Cody and I love you. Please, give yourself up. Please."

Just as we got inside the door, David stopped me. He bowed his head and closed his eyes for a moment. His face was strained. "The evil forces around here are powerful. I already feel them attacking me." He opened his eyes and I noticed the blood had drained from his face, and his usually straight posture was bowed. "They can insinuate thoughts and feelings into us and deceive our senses," David said, as if wrestling with his own doubts and fears. "Jesus is Lord. He has authority, Linda. He is all powerful. They are puny in comparison. Remember that. Nothing can separate you from the love of God in Christ. No matter what, keep your eyes on Jesus." He squeezed my arm in what felt like a feeble benediction. I hung onto these words, and kept repeating them.

Through my headset I heard scuffling, banging and muffled grunts. I was afraid one spark would ignite the fumes. The winter air outside was thick with the smell of gasoline.

"David and I are coming in," I said into my microphone. *Could Will hear me?*

"Don't light it, Lance!" Will said. "Let me cut these guys loose!"

David and I followed the beam of my flashlight past Dodie's body lying inside the door. "Oh, my Lord," David murmured. He knelt by Dodie's corpse and felt for a pulse.

"Come on, David," I said. I helped him to his feet.

"Lance, it's David!" he shouted. "Linda and I are coming in!"

"Don't come in!" Will hollered. "I'm coming out!"

Just as David and I came around the scenery flats, I heard a low monotonous chanting that made my hair stand on end. It sounded like thousands of angry bumblebees and vibrated in my stomach.

"Stop that! Stop that singing!" Lance screamed. "Get out! I'm going to..." Lance flicked the cover off the lighter. I played the flashlight beam on Rafe and George and realized Rafe was the one making the horrible sound.

Rafe's chanting built in volume, making me seasick. The gasoline fumes made the darkness shimmer. Several loud bangs startled us. It sounded like the metal beams in the Quonset hut were contracting from the cold, only the cracks were louder, like cracks of thunder. *Nothing can separate me from the love of God. Jesus is Lord.* I repeated the words over and over, resisting the mounting terror. I scrunched my eyes shut and covered my ears to drown out the horrible chanting. The sound stage seemed to spin as if I were drunk.

Suddenly, it grew extremely cold inside the hangar, though Rafe's body glistened with sweat. I glanced at David and was shocked to see him doubled over. I couldn't tell if it was shadows or gas fumes making me hallucinate, but I saw a horrible demon draped over David's shoulders, sticking talons into his back, bit-ing the back of his neck. I recoiled. *Lord, please strengthen David. Jesus is stronger. Jesus is Lord. Jesus, help me to keep my eyes on you.*

A hideous deep voice came out of Rafe, making a buzzing vibration like a chainsaw hitting metal. I winced.

"Lance, go ahead," Rafe said in that awful buzzing voice. "Blow us up." His head was twisted grotesquely, his lips pulled into a skeletal grin.

"Don't listen to him, Lance." David's voice sounded strained, weak.

"The man of God is finding it tough going in here," Rafe's new voice laughed.

Suddenly, Rafe burst from the bonds of the duct tape. His bloody face looked like rotting flesh on a skull. In shock, Lance dropped the lighter. It clattered on the cement floor and disappeared into the shadows.

Rafe laughed. The grating sound transformed into a beautiful melodious laugh. His features started to change. Despite the blood on his face he looked handsome again. The beams from our flashlights were like spotlights hitting him from three different angles. David had dropped to his knees and cradled his face in his hands.

"Worship me," Rafe demanded in the strange voice that transfixed us. Feelings of worship and awe welled up in me. I closed my eyes to resist the way my will seemed to be buckling. *Jesus is Lord. Jesus is Lord.*

"See! Your man of God is on his knees, worshipping me," Rafe said.

"He is not!" I shouted.

"Don't engage the demon," David said, though I could barely hear him. "We aren't warring against flesh and blood. Just focus on Jesus. That's enough."

I heard a crack like thunder.

David's voice wavered. "Every knee shall bow and every tongue confess that Jesus Christ is Lord." It seemed he was trying to convince himself because his own faith was failing.

I panicked. I felt so scared my knees knocked together. I felt an overwhelming compulsion to kneel and bow down before Rafe. I grabbed Will's arm. He wobbled on his feet. The evil in the room built to a huge crescendo. *The gas fumes. Are they causing a toxic reaction? Is that part of what I'm seeing and feeling?*

Rafe laughed. Lance was weeping out loud, scrambling on the floor with his flashlight, looking for the lighter.

"Lance, you belong to me." Rafe's voice sounded like a sensuous bass caress. "Your father gave you to me. Come to me."

"Lance, you belong to Jesus," David croaked. "Go outside, Lance. Please." He sounded like the breath was being forced out of him.

Rafe lunged for David and knocked him to the ground. Will jumped Rafe, who was a much smaller man, but Rafe threw him off. Will thudded against the altar, hitting George's bare leg. Will gasped for air.

Suddenly, I received another strong wordless impression. A command. *Take the crucifix. Raise it up.* My limbs seemed rooted and I still felt an awful urge to kneel before Rafe. With tremendous effort I wove toward the altar partially hidden by George's plump hairy back. Fighting an enormous invisible current I broke the upside-down crucifix off the scenery flat. With every ounce of strength I had, I turned it upright. I looked at the image of Jesus Christ suspended on the cross. *Jesus is Lord. Nothing can separate us from the love of God in Christ.* I felt buffeted by forces trying to keep me from raising the crucifix, as if unseen hands were trying to keep it upside down. I groaned with exertion. Will scrambled to his feet to help me. We marched together toward Rafe who had pinned David to the ground. Rafe pounded David's head with his free hand, bloodying his face.

"In the Name of Jesus, come out of him," Will said, his voice trembling. He didn't sound convincing at all.

Rafe turned around, gaped at Will, and started laughing. "Who do you think you are?" He smashed David in the head with his fist again, then stood up. Rafe kicked David who rolled away from him toward us. Will and I kept marching forward, using all our strength to hold up the crucifix.

I heard scuffling and the sound of the lighter opening.

"I'm going to blow the place up!" Lance said. He held the open lighter up for us to see.

"Don't do it, Lance," David gasped. "You'll belong to him for eternity if you do. It's what he wants you to do." David laboured for

breath. "He has no power except the power we give him by believing his lies. Jesus is Lord. Jesus has all power and authority."
David struggled to stand. Blood gushed from his forehead.

"And where is your Jesus right now?" Rafe asked. "You think a
plastic figure on a couple of sticks frightens me?" He roared with
laughter. "Don't come any closer or I'll kill you!" he screamed at us.

We stopped.

A series of loud cracks and rumbles reverberated through the
Quonset hut. I felt dizzy and disoriented. The crucifix seemed to
weigh a thousand pounds and Will and I couldn't hold it upright
any longer. Then David brushed against my arm. He helped us lift
the crucified Christ upright and urged us to move forward. *Nothing
can separate us from the love of God. Jesus is Lord. Jesus is Lord.*

"Thank you, Jesus, that you are here," David said, his voice
weak. "Thank you, Jesus, that you live in us. For I am persuaded
that neither death, nor life, nor angels, nor demons, nor powers,
nor things present, nor things to come, nor height, nor depth, nor
any other creature, shall be able to separate us from the love of
God, which is in Christ Jesus our Lord," David said, his voice
growing stronger and stronger.

The evil in the room built up further like a huge cresting wave.
I felt a rushing sound in my ears, like thousands of batwings beating. I glanced at Lance who seemed paralyzed with fear.

"Come out of him," David commanded. There was joy in his
voice and a smile on his face. Will broke away from David and me
and tackled Lance who dropped the lighter. It skidded into the
shadows. As David and I got closer to Rafe David shoved the crucifix toward him. Instead of trying to grab it away, to my amazement, Rafe cringed in terror.

"This little figure on a stick, this crucifix, sums up the truth!"
David shouted. "The truth that God sent His Son, Jesus, to become
a man, to take our sin upon Him and die for us! Jesus has set us
free from the likes of you! You are a conquered foe! Come out of
him, all of you! In Jesus' Name, come out of him now!" David
pressed the crucifix against Rafe who recoiled and writhed in pain,
making a horrible guttural sound.

"Come out of him and go back to hell where you came from!"
David insisted. He didn't need my help to hold the crucifix anymore.

Rafe went limp. We heard several loud bangs and another roll of thunder, but the extreme cold in the hangar had dissipated. I shined my flashlight on George who, bruised and bleeding, remained tied to the altar. Using the scissors I cut him loose.

"Let's get out of here," Will said. He gripped Lance in a headlock.

While steadying George I played the light on Rafe's inert form. "What about Rafe?" I searched for the lighter, but couldn't find it.

"Let's go!" Will said. "We can send the ERT in to get him. They have gas masks."

George could walk unaided, so I helped Will drag Lance out and prodded David ahead of us. When we reached the front door I twisted around to see if George was still following us. I swept my flashlight beam around the hallway where Dodie's body lay. No sign of him.

"Go ahead!" I yelled.

I staggered through the fumes back to the set entrance and made one last search for George. As my beam illuminated the porn set's floor I gasped. Rafe's body was gone. Suddenly, with that same calm foresight I'd experienced earlier that evening, I knew Rafe was going to blow the place up.

I sprinted outside and hollered, "The hangar's going to blow!" The fumes made me dizzy and disoriented. "Get back!" I screamed at Karen and the ERT members, waving them back.

"Rafe is gone!" I shouted to Will who was still dragging Lance. I kept running and pushed David forward.

David and I made it about fifty yards from the front door, with Will and Lance right behind us, when the hangar exploded. The blast's force knocked us to the ground. Lance wrestled against Will and seemed to be trying to charge back into the flames.

The explosion singed our hair and the backs of our parkas. ERT members surrounded us in seconds, subdued Lance, and helped us up.

Will leaned against me. "I feel like I'm going to pass out." I also felt unsteady. My head pounded.

David's forehead was bleeding and he seemed to be tottering.

I grabbed his arm. "David, you alright?"

"Praise God! That's all I can say." He grinned and embraced us.

"Rafe got out," I said.

"This place is crawling with ERT members. He won't get far," Will said.

George's fabric plane was now in flames.

I herded Will and David toward one of the ambulances waiting in front of the newly ploughed area in front of the lodge.

This isn't over.

Not yet.

the **Bust**

After Will got into one of the ambulances I ran across the trampled snow to Karen. She embraced me. "Thank God you got out safely. That was a terrible risk, Linda. You shouldn't have gone in there."

"Has anyone arrested Rafe? Or George?" I felt the heat from the fire on my cheeks. "They could have gotten out." I carried the borrowed helmet in my hands.

"I don't know." Karen pointed to a group of about twenty people huddled together, their hands bound by plastic tie-wraps behind their backs. With a flashlight I inspected their faces. I recognized the costumed actors, the makeup lady and the technicians. All the guards from South Dare melted into the surrounding woods.

It was an eerie scene. Under a bright full moon flashing lights in red, blue, and yellow from ambulances, fire trucks, and police cars illuminated dozens of people who milled around in front of the burning hangar. Water from a firehose sprayed the flames consuming George's plane. Soon it looked like the skeleton of a huge bird from hell.

ERT members found George rolling in the snow in agony from burns. They gingerly loaded his blackened body onto a stretcher. I looked away. No sign of Rafe.

I pulled his picture out of my vest pocket and showed it to the team's sergeant. He passed it along and told his men to fan out and search for him. Then the corporal whose helmet I'd borrowed tapped me on the shoulder.

My jaw dropped. "You were supposed to be watching the children!"

He whisked the helmet out of my hands. "They're fine."

But my feet were already pounding the flattened snow, my heart knocking crazily against my chest. At the lodge I bounded up the steps onto the massive porch, then barrelled through the front door, which had been left ajar. The lodge lights were still off so I groped my way toward the small den where I'd left the children.

"Grace! Grace, are you there, sweetheart?"

I heard the children crying. I took my tiny flashlight from my belt and shone it around the room, exhaustion and fear making my legs shaky. Melodie sat with one of the little boys who had his arms wrapped protectively around her. The other little girl, who was about Grace's age, tried to say something to me in French.

"Elle n'est pas ici," she whispered.

"She's not here? Where is she? Où est Grace?"

She began to speak rapidly and hysterically in French. My French wasn't that great at the best of times and her accent was different from what I was used to. The little boy tried to add something, but I couldn't understand his French either.

"Grace is missing again. I need someone who speaks French down at the lodge!" I shouted into my walkie-talkie. "Send Corporal Jacques! Please hurry!"

"That bad man took her," Melodie said.

"What?"

"The man who shot Mom."

Rafe had taken Grace. *How could I have let that happen?*

François arrived a few minutes later and spoke to the two children.

"These kids are from Belgium," he said. "Sounds like this Rafe character put on a gorilla costume or bear suit and took the girl. He's been gone about ten minutes."

"Lance beat him pretty severely." I was wringing my hands in anguish at losing Grace again. "He can't have gotten far."

The shrill sound of sirens filled the air as fire trucks pulled up along with another ambulance. A wave of despair rolled over me. I staggered in a daze up toward the hangar and the ERT members standing near Karen. She reached out and touched my arm. "We'll find them. A canine team is on its way."

"Have some coffee," she said, pouring some dark liquid into the lid of a big thermos.

I sipped some of the steaming liquid, feeling the heat on my tongue and down my throat. Until now I hadn't realized I was almost numb with cold and shock. I began to tremble. Karen had turned to speak with the ERT leaders. I finished the coffee, nudged her elbow, and handed the lid back to her.

"This is the constable whose persistence and hard work enabled this bust," she said to the ERT sergeant.

He shook my hand. "Congratulations, Linda. We've arrested men from Belgium, Australia, the Netherlands and the States. An international child sex ring."

When he let go of my hand I stumbled a little. "Did you hear the demon speaking through Rafe?"

The sergeant and Karen exchanged puzzled looks.

"What are you talking about?" Karen said.

"Did you hear that awful voice?" I said. "Inside the hangar just before we all came out? That monster has Grace!"

"We heard Lance screaming. We heard Will trying to get him to put the lighter down, but otherwise there was static or the voices were too low for us to make out."

Did I imagine the whole thing? The air stank of burning rubber. My head ached. "Rafe is demon possessed. We've got to stop him. We've got to – "

"I think you'd better call it a day," Karen said. "We'll find Grace."

I staggered toward the police cars near the lodge. Someone had turned on the propane-powered lights. A social worker from Sterling led the children outside to a waiting van to keep them warm. Terrified for Grace I kept up a steady stream of prayers.

The children had told François that Rafe had exited from the back door. I surveyed the area and tried to anticipate the direction he'd taken. A cedar grove provided a thick cover on the side of the lodge nearest the hangar. So did a wooded strip behind the house.

I took out my flashlight and looked around the bushes. Nothing. The snow was unmarked.

I wandered back up the hill toward the hangar, trying to warm my stiffening limbs. Then God showed me Rafe's hiding place.

"Has anyone checked the helicopter?" I shouted. I ran toward it.

It remained in shadows – no one was near it. Panting, I slid the door open and surveyed the inside with the narrow intense beam of my flashlight. I played the beam along the panels in the front of the aircraft, then to the passenger seats in the back. I saw a bundle of fur-like material, and gasped. The light shone right into Rafe's bloodied face. He squeezed Grace under his arm. Holding a pistol with both hands he aimed at my face.

"Don't say a word. Drop your gun."

"I don't have one. Let her go, Rafe."

"Shut up and get inside. Get into the pilot's seat."

I climbed up and sat in the pilot's seat.

"Close the door."

I did as he asked. *Where are the ERT members? Had none of them heard me shouting?*

"Put that seatbelt on," he ordered Grace. I heard the clanking of the metal buckles. Rafe, his body clad in a furry suit from the neck down, slipped into the seat beside me. I felt the gun press against my temple. I felt surprisingly calm. This time, though, I knew it was grace from God.

"Thanks for coming, Linda. Now I have two hostages. Give me that flashlight."

He took my light and examined my belt. Then he put the light down and frisked me.

"I told you, I don't have a gun." My weariness gone I assessed my options, wondering whether I could disarm him in this cramped space.

"Unbuckle your belt and throw it out the door."

I did.

Rafe swept the flashlight over the control panel. "You're going to fly this thing."

"That's insane. I've never flown a helicopter."

"I'll tell you what to do. One false move, and we're *all* dead."

"Grace, get out of the helicopter. Open the door and get out. Now!"

"Don't do it, Grace, or I'll shoot her," Rafe said.

"Be a good girl and do as you're told," I ordered.

I heard her undo the seatbelt. Rafe tried to reach behind to stop her. In that moment of inattention I forced his hand away from my head and the gun went off, shattering the windshield. The explosion blasted my eardrums. Grace started screaming. I punched Rafe's neck. As we wrestled I tried to gouge his eyes out. His arms shot to his face and the gun clattered to the floor. The door on my side slid open and Grace jumped out.

"Run, Grace! Run!" I shouted.

Rafe began his horrible chanting. "Oh, no you don't!" I shouted. "In the Name of Jesus, I forbid any demons to come near me." The authority in my own voice astonished me. I tried to jam my fingers into his eyes again.

I could feel the synthetic fur of his costume against my arm. I smashed his head into the dashboard and he yelped with pain. I spotted the gun on the metal floor. He backhanded me in the eye. I elbowed him hard in the groin. He wailed. I grabbed the gun and cracked him over the back of the head. He slumped forward. Then members of the ERT swarmed the helicopter.

It was over.

Grace was finally safe.

It's over.

Thy will...

Epilogue

The maple trees along the road to the church in South Dare had sprouted tiny leaves, their pale green flowers like lace. The birch trees, the wild pear, and the brush were budding and blossoming in glorious greens, yellows and creamy pinks. The flowering trees, the green shoots of grass, and the blue and white sky softened the poverty of the settlement. I breathed deep the fragrant May air, inhaling the scent of fresh earth and fruit blossoms, rejoicing in the new life all around me.

As I approached David Jordan's South Dare church I noticed a number of out-of-province license plates, even a few from the States. Cars lined the road on each side well past the full parking lot.

The old building showed no signs of the fire that had charred its front entrance the previous winter. Stained glass replaced the broken frosted window. Church members had laid a concrete slab and framed in a large new addition that would eventually house the worship services.

I parked my Jeep almost two hundred yards past the church and strolled along the road, the mud sucking at my rubber duck boots.

The front door was open, the church packed inside. The number of people inside violated the safety code, but I wasn't there to make arrests. I was there to worship. I squeezed inside. The first person I saw was Marie Dare. We embraced.

"Lance is here," she said in my ear. The congregation was singing *Amazing Grace.*

A small worship team accompanied the music on amplified guitars, an electric bass, a set of drums and a keyboard. I looked over Marie's shoulder and saw Lance. Thinner, looking vulnerable and awkward, he held hands with Cody who beamed with pride. Lance had just returned from an intensive drug and alcohol rehab program.

Marie released me and I extended my hand to Lance. He was reluctant to take it at first, as if he were ashamed. I smiled at him, a real smile, not one of my professional ones.

"Welcome home, Lance," I said.

Will had pushed through the crowd toward us and tapped Lance on the shoulder. He grabbed him in a big bear hug. Lance smiled shyly when Will let him go.

So much had happened. After Dodie's funeral Marie asked Children's Aid if she could bring little Melodie to live with her while Lance was in treatment. Melodie's hair was now its natural light brown and cut in a cute pixie style. Marie had told me she and Lance hoped to adopt her.

Rafe faced charges of murder, kidnapping, torture and child pornography. He also faced extradition for stealing the money the DEA had given him for the aborted drug sting. George Hall had been hovering between life and death for months, in agony from his burns, but in an even worse spiritual agony. In the meantime he had become a treasure trove of information.

George confessed he and Rafe had seeded parts of Sterling County with cocaine to distract police from South Dare. Rafe had procured the cocaine that killed Dawn Cranwell and Kerry Browning. He'd also seduced Kerry in the motel where she died.

The events in the hangar now seemed like a bad dream, especially since there was no physical evidence of any of the supernatural events we had witnessed. When the ERT did a post mortem and replayed the recording of all the talk captured by the helmet microphones, Rafe's demon voice couldn't be heard. When David, Will, and I compared notes we each remembered different things.

David said he had been seized with terrible physical pain as soon as he entered the hangar, as if his cancer had returned. When Will and I described what we'd seen and heard our colleagues thought we were nuts. They wrote it off to gasoline-induced hallucinations and the power of suggestion. But in my heart I knew what I'd seen. I'd seen the power of Jesus Christ over evil.

Money poured in for David Jordan and his family, mostly from anonymous sources. Within a few weeks he and Anne bought a second-hand trailer and placed it near where their former home had been. The church in South Dare grew, attracting spiritually hungry and broken people from all over Sterling County and beyond.

I no longer saw much of Catherine. When she returned from Florida she thanked me over and over for saving Grace's life. But after that she took time off work and appeared to be avoiding me. I respected her space. Grace still comes by and we're closer than ever, though she seems sadder and quieter now.

The little girl with hypothermia miraculously recovered. For a time it looked like she might lose her toes and parts of her fingers, but she's fine. I made it my personal project to reunite the European children involved in Rafe's sex ring with their parents. Will and I witnessed some heart-rending reunions in Halifax. Unfortunately, the thousands of children trafficked into the sex trade every year don't usually fare as well. Human trafficking brings in something like $10 billion a year. It's as big as the drug trade. And that's to say nothing of the porn industry.

Veronica's recent tests showed some promise. She's getting stronger and has put on some much needed weight. At my request she sent a letter to Jeri and Wayne asking if I could meet Meredith. I'm praying the feeling will be mutual on her part.

It was time.

And Will. He asked me to marry him. We have been planning a Christmas wedding, but both of us have been busy preparing for Rafe's trial.

As the congregation sang I mused about my new life. A year earlier, I didn't know what it was like to feel anything except anger or the adrenaline rush from the danger and excitement of my work. Now, as God had promised, He had exchanged my heart of stone for a heart of flesh. For the first time since I was a carefree

Catholic girl in Jamaica Plain I knew what it was like to feel alive. I listened to the singing, following the words projected on the white screen at the front of the church.

Through many dangers, toils and snares
I have already come;
'Tis grace hath brought me safe thus far,
And grace will lead me home.

Tears blurred the rest of the words. I pulled a small packet of tissues from my pocket, removed one, and wiped my eyes. Marie Dare nudged me, then helped herself to a tissue. She passed the packet on. When she passed it back to me, all the tissues were gone.

The Lord has promised good to me
His Word my hope secures;
He will my Shield and Portion be
As long as life endures.

The congregation sang the first verse again, a verse I knew by heart. I joined in. Thanks to God's amazing grace I now knew exactly what the words meant, and my heart overflowed with thanksgiving.

Amazing grace! How sweet the sound
That saved a wretch like me!
I once was lost, but now am found;
Was blind, but now I see.